Critics Hail Dee Davis as a Master of Romantic Suspense!

Advance praise for *Endgame*

"Dee Davis is at the top of her game in this clever and quick-paced ride over dangerous ground. With a hot love story and a cold-hearted villain, *Endgame* is romantic intrigue at its best. Davis never disappoints."
—Mariah Stewart, bestselling author of *Dead Wrong*

Dancing in the Dark

"Top-notch suspense. This story of extreme loss, treachery, and danger also adds up to great romance."
—*Romantic Times* (4 stars)

"*Dancing in the Dark* is a definite page-turner, and a story you'll want to finish in one sitting."
—*Romance Reviews Today*

"Fast-paced and intriguing, *Dancing in the Dark* shouldn't be missed."
—*The Romance Readers Connection*

Midnight Rain

"Engaging characters and lots of plot twists make for a spine-tingling romance."
—*Booklist*

"Taut suspense, wicked humor, powerful romance—*Midnight Rain* has it all."
—Christina Skye, nationally bestselling author of *Code Name: Nanny*

"Top-notch romantic suspense."
—*Romantic Times* (4 stars)

DEE DAVIS
ENIGMA

HQN™

ISBN 0-373-77048-0

ENIGMA

www.HQNBooks.com

Printed in U.S.A.

To Robert and Lexie
who always believe in me

ENIGMA

Under heaven all can see beauty as beauty
only because there is ugliness.
All can know good as good
only because there is evil.
—*Tao Te Ching*

PROLOGUE

San Antonio, Texas

THERE WAS SOMETHING off in the air. A smell, or a sound. Something that didn't feel right. And he wasn't the type of man to let that pass by—long years of practice, or maybe just gut instinct kicking in. He'd planned everything to the last letter. Position, fuse, blast ratio, timer. Everything had been perfect.

But not now.

Nolan Ryan nodded in agreement from the dashboard, the bobble-headed baseball player a reminder of everything at stake. Better to be sure.

J.T. turned his car around and headed back to the hotel. The Prager was situated in the heart of downtown San Antonio, right across from the Alamo. Twenty-three years younger than the Texas monument, the hotel was nevertheless a landmark, an elegant memoir to times gone by.

Currently, it was undergoing renovation. Which made it perfect for his purposes. An empty shell. The original design was flawless, and in destroying such beauty he'd be creating his own art. Controlled chaos.

But there was more to it than that. It was a tribute. A moment he could manipulate. Her mourning would be his pleasure—the circle completed. Yin and yang. They would be whole. Or at least a step closer.

He stopped a half block away, his eyes trained on the building, trying to figure out what was bugging him. Traffic surged past him, pedestrians waiting for a light to change, totally unaware of what was about to happen.

He took a step forward, thinking that maybe he'd recheck everything, but a glance at his watch confirmed that there wasn't time. He shifted again, searching the area.

Another step closer and he had his answer—a large black sedan parked illegally across the street. Federal plates. Someone was in the building. As if to emphasize the thought, another car pulled up behind the first, this one white with state plates. A large man wearing a suit and a Stetson stepped out of the Lincoln. He stopped for a moment, his gaze taking in the other car. Then, with a sigh, he crossed the street and entered the hotel.

J.T. forced himself to think, to try and consider his options. All the while the second man's face teased his memory. He recognized him, but had no idea from where. Not that it changed things. He glanced again at his watch. There simply wasn't enough time. Nothing he could do would change anything.

It was a regretful development. Certainly not part of the plan, and if anything he hated deviation. But the end result would be the same. And that's all that really mattered. Besides, he firmly believed that everything happened for a reason. And he smiled at the thought that perhaps destiny had stepped in with a helpful hand.

His step was almost light as he turned and headed back up the street, sliding into his car, key in hand. Less than a minute later, he was turning off of Dolorosa onto the feeder for I-10, Nolan's head nodding approval in the silent vibration of the distant blast.

CHAPTER ONE

Waleska, Georgia

ONE MORE JILTED LOVER pissed off at being dumped. At least that's the way it seemed to be playing out. Unfortunately, the jiltee knew his way around bombs, and the jilter was a preschool teacher.

Which meant a hell of a problem. And to make matters worse, Frank Ingram, the rejected suitor, had swallowed a bullet less than an hour ago. A neighbor had found the body and the note. That was about the only break they'd caught so far.

The device, located in a second floor classroom of the First Baptist Preschool, was attached to a motion detector. Too much vibration and it was all over. Which of course meant there could be no evacuation. And very little access to the bomb.

The only reason the thing hadn't already detonated was the fact that the classroom where it had been placed wasn't currently being used. A small quantity of mold had been found beneath an air-conditioning unit, and until the sample could be tested, the children had been removed from the room.

Which left Samantha Waters with two scenarios. Either the bomber hadn't been aware of the mold, or he wasn't really interested in killing anyone. Considering the alleged lethal nature of the device, and the fact that the room was normally occupied by the woman he'd wanted dead, Sam was opting for the former. And thanking her lucky stars. If not for the mold, she'd be picking through the body parts of toddlers instead of trying to figure out how to evacuate them.

The thought sent a bolt of anger coursing through her. She'd seen the aftermath of a day care blown to hell. It still haunted her dreams. And she'd be damned before she'd let the same thing happen here.

There were three other classrooms in use on the second floor, one across from the room with the bomb and two down the hall. The staircase was at the opposite end of the building, which meant there was no way to use it.

Because of the mold, the intended victim and her class had been working in a different room today, a twist of fate that probably saved her life, since the Cherokee County Fire Department had successfully evacuated everyone on that level. So Maggie Carmichael and the three-year-olds of Waleska were safe for the moment. But that left the rest of the children. And Sam didn't like their odds.

Normally she wouldn't have been involved with a local situation, but she'd been returning from another case when she'd heard the radio dispatch. And quite frankly, she wasn't a sit-on-the-sidelines kind of girl.

"We've evacuated everyone we can, and deployed the robot." The county bomb tech slid to a halt beside Sam, the fine glisten of sweat across his forehead a reflection of the slight tremor in his voice. Not that Sam blamed the man. He couldn't be more than about twenty, the fine stubble of his beard indication that he probably hadn't been shaving all that long.

Most men volunteered for the bomb squad out of some sort of misguided testosterone-cowboy need to physically stand down the enemy. Unfortunately, the rush was the kind that induced incontinence, and more often than not the bad guys won the day, the carnage in places like the World Trade Center and the Murrah building silent testimony to the fact.

"There's a problem, though," the kid was saying, and Sam forced her attention back to the scene at hand. "In order to get the robot up there, it'll have to climb the stairs, and what with the age of the building and all, there's a good chance the clatter will set that sucker off before Max has a chance to make it halfway."

Max was a TR2000 robot. The ten-wheeled apparatus weighed less than forty-five pounds and was designed to operate in tight spaces. Unfortunately, it wasn't known for its athletic grace. She sighed, eyeing the school building. It was an unusually warm spring day and all the windows were open— including the ones leading into the room with the bomb.

She lowered her binoculars, a rush of adrenaline ratcheting up her heart rate. Maybe there was a chance. "I think I've got an idea." She smiled at the young tech, and moved past him toward the cluster of emergency personnel standing in the parking lot of the building.

"Captain McBane," she called, waving at the fire chief, the ranking officer at the scene and therefore technically in charge. He turned with a frown, his expression clearly stating what he thought of women on the job, especially tiny little women who soaking wet weighed less than the bomb.

She'd heard it all before, and didn't really give a damn, except that it sometimes made getting her way a bit more difficult. She forced a smile and approached the little group. "I think I know a way we can get at the bomb."

Two other firemen, both pushing fifty, turned to face her, shooting sideways glances at their captain, waiting to follow his lead.

"Well now," he drawled, stopping just short of adding *little lady*. "I'm open to hearing anything you've got."

He probably wasn't, but at the moment Sam didn't care. "What I want you to do is move the fire engine closer to the building."

"Sure thing, and then we can all stand back and enjoy the show. There'll be body parts spread over three counties," McBane said.

One of the firemen contained a snicker, and the other spat, refusing to look her in the eye.

She bit back her frustration. "The playground's covered with recycled rubber, it's meant to absorb a fall. In fact it'll absorb most anything. Even the movement of the truck. And it's practically under the damn window. If you approach it slowly from the south—" she pointed at the open field that flanked the playground "—the bomb won't detonate."

McBane's posture was still combative, but there was a flicker of respect in his eyes.

"If we load Max onto the extension arm," she continued, pressing the advantage, "I think we can lift it close enough for me to maneuver the robot into position for an X-ray. Once we have that, I can use the disrupter to shoot out the motion detector and our bomb won't be able to spray anything anywhere."

Silence followed as the three men digested the information. She waited, knowing already they'd have to capitulate. If they didn't follow the advice of an ATF EEO and things went south, there'd be hell to pay. And if she fucked things up, then they had an out. It was a win/win situation, but that didn't mean it had to sit easy.

"I guess it's worth a try." McBane's words were accompanied by a sigh meant to insult, but Sam was already halfway across the parking lot, motioning for the young tech to follow.

"What's your name?" she asked the kid.

"Jason Briggs."

"Well, Jason, you've been drafted to help me. Got a bomb suit?"

He nodded, his eyes widening as the meaning of her words sank in. "We're going in there?"

She laughed and shook her head, stopping at the back of her open Chevy Suburban. Her suit was state of the art. A Med-Eng EOD 7-B, it weighed in at around sixty pounds— over half her body weight. "We're sending Max up there." She pointed at the fire truck, already moving into place. "But it never hurts to cover your ass, you know?"

Jason nodded, his expression solemn. "You been doing this long?"

A fair question, considering he was about to trust her with his life. She stepped into the pants, adjusting the grounder straps. "For most of my professional life. Started out in a department a lot like yours."

"How long you been with the ATF?" He reached down for the ballistic inserts, automatically tucking them into place for her.

"Couple of years." Her voice was muffled as he helped her with the helmet.

"You're EEO?"

She nodded, standing patiently while he tested her air lines. An Explosives Enforcement Officer was a coveted job. There weren't many and you had to earn the position. Sam had been selected young, but then she'd had more experience than most.

"Wow."

The word stood on its own, and with a thumbs-up, she headed over to the fire truck, indicating that Jason should follow as soon as he was suited up. The fire truck was in place now, Max precariously balanced on the extension arm of the vehicle.

She slid into place beside a similarly clad fireman and checked Max's operating panel. The signal was clear, the digital picture showing them the side of the school building. "Let's do it."

The fireman nodded, and headed for the cab of the truck, ready to hoist the arm. Jason arrived and with a last pat for Max, Sam signaled the lift. The arm rose slowly, inching over as it went upward, the robot finally swinging into place near the open window.

It took a moment for her to acclimate herself to the video,

but once she had her bearings she realized the camera lens was showing her the room's door, and across the way she could see the other classroom. And the children inside. They were huddled near the far wall, eyes wide, motion held to a minimum—as much as anyone could keep a four-year-old still.

Sam sent a silent curse down to Frank Ingram and lowered the camera to search the room. Fortunately, Frank was into hiding things in plain sight, and she found the bomb almost immediately. As improvised explosive devices went, this one was pretty straightforward—two pipes with end caps, covered in construction paper and duct-taped together. There was also a battery, various wires, a wristwatch and a blinking green light.

The motion detector.

"Whatcha got?" Jason had arrived, suitably decked out in his bomb suit.

"Pipe bomb." She gestured to the screen. "Question now is how sensitive the trigger is."

"Hell of a question." The fireman was back.

She ignored him in favor of the little screen, her mind running through alternatives, each of them carrying significant risk. There was no way to remove the device. And no way to evacuate the kids. Which left her with one shot.

Disrupt the bomb. Sever the motion detector and the device would be rendered safe. It was a gamble. But at the moment it was the only one she had. "I'm going to shoot it with the disrupter." She reached down for Max's controls, adjusting the PAN-disrupter, a machine capable of firing a variety of projectiles at variable speeds, the idea being to hit the bomb with enough speed and force to knock out the motion detector without triggering an explosion.

The primary question still being how sensitive the sucker was.

A cry filtered through the open window and Sam shifted the camera, eyes back on the monitor. A small child dashed to the door of the room across the way, obviously intent on making an escape. Sam held her breath, eyes glued to the screen. The preschooler began to step into the hallway, but before he could make the move, his teacher appeared, snagging him by the shirt, and jerking him back into the classroom.

Sam counted to ten and then sucked in a breath. At least she had an answer. Reaching down for the controls, she adjusted the speed of the water cartridge.

"You sure as hell better know what you're doing." The fireman was standing too close, and Sam glowered up at him. The man shrugged and backed away, leaving her to the machinery. Slowly she began to raise the disrupter, trying to line it up with the bomb.

A grating noise, followed by a pop, sent her heart racing.

"Something's wrong with Max." Jason's whisper held a note of fear—a healthy emotion for someone in their line of work. "The arm's not extending."

Sam swallowed a curse, and made some adjustments on the controls.

Nothing.

"I'm going to have to do it manually." Sam stood up, meeting the eyes of the older fireman. His expression held no trace of mockery now. He simply nodded, accepting that it was their only alternative, then stepped forward to pull Sam's visor into place.

"I'll lower the basket." He started toward the truck, but Sam reached out to grab his shoulder, motioning for him to move slowly.

He nodded, and headed for the cab. In a matter of minutes, the extension arm was brought back to the bed of the truck, and Sam clambered aboard, freeing the disrupter from the robot. She heard the truck's arm shift into gear as she began her ascent, but her attention was focused solely on the window, the disrupter armed and ready.

Once she was in place, she visualized the shot, and then using the laser sight, centered on the motion detector's blinking light.

One, Mississippi… She sucked in a breath and steadied herself.

Two Mississippi… She positioned the laser.

Three Mississippi… She shot.

Seconds turned to hours as she waited for success or failure. And then she noticed the quiet. Absolute complete silence.

The bomb was disarmed. The motion detector halfway across the room.

Cheers erupted below and Sam felt her knees begin to shake, the pressure finding physical release at last. Leaning over the edge of the basket she gave a thumbs-up, and watched as the firemen headed into the building, first to evacuate the children and then to dispose of the remains of the bomb.

Her job was done.

She sank down and pushed back the visor, grateful when she felt the basket sway as it was retracted. In just a few minutes she was down and with Jason's help removing her suit.

"That was really something," he said, his face red with excitement. "*Really* something."

She smiled and searched for something meaningful to say, but was saved from the exercise by the ring of her cell. Reaching into the Suburban, she grabbed the phone and flipped it open.

"Waters."

"Hey, Sam." Raymond Seaver's voice held a hint of laughter and rebuke. "I thought you were on your way back to Atlanta."

"Sort of got sidetracked." She frowned into the phone.

"So I hear."

News traveled fast, but there was no way Seaver had called just to talk about her latest escapade. Her boss was too focused for that. "What's up?"

"Got a call from a guy named Cullen Pulaski." There was a pause as Seaver waited for the information to sink in.

"The industrialist?" Sam shivered in anticipation. Something big was coming down.

"Yeah. There's been a bombing in San Antonio. Senator Ruckland and two of his colleagues were killed." Again he paused for impact.

"So?" she urged, trying to contain her impatience.

"So," Seaver drawled, "there's some kind of task force. Last Chance something-or-other. Best of the best sort of thing. And Pulaski wants you."

SWEAT DRIPPED DOWN Payton Reynolds's neck, pooling at the small of his back, his shirt sticking to him like a second skin. The hovel he currently called home was nothing more than a lean-to amidst the squalor of the Peruvian mountain jungle, the loam floor a pungent reminder that the usual occupants of the structure were sheep.

Still, it was better than sitting out in the pouring rain. A little better. He swiped at a mosquito and pulled the lantern closer to the map he was studying. According to his calculations, he was about a quarter mile from his objective.

Aimil Cortez was wanted in six countries, the combined price on his head enough to make someone a very wealthy man. Unfortunately, not Payton. His mission was to take the man out and then disappear as quietly as he'd come. By the time Cortez's body was discovered, Payton would be long gone. And the world would be a safer place. Or at least a little less repulsive.

He checked his rifle, a .50-caliber high-powered Beretta, designed to hit just about anything, but particularly useful when hunting slime. Once assured that everything was ready, Payton adjusted his pack and stepped out into the humid night air. The rain had abated slightly, turning to a fine mist, the kind one found in a sweat lodge or a sauna. Except that there was no escape when it became too cloying.

Between the moisture and the vegetation, movement was limited, but Payton had already cleared a pathway with his machete earlier in the day. He moved now with the stealth of years of training, his mind completely centered on the task at hand.

He'd been hunting Cortez for almost three months now. The man kept fading into the jungle like a fucking ghost. But perseverance always paid off, and now Payton was about to close the deal. It had been a while since he'd killed on orders, but the drug war was fought on amoral ground. And at the moment, the dark forces were winning the day, governments like the United States more interested in fighting the enemies they could see—and use as a sound bite. Which left the dirty work to operatives like Payton.

He pushed through the last of the overgrowth, stepping into a clearing. Even without the rain it would have been a moonless night, but with the clouds and precipitation, it was almost pitch black. Just the way Payton liked it.

He stopped, crouching behind a stand of feather grass and pulled out his night vision binoculars, scanning the building directly ahead, an acting gatehouse of sorts. If things were running true to form, the watchmen were in the back drinking and playing cards.

Out in the middle of the jungle there really wasn't all that much to guard against, and Payton had spent the past couple of days watching for patterns. All he had to do was wait for the man on rounds to head into the bunkhouse, then make for the fallen tree about fifty yards away.

As if on cue, the man arrived at the door, calling out to his compadres as he holstered his machine gun. Clutching his rifle, Payton ran toward the tree, crouching low to avoid detection. He waited one beat and then another, and when everything remained quiet, pulled up into the tree, climbing along its massive trunk like a spider.

With the added height, it didn't take much for Payton to

vault over the stone enclosure, and he landed silently in the soft dirt of the Peruvian compound. Lights glowed to his right, marking the bunkhouse. More, twinkling to his left, indicated the location of the house guards. All he had to do was make a beeline between the two toward the darkened windows of the bougainvillea-laden hacienda.

The whole thing took about two minutes, which meant Payton had about five more before the guard reemerged to continue his rounds. Staying low and sticking to the shadows, he crossed the courtyard and slid into the deeper gloom cast by the U-shaped walls of the building.

Sliding a climber's rope from his pocket, he tossed it in the air, satisfied when it lodged around a balcony railing just above his head. In seconds, he was up and over the railing, dropping down onto the cement floor almost soundlessly. After checking to make certain that the room behind him was empty, he turned his sights on the wing across the courtyard.

Cortez's room was directly opposite. Light spilled from the open window, the gauzy curtains lifting languidly in the water-saturated breeze. Payton waited, counting the seconds, and then released a breath as Cortez appeared through the window, crossing back and forth as he made preparations for bed.

It only took a moment to sight the gun and then Payton waited for the moving figure to hit center at the open window. One pass, two and then a third, before the man stopped to stare out into the night. With a quiet hiss, the bullet was instantly on its way, the only sign it had hit target a brief fluttering of the curtains as it passed, and a muffled thud as the body fell.

Holstering the rifle, Payton shimmied back to the ground, and moved swiftly back across the courtyard toward the fence, his mind centered now on escape. A cry from inside the house signaled his luck was almost out, and he broke into a run. Lights flashed on behind him, spilling out across the manicured lawn that stretched between the compound and its enclosure.

Dodging between bushes, he hit the fence running and was up and over in a matter of seconds, landing hard on the other side. Voices were filling the night now, trying to make order out of chaos.

Payton rounded the corner, heading back for the sanctuary of the jungle, the rain falling in earnest again, muffling the sound of his movements. He was just passing the feather grass when someone hit him hard in the small of the back. Reacting from instinct, he rolled and managed to move clear of the man, reaching for the knife in his boot, but before he could pull it free, Cortez's man hit him again.

Payton stumbled back a step, and then cut forward, surprising his assailant and connecting with the man's chin. Following up with a fist to the stomach, Payton succeeded in bringing the South American to his knees, and then, taking advantage of the opening, he grabbed the knife, moving in for the kill. But it seemed the guard had friends, and they were closing in, weapons at the ready.

Payton scanned the crowd, weighing his options, refusing to accept the fact that he was outgunned. Using the fallen man as a shield, he began to edge back toward the jungle. If he could just make his way there, he might have a chance.

Unfortunately the men with guns didn't think much of their compadre. A pock-marked man with a gold tooth and braided hair lifted his rifle, the intent clear. Payton pushed his hostage forward, sidestepping the body as the bullet ripped through the startled guard. The man fell, clutching his chest, his surprise almost comical. Except that Gold Tooth was now aiming at Payton.

Accepting defeat, or at least living with it for the moment, Payton dropped the knife, holding his hands out, palms downward, in what he hoped looked like a gesture of supplication. Not that he'd ever give up without a fight.

With a smile for the assembled South Americans, he fingered the grenade hidden in his hand. It was more than enough to blow the whole lot of them to kingdom come and back. The only downside being that he'd be a casualty as well. Still, he figured it was better than letting them take him prisoner. And it wasn't as if he had anything else particularly important to do. Still grinning, he shrugged, and was just going to throw the thing, when a shot from above took out Gold Tooth.

The others spun to look for the unseen enemy, shooting blindly into the night. Payton took the opportunity and shot off toward the jungle, but not before one of Cortez's men grabbed him by the foot.

The sound of rotors broke the night, the tall grass bending perpendicular in the manufactured breeze. The chopper appeared suddenly out of the mist like some sort of fiery bird from hell, the telltale tracers from gunfire spitting out of its yawning black maw.

Payton shook off the man and stumbled to his feet, already reaching for the rope ladder dropping from the side of the bird. A bullet whizzed by his ear, and then another, adrenaline surging as he sprinted forward, his hand closing on a white nylon rung.

The gunfire, combined with the chopper blades, was deafening, and the vibrations coming off the rotors almost shook him off the ladder. But he held his ground as the big bird pulled up into the sky, and when he was certain they were clear, he lobbed the grenade at Cortez's men—a parting gift they'd never forget—or remember.

He climbed the remaining few rungs of the ladder and accepted the offered hand into the chopper, flopping aboard like the striped bass he'd caught once as a kid. Wherever he was going, it was a damn sight better than where he'd just been.

He sat up, wiped some blood from the corner of his mouth

and turned to face his rescuer, his words of thanks dying at the sight of Cullen Pulaski sitting in the jump seat.

He might have been rescued from the devil, but he was still in hell.

CHAPTER TWO

"WHAT THE HELL were you doing out there?" Payton growled, leaning back against the leather seat of Cullen's private jet. He had washed off the bulk of the blood and grime, even changed into a clean shirt and khakis, but that didn't change the fact that he was bone-tired. The kind that even sleep couldn't completely erase. "That was supposed to have been a classified operation."

"Nothing is really classified, Payton. You should know that by now," Cullen said, his gaze assessing. "Besides, you looked as if you needed a friend."

"Don't think I'm not grateful. Although I'd have found a way out if I'd had to."

"Apparently taking half of Peru with you." Cullen shot a glance out the window, as if he could still see the explosion in the jungle.

"I was doing what needed to be done. It's as simple as that. The key objective was accomplishing the mission. Anything after that is icing on the cake."

"Apparently I value your life more than you do," Cullen said, his expression masked.

"Or you value my skills. It's not the same thing, you know," Payton said. "So I'm guessing something's happened, right? Something you're convinced only Last Chance can deal with?"

"Three senators were killed in a bomb blast at a hotel in San Antonio." Cullen as always cut right to the chase. "Although no one is claiming responsibility, we can't rule out the possibility of terrorism."

"Which is why we have homeland security." Payton took a glass of whiskey off the tray of a passing steward, thinking he could get used to this kind of opulence.

"This is bigger than that. Joe Ruckland is the highest-ranking Democrat in the country. Keith is a ranking member of his party as well. And Dawson sits on appropriations. There's more to it than just a random hit, and the White House wants Last Chance to investigate."

Payton had given up trying to understand the workings of the political mind ages ago, and he wasn't about to bother with it now. Better to just accept the facts and move on to the matter at hand. "Where's Gabe?"

When Gabriel Roarke wasn't heading up Last Chance, he worked counterterrorism for the CIA. Payton and Gabe went way back, making him the closest thing Payton had to family. In his business he couldn't afford attachments, but sometimes they came just the same.

"He's flying in from an operation in California. Something to do with a DOD leak. I didn't ask." Cullen's shrug was forced, but his expression remained blank.

Payton suppressed a smile. Evidently, not everything was accessible to the great Cullen Pulaski. "What about the rest of the team?"

"I've already briefed Harrison. Since he's based in Austin, I've asked him to supervise setting up shop at Dreamscape's offices there."

Cullen's corporation had divisions all over the U.S., which came in handy when it was time to set up an operations center. Last Chance had already based out of New York and San Diego. Austin would just be par for the course. And Harrison was more than up to the job of making their newest headquarters state of the art.

Harrison Blake spent the bulk of his career working for a

computer forensics company called Phoenix, but he was also an indispensable part of Last Chance. His abilities with megabytes and cyberspace had saved their asses more than once, and Payton, for one, couldn't imagine the team without him.

"How about Madison?" Payton sipped the whiskey, eyeing Cullen over the rim of the glass. "Can she fly?"

The mask evaporated in an instant, Cullen's face coming alive with emotion. "I was totally against the idea, but she got her doctor's okay, which didn't leave me much room to argue."

Madison Roarke was Cullen's goddaughter and Gabriel's wife, and she was six months pregnant. She was also an FBI profiler with an uncanny knack for seeing the world through the eyes of vermin, and when push came to shove, she wasn't the kind to miss out on an operation.

"What does Gabe have to say about it?" Payton's heart lightened as his mind moved away from Peruvian drug czars to thoughts of his friends.

"Gabriel doesn't know. I figured it was better to let Madison deal with him." Cullen's smile was mischievous, with a hint of regret thrown in for good measure.

Gabe was the overprotective type, which meant the sparks between him and Madison were often more than merely romantic. Still, Payton recognized that the two of them shared something really special—something he'd sure as hell never have again—and being part of their "family" was something he cherished.

"So we're on the way to Austin, too, I take it." It wasn't really a question, but Cullen frowned and sat forward, sending alarm bells clanging in Payton's head.

"Actually, *I'm* on the way to Austin. You're heading for San Antonio and the bomb site."

Payton nodded, keeping his expression neutral. "I guess that makes sense." He'd had his share of field experience with ordnance. Certainly more than anyone else on the team.

But that didn't make him an expert, and Cullen was a stickler for using only the best. There had to be something more.

"I've asked an ATF Explosives Enforcement Officer to join our team."

The use of the word "our" grated on Payton. Cullen enjoyed pretending to be part of the action, but with the exception of throwing around his political weight and his money, he really wasn't much of a player.

"Seems like a good move." Payton frowned. "So why do you need me there?"

"She's an unknown quantity. Her record is impeccable, but I'd feel better if someone I trust is on the scene as well."

"Her?" Payton ignored the last part of Cullen's little speech. Trust was the last thing the two of them shared.

"Samantha Waters. She's supposed to be a hotshot. Youngest EEO in the history of the division, and she's had experience with large-scale explosions."

"Doesn't sound like she needs babysitting to me." Payton sat back, curious to hear Cullen's logic.

"I didn't say I wanted you to babysit." He paused, staring at his hands. "I just want a second pair of eyes. I don't know this woman."

"But you know me?" Payton waited for the older man to lift his gaze.

"I know enough." Cullen raised his head, his eyes clear and steady. "Most importantly, I know you can handle the job with the discretion necessary. I've been led to believe Samantha Waters is something less than a team player."

"Then why ask her to be a part of this?"

"Because she's the best." Cullen shrugged. "She cut her teeth on the Oklahoma City bombing, and hasn't looked back since."

"All right so I'll babysit. But only because I suspect I don't have a choice." Cullen tackled life with his own rules, the rest of the world be damned. And when he wanted someone on his team he drafted them, with no chance for argument.

Although Payton had to admit Last Chance's latest incarnation was sort of a kick, in a danger and daring kind of way. And it meant he and Gabriel got to work together again. But even in the moment, there was still the shadow of the past.

As if he needed tangible proof, he traced the line of his scar, the physical pain a memory, but the memories were still excruciating. Still, life moved on—whether one wanted it to or not—and though he sometimes regretted the fact, he'd chosen forward motion.

And if Cullen Pulaski was his albatross—so be it.

THE AIR WAS RANCID, acrid smoke stinging her eyes and the back of her throat. Sam moved carefully, studying the ground before taking a step. The site had already been cordoned off, dogs, robots and bomb techs having determined that there were no secondary charges. But it never hurt to be cautious.

The seat of the explosion was a hole in the floor of what had been the lobby. An elegant room, she remembered. The foyer had been open to the second floor with a balcony running around the perimeter. Mahogany, brass, velvet—very old-world.

At the moment it was a tangled mess of broken beams, pipes and electrical wires. The blast was strong enough to have crumpled the second floor onto the first, leaving a mechanical tumble reminiscent of some twisted apocalyptic scenario.

The floor was buckled and broken, gaping holes filled with rubble from above. The cellar below had remained intact, for the most part, except in the center where the blast had originated. Outside light drifted through glassless windows and the missing east wall, still hazy from smoke and dust despite the fact the fire department had successfully extinguished all hints of fire.

She stopped near the seat and turned slowly in a circle, envisioning the blast and its path of destruction. From the proximity of the remains to the seat, it was fairly certain the men killed had felt no pain. It had been over in an instant.

Not that it made the horror any less. Plastic table tents with black numbers marked the places body parts had been found. The forensics people had already been at work, although Sam was certain there was more to find.

At least the casualties had been limited. The hotel had been closed for over a year, massive renovations from a new owner underway. The blessing was, of course, also part of the puzzle.

"It smells like death."

Sam whirled around, trying to locate the source of the voice. She'd specifically asked for time on the site alone. A chance to get a feel for what had happened without interference from anyone.

"The cause doesn't matter. It always smells the same."

A man emerged from the shadows near what had been the entrance. The haze made it hard to see his features, but he was tall and well built, his movements carrying a grace that marked him as more than a casual athlete.

He walked slowly forward, his eyes checking and rechecking the floor in front of him. He knew his way around bomb sites. But he didn't have the look of a bomb tech, or the uniform of a firefighter. In fact, she'd never seen anyone move so quickly or so quietly, at the same time maintaining constant vigilance.

The man was a panther.

He stepped into a pool of light, and she almost gasped, green eyes and sleek black hair echoing her line of thought. But it was the scar that held her attention. Jagged, and almost silver in the light, it bisected his face from brow line to chin. Whoever he was, he'd be a tough opponent.

But right now, he was on her turf.

Uninvited.

"Who the hell are you?" The question came out sharper

than she'd intended. Partly because she was angry and partly because he unsettled her, his innate quiet far more intrusive than a more vocal man.

"Payton Reynolds." He moved closer, and she fought the urge to step back a pace. She normally trusted her instincts, and at the moment they were insisting that distance was a good thing. Except that she never backed down, and he was the intruder here.

"Well, *Mr.* Reynolds—" She narrowed her eyes, her gaze meeting his. "This is a crime scene. *My* crime scene. And no one is allowed on site without my authorization." She paused, waiting for some sign of remorse, or apology.

But instead he shrugged, a hint of laughter cresting in his eyes. "Well, I think maybe you've been misinformed. You see, in point of fact, this is *our* crime scene. I know this because Cullen Pulaski told me so himself. And what Cullen wants, Cullen gets."

The irony in his voice was hard to miss. Whoever this man was, he wasn't a fan of Cullen Pulaski's. Which, at the moment, was a point in his favor as far as Sam was concerned. But it didn't excuse the fact that he was here without her permission.

"Are you a bomb expert, then?" she asked, keeping her voice purposefully neutral.

"No. But I've had my share of field experience." Again there was no hint of apology. Instead she got the distinct feeling that this man was capable of handling whatever life threw at him with very little trouble.

"What kind of experience?" she asked, her tone slightly combative. This was after all her territory and she wasn't interested in some yahoo riding in and taking over.

"Three tours with Delta Force and time served with the CIA."

That explained the panther act, and probably the scar. She'd bet her whole salary his work with the CIA was on the less-than-legitimate side. A dark horse if ever there was one.

"Well, unless you've worked a bomb site, you're not

much use to me. So if you'll kindly wait outside, I'll finish in here."

"This the seat?" He walked over to the hole in the floor, obviously not listening to a word she said.

"Yeah." She came and stood beside him, staring down at the rubble in the basement.

"Looks like about five pounds of explosive. Any indication of what was used?" He bent down to pick up a tiny piece of wiring from the rubble, silently holding it out to her.

She took it, impressed that he knew what to look for. "The forensics people were more interested in finding body parts. Now that they've been marked and removed, we're free to start putting together the evidence of what happened. I've got an ATF team coming in from Atlanta. And we've got use of the forensics team here, as well as an FBI response team. The senators are big news, and that means lots of attention."

"Including Washington."

She had to bend close to hear his words. "You're talking about Cullen Pulaski."

Payton nodded, and stood up, almost unbalancing her in the process. Automatically his hand closed around her wrist, steadying her, his touch oddly unsettling.

She pulled away, absently rubbing her wrist, not sure why exactly since it didn't hurt. "What exactly is his role in all this?"

Payton's eyebrows quirked at the question. "Haven't you talked to him?"

She shook her head. "No. I just got a call from my boss telling me that I was part of some team looking into the bombing. I thought it was a bit odd, but I never pretend to understand politics, and my orders were clear."

Truth was, she'd been too interested in the particulars of the bombing to think very much about why she'd been pulled into this or who it was that had done the pulling.

"Cullen's big with orders." He gave her the ghost of a

smile, and she wondered suddenly what it would be like to be the recipient of the full-blown thing.

Shaking her head, she frowned up at him, pushing her crazy thoughts aside. "So you're part of this Last Chance thing?"

"Duly drafted." This time his mouth definitely slid upward into a smile.

"What Cullen wants, Cullen gets?" she asked, repeating his words, studying his face, trying to make sense of it.

"Something like that. Or more accurately what Washington wants." He turned to face the ruined staircase, his expression serious again. "Last Chance is a team of experts the president calls in for special cases."

"My boss said something about the best of the best."

"A flattering observation. And probably true to some extent." There was no hint of braggadocio in his voice, just a statement of fact. "But that's not how it started. Cullen had a problem. No one would listen. So he called in favors and assembled his own team."

"You."

"And some friends." Sam wondered if a man like Payton Reynolds really had friends. "Anyway, the point is, we solved the problem. And the president liked what he saw and made our little task force permanent."

"But not full-time." This wasn't a man who sat around waiting for adventure.

"No. Let's just say in the interim we have other jobs."

"And the 'we'?" Sam asked, curious despite herself.

"You'll meet them in Austin, when we finish here." His response was just this side of curt, but she had the feeling it was more a matter of function than condemnation. He was just a business-first kind of guy.

And that was an attitude she could totally relate to.

"Anyone say what the senators were doing in the building?" Payton said, walking over to another pile of rubble. "Guy outside said it was closed for renovations."

"Ruckland was from San Antonio, so at least his being in the city isn't all that unusual. But according to his staff he wasn't scheduled to be at the Prager or to meet with Dawson and Keith. And neither of them was scheduled to even be in the state."

"So there was something going on that they didn't want anyone to know about." He was kneeling now, looking at the charred markings on what was left of the east wall. "Something someone else was willing to kill for."

"Maybe." She crossed over to him, intrigued despite her distrust. "But if they were keeping the meeting here a secret, how the hell would the bomber have known? And more to the point, why would they have been meeting here in the first place?"

"That's what we're here to find out." He stood up, rubbing his hands together to remove the dust, his gaze colliding with hers.

With a smile, she turned back to the bomb site, her mind split between the man behind her and the task at hand. Both were enigmas. And there was nothing in the world Sam loved more than a good puzzle.

She knelt to retrieve a fragment of timer, still feeling his gaze burning into her back.

Let the games begin.

CHAPTER THREE

J.T. STARED AT THE HEADLINES, his frustration building to a fever pitch. The man in the Lincoln—the one he'd seen at the hotel—his face was plastered all over the front page. *Joseph Ruckland.* Texas's senior senator. And the two other men weren't exactly chump change.

The theories were swirling—everything from terrorism to underworld plotting. But nothing about him. Nothing about the explosion. The beauty of his work had been lost in the brouhaha. That, and the reason he'd blown the building in the first place.

He sighed and looked longingly at the collage of pictures covering his wall.

Samantha Waters.

She'd been called in on the case, all right. Just as he'd planned. But instead of the focus being on the explosion, the emphasis was on the murders. And because of that she'd been assigned to some kind of task force.

Damn it all to hell. He'd planned this for years—the Prager the third jewel in the crown. His defining moment. And hers.

But now everything was different.

He hurled his beer bottle at the wall, watching dispassionately as it shattered, spattering beer across the photographs and newspaper articles. He had to change the plan. Find some way to turn this debacle to his advantage.

He'd built everything on the assumption that his latest or- chestration would lead to the discovery that he had been responsible for the others. And he'd counted on the fact that Samantha would be the one to make the discovery, eventually seeing the significance in his choices.

But now everything was focused on the deaths. And any connection to his earlier work would be lost in the fervor to find the motive for killing Ruckland and his cronies. All the planning—everything—it had been a waste. A complete waste.

He clenched his fist, surprised to find blood. Absently raising it to his mouth, he licked the droplets away and then pounded his hand on the table, the resulting pain clearing his head. He'd just have to change the rules of the game. Adapt the plan.

Samantha was involved, at least that much had been accomplished. Now all he had to do was find a way to shift interest away from the senators and back to the blast.

Or maybe he'd take advantage of the accidental raise in the stakes. He reached for the scissors and carefully cut out a picture of Senator Ruckland, then crossed to the beer-dampened wall and tacked it next to a fuzzy photo of Samantha at the Prager. A smear of blood marred Ruckland's features, and J.T. smiled, exhilaration flooding through him.

He'd never killed a man before. Never even considered it really. Except in passing. And now he'd killed three. There was power in that, surely. Even if the deaths hadn't been planned. He traced the curve of Samantha's face, his mind turning it all over, trying to figure the next move.

The deaths had definitely upped the ante. And truth was, he already had blood on his hands. What was a little more? Especially if it brought her attention back to his work. He needed her to know. To understand their special relationship. And to do that he had to become a worthy foe.

So maybe murder was the answer. Murder by explosion. But if he wanted her attention, it had to be something big.

Better even than the senators. Something—someone—that connected them. Then she'd understand.

Oh yes, then she'd have to understand.

It was like old home week—only she was from out of town.

Sam stood in the corner of the conference room leaning back against the windowsill, wishing she was anywhere on the planet but here. They'd come straight from the bomb site to Cullen's offices in Austin, the forty-five minutes in the car not yielding much information. Payton Reynolds made the strong and silent type look chatty.

She was, however, grudgingly impressed with his knowledge of explosions. He may not have had formal training, but his field work had obviously been of the intense variety, and in those kinds of situations one learned fast, or died trying.

Her eyes locked on his scar, and she wondered just what it was he'd survived, and then quashed the thought. It wasn't any of her business, and making friends with her co-workers wasn't exactly on her top ten list of things to do.

Still, she would like to at least feel a part of the team.

Unless she missed her guess, Payton was talking to the team's leader, Gabe Roarke. As dark as Payton, he lacked his friend's quiet intensity, instead coming across as a complex mix of machismo and power. This was a man one didn't cross easily. At least not and live to tell about it. The only time she saw a glint of humanity in his glacier-eyed gaze was when he looked at his wife.

Madison Roarke was tall and blond, the facade off-putting until one saw the compassion in her eyes. Add to that the way Cullen and her friend Harrison hovered, and it was obvious that she was the kind of woman who inspired loyalty among friends. She wore her pregnancy well, her hands protectively soothing the baby inside. And just for a moment, Sam felt a twinge of envy. Before it could blossom, however, she pushed it aside. She'd made her choices, and she didn't regret them.

Harrison Blake looked more like a sexy English professor than a computer dweeb, his bedhead-tousled hair curling aimlessly around his ears and neck. His eyes were an odd combination of green and brown, as if they couldn't quite make up their mind what color they wanted to be. The boy next door with intelligent eyes. An interesting combo.

Cullen Pulaski looked exactly like his photographs. His gaze probing, his mind obviously always leaping ahead to the next move. She'd probably like him if she'd met him under any other circumstances, mental chess being her game of choice, but at the moment all she felt was deep-seated irritation. She didn't belong here. And quite frankly, neither did this case.

Despite the expertise in the room, this was a bombing, pure and simple, and no matter who the targets had been, the investigation was something to be handled by ATF or the FBI.

Not that she'd say so. It wasn't worth the breath. She'd learned a long time ago that political mumbo jumbo and logic were often mutually exclusive, with rhetoric holding sway most of the time.

"Sorry if we seem a bit exclusive. It's just that it's been a while since we've all been together." Madison settled down on the windowsill next to Sam with a sigh. "There's a lot of catching up to do."

"I can see that." Sam nodded toward Payton and Gabe, the latter gesturing with both hands about something.

"They've known each other a long time." Madison's tone was quiet. Almost as if she was sharing a secret. "I don't think Payton trusts anyone easily, but when he does, you've got a friend for life."

Sam understood that kind of hesitance. Lived much the same way in fact, except that she wasn't sure she really trusted anyone. "They're lucky to have each other." She shook her head, hating the sound of wistfulness in her voice. She was just tired.

Madison's gray eyes were thoughtful, as if she could read Sam's thoughts. Then again maybe she could, that's what profilers were noted for. Sam forced a smile, needing to distance herself. "When's the baby due?"

As distracters went, it wasn't that impressive, but Madison, thankfully, followed her cue. "Two and a half months."

Sam frowned. "I thought you weren't allowed to fly that far along."

Madison rubbed her belly, shaking her head. "Eight months is when they really lower the boom, and sometimes if there are problems earlier than that. But we're doing just fine. And besides," she lowered her voice conspiratorially, "I wasn't about to miss out on the action. Even if I have to participate from the sidelines."

Sam sighed. "So you guys have been working together a long time, huh?"

"Not really." Madison shook her head. "At least not me. Payton and Gabriel go back to their days in Delta Force. But I didn't know either of them until I was drafted by Cullen. Kind of like you." Her smile was warm, and Sam found herself smiling in return.

"What about Harrison?" She nodded toward the man, still deep in conversation with Cullen.

"I'm afraid I'm responsible for getting him involved. Misery likes company."

Sam shot her a look, relieved to see that she was still grinning.

"It's not really that bad. In fact, at times it's proved quite interesting. And you'll feel like part of the team in no time. After all we'll be depending on you. You're the explosives expert."

"Well, really I'm better at the live bomb angle. I depend on a team of crack forensics people to help me with the after-the-fact work."

It was Madison's turn to frown. "But Cullen said you had

experience with forensics as well. You started with crime scene investigation, right? And then a stint in my neck of the woods with ERT?"

"You've done your homework," Sam said, surprise coloring her voice.

The FBI Emergency Response Team had been her first step from city-based work to the national scene. It hadn't been long before her proclivity for live action versus interpretation landed her at ATF.

"Occupational hazard." Madison shrugged. "Besides, it's a pretty impressive career."

It was Sam's turn to shrug. "I guess that depends on your point of view. From where I'm sitting, believe me, it doesn't seem all that extraordinary. But I can handle both ends of an investigation. It's just that I prefer the side that keeps things from going boom."

"Adrenaline junky." Payton as usual had arrived silently, and Sam jumped at the sound of his voice.

"Guilty as charged." She wasn't sure why exactly she admitted it, except that maybe she was among kindred spirits. These people obviously didn't mind living on the edge or they wouldn't be here doing what they were doing.

"Then you'll fit in fine." Payton's smile was fleeting and guarded at best, but it warmed Sam nevertheless, surprising her with the fact.

She didn't give a damn what others thought about her. In her business, success wasn't built on popularity contests. It was built on split-second rational decisions, head emphatically over heart at all times.

And to make sure she could do that, she kept people at arm's length. Anything more could spell trouble, which made her reaction to Payton not only surprising, but disturbing.

DESPITE BEING HAPPY to see his friends, Payton still wasn't sure how he felt about their latest assignment or their newest member. Samantha Waters certainly seemed to know her stuff. But it was also clear that Cullen had been right.

She was definitely a loner. And although she didn't have to love the team, she did have to buy into the concept of working together if they were going to make progress with their latest operation.

She was sitting across from him now, next to Madison, listening as Gabe reviewed what they knew so far about the explosion. She was a tiny thing compared to Madison. Probably a good six inches shorter, and built as if a good wind would blow her away. A fallacy, as he'd seen her at work, and knew that she was stronger than her frame would indicate.

Still there was something fragile about her, almost delicate, a dichotomy that Payton found fascinating. In his world there were generally two kinds of women. Those who used sex to their advantage, and those who couldn't use it because they didn't have it.

Sam had it. But apparently no one had sent her the memo.

Payton suppressed a smile. Given his current line of thought, he'd obviously been in the jungle too damn long, suppressed physical need turning his mind to mush. The woman was a team member, pure and simple. And her sexuality was simply not a subject for consideration.

Under any circumstance.

"Our biggest problem here," Gabe was saying, "is that the facts don't add up. First off, none of the three men killed gave anyone indication that they were planning to be in San Antonio, let alone meeting with each other. Add to that the fact that one of the three is considered a political enemy and things are even more confusing."

"It's not just Farley Keith who's on the outs. Even though they're members of the same party, I wouldn't expect to see Ruckland and Dawson sharing a meal," Harrison said. He'd set up on his laptop at the far end of the table, as usual more interested in the computer screen than the conversation. "They're not exactly working on the same platform."

"I had no idea you were so in touch with our reigning politicos," Gabe said, grinning.

"It's just a hobby." Harrison shrugged. "I like to know who's in charge of things."

Cullen laughed. "Sometimes I think it's better not to know."

"The point is that the whole thing feels like a setup. I mean why else would these three men have snuck off to San Antonio for a meeting they obviously didn't want anyone else to know about?"

"Unless they didn't know who they were meeting," Sam said, her gaze encompassing them all. "If this was intentional, and at this point I think we have to believe it was, then the only way that the killer could be certain that all three of his targets were present is to have invited them there in the first place. And if he did the inviting, it's certainly possible the attendees weren't aware of the other folks attending the party."

"Still leaves us with a commonality problem," Madison said, leaning forward to rest her elbows on the table. "If someone wanted them dead, there had to be a reason. And you have to admit this is an unlikely group."

"So we find the link, we find the motive." Again Sam spoke with authority.

"Shouldn't be too hard to check out," Harrison said. "I mean most of what these guys do is public record."

"It's a starting place," Gabe agreed.

"But only one," Sam interjected. "We've also got to consider the bomber. He's the one person who is most likely to know what this is all about."

"Sam's right." Payton nodded, not sure exactly why he felt the need to come to her defense. "The victims have such notoriety that it would be easy to focus solely on them."

"So in addition to looking for commonalities among the senators, we also start working backward from the scene." Madison nodded at Sam. "Were you able to determine much from the rubble at the hotel?"

"Visually it's a bit overwhelming right now," Sam admitted. "But the key is to break it down into sections. And with vigilance I think we'll be able to reconstruct the bomb. From there with a little luck we'll be able to start moving toward identifying the perpetrator."

"We've already found traces of the explosive device," Payton said, his gaze meeting Sam's. "And the seat alone is fairly indicative of what went down."

Her smile was slight, but rewarding. "Once we cull through the remains, we'll be able to be even more precise. The problem is that it takes time."

"And time is not what we have. Washington is breathing down my back for answers yesterday." Cullen, who had been silent through most of the discussion, leaned forward, his expression brooking no argument. "That's why this group was called in. We have the latitude to cut through bureaucratic bullshit, and shave corners where necessary. And that's what I want you to do."

Payton watched Sam's hand tighten on the edge of the table.

Apparently she was a stickler for the rules. Which could mean trouble. Cullen wasn't known for his keen sense of following the rules. Hell, none of them were. Except maybe Madison.

"Working with explosions is tedious work, Mr. Pulaski," Sam said, her knuckles turning white. "Cut corners and you wind up dead. That applies both before and after the fact. If you want me on the team, then the investigation into the bombing will have to proceed as I see fit or you'll have to find yourself a new explosives expert." She sat back, her gaze locked with Cullen's.

Payton contained a smile.

"Fine." Cullen wasn't the type to capitulate, but he also wasn't a stupid man. Sam was right. This kind of investigation depended on details. Taking things one step at a time. And no matter how much Cullen wanted to hurry things along, it just wasn't possible.

He liked the fact that she was right. But more than that, he liked the fact that she'd stood up to Cullen Pulaski without so much as a second thought.

Hell, truth was, he liked Samantha Waters. At least he liked what he saw. Trouble was, appearances were deceiving more often than not.

CHAPTER FOUR

THE BAR WAS DARK and smelled of stale beer and cigarette smoke. Payton leaned back against the wall, eyeing the joint. It was the kind of place frequented by locals, but then Gabe had always had a nose for dives. Even far behind enemy lines he'd been able to sniff out the local watering hole. Which served a number of purposes simultaneously.

Right now it was the perfect place to decompress. Despite Payton's change in situation, his thoughts were still back in the jungle.

"Cullen said it was pretty rough out there," Gabe said, zeroing in on his train of thought.

"Nothing out of the ordinary." Payton took a long swig of beer. "Kill or be killed, same old same old."

Gabe threw back his head and laughed, the sound loud enough to draw a couple of curious looks. "God, are we a pair or what?"

Payton raised an eyebrow. "California was hairy?"

"No more than usual." Gabe's smile hardened, frozen on his face like a shard of ice. "It never ends, does it?"

"It was our choice." Payton shrugged. "Besides, you've climbed out of the pit. You've got Madison and a baby on the way."

"I know." Gabe nodded, taking a sip of his whiskey. "And I feel damn lucky. It's just that sometimes I worry that it'll all disappear."

Payton fought against the bitterness that rose inside, concentrating instead on his friend. "Just because it happened to me doesn't mean it'll happen to you."

"Yes, but it's always a possibility."

"Or they could get hit by a bus." Payton purposefully pitched his voice to keep it light.

"The odds are better actually." Gabe's smile was small but genuine. "So, what did you think about Sam Waters?"

It seemed like a complete change of subject, but Payton recognized the look in Gabe's eyes. "*Personally,* I don't have an opinion. But professionally she seems to be on game. I was impressed with the way she handled the bomb site."

"Cullen says she's a loner."

"Couldn't say for certain. I didn't spend that much time with her one-on-one. But she'd isolated the site and was working alone when I got there."

"Doesn't matter really," Gabe said, draining the last of his whiskey and signaling a passing waiter for another. "As long as she's open about what she finds we can deal."

"Hell." Payton smiled. "We could deal with it if she wasn't. But I don't think it'll be a problem. She hits me as a straight shooter."

"She's not hard on the eyes either." Gabe grinned, and Payton resisted the urge to throw his beer.

"Look, pal, just because you've found marital bliss, doesn't mean the rest of us need to take the same road." His mood darkened. "I've been there before, and you can believe it when I tell you I've no intention of going through it again."

"Hey," Gabe held his hands up in defense, "I was only commenting on the woman's looks, not setting you up for the altar."

"Yeah, I know." Payton stared down into the beer bottle, his thoughts tumultuous. Mariam had been dead for a hell of a long time, but some days it seemed like the pain was fresh. Reflexively he ran a hand along his scar.

Gabe noticed. "I'm sorry. I really wasn't trying to open old wounds."

"They're not old. That's the problem. Every time I see Cullen, I remember." This time there was no mistaking the bitterness in his voice.

Gabe opened his mouth, then shut it again, evidently thinking better of whatever the hell he'd been about to say. Payton was grateful. "So what do you think Ruckland and his cronies were doing at the Prager?"

"Cronies isn't exactly the word I'd use." Gabe took his whiskey from the waiter, and waited until the man had set a fresh beer in front of Payton and withdrawn. "Hell, *enemies* is probably an understatement. If it weren't for the fact that they're all dead, I'd be looking at them as suspects."

"So we're back to the idea of someone else pulling the strings."

"Maybe. Or maybe our senators were working on something they were trying to keep out of the public eye."

"And a bomb just happened to go off in the process? Doesn't make a lot of sense." Payton pushed aside his first bottle in favor of the colder one.

"I guess not." Gabe shrugged. "But none of it makes a lot of sense when you get right down to it. We need to find a link between the three of them."

"And from there we'll find motive?" Payton sat back, considering the idea.

"A man can hope." Gabe smiled, the lines around his eyes making him look tired.

"Well if Harrison has anything to do with it, I'm sure we'll have something in the morning. If not, he'll still be at his computer trying." Harrison was a hell of a researcher. Sort of like a safecracker worrying at the mechanism until he finds just the right point of entry, perseverance winning the day.

"If nothing else, the case is bound to be interesting. Three senators dead has got to mean something. Even if only that the balance of power has shifted."

"You sound like a politico," Payton replied, eyeing his friend.

"Hardly," Gabe spat, leaving no question at all to his feelings on the issue. "I just like a good puzzle, and this one is looking like a chart-topper."

"We'll see. What does Madison think?"

"That the three of them were in bed together. Despite their political differences, their constituents aren't all that different. Rural and agricultural for the most part."

"So maybe there was pork to be had?"

Gabe shrugged. "Madison thinks it's possible. She's working that angle while Harrison delves into their personal lives."

"With her connections, it probably should be the other way around."

Madison's father had an industrial pedigree almost as solid as Cullen's. Between them the two men controlled a hell of a lot of power. Not that you could tell anything from knowing Madison. She'd somehow managed to miss being tainted by all that money.

"You know as well as I do she'd rather spit nails than deal with that kind of crap."

"Sure." Payton smiled. "But that doesn't mean she hasn't got the power should she choose to use it."

"True enough. But for the moment I think we'll rely on old-fashioned legwork to get our answers. Besides if we need any arm-twisting, there's always Cullen."

"That and whatever Sam finds." Payton worried the loose edge of the label on his beer bottle. "Hopefully once she's able to piece the bomb together there'll be a signature of some sort."

"A Hallmark card would be nice." Gabe raised an eyebrow, his innate cynicism showing.

"You'd be surprised what these guys leave behind. Some of it intentional, some of it as simple as tool marks. There was a guy in Namibia that actually carved lines from scripture into his work."

"All right then," Gabe laughed. "We'll hold onto the hope our man's a closet poet."

"Anyone taking credit?" Despite a gut feeling that this was about something more personal, there was no way they could ignore the possibility of terrorists.

"The usual crazies, but nothing substantiated. And I figure if it was a terrorist attack we'd have heard by now. Nothing to be gained in silence."

"I assume someone is checking the angle out anyway."

"Absolutely. I've been on the phone most of the day. So far not even a murmur of culpability. But I'm still tracking down a couple of folks."

"Underground, I presume." Payton smiled. Men in their line of work tended to fly solo, only occasionally working together, but when someone needed something, the network tended to be surprisingly strong. A certain degree of cooperation and available without question.

"It's a hell of a lot more accurate than what the computers at Langley and Quantico are spewing out."

"Don't let Harrison hear you say that." Payton's voice held a note of mock horror.

"Hell, he'd be the first to agree." Gabe grinned. "That's why he quit the FBI to work for Phoenix."

"A company that's contracted by a majority of the world's law enforcement agencies."

"They're respected for their results—not their methodology."

"My kind of company." Payton raised his bottle in salute.

"Good. Sounds like we've got everything we need except the killer."

"Yeah, all dressed up and nowhere to go."

"So might as well settle in here for the duration." Payton raised his hand to order another beer. Drinking could be dangerous in his profession, but it was also a good way to let off steam. And at the moment he had more on his plate than he wanted to acknowledge.

SAM WAS TIRED. She'd been working too hard. Of course that was nothing unusual. She'd always found work a solace of sorts, although she'd never figured out exactly what it was that she needed a reprieve from.

Life, maybe.

Although even that didn't make a whole lot of sense. Truth was, she didn't have a life. At least not apart from her work, which brought her full circle.

She sighed and slid out of the rental car, hitting the button to open the trunk. Most of her gear had already been delivered to her room. Cullen had arranged it. But she'd kept her bomb kit with her. Silly really, but like a doctor, she didn't like to go anywhere without supplies. Of course it meant getting through airport security was a little bit trickier.

But she'd found that a badge and an attitude cut through a hell of a lot of red tape.

The hotel was a nice one. One of those suite jobs that looked a lot like an apartment complex. Cullen Pulaski's budget obviously surpassed the government's. She couldn't count the number of times she'd set up camp in a motel that more likely rented by the hour than the week.

But at the end of the day, it wasn't about comfort. If it was, she'd have taken a job in the private sector a long time ago.

Sam slammed the trunk and hoisted the bag. The other members of the team were staying in the same hotel, but the parking lot was almost empty. If they were here, there was no sign of them. Probably out discussing the newest team member.

She shook her head, surprised at the turn of her thoughts. She worked with strangers all the time, jurisdictions crossing to yield a complicated hierarchy of staff and technicians. It had never bothered her before. But then again she'd never worked with men like Gabriel Roarke and Payton Reynolds.

She'd met a few, but never spent any kind of time with them. Unless she counted her father. He'd definitely been a man's man. Career army, he'd spent the better part of his life undoing the damage others left behind. First in Vietnam, and then in other war-ravaged corners of the world. A certified master blaster, there wasn't an ordnance out there he couldn't defuse. He'd spent his life living on the edge, walking a line and surviving, only to have cancer snatch him away at a time when he should have been kicking back and resting on his laurels.

Sam felt the prick of tears, wondering if it would always hurt like this. It'd been five years, but it felt like yesterday—watching her father fade away before her very eyes. He'd fought the good fight, almost beat the bastard, but in the end it had triumphed. And Sam and her mother had been left alone.

Bill Waters had been the spark in their family, the glue that held them together. And though Sam's mother had managed to make a new life for herself in Albuquerque, Sam knew that she'd never really be whole again. Bill had been the love of her life. And nothing could ever replace him.

Sam blew out a long breath and dumped the bag on the landing, fumbling for the key-card the desk clerk had given her. She'd learned long ago that the best way to deal with her loss was to sequester it away deep in her heart, and then ignore it.

If she hadn't been so tired, she probably wouldn't have thought of her father at all. Except that she'd met Payton Reynolds. The man was nothing like her father physically. And at least from first appearances, she'd say he lacked her father's joy for life. But the stillness was the same. That inner sight that had probably saved his ass more than once.

She recognized it. And respected it. And if she was honest, was intrigued by it just a little. Not that she'd ever admit the fact. There was nothing to be gained in sharing thoughts like that. Besides, who the hell would she share it with?

Her job was a solitary one. She had colleagues certainly, but no one she trusted with her innermost thoughts. It was better that way. A couple times early in her career, she'd tried to date someone on the job. But it always ended the same. Either they were freaked out by her expertise, or they couldn't handle the risks that she took every day.

And dating people from outside law enforcement only amplified the problem. At first they were intrigued, but as the relationship began to grow more serious, they'd start to pull away, claiming they weren't ready or some such drivel. The truth was they didn't want a woman like her.

After years of the same thing over and over, she'd just quit dating. It was easier. Because she sure as hell wasn't giving up a job she loved just to please some guy's need to feel superior to the little woman. Sad but true.

Hell, she sounded pathetic.

She smiled, and slid the card through the slot, then turned the doorknob. Using her hip to prop the door open, she grabbed the bag and walked into the hotel room. It was comfortable, but in a sterile, cookie-cutter kind of way. There was a tiny kitchen, a table and chairs and a sofa that no doubt doubled as a second bed.

An open door in the back wall led to an alcove that would contain the bed and bathroom. Nothing fancy, but a heck of a lot better than motel hell. She could see her suitcase lying next to the sofa, her other gear stacked against the far wall.

The door clicked shut behind her, the sound abnormally loud in the dead silence of the room. The hairs on Sam's neck rose as the tinny notes of music suddenly filled the room. Instinct took control as her gaze swept the room again, this time noticing the metal box sitting on the counter in the kitchen.

A jack-in-the-box.

Not the usual hotel decoration.

Even as she turned to find the door handle, she recognized the tune. "Pop Goes the Weasel." It was the last bar. Seconds to go.

She yanked on the door, just as the last note sounded.

A loud pop, followed by a whiz filled the air, and Sam dived out onto the landing, skinning her knees and elbows in the process. The night air was heavy with moisture, and she held her breath waiting for the fallout.

Nothing.

Except cicadas singing in a nearby live oak.

Slowly she turned around to face the room. It was shimmering in the light from the landing, bits of something fluttering through the air. Sam frowned, forcing herself to concentrate.

Confetti.

The jack-in-the-box had been full of confetti, the charge sending it spewing into the room like New Year's Eve in Times Square.

She stood up, edging back toward the doorway and the now glitter-covered carpet. Her mind insisted that there could still be another bomb. Something more deadly. But years of training told her it was unlikely. The person responsible had only wanted to send a message.

The pertinent question, of course, being…what?

CHAPTER FIVE

"WHY DIDN'T YOU CALL SOONER?" Payton Reynolds stood in the doorway of Sam's hotel room, his dark brows drawn together, the combination of scar and frown making him look somewhat demonic.

Sam, however, was merely amused. "I had everything under control." She shrugged, and turned back to the technician who was carefully bagging the remnants of the bomb. The local crime scene folks had been there almost an hour. Photographs had been taken and locations marked. All that remained was to bag the evidence so that Sam could try and recreate the device in hopes that it would yield some kind of answer as to intent.

"So tell us what happened." Gabe only looked slightly less angry than Payton. Sam bit back a smile.

"I told you pretty much everything on the phone." She leaned back against a table. "I walked into the room, heard the music, spotted the jack-in-the-box and hit the deck. The explosion was minor, shrapnel limited to the box itself. Basically it was rigged like a roman candle or firecracker, only instead of shooting sparks, it shot confetti."

"A message." Payton as usual cut right to the chase. He walked over to the charred remains of the box. Only one corner was left, the rest having broken into pieces with the explosion. "Where's Jack?"

It was a question that had puzzled Sam as well, and she felt an absurd sense of pleasure at the fact that Payton had followed the same train of thought. "There wasn't one."

She watched as he bent down to study the corner piece, careful not to actually touch it. "No fragments even?"

"Not that I've seen so far. I'll have to put it back together in the lab to know for certain. But I'm fairly certain the box was empty except for the charge and the confetti."

"So the question is whether that's significant or just a factor of constructing the bomb." Gabe, too, was right on point. Maybe this team thing wasn't going to be so bad after all.

"Exactly." Sam smiled. "Again I'm hoping that once I see what the original looked like, I'll be able to make a more educated guess."

"Any idea how it got in here?" Payton asked, turning back to face her with a frown. Despite the fact that she'd barely known the man a day, he seemed genuinely concerned. Not just generic concern, but I-care-about-you-and-don't-want-anything-to-happen-to-you concern. She was obviously misreading it, but it felt nice just the same.

"Not a clue. I talked to the manager, and he can't remember anyone requesting my key or calling the room. But it's easy enough to get access to these rooms. I mean the doors all open to the outside. All you have to do is pretend to be a maid or a repairman or something."

Gabe nodded. "And despite the electronic locks, it's still possible to break in."

"But not unless you have a pass key, or a working knowledge of electronics," Payton added.

"Considering the end result—" Sam nodded toward the box "—I'd say we can count on the guy having electrical know-how."

"That still doesn't explain how he knew you were here." Gabe had pushed away from the windowsill and was pacing, the kinetic energy no doubt helping him to think. "Cullen made the arrangements. But he sure as hell didn't broadcast where we'd be staying."

"He wouldn't have had to," Sam said. "The senators' dying is big news. I imagine every paper in the country has had a picture of me or Payton at the site. From there, it wouldn't be that hard for journalists to suss out where we're staying. And if the media knows we're here, then so does the rest of the world."

"Including the bomber." Gabe stopped, turning to face them.

"We don't know that." Payton's voice was quiet, but there was a note of authority there that Sam couldn't ignore. "Do you have any enemies?"

Sam laughed. "So many I can't count them."

"So this could be one of them." He met her gaze, his somber intensity making her shiver.

"Well, not too much of an enemy. He didn't cause me any harm."

Payton nodded to the shrapnel still littering the floor. "He could have."

"No way." Sam waved at the debris. "This bomb is hardly more than a firecracker. I certainly could have been hit by a piece of the box, but only if I walked right up to it. And that wasn't likely. If the bomber had wanted me near the box, he wouldn't have rigged it so that the music started when the door closed. This guy wasn't trying to hurt me."

"So we're back to it being a message." Payton tilted his head, eyes narrowed in thought.

"Yeah. We just don't know what the hell he was trying to say." Gabe shrugged, his frustration evident.

"We just heard. Is everyone all right?" Madison and Harrison rushed through the open door, Madison's gaze immediately locking with her husband's.

"I'm fine, sweetheart. Payton and I arrived after the fact." Gabe's expression was so full of love, it twisted Sam's heart. She'd given up on relationships, but that didn't mean she didn't have the occasional tug of envy.

"Sam?" Madison turned to look at her, her gaze assessing.

"I'm fine, too. I don't think the blast was meant to hurt anyone."

Madison turned around slowly, taking in the remaining debris and the bomb remnant. "No shrapnel?"

"None except the metal pieces that broke off the box. And they didn't carry very far."

She nodded, chewing on the side of her lip. "How was it triggered?"

"The door clicking shut. It closed a circuit that sent a signal to the jack-in-the-box. A motor started the music and when the song ended the thing went pop—literally."

"So we're talking about intelligence then. Not just a way with electronics, but someone who has the capacity to work out distance and timing. The song have any meaning for you?"

Sam shook her head. "I recognized it, though. It was 'Pop Goes the Weasel.'"

"That's pretty standard for a jack-in-the-box, isn't it?" Harrison asked.

Madison nodded. "And it shows a sense of humor. Interesting."

Sam could almost see the wheels in Madison's head turning as she tried to get a fix on the perpetrator.

"So what else can you tell us about the guy?" Gabe asked.

Madison frowned, still thinking. "Well, I'd say *guy* is right. It has the telltale markings of a male. And I'd say that considering the sophistication of the device he definitely had the ability to do more damage had he chosen to do so. The message, if there is one, will be subtle. But I predict that he'll follow up with something in writing if we don't seem to be getting the point."

"You think this is tied in to the San Antonio bombing?" Like Gabe, Payton seemed to hold Madison's opinion in high regard, and Sam marked it as a point in their favor.

"I couldn't say for certain. The timing certainly makes one think along those lines first. But I suspect Sam has made her fair share of enemies, and any limelight tends to bring people like that out of the woodwork."

"You think the guy is dangerous?" This from Harrison, his gaze darting over to Sam.

"Hard to say. Obviously he's capable of creating damage. And obviously he wanted her attention in a way that she'd appreciate. As I said before, if he really wanted to hurt her, he clearly has the necessary skills. So the fact that he didn't, tells us something. But it's all just speculation. And off the cuff to boot." Madison shrugged apologetically. "Maybe after you've examined the fallout we'll have more to go on."

"And in the meantime, I can check the ATF computer archive to look for parallels between this incident and other cases Sam's worked, including the one in San Antonio," Harrison offered.

"Sounds like a plan." Sam nodded to the tech, who had finished bagging the debris from the floor, and was now moving over to concentrate on the kitchen area where the box had exploded.

"Not tonight, though." Payton's tone brooked no argument.

"But…" Sam opened her mouth and then closed it again. She was tired, and there really wasn't anything she could do until the morning. She looked at the room, realizing with dismay that there was no likelihood of the forensics team finishing up here anytime soon.

"I got you a new room." Payton's words actually stirred the hairs at the back of her neck, and she jumped, not realizing he'd moved so close.

She spun around to meet his gaze. "I could have handled that myself." The words were out before she had a chance to think about how ungrateful she sounded.

His slow smile told her he knew exactly what she was thinking, and she bit her tongue against another retort.

"It adjoins mine." He paused, watching her, waiting no doubt for her to erupt.

She held his gaze, lifting an eyebrow.

"We thought it would be safer."

"We?" Disappointment surged, surprising her.

"It was my idea actually," Gabe said. "Until we understand what's going on here, I figure we're better off paired up. Madison and I are next door to you and then Payton is on the other side—with an adjoining door." There was no apology in Gabe's voice. He was used to making decisions unilaterally and a part of Sam actually approved.

"What about Harrison?"

"I live here, remember?" Harrison's smile was unassuming. A restful change from Payton's testosterone-laden intensity and Gabe's alpha male machismo. But then, still waters run deep. And Sam had learned a hell of a long time ago not to judge solely on surface appearances. "You're more than welcome to stay with me. I mean, Payton isn't much of a roommate."

Sam started to contradict the fact, saw Harrison wink at Payton, and then to her abject horror, she blushed.

Men.

"I'll be fine here. And if it turns out to be a problem—" she shot a smoldering look at Payton "—I'm sure they'll give me another room."

THE NEW ROOM was exactly like the old one, except that this one wasn't covered with bomb debris, and on the other side of the connecting door, Payton Reynolds slept. Or at least she assumed he was sleeping.

She, on the other hand, was not even relaxed. The hands on the clock remained stubbornly fixed in the wee hours of the morning, and she'd finally given up tossing and turning in favor of sitting in front of the bedroom's large picture window.

Facing away from the parking lot, the window afforded a view of the Colorado River. Or one of its "lakes." Thanks to a series of low water dams, the river actually formed six small lakes as it wound its way through central Texas. The last two bodies of water, Lake Austin and Town Lake, bisecting the city. Sam was staring out at Town Lake, its water reflecting the lights of the city, a sort of rippling neon affair. Picasso meets Monet.

Not that she was enjoying it all that much. The flickering colors reminded her of the confetti shower, and despite the fact that she had dealt with much worse, she couldn't shake the feeling that this was more than just a prank.

Sure, her work attracted the attention of all kinds of crazies. She'd had her share of notes, and threats, and even the occasional bomb. But so far nothing that couldn't be traced back to something concrete. Something she could either act on, or file away as part and parcel of doing her job.

But this one felt different. Whoever was behind this one, knew her—and knew her well.

Or had made a hell of a lucky guess.

Her father had given her a jack-in-the-box when she was little. He'd found the toy in a bazaar in southeast Asia. She'd treasured it, the sound of the music always making her feel closer to her father when he was away.

She'd lost it years ago in a robbery. Her apartment had been trashed, the box along with three-quarters of her belongings gone missing. At the time she'd told herself it was just an old toy. A piece of tin.

But it was more than that. It was a memory. A tie to her father. And somebody knew that. The bomb was testament to the fact. There was no question in her mind that the bomber's choice was symbolic. It wasn't a random act, or something tied to the bombing in San Antonio. No, this was personal.

And the thought scared her more than she wanted to admit.

As if to mimic her fear, an eerie moan echoed through the partially cracked door dividing her room from Payton's.

Startled, she jumped to her feet, and cautiously made her way to the opening, ears straining to identify the source of the noise. Silence reigned for a moment, and then again the night was split with a cry, this time anger combining with something so guttural she wasn't even sure she could identify it, but the hairs on her arms stood up in response to the sound.

Without stopping to think, she swung through the door, her stance defensive as she scanned the room for signs of danger.

The bed was still made, and except for a duffel thrown in the corner, the room looked uninhabited. Frowning, she moved to the doorway, her gaze scanning the adjacent room for anything amiss. The drapes were open, the harsh fluorescent light from the landing shining in through the window. At first she thought this room, too, was empty, but then another moan filled the air.

Spinning around she froze at the sight of Payton asleep on the sofa. His eyes were closed, but every muscle in his body was tensed as he fought against an unseen foe, his head tossing back and forth as if avoiding someone's fists. Sweat glistened across his skin, the moisture and light combining to turn the scar on his face silvery-white.

He wore only his jeans, and his chest, too, was bathed in sweat. An intricate pattern of scar tissue laced across his left shoulder, stretching down his abdomen and across his bicep to his elbow.

Shrapnel.

She recognized the irregular patterns and burn marks. Someone had tried to blow Payton away. Literally.

There were other scars, too. Some of them the thin lines of a knife wound, others the puckered remnant of a bullet hole. The man had fought hard, and with the exception of his nightmares, seemed to have won the day.

Payton moaned again, this time calling out, the words too garbled to understand.

Her heart twisted as she stood helplessly watching him

fight his demons, uncertain whether she should try to wake him, or leave him to his terror. He wasn't the type of man who would appreciate sharing his pain.

But she couldn't just leave him. Surely, it was worth risking his wrath to free him from whatever the hell was holding him captive?

She reached for his shoulder, thinking only to shake him awake, but some second sense must have told him she was there, because his hand closed hard around her wrist, his fingers threatening to cut off circulation.

She tried to move back, but his grip tightened as he jerked her forward, his eyes flickering open, the pain reflected there so strong and so deep that she could feel it clawing at her.

Their gazes locked and held, and for a minute, Sam forgot to breathe.

Then his eyes narrowed, and he was fully awake, the nightmare banished back to the hell it had come from. He pulled away, releasing her wrist, swinging around to a sitting position. "What the hell are you doing here?"

CHAPTER SIX

"WHAT ARE YOU DOING HERE?" Payton repeated. There was no accusation in his tone. In fact there was nothing at all. It was almost as if the nightmare had sucked away his emotions, leaving him void of anything but banality. And yet, that was wrong, too. His vitality hadn't lessened at all. If anything, his intensity was greater, his stillness almost a living, breathing thing.

"You were dreaming." She stepped back, determined to break the spell, purposefully matching her tone to his.

He waited, his breathing even now, his face impassive.

"I heard a noise, and in light of what happened earlier, I thought I ought to check it out." She sounded defensive, which pissed her off. "It sounded like you were in trouble."

"Only in my mind." He shrugged, his gaze settling again on hers. "But thank you."

The quiet words should have soothed her, but somehow they only made her feel more edgy, as if in saying them, he'd established a bond between them. A shared secret.

She shook her head, trying to clear her thoughts, to get them back to some semblance of normalcy. There was no bond between them, nothing more going on than a man having a nightmare. Period.

She'd obviously let the tensions of the day overshadow common sense.

Payton's lips curled up in the semblance of a smile, and Sam found herself wondering if the gesture was ever truly genuine. "Sometimes it gets a bit rough. I probably should have warned you."

Considering the fact that they'd barely met, it seemed a long shot to think that they'd have discussed something so personal, but then again they were practically sharing a room.

She swallowed, trying to order her thoughts, instead blurting out the first thing to come to mind. "Was your nightmare about that?" She waved a hand at the scars on his chest, then immediately wished the question back.

Payton leaned back against the sofa, the hard planes of his chest still glistening with sweat. "Indirectly." His tone brooked no discussion.

And quite frankly, Sam wasn't sure she wanted any. Still, it was the middle of the night, and they were both awake, and she *was* curious. "So how'd you get them—the scars?"

He glanced down at his chest, his face tightening ever so slightly, almost as if he'd forgotten for a moment that they were there. "Explosion."

She leaned back against the table, crossing her arms. "I'd already figured out that much. You get caught in a firefight?"

"Something like that." He hesitated, and for a moment she thought he was going to close down this line of conversation as well, but then he continued, his face still devoid of emotion. "It was a raid. Delta Force. We were trying to retrieve a package and were ambushed."

"I'm assuming the package was human?"

Payton nodded. "A friend of Cullen's. Guy got caught on the wrong side of the Iraqi border."

She frowned at the scars. "But those are old wounds."

"The fight with Iraq has been going on for a hell of a long time. This was during the first war. Our mission was to find the man and get him out. Should have been routine, but…" He trailed off, a flicker of anger flashing in his eyes.

"Something went wrong," she said, not certain why she

was urging him onward, except that she was captivated by the moment and the man.

"Yeah. Someone told the renegades we were coming. So they were ready for us. I took a grenade in the shoulder."

It had clearly been more than a grenade, but she wasn't about to push the fact.

"Lucky it didn't blow off my arm, I guess. Gabe and another guy, a British liaison, got me out of there. But we were the only ones who made it." There was stark reality in his words. The pain of the loss carefully banked inside him.

She knew that feeling. Had felt it herself every time she lost the battle with a bomb. Particularly in places like Oklahoma City where the loss of life had been so catastrophic. "The others died." The words came out on a whisper, as if saying them out loud would be irreverent.

Again he nodded. "All of them." A shadow passed across his face, and Sam frowned, there was more to the story. Something beyond Payton's injuries and lost comrades. But whatever it was, he wasn't going to share it. And she sure as hell wasn't going to ask.

"How awful." The words were inadequate, but she said them anyway, hoping he'd understand that she meant it. That in some remote way, she understood.

"It was a long time ago." He leaned forward, the motion enhancing the harsh lines of his shoulders and chest. Despite the turn of the conversation, he'd made no attempt to cover the scars. It was obvious that whatever it was that haunted the man, he was content in his own skin.

Sam felt her breathing constrict again, but this time for purely physical reasons.

Payton's upper lip quirked upward again, and she ducked her head, embarrassed, then lifted her chin, meeting his gaze full-on. "But you still dream about it." The statement brought them full circle, and though she hated to see him tense, she was relieved to have detoured around whatever the hell had just passed between them.

"I do. But not that often anymore." He absently rubbed the scar along his cheek, the motion telling.

She still had the feeling there was more to it than he was telling her, but again resisted the urge to ask. "I couldn't sleep at all. Dreams or otherwise."

It was his turn to frown. "Worried about the bomb at the Prager or the one in your room?"

"Both, I guess." She shrugged. "But the one in my room would probably edge out the other one, odds-wise."

"You said this wasn't the first time a whacko has targeted you." He was studying her now, as if her face might yield answers her words wouldn't.

"Right. But this one feels different somehow." She started to tell him about the jack-in-the-box her father had given her, but held off, not really certain why.

"Something to do with the jack-in-the-box?" he asked, his panther gaze finding hers.

She sighed, not certain she could ever accustom herself to his quiet insight. It was as if he could read her like a book. "Yeah. I had one like it when I was a kid."

"I had one, too." His words would have been condescending from anyone else, but with Payton, it was just an observation. Information added to the fray.

"I know. A lot of kids did." She frowned, trying to order her thoughts. "It's just that the one I had was special to me. A gift from my father. And it seemed a bit coincidental that a bomber would use a jack-in-the-box."

"So maybe it's someone you know? Someone who knew about your attachment to the toy?"

"Maybe. I actually had it in my office when I was first starting out. For courage." She reached for the medal around her neck, her fingers closing on the cool metal.

His eyes followed her fingers. "Like the master blaster insignia?"

She tightened her hold on the crab-shaped pendant. "It's not mine."

"I figured as much. If you'd gone through the program I'd have known about it."

Her eyebrows shot up in surprise.

"Cullen was pretty thorough in his briefing."

"I see." She wasn't certain exactly what to say. First Madison and now Payton. The idea of Cullen pulling together a dossier on her was unsettling at best, but when she thought about all of them reading it, the idea was downright unnerving. She hated being at a disadvantage more than almost anything in the world.

"Nothing you wouldn't want anyone to know." Payton's tone was reassuring. As if he understood her qualms. "Just the basics. But it didn't include military ordnance training, so I figured the crab had to be someone else's."

"My father's." She released the medal, letting it fall back into the hollow of her throat. "I wear it as a reminder of how risky it can be out there. Helps to keep me centered."

"I'm sure your father is proud."

"He would be." She shrugged again, trying to keep her emotions at bay. "But he's dead."

"I'm sorry." His green eyes glittered in the half-light, his gaze locking on hers.

From most people the statement would have been a platitude, something said automatically as part of polite conversation, but with Payton it felt real. As if he truly cared.

Maybe it was because he was a man of few words, or maybe the night had her under its spell, but she believed him. He wouldn't say something he didn't mean. And the thought was oddly comforting.

"Thank you." The words came out on a whisper. "It's been a long time, but I still miss him."

There was a flicker of understanding. And empathy that

could only come from someone who truly understood, but almost before she could identify the emotion, it was gone. "Is your mother living?"

Sam swallowed back something that felt oddly like disappointment. "Yes. In Albuquerque. They moved there when my dad retired. She still lives in the same house. Rents out rooms occasionally when she feels like company. Her current boarder is a girl named Ruth."

"Sounds like she's managed to move on."

"She goes through the motions, but my father is a hard man to forget."

"Are you and your mother close?"

Sam frowned, unsure how to answer the question. She and her mother loved each other. But her father had been the glue that held them together, and when he died, it was as if being together was simply too painful. So gradually they'd drifted apart, each seeking relief in their own way.

Her mother had never remarried. Never even been on a date. But she'd made a new life for herself. One that probably would have included her daughter more, if Sam had been so inclined.

"As close as most mothers and daughters, I guess. We talk on the phone a lot. And I try to get to New Mexico for holidays. What about you? Are your mom and dad around?"

Payton shook his head. "Mom died when I was eleven, and Dad never really was any good with kids. He stayed around until we were old enough to watch out for ourselves, then hit the road—permanently."

"We?" she asked, not certain if he would answer. Like most quiet men, he seemed to be intensely private, doling out information only on an as-needed basis.

"My brother, Kevin. He was three years younger than me." Payton blew out a breath, his eyes turning hard. "He's dead."

"In the raid." She didn't know *how* she knew, maybe it was the sudden tightening of his muscles, or the deep creases that appeared in his face, any number of things really, but whatever it was that gave him away, she was certain. Kevin had been killed in Iraq—on Payton's watch—and he blamed himself.

"Yes." The word was like a shot, reverberating around the room, the tension following it almost palpable.

There was really nothing more to say. So Sam held her tongue, wishing she had the right words, but knowing there probably weren't any.

Payton stood up, the subject clearly forbidden, and Sam started to rise as well, feeling as if she ought to go, and yet not really wanting to do so. She was surprised actually that he'd shared as much as he had. Maybe it was the moonlight. But it was clear to her that the moment of connection had passed.

She took a step toward the door, only to be stopped by the sound of his voice. "Don't go."

She turned, knowing her surprise was evident.

"I won't be able to sleep."

As explanations went it was simple enough. He wanted company. But there was something else there, an acceptance that pleased her more than it should.

Despite her better instincts, she nodded, waiting. The ball was definitely in his court.

"So what made you get into this kind of work?" he asked, walking over to the refrigerator and pulling out two beers. After popping the tops, he offered her one, and then sat back down on the sofa.

They were back to small talk. The sort of banal conversation two people have when they first meet. Which should have been appropriate. Except that it was the middle of the night, and she was wearing a T-shirt and shorts, and he was almost…well, not fully dressed.

Feigning indifference, she took the beer, pulled a chair out from the table and sat down. Sitting here with him seemed almost natural. As if they'd done it all before. A flight of fancy if ever there was one, but she couldn't shake the feeling. "I learned a lot from my dad. I guess to some extent it was inevitable."

"But you didn't start with bombs, right?"

Again with the damn dossier. "No. I started with crime scene investigation. But I kept pulling bombings and the rest, as they say, is history."

"The youngest EEO in ATF history is nothing to sneeze at."

"I didn't say it was." She smiled, taking a swig of the beer, watching him over the lip of the bottle. "I just said it was a natural progression."

"Touché." His smile still wasn't full-mast, but it was more than just a shadow. "Did you ever consider going to the ordnance school at Eglin? Really following in your father's footsteps?"

"Nope." She shook her head to emphasize the point. "I knew when I was a kid that military life wouldn't work for me."

"A free spirit?"

"Definitely not." She laughed at the thought. "I'm pretty anal when it comes right down to it. A plus in my kind of work. But I don't take orders all that well. Especially when I don't agree with them."

"There are places in the military where that can be a good thing." He was talking about Delta Force. About himself, actually. And Sam was hit by a feeling of kinship. As if they shared something in common simply because they were both loners.

"I probably wouldn't have lasted long enough to wind up there. Anyway, it's a moot point. I like where I am, and I certainly don't regret the route I took to get there. How about you?" she asked, figuring fair was fair. "You left the army after your recovery. Ever have any regrets?"

Again the shadow, and Sam wished she'd chosen her words more carefully.

"About leaving Delta Force? No." He paused to take a pull

from the bottle, the muscles in his throat moving with the action. "After what happened there was no way I could have gone back. Hell, they wouldn't have wanted me even if I had."

"So you went to work for the CIA?"

"Off and on. My work is sometimes of a more freelance nature."

"A mercenary?" The question came out on a rush of breath, her surprise evident in her tone.

His smile was cynical this time, as if he'd been asked the question one too many times. "I suppose you could call it that. Bottom line is that I take care of things that no one else wants to."

She nodded. "And you're good at it." It was a statement, not a question. She could tell from looking at him that he was the kind of man who always gave a hundred and ten percent.

He shrugged. "I'm competent. More importantly, I don't give a damn. And that gives me an edge over pretty much everyone else in the game. There's nothing anyone can hold over my head. I lost all that a long time ago."

She would have believed him if she hadn't seen the wistful expression in his eyes. It might have been fleeting, but it had been there. He might pretend to be dead inside, but truth was, he wasn't anything close. Payton Reynolds was a man who felt deeply, despite his protestations to the contrary.

"Makes for a lonesome existence, I'd expect." She wasn't entirely sure why she said it out loud.

"No more so than a woman who lives her life defusing bombs."

It was his turn to score a point, and she smiled. Maybe it wouldn't last, but just for the moment she was enjoying the connection between them. The feeling that there was someone out there who might actually understand.

"So how did Cullen rope you in? Because of Iraq?"

"No." His answer was terse, the lines around his mouth

tightening again. "I don't owe Cullen a goddamned thing. Originally I came because of Gabe."

His loyalty would be absolute. Sam envied his friends the devotion.

"But Last Chance has worked on more than one operation." She waited, curious to see what it was that kept bringing him back.

"I suppose there's the element of challenge. And there's the fact that Cullen makes it damn hard to say no. But in reality I kind of like the teamwork. Madison and Harrison are top-notch, as is Gabe. And considering I spend the bulk of my time in places where no one is supposed to even know I exist, I guess it's nice to have a place to belong."

For Payton it was tantamount to a speech. And telling to boot. She'd been right. He was a hell of a lot more than he appeared to be, and despite *her* protestations to the contrary, Sam found the idea quite fascinating.

CHAPTER SEVEN

J.T. HUNCHED DOWN in the rented car, watching as Walter Atherton alternately pushed and then dragged an overstuffed trash bin to the side of the curb. It was a big can, the kind with two wheels, and the process of getting it into place at the curb was turning into a laborious project.

If the circumstances had been different, he'd probably have offered to help. But of course that was out of the question completely. Especially since the man having all the trouble was Atherton. The truth was J.T. had no problem watching the man have a heart attack over his garbage. In a perverse way it would serve the bastard right.

But it wouldn't serve J.T.'s purpose at all. So he hunched lower, and hoped to hell that the man got the damn thing under control before anything dire happened. It would be ironic as hell if he had to use his cell phone to call an ambulance and then turn around and turn the man's house into a deathtrap.

In actual fact, J.T. was surprised to find the G-man there at all. He should have been at work an hour ago. But of course someone with Atherton's credentials probably came and went pretty much as he pleased.

Bastard.

Atherton had never even noticed J.T. He'd been too damn busy fawning over Samantha Waters. Dreaming of bedding her, no doubt. Some men did all their thinking below the belt. Fortunately, J.T. wasn't that kind of man.

And even more importantly, Samantha wasn't that kind of woman.

Atherton might have had his share of wet dreams, but that was as far as it went. Samantha would never have allowed anything more. J.T. had watched her carefully over the years, and there'd been casual flirtations with men, even a few dates now and then. But nothing more.

Samantha had more important things on her mind.

Unlike Atherton.

J.T. gripped the steering wheel, wishing suddenly that he'd brought a gun. It would have been really great to crack the window and take a clean shot.

Right to the head and Atherton was out of there.

He mimed the motion, Nolan Ryan shaking his bobble head in disgust. J.T. sighed. Nothing would be accomplished by deviating from the plan. Balance was everything after all, and in order to correct his earlier mistake, he needed to make a different kind of statement.

He thought about Sam—about the jack-in-the-box—and wondered if she realized what it was. Probably not yet.

But she would.

And if she didn't. Well, then he'd have to draw her a picture.

With Walter Atherton's blood.

The idea sent a shiver of delight running through him, and he smiled as the FBI director finally situated the garbage can, and headed back to the garage and his car. It took another five minutes before he pulled out of the drive and headed off down the street.

J.T. blew out a breath and leaned back against the car seat. Amanda Atherton had already left, beating her husband out the door by more than an hour. But that didn't mean there wasn't a maid or something. People like the Athertons always had hired help.

So far no one had arrived, and it was getting close to ten.

Still, better to be sure.

Everything had to be aligned just right. Positive and negative blending together to form a perfect whole. Patience was the key. Nothing was ever accomplished in haste.

And so he settled down to wait.

PAYTON SIGHED and put down the twisted piece of metal he'd been staring at for the past half hour. Despite his years in the field, he'd never really acquired more than an instinctive working knowledge of ordnance.

What he did know was limited to combat and espionage situations, and while there was some crossover, there wasn't enough to give him an edge in examining fragments from the San Antonio site. Especially after the fact.

Basically he preferred action to reaction, and while he had more patience than most, crime scene investigation wasn't a strong point. Still, Sam had said she needed another pair of eyes, and his were the most qualified.

They'd been hard at work all morning in the makeshift lab Cullen had set up for them. The bulk of the bomb residue from San Antonio was being cataloged and analyzed by the ATF in conjunction with local authorities, but Sam had arranged for key pieces to be sent directly to her.

In addition, she was also working with the recovered fragments from the jack-in-the-box bomb. At first the Austin police department had tried to pull rank, but a few well-chosen words from Cullen had done the trick, and Last Chance was now officially in charge of both investigations.

Rubbing his neck, Payton sat back in his chair, shooting a look at Sam working across the room. For the past hour or so, she'd been staring into a microscope, muttering to herself, and from time to time recording things in a little notebook.

Despite the fact that they'd had almost no sleep, she was alert and fully intent on her job. This was her element, and here, with no other people to deal with, she seemed more at ease than he'd seen her since they'd arrived in Austin.

Unless he counted last night. And he wasn't going to do that. In fact he was trying hard not to think about it at all, but close quarters here weren't helping anything. In all the years he'd been hiding from his past, he'd never opened up about any of it to anyone.

And he'd certainly never discussed the nightmares.

Not that he'd really said anything of significance. For the most part, he'd managed to deflect her questions. But he'd told her about Kevin. Or at least acknowledged her guess. And that wasn't like him.

He didn't like the fact that he'd allowed even a hint of intimacy between them. What had happened in Iraq was his burden to carry. Kevin and Mariam his own personal crosses to bear. Cullen Pulaski's ambition may have set in motion the events that led to their deaths, but it had been Payton's job to protect them.

And he'd failed.

He glanced over at Sam again, her silvery curls dancing around her face as she focused the microscope. It had unnerved him to find her standing over him as he'd awakened. He'd been insane to suggest that she share an adjoining suite. But hindsight wasn't worth a damn, and now he had to accept the fact that she'd broken through his defenses in a way he hadn't anticipated.

The key now was to move past it and concentrate on business. With another sigh, he picked up the fragment, turning it toward the light, carefully making a note of its weight and composition.

"Okay, I think maybe I've got something on our senators." Madison walked into the lab with a look of triumph.

Sam looked up from her microscope to see Madison's excitement reflected in her face. Payton couldn't remember the last time he'd felt that kind of enthusiasm. "What'd you find?"

"Looks like our boys were up to their necks in closed-door dealings. But details will have to wait until we're in the briefing room. Gabe wants you there in five." With a mischievous smile she spun around and waltzed back out the door.

"Well, that was enlightening," Sam grumbled, her enthusiasm tempered with frustration.

"He said five minutes, not six hours. Surely you can manage to hang on that long." He'd meant it as a joke, but based on the look she shot him, it obviously hadn't come across that way.

Whatever camaraderie they'd had last night had obviously evaporated with the sun. Truth was, she really hadn't said much of anything to him this morning, as if she, too, had regrets about the night before. Surprisingly, he felt disappointed by the thought. A sure sign he was losing his mind.

"You coming?" She closed her notebook with a snap and started for the door, oblivious, thank God, to the turn of his thoughts. Payton nodded in reply, laid the fragment carefully back in its container, and followed her.

The briefing room was nothing more than a converted conference room, complete with table, chairs and a whiteboard. It sat between the lab and what was serving as an operations room and computer headquarters. Considering the rapidity with which it had all been assembled, Cullen and Harrison had done a damn good job.

Located in the basement of the building, it was practically intrusion proof, and, with state-of-the-art equipment, better than any facility the government could have provided. There was something to be said for unlimited funding, despite the negative side effects that were part of the package.

Payton sat down next to Harrison, across from Madison who was still smiling. She wore her pregnancy well, the "glow" of motherhood suiting her fragility, lending an essence of something almost ethereal. Of course, looks were deceiving—Madison was one of the toughest women he'd ever worked with. But she kept her femininity intact all the same.

Gabe was a lucky man.

Harrison sat across from Sam at the other end of the table, engrossed as usual in his laptop. Payton wondered if the guy ever went anywhere without it, then immediately regretted the thought. Harrison was more than just a computer whiz, he was a hell of a team member, pulling answers out of nowhere on more than one occasion.

As if aware of Payton's thoughts, Harrison looked up with a grin. "Sorry, can't seem to help myself." With a laugh, he closed the laptop, and solemnly gave Gabe his full attention, prompting laughter from both Sam and Madison.

Payton found he liked the sound of Sam's laughter, which wasn't something he wanted to dwell on, so instead he focused on Gabe, whose face, despite his wife's amusement, was deadly serious.

"So, darling, why don't you tell us what you found." Despite the endearment, there was a note of censure in his voice. Gabe had always been a no-nonsense kind of guy, but Iraq had intensified the effect. Even Madison hadn't been able to soothe all of his demons. Which was something Payton understood only too well.

Madison sobered instantly at the sound of her husband's voice, although the twinkle in her eye remained. "It took some digging, but thanks to my sources I've now got confirmation that our senators were up to their necks in pork. Apparently they've been working together behind closed doors to finagle an amendment to the budget bill that would send billions their way in the form of agricultural subsidies targeted for Texas, California and Iowa respectively."

"And that's enough to make someone want to take them out?" Sam sounded skeptical.

"Hell, Ruckland and Keith working together on anything ought to put targets on their backs," Harrison said.

"From their own parties," Payton added, thinking again

how much he hated politicians. "But I agree with Sam, it seems a bit extreme."

"Well there are foreign concerns involved as well. If money goes to subsidize our farmers, then prices for consumers go down, and ultimately other markets are cut out of the picture." Madison opened a file and thumbed through the pages. "The multiplying effect could be quite devastating to underdeveloped countries relying on U.S. trade to support their economies."

"And there's only so much money in the pot," Harrison said. "So if a large portion of the funds are diverted to Texas, California and Iowa, then other agricultural states stand to lose."

"But overall isn't it a good thing to support our farmers?" Sam asked. "Save the family farm?"

"It sounds good, I'll admit." Madison shrugged. "But unfortunately the bulk of the money goes to big corporations with diverse investments."

"And let me guess," Payton said. "Ruckland, Keith and Dawson have financial interest in one or more of these diverse companies."

"Exactly." Madison nodded.

"So much for altruistic congressmen," Sam laughed. "But it still doesn't seem like this is the work of some pissed-off farmer. Or even an international conglomerate worried about selling this year's wheat crop. I mean these are high-profile American citizens we're talking about. Powerful ones. And whoever bombed the Prager would have to know that there'd be no holds barred trying to find the culprit."

"Even if they believe the payoff was worth the risk, I don't think there's any way to have planned it." Harrison had opened his laptop again.

"I take it you're giving us more than just speculation here?" Gabe asked.

"Absolutely. I've talked to all three of the senators' offices, as well as their spouses and top aides. Nobody knew they were meeting. According to his staff, Dawson was in New England at a fund-raiser. But according to the people in New England, he only popped in for an hour or so, and then rushed out claiming something more pressing had come up." Harrison tapped out something on the computer. "Apparently coming to Texas."

"So he makes a sudden trip south without telling anyone?"

"Looks that way. I've got confirmation that he took a private jet into Stinson Municipal Airport in San Antonio." He spun the laptop around. "Turns out the plane belongs to Keith."

The screen displayed the copy of a flight plan filed in Manchester, New Hampshire. Two passengers listed. Robert Keith and Farley Dawson.

"So what we've got is a low-ranking democratic senator backing out of his party obligations to fly south with the republican's lead senator," Madison restated, frowning. "I'd say that goes a long way to physically substantiating my findings."

"Yes, and due to the rushed nature of Dawson's departure, I'd say the meeting couldn't have been planned far enough in advance to allow someone to plan for the kind of bomb detonated in the Prager." Harrison turned toward Sam for confirmation.

"It was a fairly sophisticated device. And from what I've been able to put together so far, I'd say our man takes great pride in his work. And while it's certainly possible that he might have had something ready-made, so to speak, given the instability of the components he's using, I'd say it's fairly unlikely." She shrugged, and held up her hands. "I wish I could tell you definitively, but there's honestly no way to tell for certain."

"But you'd say that the odds are against this guy just throwing something together."

"Yeah." She nodded, chewing on the side of her lip. "I'd say he had to have time."

"But all we know for certain is that Dawson made the trip

on the spur of the moment. What about Keith and Ruckland?"

"Beyond their families and spouses denying any knowledge of the meeting, I've got Outlook calendars for all three, and none of them mention anything that even cryptically could be considered a memo about a meeting." Harrison pulled out a file and opened it. "And the jet took off from Southern California just about five hours before it touched down in New Hampshire."

"How about phone records?"

"This is the best part," Harrison said, producing a stack of papers from the file. "I've got LUDs on all three men and there is a call from Ruckland to Keith about an hour before the plane left California. Nothing to Dawson from either of the other two, but we know that he boarded the plane with Keith. So I'd say we have our connection." He tossed the phone records on the table with a smile.

"It's solid evidence, I'll grant you that," Gabe said. "But not enough to make a definite conclusion. We simply can't ignore the fact that the three of them were up to their asses in alligators. The very fact that they were panicked into meeting is pretty strong motivation that something had gone wrong."

"Which could mean that someone was threatening them." Sam was toying with the edge of a file folder, her brows drawn together in thought.

"Or luring them to an early grave," Madison added.

"Maybe," Payton said, leaning back in his chair. "But it doesn't track. The odds of someone discovering the fact that the three of them were involved in something shady is entirely possible. But then to have managed to lure them to Texas on the spur of the moment to a closed hotel at the exact time that the bomb he planted went off seems a bit more far-fetched."

"But the alternative is that someone set the bomb for an entirely different reason, and accidentally took out the senators. *That* seems far-fetched to me," Gabe said.

"Maybe," Sam said, looking up from peurusing the phone records. "But quite honestly, taking three high-profile men out in a bomb blast is not standard profile for the types of men we're talking about here." Her gaze met Madison's and the other woman nodded.

"She's right. A terrorist might use a bomb, but he wouldn't go through the efforts to lure them to a deserted hotel. He'd want more bang for his buck, if you'll excuse the pun. He'd be much more likely to pick a public place or maybe a senate committee meeting or party of some kind."

"Maybe someone was hoping to cover up the crime? Incinerate the bodies and confuse the facts."

"That would hold if he'd used the kind of bomb that did that kind of damage. But he didn't." Sam shrugged. "The blast was meant to destroy the building certainly, but nothing more than that. If he'd wanted to guarantee the place would be set on fire he'd have used an entirely different device."

"Besides, if the goal was to mislead authorities, there are a lot of better ways to accomplish that than with a bomb, no matter what kind." Payton turned to look at Sam, but she was back to reading the telephone file.

"Madison, you agree with this?" Gabriel asked.

"Despite the apparent improbability of this kind of coincidence, I'd have to say the idea has merit. While bombers do target individuals, there's usually a broader agenda than just killing someone. Sometimes they do try and cover up another crime. Like maybe if the senators were already dead. But we know from forensics that all three died in the blast."

"But you can't say with certainty that it was just a fluke that the senators were there."

"No." She shook her head. "But just because I can't substantiate it doesn't mean it isn't the truth."

"We see what we want to see," Payton said. "The senators are big news, and so we naturally assume that they're the reason the building blew."

"All right, then, maybe we need to come at this from another angle," Gabe said, resuming control of the conversation.

"Like was there any other reason someone would want to blow up the Prager?" Madison leaned back, absently stroking her belly.

"Or if there've been any other blasts with a similar M.O." Sam was still chewing the side of her lip, her arms crossed over her chest as she tried to put together the facts.

"I've got an answer for that one," Harrison said, pulling out another file. "I searched N-Force over the past twenty years for anything that had the same earmarks of the San Antonio blast, and came up with eleven matches. One bomber is dead. And two of the blasts were the work of a Joe Pantemo. He's in a Colorado penitentiary serving life."

"So that leaves eight more," Gabe said, his frustration obvious. Like Payton he preferred action to discussion.

"Six actually. The other two were the work of a Zachary Robertson. However, the last one left him paralyzed from the neck down and since he can't even breathe on his own, I kinda doubt he's our man. Of the remaining six, five are unsolved. And one was the work of Edwin Marcus."

"I know him," Sam said, leaning forward again. "He's a three-time loser with an uncanny way with pipe bombs. Blows things up for the pure hell of it. I helped put him away about three years ago."

"He's out on bail," Harrison said. "According to his parole records, he's currently living in Houston."

"Sounds like it's time for a road trip." Payton felt a rush of adrenaline. Hunting people was what he did best. He turned to meet Sam's questioning gaze. "You up for it?"

"I'm in if you are." Her eyes flashed, and the right side of her mouth twisted upward, the expression making her look a little dangerous.

He liked the look, found it downright arousing in fact. Not that he intended to do a goddamned thing about it.

CHAPTER EIGHT

HOUSTON WAS HOTTER than hell, the humidity upping the temperature to near intolerable levels. It was the kind of heat that made you want to shower again five minutes after leaving the house.

Sam pushed damp hair behind her ears, and wished she'd worn something cooler. Her chinos had gone from freshly pressed to wildly wrinkled, and her cotton blouse was glued to her back and breasts like a wet T-shirt, leaving little to the imagination.

She was used to Atlanta heat, but the air here was so thick with moisture that it was difficult to breathe, and from what she could tell there was no respite in sight. The piece of crap Eddie Marcus called home wasn't the kind of place that had air-conditioning.

A nineteen-twenties bungalow, the place had obviously seen better days. The porch listed at an angle that defied gravity, giving her doubts as to its stability. Payton, however, had no such qualms. Hand on the gun in his holster, he stepped over the rickety steps right onto the porch itself, a quick glance in her direction indicating she should follow.

It had taken them most of the morning to run the man down. His parole officer had produced an address, but Eddie had long since moved on, not bothering to let anyone know. Fortunately the woman who was renting his old apartment had a friend of a friend, and two hours later they were standing in front of Eddie's new place.

The question, of course, was whether or not they'd find him at home.

Payton knocked as Sam stepped onto the porch, positioning herself on the other side of the door, her weapon drawn. She didn't carry a gun that often, and it felt unnatural in her hand despite the fact that she worked hard to stay on top of her proficiency.

Payton, on the other hand, handled his gun with the ease of familiarity. Then again, she supposed, he probably had more notches on the thing than she cared to know about. They were both in the same business more or less, but on the other side of the coin. Her job was to disarm weapons, his to discharge them with lethal force.

Payton's gaze met hers, and she nodded. In for a penny and all that.

He knocked once, and then reached out to open the door. It was locked, but that didn't stop Payton and in what seemed like seconds, he'd jimmied the lock and they were inside.

Eddie's housekeeping skills weren't exactly on a Martha Stewart level, and the front room reeked of stale beer and old takeout. Sam resisted the urge to hold her nose, and moved into the room, weapon ready.

It was empty, but a telltale slamming of the back screen door signaled the quarry was on the premises. After motioning her to stay put, Payton was gone, like a shadow slipping through the house and out the door.

Sam followed suit, heading through the front door, thinking she'd cut the man off before he had the chance to hightail it out of there.

She needn't have bothered.

No more than three minutes had elapsed, and Payton was already rounding the corner, Eddie in front of him, the ex-con's arm twisted backward between the two of them. Eddie's face was an odd mix of amazement and fear, and if the situation hadn't been so serious, Sam would have laughed.

Instead, she followed them inside, watching as Eddie scrambled to a chair in the corner, trying to put some distance between himself and Payton. Smart man.

"You cops?" The words came out in a strangled sort of fashion, Eddie's fear momentarily winning the day. No one on the planet would ever mistake Payton Reynolds for a cop. Eddie was just spitting out the first thing that entered his head.

Payton shook his head, and turned a chair around to straddle it, his gun never wavering from its target—a spot somewhere in the vicinity of Eddie's wildly pounding heart. Sam walked over to the window and leaned back against the sill, wishing for just a hint of a breeze to deflect the odor of really old burgers.

She kept her gun out, but more for show than anything else. Payton had things well under control.

"You with Big John?" Eddie's skin was turning a peculiar shade of gray, and Sam figured Big John was a breaking kneecaps sort of guy. A bookie or a crime boss maybe. It didn't matter.

Again Payton shook his head. In most instances this would have been good news, but in light of Payton's steely-eyed gaze, Eddie looked more like he wanted to pee his pants.

"Then who?" he whispered, his fingers picking at the material on the arms of the chair.

"Doesn't matter." Payton kept his gaze fixed on Eddie, his body so still she couldn't even see him breathing. "What does matter is some dead senators in San Antonio."

"That wasn't me." Eddie began shaking his head vehemently. "I haven't been to San Antonio in at least six months."

"Can you prove it?"

Eddie blew out breath, defeated. "Not specifically. I mean there's people who've seen me around here. And maybe someone could vouch for me. What's the window you're looking at for the blast?"

"The bomb could have been planted anytime, Eddie. The trigger was on a timer." Payton waited for this newest bit of information to sink in.

"So there's nothing I can say that's going to satisfy you."

"You could confess," Sam said, keeping her voice light. Good cop, bad cop seemed appropriate.

"But I didn't do it."

"So you say." She smiled at him, and he narrowed his eyes, recognition dawning.

"You're that bitch that put me away."

So much for good cop. Sam shrugged. "I recognized your signature, and put the pieces together to ID you. But basically, I'd say you're responsible for putting yourself in prison."

"Yeah, well, I disagree." He lunged at her, his fear of Payton momentarily forgotten. Big mistake.

Payton was out of his chair in an instant, pulling Eddie into a choke hold. "You touch her, slimeball, and I'll gut you like a fish. You got it?"

Eddie nodded, his eyes so wide they looked like marbles glued to his face. Payton released him, and resumed his place on the chair. He hadn't even broken a sweat, and in this heat that was quite an accomplishment. Sam suppressed a shiver, not certain that she'd ever really understood the meaning of the word "deadly" until now.

Payton raised the gun again, and glanced over at Sam. The flicker of concern in his eyes pulled her thoughts back to the task at hand. She couldn't say she truly resented his intervention, but she was also fully capable of taking care of herself.

"So tell me the truth, Eddie, because you know I'll figure it out anyway." She met the man's gaze square-on, keeping her expression masked. "Did you blow up the senators?"

"No." This time there was no hedging. He was telling the truth. She could feel it in her bones. "I don't kill people."

The fact rang true with what she remembered of his cases. Three separate buildings—unoccupied—seemingly unrelated. But his methodology had nailed him in the end. A tendency to weld the end caps into place, a dangerous yet effective strategy. And ultimately they'd tied the bombings to a real estate investor who was trying to buy historic property for development. In an effort to speed the process, he'd hired Eddie to clear the properties of historic buildings, thus making an end run around community outrage.

There was potential for the Prager to fall into the same kind of scheme, but she doubted it. Downtown San Antonio was sort of sacrosanct in the historical department and destroying a building wouldn't necessarily accomplish anything except an historical reproduction.

"All right," she said, still holding Eddie's gaze. "If you didn't do it, who did?"

"How the hell would I know?" Some of Eddie's confidence had returned, his voice full of belligerence. Payton only lifted the gun a fraction of an inch, but Eddie shuddered in reaction, his bluster evaporating. "It's not like we have a newsletter."

"Yeah, but you sell your services, Eddie. Which means there's got to be a network, and I can't believe you all haven't been talking."

Eddie sighed looking down at his hands, and then up to meet Sam's gaze again. "Ain't no one taking credit for it. At least not that I've heard. I figure it's some crazy-ass dude with no desire to live. People like you lookin' for him," he shot a guarded look at Payton, "I'd say his days are numbered."

"How about speculation, Eddie?" Sam asked. "Anyone thinking it wasn't about the senators?"

"Some talk. Mainly about the insanity of a hit like that. But you know what bugs me is the firepower wasn't right for a hit. I mean if the dudes had been standing two feet different in any direction they might have lived."

"I had the same thought," Sam agreed.

"I ain't seen the site of course except on television, but

from what I could tell placement was designed to kill the building, not people. Of course I ain't no expert." He shot a sideways glance at Payton.

"You know more than most," Sam said, interested to hear his take on it. "I've seen your work, remember?"

He smiled, his fear of Payton forgotten in the wake of the compliment. Bombers were loners by nature, and the chance to discuss business was an opportunity not to be missed, no matter the circumstances. "I been around. But this guy is a real pro. I'm betting he planned this thing a long time. Meticulous work. Am I right?" He sat back, waiting, his gaze locked on hers.

"I haven't had much time to examine the fragments, but from what I've seen I'd say the guy has an almost anal need for perfection."

Eddie nodded. "Got his own tools, too, I'll bet. Like the Unabomber. Now that was one lethal dude."

"But *he* targeted people." It was the first time Payton had spoken since he'd manhandled Eddie, and they both jumped.

"True," Eddie said, his eyes thoughtful. "But I still stick by the idea that this guy was after the building. You figure out why it's significant to him, and you'll be a hell of a lot closer to finding him."

"Thanks, Eddie. I'll keep it in mind." She was always fascinated with the way people like Eddie thought. You couldn't spend as much time as she did taking bombs apart and not wonder a bit about the people who put them together.

"One more thing." He leaned forward, this time with enthusiasm instead of anger. "This ain't his first time out of the stable. It takes practice for the kind of precision he had going." This time there was a hint of admiration in his voice. "I figure he's blown before. And not just for practice. There's an art to his work that signifies a real passion for it. And believe me, once you got that kind of fever, you ain't going to sit on it."

Which meant, of course, that Eddie was most likely still

in business himself, despite his recent incarceration. But Sam was convinced he wasn't their man. And equally sure that they'd gotten all that they could from him.

She pushed off the sill, a signal that she was finished. Payton took the cue and rose effortlessly from the chair, the gun still trained on Eddie. "See that you don't go to ground. We might have more questions. And believe me, Eddie, there's nowhere you can go that I can't find you."

Sam believed every word, and apparently so did Eddie. He nodded, his gaze never leaving the gun pointed at his chest. "I ain't going nowhere."

Payton nodded, his voice devoid of all emotion. "You can count on it."

"YOU WERE pretty amazing in there."

Payton turned in the airplane seat so that he could better see Sam's face. There was no hint of mockery there. Nothing to indicate she was repulsed either. Except for Madison, he hadn't met many women who could handle what he did for a living.

Of course he hadn't killed Eddie Marcus, and that probably helped. Not that he hadn't wanted to. The little slime wasn't exactly making the planet a better place. But despite his reputation, Payton wasn't in the habit of killing needlessly. And for the most part, Eddie had been forthcoming.

"I just did what had to be done."

"In a James Bond kind of way that would have made even the most hardened criminal shit his pants. I bet Eddie's chair won't ever be the same." She was laughing now, her eyes crinkling at the corners, her mouth curled upward invitingly. It would be so damn easy to lean over and kiss her, and he was surprised at how very much he wanted to do just that.

But it wasn't the place or the time. Besides, if he was honest, her joyful abandon made him uncomfortable. He'd never been able to understand exuberance—hell, most emotions scared him to death. At least outward displays.

He felt things deeply. There could be no denying that. But he never let it show.

Never.

It was too damn dangerous.

"I'm not James Bond," he answered. "There's nothing suave or sophisticated about me or the jobs I do."

"But someone's got to do it, right?" She tipped her head quizzically, studying him.

"Something like that." He shrugged. "I gather you believed Eddie."

"I think he was telling the truth. Partly because he was so afraid of you, and partly because he sounded downright envious when he was talking about the bomb. If he'd done it there'd have been a note of bravado, and I didn't hear that." She toyed with the pack of almonds the stewardess had left. "What about you? What was your take?"

"Honestly? I think the guy was too stupid to be behind it." He leaned back in his seat. "Based on what you've said about the bomb, and what I observed at the site, I'm thinking he's not exactly up to the task."

"You've never seen his work." Sam closed her eyes. "One bomb took out an entire city block. The only reason no one was killed was that it was the middle of the night. And even with that it was a miracle no one was hurt."

"But it wasn't precise. Isn't that what you're saying?"

She opened her eyes again, her gaze meeting his. "No. I'd say he was a bigger-is-better kind of man."

"My point exactly. Our guy is very focused. Just look at the jack-in-the-box."

She frowned. "You're assuming they're tied together."

"It's the most logical explanation." He shrugged, noticing for the first time the little lines of worry between her eyes. The confetti bomb had frightened her more than she was letting on. "And until I've got proof to the contrary I think it's safer to assume it's a fact."

"I suppose you're right," she sighed. "I guess I'd just rather think it's some oddball with nothing more on his mind than testing his mettle on me."

"It's more than that and you know it."

"I do." She nodded, the worry lines deepening. "But it's easier not to go there. I don't like the idea of his targeting me."

"It could be nothing more than the fact that you're leading the investigation—the expert on bombs." He reached over to cover her hand, pleased when she didn't pull away.

"I know that makes sense. In fact, intellectually I believe that. But emotionally I'm having a little more trouble."

"Because of the jack-in-the-box."

"Yeah." She reached for the almonds, pulling her hand from his, and he resisted the urge to reestablish contact. "But I'm just being paranoid."

"We'll get this bastard, Sam. That much I can promise." He just hoped it was a promise he could keep.

"I believe that." Her gaze met his, her eyes somber. "But the million-dollar question is whether we'll get him before he has time to kill someone else."

CHAPTER NINE

"I DIDN'T KNOW you were back." Harrison walked over to the table where Sam was sorting through parts, and plopped down into a chair. "How was Houston?"

"Hotter than hell." Sam wrote a note about the fragment she was holding, and then sat back, meeting Harrison's quizzical gaze. "And pointless. Eddie didn't have anything to do with it. Although he seems to agree with our assessment of the situation."

"That the bomber meant to take out the building and the senators were just collateral damage?"

"Exactly." She pushed her hair back, and blew out a long breath. "Unfortunately, what I'm finding here seems to support the fact."

"Why unfortunate?" Harrison frowned.

"Two reasons. First off, it's easier to identify possible motives for murder. Figuring out why someone destroys a particular building is a whole lot harder. And secondly, there are all kinds of officials breathing down our necks to find out who is behind this thing. I've fielded six calls already this morning, including one from Washington. And that's just me. No telling what Gabe and Cullen have been dealing with."

"I can understand the pressure, but I don't get why it makes a difference if they were killed on purpose or for being in the wrong place at the wrong time."

"The latter doesn't play well with the media. Considering the fact that the senators were playing the system to line their state's coffers, the press is already having a field day. And they sure as hell don't want the end of the story to be that these guys were killed accidentally. Much better that it was a conspiracy. The more that gets airplay, the more pressure government officials will have to come up with that kind of answer. And the muddier the water gets, the harder it's going to be for us to figure out the truth."

"It's all bullshit," Harrison said, clearly disgusted. "That's why I left the FBI for Phoenix."

"You were in Madison's class at Quantico, right?"

"Yeah, and then I spent a couple of years as a field agent. Not bad work, really, but I think I'm more suited to do my investigating in cyberspace."

"Phoenix is a well-respected company."

"That's John Brighton. He's the force behind it all. One of the smartest men I've ever met."

"I've read about him, of course, but never met him. I've always been impressed with the fact that he uses all that brain power to help solve crimes. I mean to hear the talk, he could have been another Bill Gates or Cullen Pulaski."

Harrison shrugged. "He had that once, but it almost killed him. Literally. And I think once you've faced death like that, you're never really the same."

"Sounds like that's coming from personal experience." Sam tilted her head, studying the younger man's face, noticing for the first time the fine lines that framed his eyes and mouth.

"I guess it is." His expression had become guarded. "I lost my sister when I was in high school. She was killed by an intruder."

"God, I'm sorry." Sam reached out to touch his hand. "Were you there?"

"Yeah." The single word said it all.

"I didn't mean to..." she trailed off, struggling for the right thing to say.

"It's okay." He blew out a breath. "I should be able to handle it better. It was a long time ago."

"I don't think wounds like that ever really heal." She was thinking of her father. The thought of him still brought tears, even after all this time. And he'd died of natural causes. "Is that why you joined the FBI?"

He nodded. "I had this notion that if I fought the bad guys, it'd help me cope. But it didn't change anything really. And, as I said, I was more comfortable with computers."

"Either way, you're making more of a difference than you know." She squeezed his hand and then let go, determined to get back to more comfortable ground. "And I happen to be in need of that expertise as we speak."

"Just tell me what you need." He smiled, his gratitude reflected in the gesture.

He was more open than Payton, but in some ways they were a lot alike, preferring to bury their pain rather than deal with it. Part and parcel of the male species, she supposed.

She picked up a file from the table. "I've got photographs here of several fragments from the San Antonio site. Some are straight shots, and some are enhanced with the microscope. What I need you to do is examine them with whatever computer tools you have. Blow them up, segment them, whatever."

"What am I looking for?" His expression was back to normal, the combination of boyish enthusiasm and intelligence the cornerstone of his charm.

"Anything unusual. A tool mark. A stress fracture. Even a signature."

His eyebrows rose. "These guys sign their work?"

"Some of them do."

"You've already seen something, haven't you?" He crossed his arms, studying her face.

"Maybe." Sam smiled. The man certainly didn't miss a beat. "Just see what you can find."

"You got it." He picked up the file, then stood up with a grin and a salute and headed off toward the computer lab.

Sam returned to the fragment she'd been working on, her mind turning over the possibility that the bomber had indeed signed his work. If he had, it meant two things. First, that he was sending some kind of a message. And second, that Eddie was right. He'd most likely done it all before.

PAYTON SAT PERCHED on the arm of a chair in Cullen's office, admiring the dark sheen of the man's furniture. Mahogany antiques that had no doubt cost a fortune. But then, Cullen always acquired the very best.

Payton supposed the thought should be flattering; after all, Cullen had chosen him, in a way. But instead, the idea was repugnant. Money couldn't buy everything. Or at least that's what he preferred to believe.

"The president is riding my ass big-time," Cullen said, his gaze encompassing both Payton and Gabe. "Tell me you have something positive to report."

Gabe shook his head, his expression grim. "It's still too soon. Sam's got the NRT working on the fragments day and night. Not to mention the pieces she's got here. Unfortunately it just takes time."

"Time is not something we have." As usual Cullen was talking in edicts.

"I can't make it go any faster, Cullen. You'll just have to tell Washington we're working as hard as we can."

"How about the bomb in Sam's suite—anything there that could link it to San Antonio?"

"Nothing concrete so far." Gabe shook his head. "But I think we have to assume that there's a connection. The timing alone is indicative of that."

"Well maybe Sam can find something there that'll prove to be a lead in the other case." Cullen picked up a ball on his desk, absently squeezing it. "How's she holding up?"

"She's fine." Payton wasn't certain why he answered. Gabe could easily have fielded the question. "Apparently this kind of thing happens a lot in her line of work." It wasn't exactly what Sam had said, but it would do. And for some reason Payton felt the need to protect her. Make certain that Cullen wasn't aware of any chinks in her armor.

Not that she'd thank him for his involvement. Samantha Waters was perfectly capable of watching out for herself.

"And she's fitting into the team all right?" Cullen's question was aimed at Gabe, but again Payton felt compelled to answer.

"No problems at all. She's a straight shooter and that certainly sits well with the rest of us. And she definitely knows her job." He was bordering on effusive. And Gabe's grin wasn't helping matters any.

Cullen, thankfully, appeared to be oblivious to his discomfort. "Well, I'm glad it's working. It's important that you all work well together. Last Chance has created quite a reputation over the past couple of years, and I'd hate to see anything detract from that."

He wasn't talking about Sam anymore. And the only reputation he was worried about was his own.

"What people think of Last Chance is the least of our problems, Cullen," Gabe said, pale eyes flashing. "We've got three men dead and a building destroyed. And as you so elegantly put it, people riding our asses."

"Perception is everything, Gabriel." Cullen's expression was deceivingly bland. "Don't ever forget that."

"Right," Gabe said, his gaze dueling with Cullen's. If they hadn't both looked so serious, Payton might have laughed. But he knew better.

There was a moment of heavy silence, and then Cullen turned to Payton. "What about Houston?"

"It was a dead end." Nothing like a little more bad news.

"Goddamn it." The expletive hung in the air, Cullen's expression thunderous. "I need something. I'm supposed to fly to Washington for a press conference tomorrow. The NRT scheduled it without so much as a by-your-leave."

End runs did not please Cullen Pulaski. If there were a poster boy for control freaks, Cullen was the man. His attention to detail and personal involvement was the biggest contributor to his success. At the same time his constant meddling also meant that he was often involved in areas where he had no expertise. A double-edged sword if ever there was one.

In the case of Iraq, that lack of expertise had cost lives—Payton's wife and brother principal among them.

Payton pushed his black thoughts away, focusing instead on the present conversation.

"You've got the senators' illicit meeting, and their collusion to funnel money away from needed areas into their own backyards. That'll have to satisfy the hungry dogs." Gabe crossed his arms, his patience for Cullen and his caterwauling only slightly better than Payton's.

"I thought you'd decided that the bomb wasn't meant for the senators." Cullen frowned. "Have you found something to contradict that?"

"Nothing," Payton interjected. "In fact, for what it's worth, Eddie Marcus believes the bomb was about the building and not the senators as well."

"The point here, Cullen," Gabe said, "is that there's no need to tell the press any more than is needed. For that matter, there's no reason to let the president in on this either, although with so many people involved I'm not sure how you can stop that. But as far as I'm concerned the longer the press thinks this is all about the senators' backroom dealings, the better it is for us. It'll take the heat off, and give us time to consider all aspects of the San Antonio bombing."

"In addition," Payton said, taking his cue from Gabe, "Madison thinks that it might play to our advantage with the bomber to keep the focus on the senators."

"How so?" Cullen asked, leaning back in his chair, arms crossed.

"If this guy is trying to send a message, it's going to get lost in all the hoopla about the murders. Which, according to my wife, isn't going to sit very well."

"So you're hoping it'll draw him out." Cullen frowned, considering the possible outcomes of such action.

"Exactly."

"It's a good theory in the abstract, except that it could mean more casualties."

"Hopefully, not. If we're right, the bomber was trying to destroy the building, not take human life, which should mean his next move will be destructive but not lethal."

Cullen shrugged. "Unless he's developed a taste for blood."

WALTER ATHERTON was exhausted all the way down to his toes. It had been a hell of a day, the main order of business dealing with the San Antonio bombing. Although Sam Waters, along with Cullen Pulaski's Last Chance, was in charge of the official investigation, his agents were working as part of the National Response Team, which meant long hours and little payoff.

Everyone in Washington wanted answers yesterday, which meant he'd spent the majority of his time on the phone. Sometimes he wished he'd never become a director. Administrative work was a pain in the ass.

In many ways he'd rather have still been in the trenches. Working with people like Sam. Digging through rubble to find answers. It had been years since they'd worked together, but he'd continued to follow her career, in many ways considering her his protégée.

Although, in truth, she far surpassed him, a fact which didn't always sit well. Except that administrative work had helped pay off his home in McLean. And a summer cottage at the beach. So there really wasn't much room for complaint.

It's just that sometimes he felt so damn old. Five more years and the Bureau would be pushing him to retire. Not that they were alone in that regard. His wife was always talking about him being home. So that they could do things together. Things he had no interest in whatsoever. But he loved Amanda, and so he'd make the adjustment.

He pulled into his driveway, hitting the remote button on the visor that opened the garage. Amanda wouldn't be home until late tonight, which meant he had time to himself to unwind. The thought of a double scotch was appealing, especially when his wife wasn't around to remind him that alcohol wasn't good for his heart.

In his mind, if it helped to relieve his stress then it could hardly be bad for him, but of course his cardiologist didn't agree. And neither did Amanda.

He pulled the Acura into the garage and sat for a minute letting the silence surround him, ignoring the vibration of his BlackBerry. Technology was a wonderful thing, but sometimes it was too damn invasive.

At least it wasn't his cell phone.

He pulled it out and scrolled through the messages, stopping to read one. A press conference tomorrow. Obviously the NRT felt the need to at least pretend there had been progress. He wondered if Sam would be involved.

He doubted it. If she'd been planning to come to D.C., she would have called.

With a sigh, he pocketed the machine and got out of the car, starting for the door, stopping short when he caught sight of the empty garbage can. Amanda would have his head if he left it out.

Nothing like a little domestic peace to clue you in to your real importance in life.

He strode down the driveway, lifting a hand to wave at the

neighbor across the street. The houses here were all on big lots, which meant that it was rare to see your neighbors, and even when you did, they were too far away to talk.

Grabbing the can, he pulled it back onto its wheels and rolled it back up the driveway, deciding that he'd have two double scotches. Hell, after his day, he'd earned them. He pulled the bin over the bump that divided the garage from the driveway and maneuvered it into the open space between the door and some shelving.

Everything in its place—just the way Amanda liked it.

With a smile, he walked through the garage to the back door, and reached up to press the button to close the garage. Instead of the usual grinding noise that signaled the grudging descent of the door, there was only a hollow click.

Frowning, he tried again, this time pressing and holding the button.

The fireball crashed out through the open garage door and up into the twilight sky, taking half the house and its owner with it in less time than it took Walter Atherton to draw his last breath.

CHAPTER TEN

SAM STARED DOWN at the half-assembled model on the table. She'd cast the major pieces of the recovered bomb fragments and filled in the rest using a combination of experience and intuition. Her lab in Georgia was doing the same thing, and between the two of them, Sam was confident they'd soon have an accurate replica of the bomb used at the Prager.

In seeing how the bomb had been put together, it was possible to gain insight into the man who had built it. And right now that was of paramount concern.

She took a piece of putty and used it to connect two fragments, the entire thing beginning to take on lethal proportions. There was an odd kind of beauty at work, and despite the fact that the thing had killed three people, Sam couldn't help but admire the ingenuity involved.

She'd been fascinated with things that went *boom* since she'd first discovered firecrackers as a kid. And listening to her dad's stories had only fueled the fire, so to speak. While other kids were building forts or windmills with their Tinker Toys, Sam had been building explosive devices. Some of them even operational.

She'd been grounded once for a month after an experiment had gone wrong and blown up her mother's washing machine. From that point on, she'd been a hell of a lot more careful where she tested her work.

After high school, she'd moved on to college and engineering. Texas A&M had opened a whole new world, and, except on paper, there hadn't been time for explosives. But then once she'd landed with the crime scene unit in Abilene, she'd found her way back to what she loved most—the intricate combination of chemistry, physics and pyrotechnics that yielded a bomb.

That and the psychology of those that made them.

There was a certain symmetry in the fact that what she had once loved to create, she now spent the major portion of her life destroying. Most people thought she'd just followed in her father's footsteps, but Sam knew better. There was something else there—something inherent in her makeup. Her father had had it, too. So maybe it was in the genes—or maybe it was a quirk in personality.

Either way, pure and simple, she loved her job. Even when it seemed to be going nowhere.

She dropped the piece she was working with and picked up another, turning it to see if maybe it would fit with the already assembled parts. Tedious work, but she was convinced the payoff would be worth the effort.

"You're working late." Payton as usual had arrived on silent feet, and Sam jumped at the sound of his voice.

"You scared the crap out of me." Her words came out harsher than she'd meant them, but her heart was pounding and, quite honestly, she didn't appreciate being interrupted.

"Occupational hazard." He shrugged, not looking even the slightest bit apologetic. "You had anything to eat?"

"No time." Sam shook her head, rotating the fragment to try and match it to another piece.

"That's what I figured." Payton produced a large paper bag that smelled of cumin and chili. Sam's mouth watered and her stomach clenched in anticipation. Her brain might want to keep working, but the rest of her body was obviously in revolt.

"Harrison swears this is the best Mexican food in Austin." He pulled out a plastic container and handed it to her, then pulled out another for himself. "I didn't know what you'd like so I went for variety. Two Chuy's Comida Deluxe plates at your service."

"Thanks." She opened the container and inhaled appreciatively, then picked up a taco bursting with meat and cheese. "It looks wonderful. Between our trip to Houston and working here in the lab, the day sort of got away from me."

"Totally understandable," he said, sliding into the chair next to hers, his thigh brushing against hers. "But starving yourself isn't going to help you find answers."

She nodded, her mouth too full of guacamole to answer with words. She was touched by his thoughtfulness. Surprised by it, too. Payton didn't seem like the kind of man who spent time thinking about other people's needs. Obviously she'd misjudged him.

She reached for her Dr. Pepper, and in the process moved her leg. The contact was distracting. Payton didn't seem to notice and she couldn't decide if she was relieved or offended. Basically she was overanalyzing the whole thing. He'd brought her dinner.

Big freaking deal.

"What are you working on?" He motioned to the partially completed model with an enchilada-laden fork.

"I'm trying to build a model of the San Antonio bomb. But it's tricky. There were only a couple of fragments large enough to work off of. So I'm trying to guess the proximity of the rest."

"An educated guess, I'd assume." He was studying the pieces now.

"Well, I have seen a lot of bombs in my day. But the real key is the computer. Both the ATF and the FBI have extensive databases recording blasts and the apparatus used. By comparing my parts with the database, I can be a hell of a lot more accurate." She motioned toward a laptop she had set up at the end of the table.

"Still, seems like frustrating work." He turned back to his plate of food, already more than halfway through it.

"It can be. But for the most part I like it. Particularly the challenge of working backward to solve the puzzle. It's interesting to try and get into the bomber's head."

"You sound like Madison."

Sam smiled. "I guess there are similarities. Only her job is a lot harder."

"No. Just different." His smile was still only half-mast, but it was genuine. "Once you get that done, what will it tell you?"

"Hopefully it'll help establish a signature. Which is the best way I know of to try and nail a bomber. The methodology may vary from incident to incident, but, for the most part, there are peculiarities that hold true every time a particular bomber produces something. If we can find those idiosyncrasies, we can start to build a history for the guy and work from there."

"Sounds like an indefinite science." Payton put his trash back in the bag, wiping his hands with a napkin.

"In some ways it isn't science at all. I mean the principles of chemistry and physics apply, certainly, and without a working knowledge of both, a bomb can't be constructed. But there's also an art to it. And sometimes these guys are a lot more about the sheer beauty of combustion than the more technical aspects."

"And reconstructing the bomb can tell you how this particular bomber fits onto the scale?"

"Exactly. You start with specific components he chooses, then work through the way he connects them together, right up to the way he perceives the impact of explosion. It's a detailed process, and the construction of the bomb can tell it all." She smiled up at him. "Sounds certifiable, huh?"

"On the contrary, I find it fascinating." His hooded gaze held hers, and though the message there was all about chemistry, it had nothing to do with bombs or bomb fragments. Her stomach tightened and her pulse pounded in her ears.

Just looking at him made her dizzy. The idea of him touching her set off every nerve synapse in her body. She leaned forward, not certain what exactly she was planning to do, intent only on the green of his eyes and the battle-scarred line of his jaw.

She knew she should back away, break the connection, but she couldn't bring herself to do it. She wanted to know what he tasted like, what his lips would feel like against hers. She'd wanted it since last night. His vulnerability touched her in a way she couldn't have imagined.

Her heart beat wildly as she closed the distance between them. His lips brushed against hers, the contact more exquisite than anything she could have imagined. She closed her eyes, and simply let the sensation surround her.

Minutes seemed to stretch to hours, and then, with a groan, he threaded his fingers through her hair, his hands holding her captive as he tasted and teased. With a sigh, she opened to him, their tongues tangling together, the kiss deepening, desire burgeoning from deep within.

There was no trace of gentleness now. This was a man who took what he wanted. No quarter spared. In any other man it would have offended her, but with Payton she found the idea enticing.

Then reality reared its ugly head and she realized where they were.

Pushing away, she fought for breath, her gaze locking on his.

His smile was slow, his gaze still clouded with passion. "I've wanted to do that since the first time I saw you."

"I can't say that the thought hasn't crossed my mind, but you know as well as I do that this isn't a good idea." Her voice was raspy, her breathing still labored.

"It was just a kiss."

"It was a hell of a lot more than a kiss, and you know it," she snapped, immediately wishing the words back, her anger clearly overriding good sense.

Damn the man.

"Well one thing is for certain, if we don't explore our options we'll never find out." He reached over to wipe a smear of guacamole from her cheek, the intimacy of the act sending shivers chasing through her. "Consider the kiss an invitation. If you're interested, you know where to find me."

She wanted to tell him to drop dead. To forget the whole idea, but instead she nodded, not certain at all what she was agreeing to. The truth was, she'd never in her life met a man who managed to put her at such a disadvantage.

She reached for the remains of her dinner and started stuffing things back into the sack, the action giving her time to pull her rioting emotions into control.

"I'm glad you guys are still here." Gabe's voice was like a bucket of cold water, and despite herself, Sam jumped back, dropping the bag, her guilt no doubt playing across her face like a neon sign.

Payton bent down to help her retrieve the sack, in the process reaching out to squeeze her hand. "He didn't see a thing."

His whispered reassurance was oddly more disconcerting than his earlier words had been, and Sam wondered if perhaps she'd stumbled down Alice's rabbit hole.

Forcing a calm she did not feel, she straightened and turned to Gabe, who fortunately seemed to have other things on his mind than the dinnertime philandering of his teammates. In fact, now that her head was clearer, she noticed the stark lines on his face.

"What's happened?"

Gabe's expression, if possible, turned even more grim. "There's been another bombing."

"Where?" Payton stepped around the end of the table, his attention fixed solely on Gabe.

"Virginia, just outside of D.C."

"Any casualties?" Sam sank back against the table, trying to process this newest information.

"One. Some director with the FBI. His garage was booby-trapped. Poor bastard didn't stand a chance."

"So what's the tie-in to San Antonio?"

"Logistically there's nothing yet. But the guy killed was heading up the NRT for our bomb. Seems like something more than coincidence."

Sam's stomach roiled, her dinner threatening to do an encore performance. "You're talking about Walter Atherton." It was a statement, not a question, but her heart refused to believe the obvious without verification.

"Yeah, why? You know him?"

She nodded, surprised that the muscles were working. "He was my boss when I worked in evidence recovery. A lot of what I know I learned from him. He and Amanda were like a second family."

Payton moved to stand beside her, his physical presence giving her needed support.

"Was…" She paused, trying to order her words, her emotions blocking the transmission of cognizant thought. "Was Amanda there?"

Gabe shook his head. "Just Atherton. You going to be able to deal with this?"

It was a valid question and one she wasn't completely sure she could answer, but compartmentalizing her feelings was part and parcel of the job, and if anything she owed it to Walter to pull herself together. "I'll be fine." She sucked in a breath and squared her shoulders. "I assume we're heading to McLean."

Gabe searched her face, and then nodded, seemingly satisfied with what he saw. "Cullen's plane is standing by. We'll leave as soon as you're ready."

She reached across the table for her bomb kit, tucking a

couple of files from the table into the bag. Everything else she needed they'd have on site. "I'm ready."

Flanked by Gabe and Payton she walked out of the office mentally preparing to do battle with the devil.

Only this time, it was personal.

J.T. SAT CROSS-LEGGED on the bed of his hotel room, watching the evening news. The blast had made all three networks, not to mention blow-by-blow details on CNN. He should have been pleased that things had gone according to plan, but he wasn't.

Instead, he had once more unwittingly tied himself into the senators' wrongdoings. The press had already concluded that the hit on Atherton was precipitated by his involvement in the investigation. The logic following that the bombing was either meant to slow the investigation or send a message, quite probably both.

There was an element of truth in the latter. He *was* trying to send a message, but the world was intent on translating it completely wrong.

According to the news, Samantha's team was on its way. The film footage of her and one of Cullen Pulaski's flunkies was disconcerting at best. He didn't like the possessive manner in which the man cupped Sam's elbow, although she seemed oblivious to the fact, concentrating instead on the plane they were boarding.

Knowing Samantha, her mind was firmly fixed on the task at hand—deciphering the clues his handiwork had left behind. Even before she reached the site, she'd be examining other experts' reports: the medical examiner, the preliminary site team, probably even interviews with Atherton's widow.

She'd want to pull together as much information as she could, then let her senses do the rest, filtering the visceral reality of the bomb impact with the conclusions of others. She was meticulous to a fault. And at the end of the day, J.T. had no doubt she'd work out the implications of what he'd done.

Unfortunately, Atherton's ties to the investigation would no doubt confuse things. He should have anticipated the outcome. Done something to make certain there could be no confusion. But in the heat of the moment, he'd allowed his emotions to carry him away, his need to reach Sam more pressing than the minor details of Atherton's professional life.

In the course of a day Walter Atherton oversaw a myriad of cases. Still, J.T. should have realized that the San Antonio bombing was a priority. And that the press would see the attack as part of the alleged conspiracy involving Ruckland and the others.

He sighed, allowing his body to settle into the familiar lotus position. What he needed was to find inner strength. To cleanse his body of all emotion. His attachment to Samantha was something that couldn't be denied, as intrinsic to his being as breathing and blood flow. But it couldn't become a distraction.

The senators had been a mistake, but he should have predicted the media's reaction to Atherton's death. He wouldn't make the same mistake next time.

He closed his eyes, intent on traveling the pathways of his mind. He chanted softly, letting the monotonous tone pull him deeper into his own subconscious. Peace beckoned, the circle curling in on itself until he felt whole.

As always, she was there waiting, the smile on her face knowing, the promise of completion pulling him deeper and deeper until he could no longer tell where he ended and she began.

CHAPTER ELEVEN

PAYTON STOOD on the remains of the Athertons' driveway, watching as Sam studied the burnt-out casing that had once been a wall-mounted garage door opener. She stopped for a moment, writing something in the spiral notebook she carried everywhere, then resumed her inspection. They'd been on-site for less than an hour, but already she'd taken control with a seamless efficiency that left no ruffled feathers.

And considering the number of high-ranking FBI personnel present, that was no mean feat.

The medical examiner's office had already been by to collect what remained of Walter Atherton. Although there hadn't been much left, there had been enough to establish tentative identification. Which meant that Sam's friend had been the man caught in the blast.

Sam bent to pick something up, then discarded it, her expression remaining carefully neutral, but Payton knew her well enough now to recognize the signs of stress.

On the plane ride to Virginia she hadn't said much, just reiterated that Atherton was a friend. The world of ordnance retrieval was small and when one factored out the military it was miniscule, all personnel interconnected in some way or other. But this was more than that—she'd truly cared for this man.

And Payton hated the idea that she was hurting. He'd known her for such a short time, yet he felt connected, bound in the pheromone-laden way that nature had created to assure survival of the species.

But it was more than that. He recognized something of himself in her. Like him, she kept the world at arm's length, preferring to live in the moment with little thought to the future. And no thought at all of the past.

But unlike him, Sam had nothing to hide. No internal flaw that destroyed the people he loved. Sam was simply a loner more comfortable in her own company than anyone else's.

He could respect that—to a point. But he'd meant it when he'd invited her into his bed. He wanted to feel her moving beneath him. Wanted to drive deep into her heat, losing himself in the moment, forgetting just who and what he was.

He was realistic enough to understand that the road might end there, that neither of them was particularly inclined to enter into something long-term. Which in some ways suited him just fine. But there was another part of him that was intrigued with the idea of something more. Something permanent.

Yeah. Right.

He shook his head, clearing his brain of romantic bullshit. No matter how big the hole inside him, it wasn't worth it to try and fill it again.

Except temporarily.

It was a rationalization. He was honest enough to admit that. But hell, the truth was he wanted her. Simple as that. In the meantime, however, they had bigger fish to fry, starting with the big black limo that had skirted the barricades to arrive at the Athertons' curb.

Sam had seen it, too, temporarily abandoning her examination of the site to cross over to him, her face awash with a mixture of trepidation and curiosity. "Any idea who that is?"

He shook his head, trying to ignore the jump in his pulse at her nearness. "Someone with clout, though. The limo waltzed right through the checkpoint."

Sam nodded, shading her eyes as the back door opened. Payton followed the line of her gaze. The door opened and a man in a blue suit stepped out. *Cullen.* He should have known. Leave it to him to arrive like the king of fucking England.

Sam's eyes narrowed as she realized who had emerged from the limo, her quick intake of breath a sign that she viewed the man as nothing more than an unnecessary intrusion.

"Great," she murmured, already striding toward the limo.

Payton followed in her wake, watching as Cullen turned to lean back into the limo, helping a woman disembark. The lady was of indeterminate age, dressed in an expensive green suit. She clung to Cullen, her ringed hand lined with age.

"Amanda," Sam called out, shoving past the gathering crime scene folks as if they were of no more substance than paper dolls. The two women embraced, and as Payton drew closer, he could see the tear-ravaged face of the older woman.

"You shouldn't be here," Sam said, shooting Cullen a murderous glance, then returning her worried gaze to Amanda Atherton.

"I had to come." The older woman shook her head. "I needed to see this."

"The deputy director told her about Walter," Cullen said by way of explanation. "But then left her at her club to wait. I found her there and volunteered to bring her here."

Sam opened her mouth to say something, and then evidently thought better of it, putting an arm around Amanda instead.

Payton could understand why Sam would want to shelter her friend, but at the same time he couldn't fault Amanda for wanting to see firsthand what had happened to her husband. There was a masochistic kind of closure in the act, something he often wished he'd been allowed in Iraq. But circumstances had prevented it. Circumstances and people.

He fought a surge of bitter resentment and kept his gaze away from Cullen's.

"Is he here?" Amanda asked, her voice barely above a whisper.

Sam shook her head. "They took him to the medical examiner's office. I'm sure they'll release his remains as soon as they can."

"Won't they..." Amanda paused, sucking in a deep breath. "Won't they need me to identify the body?"

Sam shot a look at Payton, her gaze beseeching.

"No, ma'am," Payton said, trying to keep his voice even. "They've already had a visual ID. They'll want to verify using DNA. But they're certain it's him."

"I see." The words were quiet. Accepting. This was a woman of strength, and Payton admired her for it. "Have you found out what caused the explosion?" Again she looked to Sam for an answer.

"Not yet. I think the detonator was in the garage door opener. But that's as far as I've gotten."

Amanda frowned, the gesture deepening the lines around her eyes and mouth. "But I used it this morning when I left for my meetings. And I'm sure that Walter did, too."

"That doesn't necessarily mean anything, Amanda. The bomb could have been set later in the day, or maybe it was attached to a timer." Sam looked as if each word were twisting her heart. Payton's anger at Cullen grew exponentially. It was his fault she'd been put in this position. Sam would no doubt have wanted to see Amanda before they went back to Austin, but it would have been in a setting far different from this.

"You're saying the thing could have been there all along. That we should have seen it?"

"I'm not saying that at all. If it was already in place it would have been well hidden." Sam squeezed Amanda's hand. "Look, Cullen, this isn't the time or place to discuss this. We need to finish our site investigation, and then analyze the data. All of which takes time. It could be weeks before we have definitive answers."

Amanda met Sam's eyes head-on, and again Payton was

impressed with the woman's strength. "Just tell me one thing. Do you believe this is connected to the bombing in San Antonio? Walter was working on it day and night. I've never seen him so driven."

"There are similarities in the materials used. And in the execution." Sam flinched at her choice of word, darting a glance at Payton. He subtly shook his head, satisfied that Amanda had missed the double entendre. "I'll know more when I get the fragments back to the lab."

Amanda nodded, obviously turning Sam's words over in her mind. "And you're in charge of this investigation. You and Mr. Pulaski, here." She tipped her head toward Cullen, who had been uncharacteristically silent since his arrival.

"I've got a crack team of experts working on it, Mrs. Atherton," Cullen inserted. "Sam and Payton here are two of the team. Sam of course is taking lead because of her expertise in dealing with this type of situation."

"Bombings, you mean." Amanda's tone was dry, as if she loathed the word. But then again, considering what had just happened, she probably did.

"Yes. She's one of the best in the country." Cullen's response bordered on patronizing, and Payton waited for Amanda Atherton's reaction, expecting fireworks.

"I assure you, Mr. Pulaski, I'm quite aware of that fact. My husband is in large part responsible for her career, as well as her expertise." Amanda turned her concerned gaze on Sam, reaching out for her hands. "You be careful, Sam. Whoever this is, he's lethal. And he's already killed one investigator. You could be next. I don't want to lose you, too." The woman's eyes filled with tears, and Sam reached out to hug her again, the two women holding on to each other, giving and getting support.

Sam met Payton's gaze over Amanda's shoulder, her eyes filled with tears. And Payton felt a rush of emotion that surprised him with its strength.

If the bastard ever tried coming after Sam, he'd have to get through Last Chance first. He might not trust Cullen—hell, he didn't even like the man—but he had put together a crack team, and none of them, Payton most particularly, was going to let anything happen to Sam.

Of that much he was absolutely certain.

SAM LEANED BACK against the cool leather seat of Cullen's private jet, trying without success to get some sleep. It was late. Almost morning, actually, and she'd been up for almost thirty-six hours. But despite utter exhaustion, her brain simply wouldn't turn off.

This was her fourth trip in the jet, and she had to admit it wasn't a bad way to travel. Still, she'd rather go by bus if it meant that she wouldn't have to deal with Walter Atherton's death.

There weren't many people that had touched Sam's life. She was too self-contained for that. But her father had been one, and Walter Atherton another. Maybe if she was really generous she could add a couple other names, but basically, when she thought of the people instrumental in her life, her dad and Walter summed it all up.

And now they were both gone.

She hadn't allowed herself to cry. Wasn't going to do it now, either. Despite the fact that Payton was sound asleep in the seat next to hers.

Cullen was sitting several rows back, and the last time she'd checked, he too was out like a light. Gabe and Madison were still in Austin, coordinating things from that end. And Harrison was sitting a few rows up, tapping diligently at his computer. Nothing new in that. But Sam had to admit there was a certain comfort in the sound of clacking keys.

She closed her eyes, willing herself to relax, but she had no more luck than she'd had the first hundred times she'd tried. It had been hard to leave Amanda, but her daughter had arrived from Radcliffe, and her son should be there by now. They needed time alone. Time to grieve. And despite Sam's relationship with the family, she was still an outsider. Besides, there was work to do.

If they were going to nail the bastard behind all of this, she had to stay focused on the evidence. Piece together the puzzle. There were definite similarities. She just had to tie the two bombings together. Once she'd established a pattern, then they could start to look for other incidents.

Harrison had already found five. She could start there. Maybe if she understood a little more about them, she could begin eliminating. In addition to that, she needed to get Harrison's take on the photos of the fragments she'd given him.

She doubted he'd had time to analyze much since they'd just spent the last twenty-four hours in Virginia, but there was no time like the present. And at least talking to him, she'd feel like she was doing something constructive.

Moving carefully so as not to wake Payton, she slid out of the seat and made her way up the aisle to Harrison, leaning on the armrest of the seat across from him. "Burning the midnight oil?"

Harrison looked up with a rueful grin. "I know, I should be sleeping, but this stuff just sticks in my head and won't go away."

"I know what you mean." Sam smiled. The first genuine one she'd had all day. There was just something comforting about Harrison Blake, like a favorite blanket or sweatshirt or something.

She shook her head at her musings. It seemed that Last Chance was full of intriguing men. Score one for Cullen.

"So tell me what you know about the five unsolved bombings?"

"Not much really." Harrison hit a couple of keys and brought up a report. "They're all in Texas." He shot her an apologetic look. "I figured these guys typically stay close to home, so I used San Antonio as the center. With Virginia in the mix I probably ought to take the search national."

"I searched the databanks myself for anything as big as San Antonio that might match up, and came up with zilch. So I think you were right to stick to Texas. We're looking at priors here, and so whatever we find might have a similar M.O., and should certainly have the same signature, but it won't necessarily be as big or as well done. So you did fine," she said, stifling a yawn.

"Maybe you're the one who should be sleeping," Harrison said, his gaze meeting hers, his smile crooked.

"I've been trying, but my brain and yours are on the same wavelength, I think. So tell me about the possible incidents."

He turned his attention back to the screen. "They're all across the state. Two in west Texas, two on or near the coast and one in east-central Texas. Nothing in the immediate area around San Antonio."

"Let's start with the ones in west Texas." She leaned over so that she could see the computer screen.

"Sure." Harrison hit a button bringing up a more detailed screen. "The first one was four years ago in Lubbock. Pipe bomb. Welding." He paused to look up at her. "That was part of my search parameter."

"Did you specify detonation?"

"I said electrical. And described what we found in San Antonio."

Sam nodded as Harrison turned back to the computer screen. "Anyway. This one happened at a bus station. The investigation shows three deaths. Two transients and the night watchman. The bomb was triggered by the man's radio."

"Battery-powered or electric?"

Harrison scrolled through the report. "Electric. Which would be why the computer spit it out. Investigation centered on the night watchman since it was his radio. Although according to the police report, the radio never left the bus station."

"So it could have been about something else."

"Exactly. But our guy would have known he was killing someone, since it required turning on the machine to close the circuit for the blast."

"All right," Sam said, frowning. "Let's hear about the other one."

"This one was in Abilene."

Sam's frown deepened. "When was the bombing?"

"Almost three years ago. The city office complex across from the courthouse."

"Common target. I actually defused a bomb there something like twelve years ago when I was working CSU. What are the specifics this time?"

Harrison brought up another screen. "Same type of bomb as Lubbock, this one detonated by the security system. Once the security system was activated for the night, a timer started, three hours later, there was no need for the system. It was assumed that it was some local group at odds with the government, but nothing was ever proved."

"Any casualties?"

Harrison shook his head. "You want to hear about Brownsville?"

"Yeah." She chewed the side of her lip, trying to put the newest pieces of information into coherent order.

"This one was a year and a half ago. Same M.O. for the bomb. Detonator was also a security system. This time to the computer room of the city building. A janitor punched in the code and *kaboom*. Two fatalities."

"Both janitors?"

Harrison nodded, opening yet another screen. "The other bomb on the coast was in Refugio. It was the longest ago. Sixteen years. And barely fits our parameters. The bomb construction fits the bill, but the work is a lot cruder. The target was the county museum, specifically an exhibit of Nolan Ryan memorabilia. He was born in Refugio. Anyway, the bomb was detonated with a kitchen timer hooked to an electrical circuit powered by a battery."

"You're right, it isn't as sophisticated as the others. But let's not rule it out. It could have just been part of his evolution. Anyone killed?"

"Nope. The explosion occurred on a Saturday night just after closing. No one was on the premises."

"So we've got four possibilities. What about the last one?"

"Bryan." Harrison hit a button to display the final screen. "This one occurred six years ago in a barbeque restaurant. At first they thought it was a fire, but later investigation turned up bomb fragments. The place was small and evidently a hell of a tinderbox, so there wasn't much left. Nothing to firmly tie to a detonator. But there were fragments of wiring there that indicated an electrical detonation of some kind. It fits the pattern the least."

"But part of that's because there wasn't much to go on."

"That and the fact that there wasn't a lot of investigation. Apparently the owner was suspect from the get-go. He evidently owed a lot of money to the wrong sorts of people. Speculation was that either he did it himself for the insurance money, or his loan sharks did it to teach him a lesson."

Sam sighed. "We're going to need something more definitive to tie any of these to our guy. You get a chance to look at those photographs yet?"

"Not much. I started, but then this thing in Virginia happened, and it sort of got crazy...." He shrugged, his expression apologetic again. "I need a better computer than this one," he waved at his laptop, "to properly enhance what you gave me. But I did notice something right off. In comparing the San Antonio photographs to other fragment photos in the FBI database, I was surprised to see no tool marks. It's like the guy polished the pieces after he'd assembled them or something."

"The Unabomber did that. Meticulous to a fault."

"So maybe we're dealing with a similar personality?" Harrison's eyebrows raised with the question.

"God, I hope not." The Unabomber had gone undetected for years. And Sam wasn't about to entertain the notion that this guy would follow a similar path. She wanted to nail the bastard now. Before he managed another attack.

People like him didn't stop. The need to demonstrate his power would be like a virus growing inside him. Which meant there was potential for it to get a hell of a lot worse before it got any better.

CHAPTER TWELVE

"I DON'T KNOW what the hell we're dealing with here, but whatever it is, it's getting attention from everyone in the free world." Cullen stood in the operations conference room, his hands waving through the air underscoring his words. "Which means the fire under our butts is reaching the broiling stage."

"I'd say that's hitting a little too close to home." Gabe grimaced, glancing down at the photographs he held in his hands. Pictures of the remains of Walter Atherton. Payton had just spent the past half hour bringing Gabe up to speed. They'd communicated by telephone in Virginia, but it wasn't the same as a firsthand account.

"If the shoe fits…" Cullen's face had turned red, his frustration building into anger.

"Come on, Cullen, you know we're working as fast as we can," Madison said, her voice soft and unaffected. She was the only one who seemed completely impervious to Cullen's outbreaks. But then she'd been dealing with the man for years. "You've got to remember the guy on the other side of all this knows why he's doing what he's doing. We don't have that luxury."

"I thought that's what you were supposed to excel at. Thinking like this vermin."

Madison smiled, her hand on her stomach, the gesture touching somehow, as if even in utero she was protecting her child. "It's not as easy as all that and you know it. I have to have more to go on than just his handiwork."

Cullen sank down onto a chair, running a hand through his hair. "I know that. And I didn't mean to lash out at you." He shot her a chagrined look, and for a moment Payton almost forgot he hated the man.

"We're all under a lot of pressure here." This from Gabe, who was holding on to his temper by a hairsbreadth. Cullen and Gabe had never been the best of friends, but things had eased a lot with Madison's intervention. However, in light of her current condition, Gabe was more protective than usual.

"Well maybe we can help." Harrison and Sam stood in the doorway, Harrison waving a sheath of photographs for emphasis. "We may have a signature."

"Let me see." Cullen stood up and was across the room in two paces. Harrison however, was one step ahead of him.

"Hang on," he said, lifting the photos over his head, well out of Cullen's reach. "This is Sam's show."

She shot Harrison a warm smile, and Payton swallowed a surge of irritation. The two of them had been thick as thieves since they'd boarded the plane back to Austin.

"Why don't you quit with the histrionics and just tell us what you've found." His words sounded harsh, but there was no taking them back.

Sam's eyebrows rose, her gaze knowing, and he silently cursed his own weakness. "Believe me, it'll be better if we show you. And thanks to Harrison and all this amazing equipment, that's exactly what we want to do." She nodded to Harrison who had attached his computer to some audio/visual equipment, the enlarged image of a bomb fragment projected on the whiteboard.

Sam moved over to stand next to him, a laser pointer in her hand. "This is fragment 18A from the San Antonio bomb site." She circled the image on the screen with the red laser line, as Harrison turned out the lights. Cullen and Gabe had taken seats flanking Madison, the three of them intent on the projected image. "This is the largest fragment we found. A part of an end cap. At first I thought it was a fluke that it survived. The evidence indicates that our bomber welds his end caps. And if that's the case, this piece should never have remained intact."

Payton leaned forward, squinting until his eyes adjusted to the newly created gloom. The picture changed, the computer acting as slide projector. "This is a picture of a fragment of the other end cap. You can see that it's a lot smaller. We found three fragments like this one."

"And the rest of the end cap?" Cullen asked.

"Was destroyed in the blast. Exactly as the other one should have been." The photo switched again, this time to a close-up of the previous slide. "The markings you see at the bottom of the fragment are welding marks."

"I don't see anything," Madison said.

"That's because they're really faint," Sam said. "Harrison, can you enlarge the picture any more?"

"Sure." The picture obediently changed sizes, this time the markings becoming more apparent.

"They're right here." The laser's red dot highlighted each of the marks. "I didn't see them myself at first. One of the interesting things about this guy's work is that there are no tool marks. Harrison thinks maybe he's polishing the parts after he makes them."

"Like the Unabomber." This again from Madison.

"Exactly." Sam shot her a triumphant smile. "But a weld isn't as easy to get rid of. The metal itself is chemically altered. And so even though he did his best to remove them, the marks remain."

"So what if the guy welds his end caps? Madison just said someone else did it, too, that hardly makes it a signature," Cullen interjected, his impatience showing.

"It's not the welds themselves that are important. It's the lack of welds on the other end cap." The image on the screen changed back to the original one. "Enlarge it, Harrison."

Again the image came into sharper focus, the edge clearly unmarred.

"What I'm thinking is that he only welded one side. Which would pretty much guarantee that the unwelded end cap would survive a blast. The pressure inside the pipe builds against the welded side until it blows the other end off like a pop bottle top when you shake it."

"Where was the fragment found?" Gabe asked, his dark brows drawn together in concentration.

"About twenty yards from the seat of the explosion."

"Fits the facts." He nodded, obviously processing the new information. "So is welding only one side unique?"

"It's not as common as a double weld, but it's certainly not unique. What is unique is the fact that I think he wanted this fragment to survive for a reason." She shot a look at Harrison, who hit a key on the computer, bringing up the same fragment shot from the opposite side.

This side was clearly scratched. A circular mark located center right on the fragment.

"So what are we looking at now?" Payton asked.

"The inside of the cap."

"I thought you said there weren't any tool marks." Cullen still sounded frustrated.

"Not any that reflect the tools used to make the bomb." Sam smiled at him. "This one was put there to identify it. To sign it, if you will." She nodded at Harrison again, and the image enlarged, then enlarged again, the scratching coming clear.

It was a circle, the interior divided by a curved line into two equal parts forming a paisley shape. One side was darker, the metal altered to create the sense of color. Two dots—one dark and one light—occupied mirror opposite positions in each half of the circle.

"What the hell is that?" Cullen asked.

"Tai Chi Tu," Payton answered. "Sometimes it's just called the Tai. It's the symbol for yin and yang."

"That's what I thought, too," Sam said, smiling in his direction. "But I wanted confirmation. So I had Harrison look at it, and he agreed."

"Except that I didn't know what it was," Harrison admitted.

"Well, I still don't. I mean I've heard the terms yin and yang before, but I don't know what they mean exactly. Something to do with opposites, right?" Cullen turned to meet Payton's gaze.

"That's certainly the Western interpretation. But the Chinese interpretation is more complex. The two are opposites in a literal sense, but they are also interdependent. One cannot exist without the other. As one ebbs the other flows and vice versa. The idea of yin and yang dates back to the earliest Chinese philosophy. It's part of *I-Ching* and the *Tao*."

"All of which is well and good," Cullen said, his voice reflecting his impatience, "but how the hell does it relate to the bomber?"

"We don't know." Sam shrugged.

"But we do know that the bomber put it there for a reason." Madison was leaning forward, studying the symbol. "The image is definitely intentional. And I'm betting it wasn't present before the bomb was made."

"So what, he left us a clue?" Gabe asked, his frustration evidently on a par with Cullen's.

"Most likely," Madison said, unaffected by her husband's outburst. "A symbol like this wasn't chosen randomly. For one thing it's quite intricate, and I'm betting he did it himself. The circle is just a little off, and the lines waver a bit."

"So you think the work was done by hand."

"It makes sense. After all the effort this guy has gone to to remove anything that might identify his work, he's not going to go out and buy a traceable metal stamp."

"Well, we damn well better be sure of that," Cullen barked.

"Already on it," Harrison said.

"So what is it saying to you?" Payton asked, curious to get Madison's take on things.

"Of course I can't say definitively. But I think it's telling that it's an Eastern symbol. There's a certain mindset involved in Eastern philosophy. If our guy is actively involved in Eastern beliefs, then he's going to behave in dramatically different ways than someone who is a participant in Western ideology."

"But for all we know he could just be entranced with the artwork." Gabe was pacing behind his wife, his agitation reflected in his movements.

"It's possible of course." Madison reached out to lay a gentle hand on her husband, and he stilled, covering her fingers with his own. "But it's more likely that the symbol has intrinsic meaning for him. And that its placement is reflective of a higher purpose. Quite possibly tied directly to his motivation for setting the bombs. To be certain, we need to know if the same symbol exists on a fragment of the Virginia bomb."

Sam nodded. "I've already called to request photos of all the fragments they've found. According to the NRT tech I talked with, there was a large fragment of end cap recovered. They're going to fax the pictures as soon as they can and will be shipping the fragment overnight."

"What about the other bombs?" Payton asked, his mind leaping ahead, trying to solve the puzzle.

"What other bombs?" Cullen asked, clearly still floundering.

"I found five unsolved cases involving bombs similar to the ones used in both San Antonio and Virginia. We've already called to request that all information about these incidents be forwarded to us in the hopes that maybe they overlooked the symbol in their investigations. In addition, I've requested actual frags if they still exist," Harrison said.

"I doubt they kept them. It's only been in the past few years that we've recognized the value of recording and in some cases preserving fragments from unsolved bomb cases." Sam sounded regretful, as if the omission had been her fault.

Payton contained a smile.

"At least they should have retained the files on the cases," Harrison continued. "Which means that the evidence photos should still be there. And with today's improved technology, we ought to be able to find the symbol if it exists."

"And if it does?" Cullen asked.

"We start trying to figure out what the hell it means to our bomber," Sam said, her tone matter-of-fact. "And until then, we keep sorting through the evidence. His methodology may also give us a clue to his identity. In both cases, he's used existing electrical devices to trigger the bomb. A garage door opener in Virginia and an air-conditioning thermostat in San Antonio."

"Interesting choices," Madison said, her nose wrinkled in thought.

"So the guy is some kind of lotus-worshiping air-conditioning repairman," Cullen spat.

"More than that, I'd say," Madison said. "The choices show an improvisational ability. Using something available on-site to detonate. In addition, I'd say our man is more than a mechanic. In order to successfully use either of those items, he'd have to have a working knowledge of the electrical components of both devices."

"So you're thinking an engineer." Sam was sitting on the corner of the table, arms crossed, one shapely leg swinging idly.

"I think it's probable. Which would follow with the Eastern orientation."

"Because all engineers are Buddhists." Cullen had moved from frustration to sarcasm.

"No," Madison smiled at her godfather, "because one has to be well educated to fully understand the nuances of Eastern philosophy."

"And in order to comprehend engineering, a person has to have something upstairs." Harrison tapped his head for emphasis.

"Exactly. So I'd say the man we're looking for is of above-average intelligence. Possibly even chart-breaking IQ. Despite his intelligence, he's still going to be something of a loner. Not good in social situations. And I'd predict that although he attended college, he probably never finished. Or did so with undistinguished marks. He's going to have tried to find work with explosives. Possibly a stint with the armed services, or maybe police work. He's going to be disdainful of authority, and not prone to making relationships. Although I'm betting when he does connect, he's incredibly loyal." Madison sat back, shifting to find a more comfortable position on her chair.

"You doing okay?" Gabe put a hand on her shoulder, his expression full of concern, and Payton had a moment's envy wishing for a connection like that. Almost as if he'd been pre-programmed to do so he turned to look at Sam, surprised to find a similar expression on her face.

Maybe they were kindred spirits. Or maybe he was seeing what he wanted to see. Either way, this wasn't the place to examine his emotions. He turned back to Madison in time to hear her assuring Gabe that she was fine.

"Sounds like a solid profile," Sam said, purposefully avoiding Payton's probing gaze. "I'd definitely have to agree with the intelligence factor. These bombs weren't the work of an amateur. This guy knows his stuff."

"All of which makes wonderful conversation, but gets us no closer to identifying him or his motivation." Cullen sounded almost petulant. "I don't mean to be the squeaky wheel here, but we need to figure out where this guy is going to strike next. Assuming we're all in agreement that he will strike next."

"He will," Payton and Sam said simultaneously.

"And probably sooner rather than later," Gabe said, his expression grim.

"I still think he's likely to send us a message. He wants us to understand why he's doing this. That's what the Tai Chi is all about. Remember?"

"What about the confetti bomb? Could that have been his message?" Harrison asked.

"If it is, the meaning was sure as hell obscure." Sam ran a hand through her hair, suddenly looking exhausted. "But I'll go over it again and see if I can find anything new."

"I've been checking out Sam's enemy list. The majority are still behind bars." Harrison shot her an admiring smile. "When you nail a guy, you do a damn good job of it." He turned his focus back to the group. "But I'll keep on it."

"I don't think it should be a priority." This surprisingly from Cullen. "It seems like the most important thing to concentrate on for the moment is the Virginia bomb. Until we've examined all the evidence thoroughly there's no way to know for certain that the two bombings are connected. If we can find the symbol on the end cap fragment from McLean, it'll go a long way toward proving the fact. And I also think we need to find out if there's any connection between the Tai Chi and the senators."

"Like one of them is into feng shui?" Harrison quipped, the joke falling flat.

"No. Like maybe there's some sort of connection between the pork arrangement and the Chinese," Gabe mused. "Payton, you can check that out, right?"

Payton's connections in the Far East had helped them on more than one occasion. However, this time he had the feeling they were looking in the wrong direction. Still, it couldn't hurt to check. "I'll make some calls. I'll also check to see if the symbol is associated with any kind of terrorist organization. It's a long shot, but probably worth eliminating the possibility just to be sure."

"Makes perfect sense to me," Sam said, nodding. "I tend to agree that this guy is local. Or at least national. And I'm betting he's operating solo. But I do think we need to look at all the angles."

"Along those lines, I've finally got Ruckland's head man to agree to sit down and talk," Gabe said, looking at his watch. "He's driving in from San Antonio."

"Mind if I tag along?" Sam asked. "I'd like to hear what he has to say firsthand."

"Fine by me," Gabe said. "Probably better to have two sets of ears anyway. In the meantime, Harrison, you keep working on getting the evidence from the other bombings. Maybe we'll find a tie-in there."

"If there's something, I'll find it," Harrison promised.

"If only it were that easy," Madison sighed. "Still, it feels as if we're making at least a little progress."

"I don't know," Gabe said, "it seems to me the guy has us by the balls. I mean he knows what he's doing and we don't, which is like playing chess blind against a sighted opponent. Odds don't seem to be in our favor."

"Exactly why we have to do everything in our power to make sure that we figure out what the hell his game plan is." Sam's words were matter-of-fact, but the intensity in her eyes spoke volumes. "Once we know that, then we can start playing offensively."

"Until then," Payton sighed, "we'll just have to play defense."

Gabe raised an eyebrow, his gaze encompassing them all. "And pray to God that'll be enough."

CHAPTER THIRTEEN

Z TEJAS WAS LOCATED in an old house on Sixth Street, the kind that should have been a family home, but had long ago given way to the urban crawl of commerce. Still, the restaurant had a certain charm. A holdover from the hippie days of Austin, the street housed some of the best music venues in the country.

Sam had spent a lot of time in said venues in college. It was always a lark for Aggies to invade University of Texas haunts. And although College Station had its share of good places to dance and drink, it couldn't hold a candle to Sixth Street.

This end of the street, though, was more about swanky places to eat and little art boutiques, a sure sign that Austin was changing, moving into the twenty-first century with sophisticated flair. Sam had left long ago, but she firmly held to the old saying that you could take the girl out of Texas, but you couldn't take the Texas out of the girl.

She smiled at her own whimsy and followed Gabe into the restaurant. The place was fairly deserted thanks to the fact that they were coming in between the lunch and dinner rushes.

A man in an Armani suit and wire-rimmed glasses stood up when they entered, his face a banal mask of cordiality. "Gabriel Roarke?" His tone held just the right blend of approachability and reserve. "Jack Sloane." He held out his hand and Gabe shook it.

"This is my associate, Sam Waters." Gabe tilted his head

toward Sam, and Jack held his hand out to her as well. She took it, grateful that he shook it with the same firmness he'd exhibited with Gabe. So often men assumed a woman wasn't up to a *real* handshake, and the notion irritated her.

"I've seen your picture in the paper," Jack said, his gray eyes warming as he let his gaze travel the length of her body.

She pulled her hand back, keeping her smile chilly. "Unfortunately there's been an inordinate amount of press. I'm afraid it always makes our job more difficult."

He held out a chair for her, and she had no choice but to sit next to him. Gabe took a chair across from her, his lips quirking as he tried to contain his laughter. Obviously, Mr. Sloane thought of himself as a ladies' man.

They perused the menu, ordered their meals, and continued making small talk until the waitress brought their food. Sam's stuffed pork tenderloin smelled delicious, and as she put the first bite in her mouth she realized she hadn't eaten since the night before when Payton had brought her food from Chuy's.

Payton's face flashed in her mind and she wished he were here. Not that she needed him; it was just that she was growing accustomed to his quiet presence. There was a strength there a woman could easily come to depend on.

She shook her head, taking another bite, forcing herself to focus on Gabe and Jack's conversation.

"As I'm sure you're aware, the focus of the investigation to date has revolved around the backroom alliance between Senator Ruckland and his two esteemed colleagues."

"I believe *alleged* alliance is a much more accurate description. Although it seems to be a forgone conclusion with the press." Sloane was obviously attempting to sidestep the issue, but Gabe wasn't about to let that happen.

"I couldn't give a rat's ass if the alliance existed or not. What I do care about is the fact that Senator Ruckland places a call to Keith that sends him running across the country to pick up Dawson and then fly into Stinson. An hour later, all three of them are dead. There was a reason they were meeting and I need to know what it was."

Sloane's face tightened, his eyes narrowing for battle. "And I told you on the phone I knew nothing about the meeting."

"Mr. Sloane—Jack," Sam said, her tone cajoling, "we're fighting an uphill battle here. We've got four people dead, and I suspect more to come if we can't get to the bottom of what's happening. Anything you know can be a help to us. And you have to understand our interest has nothing whatsoever to do with finding fault with Senator Ruckland. We just want to get the guy who killed him. And we can't do that without your complete cooperation."

Sloane eyed them both for a moment and then sighed. "I really don't know all that much."

"Just tell us what you do know." Gabe sat back, crossing his arms over his chest, his dark brows drawn together in a frown.

Sloane sighed again and laid down his fork, his gaze encompassing them both. "Joe was working with Dawson and Keith. The droughts over the past few years have severely crippled the nation's agricultural industry. And three of the hardest hit were Iowa, California and Texas. The three states comprise a large percentage of the nation's food production, but to date they're only receiving a small percentage of the federal relief package."

"So the senators took matters into their own hands."

"It's the basic principle behind our constitution." Sloane shrugged. "A you-scratch-my-back-while-I-scratch-yours sort of mentality. Compromise gets all kinds of things accomplished."

"If we agree that compromise is the same as collusion," Gabe said, his face impassive. "But I meant what I said. I'm not here to judge the process or senators. I just need to understand what it was that spooked them."

"You mean the meeting."

"I thought you didn't know about it." Gabe's eyebrows rose until they formed one solid line across the top of his forehead. It made him look even more threatening than usual, and Sam contained a smile when Sloane pushed back his chair as if to physically increase the distance between him and Gabe.

"Of course I knew about it, I just wasn't going to tell you."

"So why the one-eighty?"

"Because Ms. Waters asked so nicely." He shot her an ingratiating smile. "And because you're right. We need to catch this bastard before he hurts anyone else."

Underneath all the political razzamatazz it appeared that Sloane actually had a streak of humanity. That, or telling the truth played into his political needs. Either way it was possible he had information they desperately needed.

"So why the meeting?" Sam asked, her food forgotten as she focused on Sloane.

"Bud Walker."

"The senator from New Mexico?" Gabe was getting impatient. Sam recognized the signs, but Sloane wasn't a man to be hurried.

"He's a republican, right?" Sam interceded, shooting a warning look at Gabe. "Been around forever."

"Yes." Sloane nodded, his attention now on her. "Fifth term. His main claim to fame is his longevity. Other than that I can't say that he's contributed a lot to the process, although there are republicans who would no doubt argue the fact."

"Particularly the ones from the Southwest." Sam smiled, her own patience waning. "I'm assuming that Walker got wind of what was going on between Ruckland, Dawson and Keith."

"More than that. He actually had proof of the agreement's existence. And he was threatening to blow it all sky-high unless New Mexico was included in the deal."

"Which Ruckland didn't want to happen."

"New Mexico isn't even in the same league as Texas when

it comes to agricultural production. And Senator Ruckland wasn't about to see the money funneled into a losing proposition. Besides, Walker and Keith have been sworn political enemies for years. If the senator had let Walker in, Keith would definitely have wanted out. And his participation was crucial."

"So the meeting was to try and figure out how to handle Walker?" Sam reached for her iced tea and took a sip, trying to sort through the implications of what Sloane was telling them.

"Exactly. The three of them had to come up with a strategy to appease the old man without actually giving in to him."

"What would the ramifications have been if the agreement had come to light before fruition?" Gabe asked, turning his fork idly in his hand.

"Disastrous. First off, Senator Ruckland would have lost credibility, which would have damaged not only his work on appropriations, but any number of other alliances he'd been cultivating in order to get certain bills passed this session. Everything in the Senate is about power. And without it, you can kiss your job goodbye."

He paused for emphasis, then continued. "Second, the economic ramifications for the state are huge. We really have been hurt by the drought. More than most states, in fact. But as I said earlier, federal relief plans are geared toward the nation as a whole, not one particular state. So without this particular line item, Texas, as well as California and Iowa, stands to lose a great deal of much-needed cash."

"None of this seems enough to make someone want to kill the senators, and certainly not in such a public way."

"There are factions out there that would stop at nothing to funnel the money elsewhere. The senators' deaths, if nothing else, will make certain that status quo is maintained as far as agricultural reparation is concerned."

"Do you suspect Walker?" Gabe asked.

"Personally? No. It would be too big a risk for someone of his stature. However, I wouldn't put it past his people."

The statement hung between the three of them for a moment, Sam finally breaking the silence by pulling out a drawing of the Tai Chi. "Have you ever seen this symbol before?"

Sloane took the piece of paper, and held it up to the light for a closer look. "It's that opposites-attract thing, right? Ying-yang or something like that?"

"Yin, yang," Sam corrected. "And it's more than just opposite attraction. It's about the interrelationship between both sides of opposing forces. We have reason to believe it may be connected to whomever is behind the bombings."

"So I was right. It's some fanatical group."

"There's no indication of that. But I do need to know if there's any way you can think of that the symbol, or the idea, or even the actual Chinese philosophy itself might be attached to Senator Ruckland or one of the others."

"Lady, if you only knew just how unlikely that possibility was." Sloane tipped back his head, laughing. "Joe Ruckland fought in Vietnam. And his father fought on the Pacific front in WWII. Not to mention the fact that he's a good ol' boy from way back. There is absolutely no way that he was in any way involved with anything Asian. Particularly religion. I'm not sure what his true feelings about God were, but I can tell you he never missed a Sunday in the First Baptist church."

"What about Keith or Dawson?"

"Episcopal for Dawson and I can't say that I know much about Keith's religious predilections. But I don't think it was anything too far-flung or Senator Ruckland wouldn't have allowed himself to get in bed with the man. He was taking a hell of chance just because he was a republican. I can't imagine him pushing the envelope much further than that."

"Well, it was worth a shot. And we'll confirm of course with Dawson and Keith's people."

"I felt certain you would." Sloane shot a not-so-subtle look at his watch. "I really should be heading back. I've got a staff briefing this evening." He handed back the drawing of the Tai Chi. "Of course it goes without saying that our conversation here was off the record."

"That goes both ways, Sloane." Gabe's tone brooked no disagreement.

"I have no problem with that." He stood up, and with a sly smile for Sam, headed for the door. They waited until he was no longer in sight and then resumed their seats.

"So what do you think?" Gabe asked, pulling out his wallet to pay the bill.

"About Sloane in general, or his sudden memory of the meeting between the senators?"

"Both, I guess."

"I think Sloane is a sleazeball." Sam shrugged. "And I think he's very good at what he does. I think he came here to give us information, and any reticence we might have perceived on his part was part of the show."

"You think he led us down the garden path?"

"No, I think he just tried to manipulate things to his benefit. I wouldn't be surprised at all if we see Mr. Sloane running as Ruckland's replacement. And in the meantime, I think we need to find out what, if anything, Senator Walker had to do with the bombing."

"I agree," Gabe said. "But I need to talk to Cullen about how to handle it. We can't just go down there and accuse the man of killing three of his fellow statesmen."

"Well I wasn't exactly suggesting that we should." Sam grinned and shook her head. "I may not be much on people skills, but even I can recognize that it's not wise to poke a sleeping tiger."

"You know a hell of a lot more than you let on, Sam." Gabe's expression had grown speculative. "In fact, at times you remind me a lot of Payton. And I mean that as a compliment."

"Thanks, I think." She smiled, delighted to be put in the same category as Payton. His strength of character was definitely something to emulate. "You've known him a long time."

"Since Delta Force days." Gabe nodded.

"He told me a little bit about Iraq. It must have been awful."

Gabe's gaze turned speculative. "I'm surprised he told you anything. He doesn't like to talk about it."

Sam started to tell Gabe about interrupting Payton's dream, but decided against it. Somehow it seemed as if that night ought to stay between then two of them. "He didn't say all that much. Just that Cullen roped you into a dicey situation, and that his brother and most of the team died as a result."

"He told you about Kevin?" Gabe's brow rose in obvious astonishment.

"I think he probably said more than he meant to," she admitted with a shrug. "It was late, and it was just one of those moments."

"Had to have been more than that for him to have talked about Kevin."

She blew out a breath, still determined not to talk about the dream. "It must have been awful."

"It was. We almost lost Payton, too." Gabe's face tightened with memory. Payton evidently wasn't the only one with nightmares. "I assume he told you we were betrayed. They let us get in. Even let us liberate the hostage, and then they started shooting. It was an old villa. The kind built around a courtyard. They had men stationed on the balconies, on the roof, everywhere. We were sitting ducks. You could hardly see through the smoke from the gunfire. We didn't stand a chance."

"But you got out alive."

"Thanks to Nigel." Gabe blew out a breath, lifting his gaze to hers. "Nigel Ferris was British Special Forces. Their equivalent of Delta Force. He'd been assigned to our unit as an adjunct and so was part of the mission. He and Kevin were acting as lookouts, watching our backs.

"When we came out with Cullen's man, the shooting started. Nigel was the first to recognize it for what it was. He clued Kevin in and the two of them started taking out the men on the balcony. Then, when it was clear enough, they fought their way into the courtyard.

"By then we had four men down. Three dead, one wounded. Kevin and Payton went in to get the wounded man out. But by the time they got there he was dead. Then someone dropped a grenade and the place erupted in fire. Kevin caught the brunt of it, but Payton was hit pretty hard, too. Nigel and I positioned ourselves to give protecting fire."

"Where was Cullen's man?"

"I had him. And believe me it was tempting to leave the fool to his own fate. He never should have been in Iraq in the first place. It was his arrogance that started the entire process. But I'd given Cullen my word. And besides—" he shrugged "—it was our mission.

"Payton grabbed Kevin and threw him over his shoulder. They were both on fire, and the Iraqis had reinforcements. Nigel and I flanked Payton and Kevin and we began to work our way out of the courtyard. Somewhere along the way, we realized Kevin was dead. I tried to get Payton to leave him, but he wouldn't. He simply couldn't accept the fact that his brother was gone. There was no time for argument, so Nigel took matters into his own hands. He knocked Payton out, and threw him over his shoulder. We left Kevin there. Believe me, there was no choice.

"I'm not really sure how we made it to the helicopter. The whole area was hot. And even once we were airborne it was risky, antiaircraft gunfire coming from everywhere. But we bugged out, leaving a hell of a lot of good men behind.

"We were all injured except the bastard we'd come to save. Isn't that always the way of it?" His face hardened, his voice bitter. "Nigel had taken a bullet in the shoulder, and I'd been shot in the leg. But it was Payton who'd suffered most. He was burned on one whole side of his body, shrapnel slicing gouges in any skin that was left. An eight-inch piece of metal bisected his face, and he'd taken a bullet in the chest, and another in his hip. Quite honestly, I didn't think he'd make it through the flight."

"But he did." Sam's voice was tight as she fought against emotion, the vision of the battle almost too real.

"Yeah. He's a hell of a fighter. But he was never the same. Too much had happened. He'd lost Kevin. And then Mariam."

"Mariam?" Sam frowned, trying to remember if Payton had mentioned her.

"I thought you said he told you about it." Gabe stopped, studying her face for a moment.

"He did. At least about the raid, and Kevin and Cullen's part in it. But he never mentioned this Mariam."

"She was his wife." Gabe sat back, crossing his arms across his chest.

"He was married?" she repeated, sounding like a stupid schoolgirl. "I...I didn't know." She felt betrayed. A stupid notion, surely, but there it was nevertheless. She'd felt close to Payton, certain that they shared a bond of some sort, but obviously she'd been wrong.

"Sam," Gabe said, cutting through the wild thoughts racing in her brain, "Payton doesn't talk to anyone about anything. The fact that he told you about Kevin says a hell of a lot. Believe me."

She nodded, but couldn't find words. This really shouldn't be affecting her so strongly. But the fact remained that it was.

"Look." Gabe's expression was gentle. "They weren't married long. It was one of those fast-and-furious things. He met her on leave, and she entranced him."

"You don't sound like you liked her very much," Sam said, pushing her own feelings for the woman firmly to the side.

"It wasn't for me to judge." Gabe's expression closed. "She was a French journalist. Very smart and very beautiful. And like Payton, she loved living on the edge."

"So what happened to her?" Sam wasn't certain she really wanted an answer, but she had a feeling knowing would offer insight into Payton that couldn't be gained any other way.

"Cullen asked her to help with the raid. To use her sources to gather intel. She agreed. Payton tried to talk her out of it. But as I said, she liked dancing on the edge. And unfortunately, whoever turned on us turned on her as well. She was shot to death in her hotel room. I didn't find out until we were safely out of Iraq."

"And Payton?"

"I couldn't tell him. At least not then. She was the reason he was hanging on, and believe me, he needed a reason. Most men wouldn't have been able to survive what he did even with the strongest of motivations, but Payton has a stronger will than anyone I've ever known."

"And when you did tell him?"

"It almost destroyed him. Kevin's death had already taken a hell of a lot out of him. Not to mention his injuries. The news of Mariam's death sent him over the edge. He blamed Cullen and he blamed me. But mostly he blamed himself."

"But he couldn't have prevented any of it."

"No. He couldn't have. But he's never been able to see that. He thinks that if he could have moved faster, or been stronger, Kevin would have lived. And that if he'd just been more forceful, Mariam wouldn't have agreed to work with Cullen."

"But surely he can see that she made her own decision."

"I think intellectually he understands that, but in his heart, he believes he failed them both."

Sam's heart twisted, her chest tightening with unshed tears. She couldn't imagine what it would be like to carry that kind of burden. "So what happened to him when he left the hospital?"

"His injuries allowed him an honorable discharge. And

shortly after that he disappeared. I tried to find him. Nigel did, too. But Payton wanted to stay lost, and we couldn't track him. Then several years ago he popped back onto the map. In Asia, working freelance."

"As a mercenary." She nodded. "He told me that much."

"You have to understand that before Iraq, he was totally different. Boisterous, and funny. Always with a story. Making everyone laugh. But all that was gone. He was a different man. So quiet it was as if he weren't bothering to breathe. He'd turned inward, using his strength as a shield against the world. His new persona only made him better at what he did. In his mind, he had nothing to lose, which meant that he was a very valuable commodity."

"For difficult assignments." Sam tried to picture his world, but even with all her experience, she couldn't.

"The most difficult. We worked together a couple of times. And I think he's forgiven me for waiting to tell him about Mariam. There's a bond between the two of us that can't be severed, no matter how dire things get. Nigel, too, for that matter."

"What about Nigel? Why isn't he here?" She'd heard the man's name in passing a couple of times, but hadn't understood the significance until now.

"There was a conflict of interest on our first case. Nigel works for MI6. And his loyalties lay there."

"He betrayed you?"

"In a manner of speaking. We're working through it." Gabe's smile was more relaxed, some of the shadows retreating. "Payton's going to kill me for telling you any of this."

"I already knew most of it." She tipped her head, searching Gabe's face. "Why *did* you tell me?"

He shrugged. "Because I think you care about Payton. And frankly, I think he cares about you. It's important that you understand where he's coming from. What he's been through. And quite frankly, who he is. I've spent my entire professional life walking in the shadows, Sam, and it's taken a toll. Take my life and multiply it by a thousand and you have Payton's. If I'm in the shadows, he's in the dark. And I'd hate to see him go through the rest of his life alone." Gabe laughed, the sound tinged with self-mockery. "Impending parenthood has made me too damn introspective. All I'm trying to say is that I think you could be good for Payton. And in order to understand him, you needed to know about Iraq. All of it."

They sat for a minute in silence, Sam trying to think of something to say to ease the tension hanging between them. But everything she thought of seemed trite. Finally, she just said, "Thank you."

Gabe smiled. "If I were you, I'd hold your thanks until Payton finds out what I've done. After that, you may wish you'd never met me."

"You're a good friend, Gabe. Payton is lucky to have you."

"Goes both ways, Sam. I'm lucky to have him, too."

CHAPTER FOURTEEN

SAM WALKED INTO the operations room, grateful to see that Payton wasn't there. After Gabe's revelations, she wanted some time to herself. Time to process all that Gabe had told her. And most importantly, time to sort through her feelings for the man.

The fact that Payton had been through so much should have scared her, but it didn't. It only made her admire him all the more. But she was realistic enough to recognize the fact that despite Gabe's words to the contrary, Payton's interest in her was most likely only superficial. Pheromones calling to pheromones.

It simply didn't make sense to believe that he'd risk any kind of involvement beyond that. Which meant that if she allowed things to progress, she had to be damn certain her heart wasn't involved. At least not at a level that meant she'd be hurt when it was time to move on. A couple of days ago, she'd have been certain she could handle that.

Just at the moment, she wasn't as sure. Payton had jump-started emotions she'd thought dead and buried, and she wasn't certain what would happen if she allowed them to develop. So she needed to think long and hard about the costs of allowing herself to become any more involved with him. And the best way she knew to clear her head was to go to work.

Harrison looked up from his computer console as she passed. "How'd things go with Ruckland's man?"

Sam pulled her thoughts away from Payton, thinking instead about the meeting with Sloane. "Interesting twist. It seems there was a fourth senator. Bud Walker from New Mexico."

"He was in on the pork?" Harrison frowned.

"More like he wanted to be in on it. He's the reason the other three panicked. To hear Sloane tell it, Walker wanted in on the deal, and Ruckland was saying no."

"And Walker wasn't taking it gracefully, I assume."

"Something like that. Gabe is going to talk to Cullen about how best to approach Walker. I'm hoping we'll head that way tomorrow."

"Sounds like a plan," Harrison said.

"Did the NRT photos arrive of the McLean fragments?"

"Better than that. The fragment is here. Seems they decided to put a rush on it and sent it via courier." Harrison sounded more put out about the fact than excited.

"And you're not happy about it?" Sam queried.

"Well, I'm delighted that the frag is here, but I didn't get the chance to look at it. The courier turns out to be an NRT flunky by the name of Elliot Drummond. And Elliot won't release the fragment to anyone but you."

"He's not a flunky." Sam smiled. "He's a friend. I used to work with him at the Bureau. We were on ERT together."

"Well he still could have let me look at the frag," Harrison said.

Sam shrugged. "He's cautious." An understatement actually. Elliot was a by-the-book sort. Everything in its proper place and time. If he'd been told to release the fragment to Sam, that's exactly what he would do.

"Where is he?"

"In there." Harrison tipped his head toward the lab, his attention back on his computer.

Sam turned and walked into the conference room, almost running down the tall, lanky man hovering in the doorway.

"Elliot. My God, it's been forever." She reached up to hug him, surprised when he didn't immediately respond. Pulling back, she searched his face, the lines and shadows there making him seem much older. "Are you all right?"

"I'm fine. Just a little tired. Ziggy's got us burning the candle at both ends."

Carl Ziegler had taken over ERT when Walter Atherton had been promoted. The man was as good as it got when it came to hazardous device forensics, but he was also a hell of a taskmaster. "Nothing ever changes."

"You look good." He smiled, the action lightening his features. "But then working under pressure was always your preferred methodology."

"I don't know." She shrugged. "A little less intensity might be nice. You've got the fragment?"

"Right here." He held out a plastic bag, the gray metal inside shining in the fluorescent light.

"I think you hurt Harrison's feelings. He really did want to see it."

Elliot's smile broadened, mischief cresting in his eyes. "I was told to put it directly into your hands."

Sam laughed, and took the bag. "All right then, consider your mission accomplished." They walked into the lab, and over to the microscope. "Can you stay?"

"Not for long." Elliot shot a surreptitious look at his watch. "Ziggy was adamant about my getting back ASAP."

"Can't live without you?" Sam said, sliding the fragment out of the evidence bag.

"Yeah, right." Elliot's laugh held a note of bitterness. "More likely he just wants to be sure I'm not using this trip as an excuse to get out of work."

Sam looked up at him, trying to read between the lines. "You're sure nothing's wrong?"

He shook his head, reaching out to give her hand a squeeze. "Just too much time in the lab. Sorry. Did I hear you say something about Senator Walker?" It was an obvious change of subject, but Sam didn't want to push.

"Yeah. One of Ruckland's aides says he was in bed with the senators."

"So you're thinking Walker could be behind all of this?"

"I haven't formed an opinion, yet. But we need to talk to the man. He's part of the chain of evidence."

"Makes sense." Elliot pulled his stool closer as she flipped the fragment, situating it so that the inside was facing up. "So what are you looking for?"

"There was a symbol etched into a fragment of an end cap from the San Antonio bomb." She focused the microscope and began to methodically search the twisted piece of metal. "If I can find the symbol on this end cap fragment, it will definitively tie the two explosions together."

"But I thought we already knew they were connected." His brow wrinkled in concentration. "I mean Atherton was heading up the investigation for the FBI. And the similarity between the two bombings is significant."

"On the face of it, I'd have to agree, but you know as well as I do that commonality of technique alone isn't enough to establish a credible link—at least not one that will hold up in court. And I want to nail this bastard for what he did to Walter."

"Amen to that," Elliot said, moving closer. "Atherton was a stand-up guy. I think everyone in the Bureau wants a piece of the man who did this."

"So we have to build an airtight case," she said, and turned back to the microscope, moving the fragment in a circular pattern, stopping when she found the indentation she was looking for. Her heart rate accelerated with the discovery, and she increased the magnification accordingly. The edges of the Tai came clear, the image an exact copy of the one they'd found in San Antonio.

"You got it?"

Sam nodded, distracted by the implications of what she'd found.

"Can I look?" Elliot was already standing behind her, ready to take her place at the eyepiece.

"Sure." She moved off the stool. "Have at it."

"It's the Tai Chi," Elliot said, staring down at the fragment. "Is this what you found in San Antonio?"

"Yeah." Sam nodded, chewing on her lip. "It's got to have some kind of significance for the bomber. But I don't know what."

"Maybe he considers himself the diametric half of something? You know, like good versus evil."

The thought had occurred to her as well, although she couldn't see how it related to the senators, but then sometimes patterns were so obvious it was possible to miss them amid all the details.

"You found it." Payton's voice danced along her spine, sending inward tremors of something she wasn't certain she wanted to identify. As usual he'd managed to arrive without a sound.

"Yeah." She smiled up at him triumphantly. "No idea what it means, but we've definitely got a match. Did you reach your contact?"

Payton nodded, then shot a questioning look at Elliot still looking through the microscope.

"He's a friend," Sam said, ushering Payton into the conference room. "We worked together on ERT. He came with the fragment. So what'd you find out?"

"There's no record of any terrorist group relating to the Tai. There are a couple that could be attached to the concept if you really stretch things, but they aren't involved with anything that would connect to the senators." He was standing so close to her, she could feel the rhythm of his breathing. The proximity was intoxicating.

"So there's no talk out there of outside involvement?"

"Not on the international front. General consensus was that if this was the work of terrorists, they'd have taken credit for it. And if it was about foreign trade, someone I know would have gotten wind of it."

"So we have nothing." She swallowed her disappointment.

"Actually, I think you have to look at it as a process of elimination. My sources just confirmed what you already suspected. That this is the work of an individual."

"Except that we still don't have any idea why he's doing this."

"Something to do with the Tai." Elliot was standing in the doorway. "Maybe Senator Walker will be able to make the connection. You're going to see him tomorrow?"

Payton shot Elliot a pointed glance, and he actually took a step backward.

"I, ah, didn't mean to interrupt."

"You're fine." Sam smiled at Elliot, shooting a frown in Payton's direction. "We were just talking about it." She turned her attention back to Payton, her expression pointed.

"We're going tomorrow evening," Payton said, accepting Elliot's presence without further comment. "I just got word from Gabe. It seems the illustrious senator is a bit pressed for time. He's in the middle of a reelection campaign. But his aides arranged for us to see him after tomorrow's fund-raiser in Albuquerque."

Sam's stomach lurched at the thought of going to New Mexico. Her mother would no doubt be delighted to see her daughter, but Sam wasn't exactly sure she was in the mood for her mother's scrutiny.

Elliot cleared his throat. "I'm afraid I've got to be going."

"So soon?" Sam pulled out of her thoughts, wishing he could stay. It was nice to have someone here that she had history with.

"No rest for the weary." He shrugged. "My flight leaves in an hour."

"It was great seeing you." She reached out to take his hands, and he pulled her into a bear hug.

"Be careful, Sam," Elliot whispered. "Watch your back."

The last was a standard phrase. Something she'd said a million times, but she couldn't shake the feeling that Elliot was trying to say something more. He released her, and she searched his eyes for explanation, but there was nothing there.

"I'll see you on the flipside." His smile included them both, and with a casual wave he headed through the door.

"Looks like the two of you were pretty cozy," Payton said, his eyes narrowing in thought.

"We were good friends once. But it was a long time ago." She sighed, dismissing Elliot from her mind. There were more pressing issues.

Payton laid his hands on her shoulders, his palms warm through the thin fabric of her shirt. "You look tired."

"I am," she sighed. "We've been at this nonstop. And there's no end in sight." Their gazes met and held, and her heart started pounding. Lord, just standing close to him set all her nerves on edge.

He reached out to push a strand of hair behind her ear, the gesture somehow more intimate than a kiss. "Sounds like you could use some rest. Maybe we ought to go back to the hotel."

She wanted to say yes, to throw herself in his arms and damn the consequences. Just the idea of him moving inside her making her weak at the knees. But there were photographs to examine, and Harrison's cases to discuss.

She couldn't just abandon it all for pleasure.

As if she'd conjured him up, Harrison walked into the conference room, and Sam sprang back guiltily, more than aware that both men smiled in response.

"Elliot certainly left in a hurry," Harrison said, his mouth still quirking with amusement.

"He had a plane to catch." Payton shrugged.

"I'm sorry he couldn't have stayed longer," Sam said, pushing her hair out of her face. "But he did give me food for thought."

Payton and Harrison both looked at her expectantly.

"It's not a burst of brilliance or anything, but he mentioned the fact that maybe the bomber sees the Tai as a link between good and evil."

"So what?" Harrison asked. "He's evil?"

"Or maybe he thinks he's good. There are a lot of people who believe that government is evil. Maybe he believed stopping the senators was part of the pattern. That he was counteracting their bad deeds with something good."

"Their destruction?" Harrison was frowning, trying to think it through. "That seems a little harsh."

"It's a cruel world," Payton mused. "And sometimes the greatest good is only achieved by force. The central idea of the Tai is that everything has an opposing force and that together the two forces are part of a greater whole. So maybe our guy views himself as the righteous half of the political circle."

"Government versus the bomber?" Harrison quipped.

"More likely government versus the people," Sam mused. "Maybe he sees himself as an avenger."

"But that doesn't explain Atherton's death."

"He was in the way?" Harrison sat down on the corner of the table. "Or maybe he was connected to the senators in some way we haven't discovered yet."

"Which is why we need to get back to work." The electric tension between her and Payton hadn't dispersed, but it had lessened. And for the moment, she was determined to ignore it.

"We're at your command." Payton's smile was limited to his mouth. His eyes flashed a completely different message, a promise of things to come. And despite herself, Sam shivered in anticipation.

ELLIOT DRUMMOND stepped out of his rental car into the humid Texas night. It hadn't been easy to find this place. His instructions hadn't mentioned the fact that there were two Spicewood Springs Roads. It was only by sheer luck that he'd found the older one. And even after finding the road, he'd almost missed the park entrance, the parking lot no more than a rough graveled area surrounded by a hewn log fence.

The other car in the parking lot fit the description he'd been given, and he pulled out the photocopies he'd made. There wasn't much, but he hoped, coupled with the information he'd managed to glean from Sam, he'd have enough to earn his money.

A shadow detached itself from the fence. A wiry man wearing jeans, boots, a denim jacket and baseball cap moved into the lamplight. It seemed awfully hot to be wearing a coat, but Elliot figured it fit the image of a Texan to a T. The brim of the man's hat kept his face in shadows, but Elliot could see the line of his jaw, and the stubble of his beard.

"You don't look like a reporter." He was surprised at how shaky his voice sounded. And immediately cleared his throat in an effort to sound more authoritative. The man had been clear on the phone. No information, no money. And Elliot needed money.

Badly.

"What exactly am I supposed to look like?" The man laughed, the sound hollow in the stifling heat of the parking lot. They were deep in a canyon cut by a meandering stream, trees hanging heavy on both sides of them, the dark threatening even the streetlight. "You got something for me?" The reporter moved across the gravel and stopped by the trunk of Elliot's car, waiting.

"I have a file here. And some things that I heard. You have any proof you're who you say you are?"

"A duffelbag full of Ben Franklins." The reporter lifted the bag in testament to the fact, and Elliot's jaw dropped. A hundred thousand dollars would solve a hell of a lot of problems, and get his bookie off his back once and for all.

He smiled at the man and held out the file. "I made some copies from her files. I didn't get as much as I'd have liked. She interrupted."

The reporter reached for the file and just missed the edge. The papers fluttered to the ground, and with a curse the man bent to retrieve them before they were lost in the dark.

Elliot didn't offer to help. Somehow that was going too far. So he watched as the man crawled under the car to get the most elusive piece, trying to contain his guilt. It wasn't as if he was really hurting anyone. So the information hit the news a bit sooner than anticipated—in the end it wouldn't really change things.

At least he hoped not.

The man stuffed the last of the papers into the file, and pushed back to a standing position. "What else you got?"

Elliot could see his eyes glittering beneath the cap. "Give me the money first."

The man shook his head. "Information, then money. That's the deal."

Elliot swallowed nervously, then nodded. "I don't know if it matters but they've isolated some kind of symbol on fragments from both bombs. Some Chinese thing. Yin and yang."

The guy seemed to absorb the information with only minimal interest, and Elliot felt his stomach sink. Maybe he didn't have enough. "There's one more thing."

The man crossed his arms, the file still in his hand, waiting.

"They think there may be a link to a senator in New Mexico. Bud Walker. They're going to talk to him. Something about a fund-raiser."

"When?" The man had gone still, his interest apparent, and Elliot sighed with relief.

"Tomorrow night. They're meeting with him afterward."

"Who?"

"Sam and Payton—at least I think that was his name. Someone named Gabe is sending them."

The man nodded, clearly contemplating the information.

"Is it…is it enough?" Elliot said, the silence getting to him.

The reporter jerked his head at the sound of Elliot's voice, his face still in shadow. "Yeah. Here, take the money."

Elliot grabbed the bag, and tossed it into the back seat through the open window. All he wanted now was to get the hell out of here.

"You're not going to count it?" The guy seemed to be goading him. As if he knew that Elliot wasn't up to handling this kind of thing.

Elliot narrowed his eyes, trying to imitate Payton's piercing gaze. "I don't need to." He tried to keep his voice flip, but to his dismay, it cracked instead.

The reporter's mouth quirked at the corner, and then he shrugged. "Nice doing business with you." Without waiting for a response, he headed for his car.

Before the man could even open his door, Elliot had the key in the ignition, his car's engine jumping to life. With a peel of rubber on gravel, he pulled back out onto Spicewood Springs Road. Euphoria made him feel reckless, and he pressed his foot to the pedal, delighted when he saw the reporter's car turn in the opposite direction.

Wind whistled through the open windows, and for once Elliot felt on top of the world. Things would be better now. First off he'd pay his debts. Get his bookie's bruisers off his back. And then he'd figure out a way to start over.

Maybe he'd head for Vegas. Somewhere where the cards were hot and the women hotter. Truth was, he'd never really mastered either one. But he was willing to give it a go.

Sam's face flashed through his mind, but he pushed it away. He hadn't had a choice. Besides, she'd moved on to bigger and better things. He had the same right, didn't he? And really, he hadn't given the reporter a damn thing. The file was worthless, just a bunch of mumbo jumbo he'd copied randomly from who knows what file.

The only interesting bit was the Chinese symbol. But that could mean anything. Or nothing. Hell, there was no predicting the way a bomber's mind worked. It was easy money, pure and simple. And no one was going to get hurt.

With a smile, he floored the pedal, feeling the surge of power through the car. It shimmied slightly, and then as the needle crept higher, the steering wheel visibly shook.

Piece of shit rental car.

The needle hit seventy and the car exploded, the force ripping Elliot from the seat and tossing him around like a bean bag. The sedan hit the embankment, breaking through the guardrail and rolling in a fireball into the thick woods that cloistered the road. Elliot Drummond's body flew through the window to land at the foot of a live oak, his charred remains staring sightlessly at the wide Texas sky.

CHAPTER FIFTEEN

"WELL, I'VE RULED OUT Brownsville." Harrison stood in the doorway to the lab, holding a stack of photos in his hand. "I've been over all the photographs and there isn't any sign of a Tai anywhere on the fragments. In addition, I've got clear tool marks on several fragments, as well as apparent welding on both end caps."

Payton looked up from the report he was reading. "There's nothing in the bomb squad's report that contradicts that. No mention of any kind of symbol, and the report confirms the presence of tool marks. In addition, there's some question as to whether the security system was actually the trigger. The responding police officers are the ones who tagged the system as the point of origin, but the bomb folks never found anything to tangibly support the fact."

"So it's not the same guy. He might not use the symbol if it's honestly linked to the senators. But there's no way the rest of his M.O. would have changed that much. Once a perfectionist, always a perfectionist." Sam blew out a breath, pushing her hair behind her ears. She looked as tired as Payton felt. "Maybe we're not going to find any priors. At least not with the Tai symbol."

"Which means we'll have trouble establishing a direct link."

"There's still four more to investigate," Harrison said. "I should have most of the paperwork in the morning. Except Refugio. They can't seem to locate the file."

The phone rang, and Harrison reached for it, moving away so that his conversation wouldn't disturb.

"Gabe was right," Sam said. "There's no way to figure out where this guy is going next. Whatever his agenda is, it's not making any sense at all from this end. Even with the addition of Walker to the mix, I still have trouble believing this guy's only agenda is some agricultural wheeling and dealing. I mean if it was something really insane like nuclear testing or embryo experimentation I could see the logic. But not this."

"So you're still thinking the senators were just in the wrong place at the wrong time." Payton tried to keep the skepticism from his voice. She was the expert after all.

"No. I don't see how that tracks either. Not with Walter's death. That was definitely intentional. And the only connection I can see to San Antonio is through the investigation. Walter was a career bureaucrat. And while I'd say he played the political game well, he wasn't at a level where he'd have been hobnobbing with men like Ruckland. Amanda didn't think he'd ever even met the man."

"What about Dawson or Keith?"

"Same answer. Neither had anything to do with defense committees or law enforcement legislation, and as far as I know Walter was never asked to testify before Congress. There's always the possibility that he had met them socially. Washington's a small city. But it can't have been anything lasting or Amanda would have known about it."

"Which leaves us with one of two possibilities. Either this is in fact related to the senators and their pork barreling scheme…"

"Or?" She leaned back against the table, waiting.

"Or there's something else going on and everything we're seeing is just a spurious connection. Forest for the trees kind of thing."

"Holy shit," Harrison said, clicking off the phone, his expression grim. "That was Gabe. He just got a call from Cullen. Elliot Drummond is dead."

"What?" Sam said, pushing off of the table, her stomach tightening in revolt. "He was just here. What happened?"

"Apparently his car crashed. They found it on old Spicewood Springs Road. Looks like he must have lost control and plowed into the woods. The car flipped and then caught fire. Elliot was thrown clear, but not before he was pretty badly burned."

"They say anything about an explosion?" Sam was standing in the center of the room, her focus turned inward, tension radiating off the line of her shoulders.

"Gabe didn't mention it." Harrison shook his head, frowning.

"Take me to the accident site." She was already heading out the door, Harrison and Payton following in her wake.

"You think it was the bomber?" Harrison asked, his brows raised in surprise.

Payton already knew the answer. If there'd been a fire, then they had to expect the worst. Elliot Drummond worked for ERT. Hell, he'd worked for Atherton. And he'd worked with Sam.

But even barring that connection, there was the fact that something had been off with the man. It had been there in his eyes. A haunted look Payton had seen before. Desperation. And desperate men did desperate things.

Payton shook his head, focusing on the facts. First thing they had to determine was if the messenger had indeed been sacrificed. Maybe the man had simply pushed his luck a step too far.

THE CAR, or what remained of it, sat about fifteen yards off the road. It had flipped over, the roof caved in so that the body of the sedan sat almost flat to the ground. The paint had bubbled off in the heat, and a trail of parts was strewn along the road for something like twenty feet.

There was no question in Sam's mind that the car had exploded well before it left the side of the road. In fact, in examining the pathway from road to car, she saw very little to indicate that the sedan had actually traveled the route. More likely, the momentum had actually lifted the car and flipped it into its current position.

Elliot had been dead well before he'd been thrown from the vehicle. Even if the coroner hadn't confirmed it, Sam would have been certain of the fact. There was a pattern to the damage a bomb left on a body. She could see it in the burn pattern, as well as the fact that he was missing an arm and part of a leg.

The car was too hot to examine. Thanks to some freak act of physics, her friend's wallet had been thrown clear. If not for that, the police wouldn't even have been able to tell who he was for a couple of weeks. Not without DNA and dental analysis.

They'd still have to check for certain of course, but there was no doubt in Sam's mind that she was looking at Elliot's remains. It was hard to believe he'd been standing in her lab just a few hours earlier. For the second time in two days she was looking at the body of someone she'd cared about.

She shivered, then forced herself to focus. The real question here, beyond why someone would target him, had to do with why Elliot was here at all. He'd obviously driven north from their headquarters—away from the airport. He'd said his plane was leaving in an hour, which meant that his choice of a decidedly rural and therefore deserted area in the middle of thriving urban sprawl was more than a bit odd.

"Where does this road lead?" Payton asked, evidently following the same line of thinking.

Harrison looked up from the rubble. "To a housing addition, and eventually to the highway. But it's hardly a throughway. In fact if you're not from Austin, I doubt you'd even know this was here."

"Well somebody told him about it." Payton bent down to

pick up a fragment in the grass. He studied it for a moment, and then flicked it away.

"So you think he was meeting someone?" Sam asked, her stomach churning with the smell of burned rubber and human flesh. No matter how many scenes like this she worked, the olfactory onslaught always caught her off guard.

"Makes sense," Payton said. "We passed a park on the way. Public space, out of the way access. Maybe he was trading information about our investigation."

"No way," Sam said, anger rocketing through her. "Elliot wouldn't do something like that."

"He could have been in trouble, Sam. You saw his face."

She blew out a breath and nodded. Something had definitely been off. "I still don't believe he'd sell me out."

"Desperate times…" Payton shrugged. "Look, I'm just calling it the way I see it."

Sam shook her head, her heart still rejecting the idea. "But in order for that to work, someone had to know he was coming."

"He flew commercial," Harrison said. "It was the fastest way to get here with the frag. It would be easy enough for someone to find out who he was. Especially if they were looking for a way to access our findings. And if he did have problems, it would make him an easy mark. All the killer had to do was identify him, and then make him an offer he couldn't refuse."

Payton moved closer to the car, nudging the smoldering remains of a canvas bag with his foot. The duffel had obviously been thrown from the car, its side splitting in the process, charred stacks of bill-sized paper flapping in the breeze. "Looks like whoever it was took him for a ride. This stuff is bogus."

"You think that's the payoff?" Sam bent down to examine the bag, using a stick to lift the side. A piece of paper fluttered up with the motion, and she reached up to catch it. "At least some of it was money." She held out the burned bill, the number one hundred still visible on the corner. The evidence certainly supported the idea that Elliot had sold information. Her heart twisted at the thought, but she couldn't ignore the facts.

"So someone contacts Elliot and offers money for information." Harrison squatted down to examine the bag.

"We don't have proof of that, but it follows with what we're finding here," Payton said.

"But we still don't have a motive," Sam insisted, some small part of her still hanging onto her faith in her friend.

"We'll find it." Payton's gaze held hers for a moment, and then he turned back to Harrison. "So following your scenario, Elliot gets the information, contacts his source and is told to meet him somewhere along this road. Maybe at the park. And the guy takes the information, gives Elliot the bogus money and drives away."

"Finding time somewhere in there to booby-trap the car? That doesn't seem likely." Harrison's expression was skeptical.

"You'd be surprised how easy it is," Sam said on a sigh. "All he'd have to do is drop something, pretend it rolled under the car, crawl under to retrieve it, attach the bomb and voila."

"Sam's right," Payton agreed. "It's an easy way to get rid of someone. And if this guy is as smart as we think he is, he wouldn't want to leave anything to chance. Including a witness."

"But why would the bomber want to know what we know?"

"To see if we're getting his message." Sam shivered, her gaze taking in the carnage of his most recent handiwork. No matter what he'd done, Elliot had still been her friend. And no one deserved to die like this.

"But we're not," Harrison said, frustration cresting in his eyes.

"Oh we're getting it, all right," Payton said, his scar highlighted in the faint light. "We just don't know what the hell it means."

"He's here though. Or he was. Still running two steps ahead of us." Sam scanned the woods as if perhaps he'd be standing there, waiting for her to find him. This was starting to feel personal. As if he were goading her. And she didn't like the idea one little bit.

The tech team moved in silence around her, measuring and photographing. Sam shifted out of the way, stepping back into the relative solitude of the woods. There'd be more answers in a day or so. Confirmation of what she already knew. Elliot had been used and destroyed with the callousness of a soldier. Whoever this guy was, he was good, but he was also arrogant.

To kill Elliot right under their noses indicated the man was getting cocky. And his need to know how the investigation was progressing marked him as paranoid. And that combination ultimately would lead to mistakes.

"He's long gone." Payton slipped up behind her, his hands on her waist, his breath warm against her neck.

"I know," she sighed. "I just keep thinking that if I stare into the darkness long enough I'll find answers. Figure out what this bastard is all about."

"We'll get him, Sam. It's just going to take time."

She nodded, resisting the urge to lean back into his arms. She was so damned tired. And the circus showed no sign of ending.

"Let's go home."

The words were simple but their meaning was oh so complex. And suddenly Sam didn't want to analyze anymore, she just wanted to find solace away from all the death and destruction. Tomorrow would be another day, and she'd rise to the challenges just as she always did.

But for tonight, she simply wanted to take what Payton was offering. No questions asked. No strings attached.

She turned to face him, reaching up to trace the line of his scar. "I'm ready if you are."

THE ALBUQUERQUE AIRPORT wasn't all that different from Austin's. Maybe a little larger, but basically similar in design. The flow was more organized than older airports, and J.T. appreciated the fact, the orderly arrangement of things flowing together into what was actually a pleasing design.

He wondered for a moment what his life would have been like if he'd been an architect, then dismissed the thought before it had time to grow. A person must live with the choices he made, for those decisions came together to equal the sum of the man.

He smiled, realizing that for the first time in several days he was actually happy. He regretted having to kill Elliot Drummond. Not because he felt anything for the man, but because it had been a deviation from plan. And because it had been messy.

Last minute things always were.

But if he was going to accomplish his goal, he had to be willing to improvise. Everything he'd worked for had altered the minute the senators had died. And if he was going to get things back on track, he had to know how much Samantha had managed to put together. Elliot had been a means to an end, nothing more.

J.T. stopped at the sliding doors leading to passenger pickup, trying to decide between a rental car and a taxi. A taxi was less likely to be traced, but it limited his mobility, something he really couldn't afford considering all that had to be accomplished here.

With a sigh, he turned toward the line of rental car companies, choosing the busiest, the bustle of business travelers hopefully diluting any memory of him. Not that they were looking for him.

Eventually it would come to that, but for the moment he

was still anonymous. Which meant that as long as he didn't do anything memorable, he'd most likely be all right. A calculated risk. But then what in life wasn't?

He stood in line, keeping his head at a neutral level, his body purposely relaxed. Any deviation from the norm would be remembered. Too nice, too mean, too anything. All he had to do was keep his actions to the point, and nondescript.

He hoisted his bag onto his shoulder, and moved forward in the line. He'd had to check the duffel. Which wasn't something he'd been comfortable with, but he'd had to bring some of his components with him, and taking them through security would have been too much of a hassle. There'd been an X-ray of course to prescreen checked luggage, but his components separately weren't something that would cause concern.

Everything else he needed, he could to buy here in New Mexico without threat of being traced. They were all common items that could be purchased anywhere. It would have been easier to drive. Then he could have brought everything with him preassembled, his preferred methodology. But time was of the essence and concessions had to be made.

He reached the front of the line and with a half smile at the agent, plopped down his money. Five minutes later, he was walking toward the parking lot, a set of keys jangling in his hand.

So far so good. Everything was going according to plan. A sense of confidence mixed with elation filtered through him. After tomorrow night, Samantha would finally be on the right track. She still wouldn't understand. That would take a little more connecting. But he knew she was more than up to the task.

He glanced up at the stars. Everything seemed bigger out here, especially the night sky. The moon hadn't risen yet, but the stars glittered brightly, their whirling patterns a signal that everything was pulling together, the circle almost completed.

He had only to do his part and all things would be as one.

Soon Samantha would understand the order of things. She'd know what was written on the stars. For every man there was a woman. A yin to a yang. And when the halves were joined, the world was in balance. Harmony reigning. Destiny at hand.

J.T. smiled and slid behind the wheel of the rental car. All he had to do was start the wheels in motion. Beginning with Senator Walker's fund-raiser.

CHAPTER SIXTEEN

"THE BODY COUNT IS RISING," Sam said, sinking onto the sofa in Payton's suite. "And I've got the feeling we're not finished."

Payton reached into the refrigerator and produced two beers, handing one to Sam. She took it and popped the top, letting the pungent beverage soothe her throat. Exhaustion radiated through her like the hot Texas sun, yet she knew sleep was not imminent. Not while there was a bomber out there. A bomber who was taunting her.

"We're not going to solve anything tonight." As usual, Payton was reading her mind. In an odd sort of way she was actually getting used to it. If someone had predicted a relationship between her and Payton, she would have scoffed. Two loners like magnets with the same charge, repelling each other by definition, there was no way in hell she would have predicted attraction.

But nevertheless it was there, at times overwhelming every ounce of common sense she possessed. She tipped back the beer bottle, watching him over the rim. He reminded her of a lake she'd visited once as a kid.

It was breathtakingly beautiful, so still it reflected the splendor of the mountains around it like a mirror. She'd been awestruck. But in seconds she'd seen the darker side of the lake when a storm had blown in, churning the fathomless waters into a frenzy, their canoe flipping, the icy water threatening to suck her down into its depths.

Her father had pulled her to shore, and other than a week

or so of nightmares, there'd been no lasting harm. But after that she'd maintained a healthy respect for water. Especially the deceptively calm type.

"I should go back to the lab. If I recheck the data on the fragments maybe I'll find something I've missed." She leaned forward, starting to stand, but Payton held out a hand.

"Tomorrow will be soon enough. Right now you need to relax." There was a note in his voice that struck a chord with her. The same note she'd heard at the car-bomb site. Despite the fact that Payton was a dangerous man, he was also a man of perception. She had the feeling that if he ever cared for someone, it would be deeply.

The thought made her shiver, and their gazes collided, the heat she saw reflected in his eyes nothing at all like a cold mountain lake.

"Turn around."

She paused, suddenly uncertain of how to proceed. She'd opened the door, even stuck her foot in it, but suddenly she was having second thoughts. She was out of her depth. She didn't have casual affairs, and despite her desire for the man, the general idea scared the hell out of her.

"It's just a massage." He smiled, his tone reassuring. He motioned for her to swivel on the sofa, and although she held her ground, she was fast losing willpower, the idea of his strong fingers massaging her aching muscles more than appealing. Maybe it was fate. She didn't believe in that sort of stuff, but then again, not believing didn't always make something untrue.

Rationalization was also the quickest way to hell.

He put his beer on the table, and with a sigh she gave in. What the hell, it had been a long couple of days. Surely she deserved this.

The little voice in the back of her head was screaming something about emotional entanglements and the pain of failed relationships, but she silenced it with an internal shrug and gave in to his ministrations.

His fingers were better than anything she could have imagined, stroking and kneading her muscles into compliance. She tipped her head forward, allowing him better access, and his hands circled her throat, massaging the skin covering her collarbone with his fingers.

These were hands that could easily kill, but she'd never know it from the gentle way he touched her. The heat of his fingers melted into her skin, sending ripples of pleasure shooting through her, and she could feel his breath on the back of her neck.

He shifted then, using his palms to knead the small of her back, her body stretching like a cat in response. God, he was good. Magic fingers. She closed her eyes, letting the sensation fill her, surround her, her muscles unwinding despite themselves.

He massaged her shoulders, her arms, even the tender skin around her rib cage, his hands encircling her waist to caress the soft skin of her belly. And then he bent his head, kissing her neck, sucking slowly against the corded muscles until she was quivering with anticipation.

Heat pooled between her legs as his hands slid low to knead the curve of her rear, and she squirmed against him, impatient now. When he reached for the hem of her shirt, she obediently raised her arms to help, relishing the friction as it slid away from her body.

Her bra followed her shirt, and she swallowed a moan as his hands closed over her breasts, his thumbs circling her nipples, bringing them to hard pebbled points. His mouth resumed tasting, his tongue tracing the line of first one shoulder, then the other.

It was as if he were learning the feel of her, his hands and mouth everywhere at once. He followed the curve of her spine, his mouth sucking and teasing against muscle and bone. Shivers spiraled downward, her oversensitized body reacting to every touch, every nibble.

And then he was kissing her ear, his tongue moving in and out until she was writhing against him, his hands still massaging her breasts, tormenting her nipples. She wanted to turn, to face him, to give him some of what he was giving her. But instead, he pulled her onto his lap, her back tight against his chest, her bottom against his rising erection. Even through his jeans, she could feel its pulsing strength.

He released a breast, and she groaned in complaint until his fingers slid lower, making short work of the button at her waistband, the zipper following suit without any argument at all.

He cupped her mound and then slipped a finger inside, his thumb stroking her clitoris as he moved languidly in and out. She pushed against him, wanting release, wanting him inside her now. But he held her firmly, his fingers moving faster, the pleasure building in intensity until she wasn't certain she could stand another minute.

She tried to move away, her breath coming in gasps, but he held her tight, his lips sucking her earlobe, pulling and teasing to the rhythm of his fingers. It was as if she were an instrument, and he the musician, each part of her responding to his touch in a way that blended together into one amazing moment. One perfect piece of music that filled her senses, ringing in her ears and dancing along her synapses.

She started to move against him, accepting the inevitable, losing herself to sensation, allowing him to carry her higher and higher, each stroke of his fingers bringing pleasure beyond belief. And in that moment she let herself go, wanting only to find release, to fall from the edge. To fly.

She moaned his name, half in praise, half in thanks, and fell back against him, tremors of pleasure still washing through her with the power of an ocean tide. She clenched around his fingers, not wanting it to end, understanding for the first time why someone would want a multiple orgasm.

His arms closed around her, his heartbeat strong against

her back, and she leaned into his warmth, grateful for the soft place to land. She sat like that for a while, held tight in his arms, satiated for the moment, and then he started to kiss her neck, and the heat inside her began to build again.

This time she demanded they meet face-to-face, pulling away long enough to turn around, meeting his hungry gaze with her own. He closed the distance between them, his kiss claiming her. There was no gentleness in his touch, only driving need matched stroke for stroke by her own desire.

She wanted him like she'd never wanted a man before. Wanted to feel him moving inside her, feel his excitement building to climax. With deft fingers she pulled his T-shirt free of his jeans, and, like her, he raised his arms, waiting for her to remove the thing. In one swift movement it was gone, and she pressed her breasts against him, eager to feel his skin against hers.

Their lips met again, their tongues dancing together, jockeying for position, for strength. She couldn't get enough of him, stroking the scarred skin of his shoulder and chest, the new skin surprisingly supple and soft.

He was such a contradiction, this man. Leather and velvet. One moment capable of defeating the most frightening of enemies, the next worrying about when she last had a meal. Her heart twisted with longing, and she framed his face in her hands, losing herself in the intensity of his fathomless green eyes.

"You're sure?" His words were whispered, his voice raw with need.

She wasn't certain exactly what he was asking. There was something beyond passion reflected in his eyes. Hope, maybe. The thought scared her, but she wasn't about to back away. Whatever path they took, she was more than ready to start the journey. If there were consequences, then she'd face them tomorrow. But for tonight, she wanted only to be with him.

"I'm positive," she whispered back, her thumb caressing the line of his scar.

Payton groaned deep in his throat, the sound animal, and crushed his lips to hers, at the same time scooping her into his arms. In three strides they were through the bedroom door, and in what seemed like seconds they'd removed the rest of their clothing, desire arcing between them with electric force.

He was even more magnificent than she'd imagined. His body hard and strong, his scars only accentuating his masculinity. His erection sprang up against his groin, and her breath caught in her throat at the sheer male beauty of it.

She reached out and stroked the velvety head, her fingers closing around the shaft, moving gently up and down, teasing him with every movement. His jaw clenched and he closed his eyes as she knelt in front of him, taking him in her mouth, her tongue tracing circles around the skin of his penis.

He smelled of soap and man, and tasted salty. She reached up to cup his buttocks, pulling him closer, and felt him tense, trying to maintain control. Using both her hand and her mouth, she teased him, feeling him grow even harder, his muscles taut, wanting release.

Then laughing, she pulled away, taking his hand and leading him to the bed in a show of seduction that was unlike her. Something in Payton released her inhibitions. He made her feel beautiful, and slightly wicked.

She lay on the cool cotton sheets, spreading her legs invitingly, and he lowered himself on top of her, his penis resting hot against her. He braced himself on his elbows, his eyes locking with hers, and all frivolity vanished. She wanted only one thing, and with a crooked smile, he acquiesced. One slow stroke and he was inside her, his penis penetrating only to the head, allowing her to accustom herself to his size and heat.

But she didn't want to wait, and with an impatient sigh, she pushed against him, taking him to the hilt, the feel of him deep inside her more pleasurable than anything he'd done to her before.

Holding perfectly still, he bent his head and sucked first one breast and then the other, taking her nipples between his teeth, the sensation sending shards of white heat pooling between her legs.

She tried to move, to get him to engage, but he held her firmly, his tongue circling one nipple and then the other, his teasing touch making them so hard she thought they might burst. His thumb found her clit and resumed the magical flicking, the rhythm matching the movement of his tongue against her breasts.

She writhed against him, mewing like a kitten, the sounds emanating from deep inside her. Colors washed through her head, and she fought for control, the power of his hand and mouth driving her closer and closer to the brink.

Then suddenly he moved, his penis thrusting in and out, building a tension so sweet and so tight that she felt as if she was going to shatter. She matched his pace, her body pounding against his, the ferocity of their mating earthy and primal. Their scents mixed together, heated and sweating, and she wanted more, still more.

As if reading her mind, he withdrew, the separation almost making her weep, but before she could protest, he flipped her over and entered her from behind, the contact even more intimate than before, his scrotum rubbing against her bottom in a seductive slide that felt so damn good.

He covered her breasts with his callused palms, squeezing and kneading in time to his thrusting. Again she spiraled upward, sensation reaching a fever pitch, and she tossed back her head, moaning his name.

"Payton, please. I need to see you." Her voice was rough with passion, barely more than a whisper. "Please."

He broke contact again, leaving her shaking with desire, and turned over so that she was on the top. His breathing was as labored as hers, his green eyes dark with passion and his erection if possible even harder.

She slid down on him with a delicate sigh and began to move. Up and down, in and out, the movement creating exquisite agony. She was in charge, his fate in her hands, and the power combined with her passion was heady. She slowed, teasing him with the motion, torturing herself as well as him.

Her body strained to find release, even as her mind fought to control it. She bent to brush her lips across his. He reached for her head, deepening the kiss, drinking her very essence. And with the contact, the power shifted.

He grasped her hips, forcing his own rhythm, thrusting harder and deeper, faster and faster, the friction of their bodies together ratcheting her need higher and higher, until she felt as if she might explode.

And still he thrust, her passageway tightening around him, holding him inside her, until she could no longer tell where he ended and she began. And still they climbed higher, locked together in an endless dance. A kaleidoscope of emotion and sensation that seemed beyond endurance. Yet she wanted it—needed it—more than breathing.

She felt his hands tighten hard against her hips, and then the world exploded, light and heat combusting into sensations so intense she felt as though she might be ripped apart. Wave after wave washed through her, pleasure and pain so intricately bound her body shook with the impact.

And then he called her name, the sound sweet and compelling, completing her in a way she'd never imagined possible. His hands found hers, and together they rode the storm, cresting the waves, until the tempest was gone, and there was nothing but contentment. Two people alone in the dark, their bodies linked, their fingers intertwined.

Sam sighed, nestling against the warmth of his chest, allowing herself to drift to sleep, her last thought that maybe there were some things in life worth fighting for.

And Payton Reynolds topped the list.

CHAPTER SEVENTEEN

PAYTON STRUGGLED against the dream, part of his brain aware that it wasn't real, that it was only a twisted memory. Unfortunately, the rest of him was convinced it was dead-on reality. The shadows of the building seemed elongated, darker and more menacing than they should be, Kevin's silhouette showing only in the staccato flash of machine-gun fire.

There were already four men down, and if they didn't get the hell out of here soon, there'd be more.

Payton followed his brother back into the courtyard, crouching low. They reached Mackenzie but he was already dead. Same for Tyler and Goodacre, but Wallenski was still moving, holding onto his side, the blood already soaking through his fatigues.

Another burst of gunfire erupted from the balcony to Payton's left, the bullets sending dust flying. There was an answering volley from behind, Nigel and Gabe covering their asses. Kevin reached Wallenski, and then bent to take a pulse. In the few seconds it had taken them to reach him, the kid had died.

Payton swallowed a surge of anger, knowing that it would only get in the way of their survival. Bullets danced along the edge of the building, sending fragments of masonry flying through the air.

Kevin signaled a retreat, and Payton shifted toward Gabe and Nigel's position, using the wall to cover his back. He'd barely taken a step when a soft thud, preceded by a quiet whis-

tle, sent him diving for nonexistent cover, years of experience
sending his muscles a warning long before his brain had time
to react.

The grenade exploded with a burst of heat and fire that en-
gulfed both him and Kevin. Searing pain bit into the left side
of Payton's chest, and he could smell his shirt and flesh burning, but it was his brother who needed help. Kevin had been
knocked to the ground, flames leaping around him, mortar
cutting through him like slicing knives.

Payton dashed forward, shooting blindly off his left hip toward the balcony. But the bastards kept firing. Another grenade followed in the wake of more bullets.

This time Payton hit the ground rolling, using Wallenski's
body for cover as he crawled toward his brother. Seconds
passed, but they seemed to take forever. Then he reached
Kevin's side, machine-gun fire pounding the turf beside him.
A bullet found home, digging deep into the side of his chest,
the impact dizzying. But he pushed the pain away, concentrating on his brother. Using field training, he quickly assessed Kevin's wounds, signaling to Gabe that he would carry
his brother out, praying his friend could make out the motions
through the smoky haze.

He slid his arms under his brother, squatting so that he
could more easily bear the weight, but Kevin's hand closed
on Payton's, his pain-glazed eyes, fluttering open. "Let me
go, Payton. You have to let me go."

Payton clenched his jaw, shaking his head. "Not a chance
in hell. We're getting out of here." He tightened his hold and
lifted his brother, clutching him to his chest, only to find himself looking down into Mariam's dark eyes.

"Help me, Payton. *Please.*"

Blood dripped from her face onto his hands, and he felt the
sting of tears. "I won't let you go," he yelled, as another volley of machine-gun fire hit the walls around him. "I promise."

"It's too late," she whispered, the light already draining from her eyes, her features changing yet again.

Payton shook his head, trying to clear his head, concentrating on survival. But suddenly it was Sam that he was holding, her face mutilated almost beyond recognition. He fought to revive her, to stop the blood, but she was gone.

Dead.

They were all dead.

"No." Payton threw back his head, his scream filling the courtyard. He screamed for Kevin, for Mariam and now for Samantha.

But it was too late.

He couldn't save them. No matter how much he loved them, it was too late. Everyone he loved died. He screamed again, heedless of the renewed gunfire. He wanted to die, wanted the bullets to tear him apart. Maybe in death he'd at last find peace.

"Payton." The sound of Sam's voice broke through the nightmare like a lantern, the cool light banishing his tortured memories to the dark recesses of his mind. He pulled against the power that held him, struggling to wake up, to release himself from his self-imposed hell.

"Go," Kevin cried.

"Don't leave me," Mariam begged.

"Wake up." Sam was shaking him now, and the voices faded away as he surfaced to reality, sweat drenching his body.

He sat up, running his hands through his hair, torn between remnants of his fear, and mortification that he'd had the dream—tonight of all nights.

"Let it go, Payton. Let it go." Sam's arms encircled him, her breasts pressed against his back, he could feel each breath, testament that she was uninjured and alive. "It's over."

He shook his head. "It'll never be over."

"Yes, it will. But you have to let it go." She laid her cheek against the scarred skin of his back, her touch both comforting and arousing. "You have to give yourself permission to go on. I can't believe that Kevin and Mariam would have wanted it any other way."

He pulled away, turning to face her, anger threatening to override other emotion. "How did you find out about Mariam?"

"Gabe told me," she said quietly, her look unapologetic. "He thought I had a right to know."

"He shouldn't have said anything," Payton snapped, then bit back the rest of his retort, his anger dissipating almost as quickly as it had formed. "It wasn't his place."

"No," she said, her eyes still steady and clear. "It was yours. You should have been the one to tell me. But you wouldn't have, would you?"

"Probably not." Her face tightened as she tried to control the hurt, and he cursed his lack of sensitivity, looking for some way to soften what he'd said. "I don't talk about it much to anyone."

"Especially a one-night stand." The words were mumbled, but he heard them just the same.

"You mean a hell of a lot more to me than that, and you know it." The anger was back, but this time because she doubted him. Doubted *them*. He hadn't really admitted to himself how he felt until now. Wasn't sure what the hell it meant even at that. But it was real, and he wouldn't let her belittle it.

"Then don't be afraid to share it all with me, Payton. The good stuff and the bad," she dared him, her anger rising to match his. "I don't need to be protected."

"I wasn't protecting you," he said. "I was protecting *me*."

"From what?"

"I don't know. Rejection. Or maybe condemnation for what I've done." Fear clutched at his chest as if it had flesh-and-blood fingers, and he closed his eyes, willing away his vulnerability.

"You didn't kill them, Payton." She reached up to stroke his face, her fingers tracing the pattern of his scar, the gesture oddly intimate. "It wasn't your fault."

"The hell it wasn't." His eyes flickered open, his gaze battling with hers. "They trusted me. I was supposed to take care of them."

"Loving someone doesn't mean you can keep them safe, Payton. It's a nice idea in theory, but in actuality it doesn't make a lot of sense. I mean, you weren't even there when Mariam died. And from what Gabe told me you did everything you could to save Kevin."

"It wasn't enough." His brother's face flashed in his mind again, and he clenched his fists, his heart twisting in agony. "It wasn't fucking enough."

"Oh, God, Payton. I wish I could take away the pain. Make you see that there wasn't anything more you could have done. But I don't have that kind of power. All I can do is hold you, and let you know that I'm here, and that I care. And that you don't have to protect yourself from me." She met his gaze unflinchingly. There was no cynicism, no pity, only compassion—and something more, something that he scarcely dared to put a name to. "Let me be your safe place, Payton."

With a groan, he pulled her to him, his kiss restrained, a renewal of sorts, as if she alone had the power to sustain him. And maybe she did. He marveled at the fact that she had come to him, knowing about his past. Had witnessed his nightmares, not once but twice, and hadn't turned away in disgust.

Instead she offered herself, freely, without asking for anything in return. It humbled him. And excited him. And created feelings he wasn't even sure he understood. But he knew one thing: he needed her. And he'd be a fool to turn away from so precious a gift.

He pulled her back into the soft comfort of the bed, determined to show her with his mouth and hands and body all the things he couldn't find voice to say. And she answered him in kind, the two of them delighting in the discovery of each other, tasting and exploring, kissing and teasing, his body responding to hers as the fears and anxiety of his nightmares were pushed aside in the wake of their rising passion.

He braced himself above her, marveling at the beauty of her smile, the hazy blue of her eyes, the dusting of freckles across her nose. This was a woman a man could lose himself in. And at the moment, that's all he wanted. Refuge in the storm. A place where the demons couldn't find him.

With a single thrust he was inside her, his body establishing a rhythm. She arched against him, taking him deeper, her body rising to meet his in a dance to music only they could hear, the melody building in tempo and complexity until there was nothing but the two of them.

He closed his eyes and let himself go, surrendering to the moment. Together they moved, two souls joined together in a sensual spiral of passion. And together they found release, the world breaking apart in a frenzy of sensation, the climax beyond anything he'd ever believed possible.

And in that moment of ecstasy, he held on to the fact that it was his name she called. His body she clung to, his soul she held in her hands. And there in the soft beauty of her smile, he found sanctuary, and rejoiced in the fact that, at least for the moment, together they held the darkness at bay.

SAM LAY COMPLETELY STILL, content for the moment to simply feel the rhythm of Payton's breathing. The sun was only a hint of color at the window, and she was loath to break the spell. Whatever it was that had passed between them in the night, she was afraid it would fade with daylight, and her heart wasn't certain she could take the loss.

So she held on to the moment, letting the pink rays of the sunrise deepen, casting their warming rays across the sheets. So many things had passed between them last night. Her body was testament to the physical aspects, and her heart was heavy with the emotional part.

Payton was every bit as complex as she'd imagined. And every bit as compelling. The ghosts that haunted him wouldn't easily let him go. Even if they agreed, she wasn't sure that he'd let *them* go. All of which made a relationship tricky at best.

She sighed, and allowed herself a moment to simply hold him. To feel his chest rise and fall, his breath on her face, his hand thrown possessively across her chest. Their bodies fit together like two halves of a whole. She laughed at the cliché, even as she recognized its truth.

Opposites might attract, but kindred spirits welded together in a way that made it hard to separate. But separating was exactly what she had to do. There was business at hand, a job to do. And nothing, not even the magic of last night, could be allowed to get in her way.

Carefully extracting herself from beneath his arm, she slid out from beneath the covers, immediately regretting the loss of his warmth. Despite the Texas heat, the hotel room felt cold and suddenly empty.

She shivered and gathered her clothes, then walked into the living room, slipping into them with less grace than she'd removed them, her mind lingering on the memory of his hands against her body, his lips against…

She shook her head, pulling her thoughts to the present. She'd deal with the fallout later. At least for the moment they were together. There was some comfort in the thought. Sam bent to retrieve her shirt, sliding it over her head.

She wasn't going to let her emotions get the better of her. It wouldn't help anything. What she needed was to focus on the case. On finding the bomber.

"Where're you going?" Payton stood in the doorway, stark naked, his eyes narrowed in concern.

"I've got work to do." Despite the reality of the statement, it sounded lame. And she turned to face him, her lip caught between her teeth.

His frown was flattering, and sexy, his anger somehow more palatable when it concerned her leaving. "It's early. I don't think Cullen expects you to punch a time clock."

He looked so damn at ease that it made her angry. "In case you've forgotten, there's a bomber on the loose, and I don't think his next victim will appreciate it if I spend my day in bed with you instead of trying to figure out who the hell he is."

The frown deepened. "I didn't mean to piss you off."

She wondered where the easy camaraderie of the night before had gone, but knew the answer. She'd created the awkwardness, her fear creating chasms where there had been none. Story of her life.

"I'm not mad. I'm just concerned about doing my job. Look, last night was wonderful. I—*we* needed the escape. But it's morning now, and reality demands that I concentrate on the reason I'm here."

"Last night was more than wonderful." He crossed the room in two strides, his fingers lifting her chin, forcing her gaze to meet his.

"I know." Tears threatened, and she silently cursed. "But it wasn't real."

"You can't be sure of that." His eyes were dark with emotion, and she wished she could believe the things she saw there.

"And you can't tell me for certain that I'm wrong." She waited, knowing that he wouldn't disagree.

"No, I can't." His gaze still held hers. "But I'm not willing to give it up without at least trying." He made it sound so easy. Like climbing a tree or deciding what to have for breakfast.

"I don't want to get hurt."

"The only way you find the things in life that matter, Sam, is by risking hurt." This from the man who couldn't let go of his dead brother and wife. But then maybe that was the point. Maybe Payton had risked and lost, and in doing so won the prize that mattered most of all.

She reached up to touch his face, loving the fact that it felt so familiar. "I'm not going anywhere. At least not metaphorically." This time her smile was self-mocking. "But I am going to my room. I need a shower, and I need to get to the lab. This guy is gaining on us, and I don't like the idea of his winning even an inch."

"When you put it that way…" Payton's grin was still intimate, and he bent to brush a kiss against her lips, the simple act stealing her breath away. God, she had it bad. She smiled up at him, feeling all of about fifteen, then squared her shoulders and turned her back, walking into the bedroom, heading for the connecting door between their rooms.

"Wait."

She turned, the protest dying on her lips when she saw the expression on his face.

"You haven't been in your room since we got home last night." The statement seemed innocuous, but she followed his train of thought immediately.

"You think the bomber left me another present?"

He shrugged, walking toward the door.

"Hang on," she said, her voice louder than she'd intended.

He turned, his eyebrows raised in question.

"You can't go in there like that." She allowed herself the luxury of perusing his naked body, the memory of last night sending heat rising to her cheeks.

His mouth quirked with laughter. "I hardly think a pair of Levi's is going to be protection against a bomb. But I'll humor you." His gaze collided with hers. "Don't move."

Usually when someone issued an ultimatum, she was inclined to ignore it, but nevertheless she waited until he'd pulled on his jeans and come back to the door.

"I'll go first," she said, her eyes already scanning the frame for signs of wiring or tampering. "If he has done something, I'd lay odds it doesn't involve this door. Access is too difficult. Besides, he used a door last time, and this guy doesn't seem to be one for repeat performances."

Payton flanked her, his eyes also following the line of the frame. "So you've accepted the idea that the confetti bomb could be the work of the same guy."

"Having seen more of his work, I've got to admit the possibility. But until I've got definitive proof, I'm not going to speculate."

He smiled. "No speculating I can accept. As long as you treat it seriously."

She turned to him, her face impassive. "I'm always serious when it comes to bombs and the people that produce them. That's how I've lasted as long as I have in this business."

"You mean people would have run you off?"

"No." She shook her head, "I'd be dead."

She reached for the knob, and turned it, holding her breath. Nothing happened. "I think we're okay."

"You *think?*" Payton repeated.

She allowed herself a smile, watching as he reached for the light switch. Then some instinct sang out in warning, and she dove for him, the two of them hitting the floor just as a *whoosh* filled the air, followed by a *pop* as the lightbulb shorted out and an object on the far side of the room exploded.

CHAPTER EIGHTEEN

"WHAT THE HELL WAS THAT?" Payton's voice was muffled, and Sam shifted slightly so that she could see, her body still covering his.

"Something over there blew." She tipped her head toward the table across the room, smoke still emanating from the center. "My guess is it was triggered by the light switch."

"That would explain the lamp," he said, nodding toward the floor lamp next to the table, its shade warped and in places completely disintegrated, the broken stub of the lightbulb the only thing remaining in the socket. He started to roll out from under her, but she held her hand up to stop him.

"Don't move yet. There could be a secondary device." She was already visually searching the room, trying to locate anything that looked unusual. The wall plate of the light switch was singed, and there were pieces of metal scattered around the floor near the table along with something white lying halfway between the table and the connecting door.

She could see from here that the lock was in place on the front door, the curtains drawn and the bedroom door closed. She didn't remember leaving the door closed, but then she obviously hadn't been the last one in the room.

"I think it's clear." Payton, too, had been scanning the room.

She nodded, studying the remains of the bomb, then returned her gaze to his, suddenly aware of their proximity. She'd hit him with full force, ending up straddling him on the floor. "You all right?"

"It was a hell of a tackle." His mouth twitched once at the corner, then he sobered. "But overall, I'm fine. Thanks to you." He reached up to trace the line on her cheek, the contact sending shivers of fire racing through her. Last night, it seemed, had been only a prelude. She still wanted more.

"Nothing to thank me for." She forced herself to ignore his touch. It was important to stay focused on the task at hand—the bomber's message. And impossible to do so lying on top of Payton.

She rolled off him, moving slowly to a sitting position, scanning the room for any reaction to her movement. Everything was still.

Payton followed suit, leaning back against the wall, his gaze still raking across the room. "Seems stable."

"Yeah. I think we're good to go. Although I'd prefer to leave the bedroom door closed until the technical team arrives."

"You think he was trying to hurt you?" Anger sparked in his eyes, his tone possessive.

"No." She shook her head, ignoring the sparks still flying between them. "I don't think it was meant to hurt anyone. The debris is limited to the area around the table. Which means that whichever door I'd entered from, the odds were I'd be too far away to be in any real danger."

"What if you'd gone directly for the lamp?" He asked, pushing to his feet and offering her a hand.

"That's why the drapes are pulled and the bedroom door closed," she said, allowing him to pull her up. "He wanted to force me to use the light switch."

"Smart man." Payton's expression had turned grim, and he walked toward the lamp.

Sam followed in his wake, stopping at the edge of the table. The seat of the explosion was an eight-inch rectangle scorched permanently into what remained of the table. It had split in two, but because of its position against the wall, it hadn't fallen. Secondary scorch marks ran in streaks radiating from the rectangular burn like a sunburst. One on the left side of the table seemed particularly long, and Sam wondered if it had been made by a fuse.

She turned to face the room, trying to envision the explosion, marking the distances pieces of shrapnel had traveled. Nothing had gone more than about four feet from the table, which meant a controlled blast.

She'd been right. There'd been no intention to harm. Just a message.

But what the hell was it?

She bent to the carpet, brushing her fingers against something red and sticky. Lifting her finger to her nose, she sniffed cautiously.

"Paint?" Payton asked, coming up behind her.

Startled, she started to spin around, then checked herself, wondering if she'd ever get used to the way he moved. "Looks like it. I'm thinking the bomb's container was painted, and the heat of the explosion melted the paint." She reached down to pick up a twisted fragment, the metal still warm to the touch. "See?" she offered, holding it out. "It's still got streaks on it."

"I'll call Gabe," Payton said, already walking toward the phone.

Sam nodded, still studying the fragment in her hand, then her mind caught up with the conversation. "Wait."

Payton turned, his gaze quizzical.

"Better use the phone in the other room. I'm sure this one is fine. But no sense taking chances."

His smile was crooked as he walked back toward her, stopping to give her a kiss. "Thanks for watching out for me."

"It wasn't about you, believe me." She smiled, her teasing tone matching his. "I just didn't want to clean up the mess."

"Nah, you'd miss me." He turned to go, and she realized with gut-wrenching surety that he was right.

"Make sure Gabe sends a full technical team. I want this room gone over with a fine-toothed comb. If there's something here to identify this guy, I want to find it."

"Sam?" Payton had stopped in the middle of the room, bending to pick something up. "You recognize this?"

She glanced down at the thing in his palm, her heart stuttering to a stop. It was roughly the size of a golf ball, its painted face still intact, its little hat frayed and crooked. "Oh my God." She took a step away from it, waving her hand as if she could make it disappear. "It's Jack. *My* Jack."

The little clown had been her best friend for three quarters of her life. The sound of the music and his jaunty *pop* always making her laugh, no matter how bleak her life might have seemed. He'd seen her through the ups and downs of childhood, the angst of adolescence, the insecurities of young adulthood, and then he'd gone—just like her father.

"It isn't your Jack, Sam." Payton reached out to steady her, his touch bringing her sharply back to the present.

"I know." She closed her eyes and blew out a breath, fighting for a calm she didn't feel. She opened her eyes again, her gaze meeting his. "It's just that it looks so much like mine."

"The guy's playing mind games." He framed her face with his hands, searching her eyes. "You can't let him get to you."

"I won't." She pulled away, shaking her head. "I just had a weird moment. Sorry."

"It's understandable. I don't like the idea that the prick was in your suite any more than you do."

"It's par for the course, I guess. I just let it spook me." She squared her shoulders, forcing a smile in an attempt to erase the worry creasing his face. "We already established that he wasn't trying to hurt me. Just jerk me around a bit. And tell me something."

"So how do we figure it out?"

"The tech team will be a start, and from there I'll try and reconfigure both bombs. He's left marks before. Maybe there's something embedded in a fragment that he wants me to see. Or something that will tell us where the box came from."

"You think it's the one that was stolen from your apartment?"

"I know it's not likely. But I can't rule it out. At least not until I've thoroughly examined what's left of it."

"All right. I'll make the call." He laid the little head back where it had landed, and walked into his suite.

Sam stared down at the little clown, his sad eyes staring up at her, trying to tell her something—something only she could know. The bomber obviously had done his homework. Knew enough about her life to send a personal message. Problem was, she hadn't a clue what the hell he was trying to say.

"I WANT ROUND-THE-CLOCK protection, damn it." Payton slammed his hand down on Cullen's desk, satisfied when the other man jumped.

"She's got you, Payton. I don't think it gets much better than that. And I've arranged for the two of you to move into a secured house. It's gated and most of the property is fenced, plus there'll be security stationed everywhere. I'm moving the rest of the team as well." Cullen spread his hands. "But you said yourself that this man, whoever he is, isn't trying to hurt her."

"Yet." Payton let the word hang in the air, gripping the edge of the desk, his anger barely leashed. "I don't want to take any chances."

"You could lock her in a room." Cullen's quip fell flat, and Payton exchanged glances with Gabe who was standing in the corner, leaning back against the edge of Cullen's bar.

"I hardly think that will be necessary," Gabe said, one eyebrow raising. "Don't forget she's perfectly capable of taking care of herself."

"I know that," Payton growled. "But it's not enough."

"I agree, Payton," Cullen said, his voice placating. "That's why I've arranged for the safe house. And in the meantime, you and the rest of the team will have to make sure you have her back. That's as good as it's going to get. I need her on this case. Especially if she's connected to it somehow. Hell, she may be the only one who can figure it out."

"And you always get what you want." His words held scorn, but his tone lacked conviction. Truth was he didn't have the energy to fight Cullen. Besides, even if he did, there was no point. Sam wouldn't quit even if Cullen told her to. Better to keep her on the team—at least that way he could watch over her.

"She's going to be fine." Gabe reached out to pat his shoulder. "We'll see to it."

"Like we did in Iraq?" Payton met his friend's gaze, his own searching.

Gabe shook his head. "We did the best we could at the time. You know that."

"Yeah, I guess I do." Payton rubbed the bridge of his nose, the seeds of a headache starting to pound at his temples. "I just don't want her hurt."

"None of us do," Gabe said. "And I'm not saying we can ignore the fact that this guy seems to know a lot about Sam. But even assuming the incidents in her room are part of some bigger plan, it still doesn't mean he's targeting her specifically. She's the lead investigator. If he wanted to send a message, she's the logical target."

"And to that end, she's also the logical person to help us figure out what the hell he's trying to say." Cullen steepled his hands, his expression impassive.

Payton knew the guy had feelings, he'd seen them when Madison was being threatened. But apparently his need to protect only extended to people he cared about. Payton swung around to go, working to swallow his disgust.

Sam was standing in the doorway, an odd expression on

her face. His heart sank, and he wondered how long she'd been standing there, cursing Cullen for not saying anything.

"I've reconstructed the shrapnel from the bomb in my room." She pushed past him without meeting his gaze, her attention on Cullen and Gabe.

"Another jack-in-the-box?" Cullen asked.

"No. It was a car. A miniature of the one Elliot Drummond was driving."

"Well I'd say that makes the message pretty damn clear," Gabe said, frowning. "He's taking credit for his handiwork."

"It certainly looks that way," Sam agreed. "Hopefully I'll know more after I reconstruct the first bomb."

"Any sign of the Tai on the fragments from this most recent attack?"

She shook her head. "Nothing that's visible to the naked eye. I didn't have time for anything more than reconstruction. Harrison's going to do a more detailed search. And when I get back I'll start looking for evidence to link the San Antonio and Virginia bombs to the ones in my hotel room and the one that killed Elliot. In the meantime though, in light of the model car, it seems like we can assume a connection to Elliot. And, through him, a connection to the other bombs."

"One thing's for certain," Payton said, shifting so that he could see Sam's face. "This guy is playing for keeps. He's killed five people already. And there's no sign that this is the end. So as far as I'm concerned until we know something different, we have to believe he's after you."

"You're jumping to conclusions." Her voice was deceptively soft, a little muscle ticking in her jaw. "He obviously knows something about me, but to date he's only used it as a means to get my attention. There's nothing we've seen that makes me believe the guy is doing anything but toying with me. It's not something I like. But it also isn't something that makes me think I should be running for the hills."

"What about Jack?" Payton asked, his anger rising. "You said yourself you thought it was yours."

"I overreacted. Heat-of-the-moment response." She shot him a telling look, her eyes glittering with anger. "He's definitely of the same vintage as the remains of the jack-in-the-box found in my room. But that's all I can be sure of right now. I've got Harrison working on a comparison to try and prove that he actually came from the same box as the first bomb."

"How about the box itself? You said it resembled the one you had, right?" Gabe's brows were drawn together in a frown.

"Yeah. I had Harrison check into that, too. And it seems like the toy was pretty standard issue at the time. And most of them were made in China. My dad picked it up while he was on a mission in the Far East. So that means my box was far from unique."

"Even so, it was old. That could make it rare," Payton insisted, still trying to get her to take his concerns more seriously.

"Actually, no. I looked on eBay just to see, and pulled up about twelve. Two of them identical to mine." She shrugged, but her tight smile signaled the fact that she knew she'd won the point. "I'm not saying his using the box is a coincidence. Just that I don't think he chose it for any other reason than to get my attention."

"Well, it's working." Payton caught her gaze and held it.

"Look, the thing that's important here is the fact that Jack survived the blast relatively untouched. At least his head did. Which tells me the bomber wanted it that way." She walked to the window and leaned back against the sill.

"Blast patterns are predictable. Attach a component this way or that and you can pretty accurately guess where it will land and what condition it will be in. All the variables have to be taken into consideration, and even then there is the possibility of a miscalculation, but overall, if a piece survives intact, especially in a situation like this one, it can be concluded that it survived because the bomber wanted it to."

"Which means that he planned for you to find it." Cullen sat back, steepling his fingers on his desk.

"Exactly." She nodded to emphasize the point. "And that tells us that at the very least Jack's presence at the second bomb site ties the two incidents together."

"What about your list of enemies?" Cullen queried.

"It's not as long as you might think," Sam said with a half smile. "But I'm still working on eliminating folks. Like Harrison said, most of them are still incarcerated, and so far the ones who aren't either don't fit our M.O. or they've got alibis."

"You'll keep checking?" Cullen asked.

"Of course. But in the meantime, I think we need to concentrate on the leads we have. Like Walker."

"And just ignore the fact that this guy seems to be gunning for you," Payton said.

"I'm not trying to ignore it. I'm just trying to keep it in perspective." She stood up, hands on hips, her blue eyes shooting sparks.

"He set two bombs off in your room, for God's sake," Payton said, closing the distance between them, forgetting for the moment that they weren't alone. "What more do you want?"

"I want to do my job. Without interference." She stepped back, her gaze including all of them now, her expression fierce. "And I can't do that if the three of you are plotting to sequester me against my will. I've dealt with this kind of thing before, and I can deal with it now."

"We're just trying to get your back," Gabe said, his tone unapologetic.

"I can live with that. But I won't stand for anything else. All right? I'm not some helpless victim that needs someone to ride to her rescue. Got it?"

They all nodded, but it was clear the message was for Payton.

"Fine, I'll back off." He held up his hands, not certain if he wanted to throttle her or kiss her. Either way he was lying between his teeth, because there was no way in hell he was letting her walk into some madman's plot. Even if it meant tying her to the bed.

Now there was a thought with definite appeal.

"WHAT THE HELL were you thinking?" Sam stared out the window of Cullen's jet, tired of containing her anger. This was the first time she'd had the chance to face Payton alone since she'd overheard his high-handed conversation with Cullen and Gabe in Cullen's office, and she'd been seething ever since.

"I was trying to protect you." Payton turned to face her, his scar making him look fierce. But she knew him too well to be afraid.

"From what? Myself?" She clenched the armrests, her fingernails digging into the soft leather. "I don't need that kind of protection." She wasn't sure why she was so angry at him. Every man she'd ever met had tried to protect her. Even her father. Maybe it was that she'd expected better of him.

"I didn't say you did." His look bordered on mutinous. "I just don't think you're taking the incidents in your hotel room seriously enough."

"So what, you want me to cower in the corner until it's all over?" She didn't mean to sound so waspish, but he punched her buttons.

"No." He reached out to take her hand, simply tightening his grasp when she tried to pull away. "I just want you to quit acting like a superhero. Everyone needs someone to watch their back now and then."

"You wanted more than that. I heard the three of you. You wanted to bench me so that you could play big hero and slay the dragon." It had been the theme of her life with men, and somehow it goaded her more now than ever.

"You're punishing me because I care about you."

"No," she spat. "I'm punishing you because you won't believe in me. I can handle this."

"Not alone."

She frowned in frustration. "I never said I wanted to handle it alone. I just want to continue to be an active part of the team."

"The leader."

"I'm best qualified for the job." She stared at him intently, daring him to argue with her.

Payton sighed. "I don't want you to run for cover just because some maniac is calling your bluff. I just want to be certain that you're not blindly running to him because you refuse to face the possibility that he's got your number."

"What the hell is that supposed to mean?"

He ran his hand through his hair. It was the most flustered she'd ever seen him, and if she hadn't been so angry, she would have been delighted that she'd gotten that kind of rise from him. "You could try the patience of a saint, Samantha Waters." He spoke through clenched teeth, his fingers wrapped around hers contradicting his tone.

"I try." She shrugged, feeling obstinate, but not exactly sure why.

"Look," he said, his green eyes serious, "your job is to find this bomber and to bring him to justice. My job is to make sure you can do your job in one piece. It's that simple."

Her obstinacy deflated. "And that's it?" The words were out before she could stop them, sounding a lot like a disappointed adolescent.

"You know it isn't." His thumb was stroking her palm, saying a hell of a lot more than words could ever convey.

"I don't know what to think." She leaned back against the seat, closing her eyes. "I just want my chance to find this guy. And I don't want anyone riding roughshod over me."

"I'm not trying to get in your way, Sam. But you can't shut me out either. You've got to trust me." His words echoed through her brain, and she knew she wanted to believe. Not only that he could be trusted, but that he could honestly stand beside her. As a partner.

But she'd heard him in Cullen's office. They'd been talking about locking her in a room. Which made him just the same as all the others, certain that she couldn't handle the life she'd chosen on her own. Certain that she needed someone to watch over her.

Well, she didn't need anyone. She never had. Her father had instilled that notion a long time ago. Stand on your own two feet, or fall.

She opened her eyes, ready to refute all that he was saying, to tell him she owed nothing to anyone, and liked it that way. But there was something in his eyes, something that reminded her that in asking her to trust him, he was opening himself up in a way no more comfortable for him than it was for her.

"I want to trust you. But I can't have you going behind my back like that again." He opened his mouth to contradict her, but she held up a hand to stop him. "I mean it. I've been doing what I do for a hell of a long time. And I'm not a novice. If I'm going to trust you, you have to trust me. You have to believe that I'm making informed decisions based on a hell of a lot of experience. I'm not about to let this guy get the better of me. So you've got to shelve that chauvinistic streak if we're going to continue to work together."

She'd purposely used the word *work,* but they both knew she meant more than that.

Payton was silent for a moment, letting her words sink in, but he didn't release her hand, the contact binding them together in some wordless way that went far beyond the semantics of their discussion.

Finally, he nodded. "I agree. But if I'm going to accept who you are, you've got to take me as I am as well."

She wasn't sure exactly what he meant, and waited, holding her breath, not certain she was going to like what he had to say.

"I grew up in the army. I believe in chain of command, and the wisdom of my superiors. Despite the fact that I've been on my own for a hell of a long time, I still have a set of standard operating procedures I live by. A code of honor if you will. And part of that code is to protect the people I care about—and I care about you." His eyes met hers, the intensity robbing her of breath.

She nodded, for once totally speechless. There was nothing she could say that would top the quiet eloquence of this man. She was honored, and frightened, and incredibly in love.

The emotion blindsided her. Uninvited, unwanted and probably unrequited.

But, in that moment, she knew that she would honor Payton Reynolds's request. She would accept him as he was. No matter how much he infuriated her. Because to do anything less would mean losing him.

And suddenly nothing in world seemed worth risking that.

CHAPTER NINETEEN

THE HYATT REGENCY was one of the ritziest hotels in Albuquerque, but the security was nonexistent. J.T. had planned his attack as if he were breaching Ft. Knox, but at least some of the preparation hadn't been necessary. He'd taken the precaution of raiding the hotel laundry to procure a workman's uniform, even managing to lift an ID badge from the laundry supervisor's desk.

It had obviously been left on a uniform, and despite the fact that it said it belonged to one Jorge Rivera, as long as nobody paid attention he was home free. He'd taken the time to replace the picture with his own, but so far no one had even spoken to him, let alone asked for ID.

The senator's benefit was being held in the ballroom. Capable of seating up to a thousand, the room was already set up with round tables and chairs, the dais at the front backed by two huge flat panel monitors.

For two thousand dollars a plate, the senator's guests were going to get one hell of a show. J.T. smiled to himself as he slipped up into the control room. Just a few minor adjustments and everything he'd set into motion earlier in the day would be ready for action.

He'd waited until the crew had performed all their technical checks, watching as they'd tested the sound and the monitors. Everything was perfect. Which meant that there should be nothing else standing in his way—except the possibility that Samantha would cancel the event. But unless he'd miscalculated, she hadn't made any conclusions that would lead her to decide that the event itself was dangerous.

Only that the senator was worth talking to.

J.T. might not have started out with this scenario in mind, but he was more than capable of adaptation. Who was anyone to question the ways of fate? Certainly not him. Truth was, he prided himself in allowing Ming to be a part of his world. He had only to take advantage of it. To shape fate the way he saw fit.

Balance and order, that was what mattered.

Besides, if Samantha cancelled the event it would change nothing. Only the beauty of his planning would be lost, and while he would mourn the fact, he would rise to the challenge—just like he had in San Antonio.

Of course nothing was going to go wrong. He was letting his imagination carry him away, worrying about nothing. Fate was on his side. He was, after all, structuring order from chaos, and considering how many parameters had already changed, he was lucky to have made it this far. Surely that meant that his plan was blessed. Ordained by the holy ones. The fact that he'd managed to escape detection so far was a testament to the fact that he was still in charge of the game.

The balance might change, eventually. Indeed, in some intrinsic way he wanted it to. But not yet. First he had to prove his power of manipulation. He'd demonstrated it in small ways already, but nothing of this magnitude. He'd thought the pyrotechnical display at the Prager had been his life's work, but he'd been wrong. It had been only a primer.

And this time he'd have an audience—the senator's adoring public, decked out in diamonds and designer threads, the elite of New Mexico. There was a certain *je ne sais quoi* in the fact that the very people to witness his masterpiece were representative of the type who had scorned him so often.

Not that any of that mattered in his grand scheme. Only one pair of eyes was necessary for success. His display was for her alone. And this time she would not be able to escape the fact that everything he'd done had been for her. It would no doubt take her time to figure out who exactly he was. How he was connected to her. But that was part of the game.

He smiled and pulled out a console, using a pair of borrowed pliers to replace three of the wires with his own. Fifteen minutes later, everything was ready, and nothing was detectable. The senator's dinner would proceed as planned—with one slight detour.

But first, J.T. had to make certain that the guest of honor would in fact be present.

He walked to the door, reaching up to flip off the lights, wondering how she'd liked his last present. It had been fun finding the right car and rigging it so that the little clown would survive his journey.

It was almost sad that J.T. hadn't been able to see it fly, but then he wouldn't have been able to be here, placing the dots for her to connect, leading her on her most difficult case. His creation, her undoing.

There was symmetry in the thought, and J.T. closed the door, walking away from the ballroom with a light step. Life was going exactly as planned. And nothing could make him happier.

THE SENATOR HAD one hell of an impressive turnout. Payton figured half of Albuquerque must be in attendance. It was the kind of affair he abhorred. Everyone making nice when no one really gave a damn.

The best of the best, none of them with anything at all to recommend them, and quite frankly he'd rather be anywhere but here. But they needed to talk to the senator and according to his aides, this was their only chance. The senator's people had left tickets for them.

So grudgingly, Payton had donned his tux and feigned interest in the affair, the only benefit to the evening being that he got to see Sam in an evening gown. She was sexy in jeans and a T-shirt, but in the clingy black sheath she was wearing now, she was a knockout. Not exactly great for keeping his mind on business.

There was extra security everywhere, and Sam had organized a bomb sweep. Best they could tell, the room was clean. Which had comforted the senator, but not Payton. The bomber was smart, and Payton wouldn't put it past him to have devised something that could slip by security unnoticed. Even under eyes as watchful as Sam's.

"Everything seems secure," Sam said, waving away a waiter with a tray of champagne. "Although I admit I would have felt better if Senator Walker had called the whole thing off."

"That was never going to happen. He wouldn't have gotten as far as he has if he scared easily. Besides, canceling something like this at the last minute for anything less than total disaster would cost him far more than the risk of something going wrong tonight. We've just got to make sure that risk stays minimal."

"I walked the perimeter again, and everything seems fine. We've got security people posted at every entrance, someone triple-checking invitations, and just to be certain, about twenty undercover policemen manning the party itself."

As if to underscore the fact, a tuxedoed gentleman sporting an earplug walked past, the coil snaking down his neck a dead giveaway.

Sam smiled. "Okay, maybe not so undercover. But the point is that they're here."

"Look, we're making a big leap here anyway, assuming Elliot revealed our plans."

"Unfortunately, it just seems logical." She fiddled with her bracelet, clearly as uncomfortable as he with the fancy clothes. "Unless Walker's the one behind all of this."

"If that's the case, then this has all been an exercise in futility." Payton shifted slightly so that he could better see the room. "But I don't think he's pulling the strings."

"Why not? We know he was causing problems for Ruckland and company."

"Because if he's behind the bombings, then the killer is a hit man. And I don't believe for a minute that someone like that would take the time to play mind games with you. It just doesn't fit the profile."

"Now who's sounding like Madison?" She smiled, for a moment looking as if there were nothing more pressing on her agenda than a night on the town.

Unfortunately it was nothing more than an illusion, one that he wanted to preserve if even only for a moment. "You talk to your mother?"

"Yeah. She and Ruth were planning to settle in for a round of Katherine Hepburn movies."

"You tell her why you were here?"

"I skimmed over it." She shrugged, her expression impassive. "My mother doesn't really approve of what I do. I think one risk-taker in the family was more than enough."

"Your dad."

Sam nodded. "Anyway, I told her I didn't think there'd be time for a visit since we're planning to fly out as soon as this thing is over and we've talked to the senator."

Payton nodded, taking her cue to drop the subject. Whatever the relationship between Sam and her mother, it wasn't for him to interfere.

"Ms. Waters?" A bespectacled young man in a perfectly tailored tux appeared at her elbow, his smile of the obligatory nature. "The senator has a few moments now if you'd care to talk to him."

Sam shot Payton a glance, and he nodded, the two of them turning then to follow Walker's flunky. Sam moved with smooth fluidity, her rear outlined with mouthwatering clarity by the silky material of her dress. Payton forced himself to focus instead on the little man in front of her. No point in meeting the senator with a hard-on.

Their escort ushered them into a small but elegant ante-room off the ballroom, a security guard flanking each side of the door. Senator Walker had his back turned when they entered, shaking hands with a well-endowed woman in a white dress that was just a bit too snug for acceptable standards.

She cooed up at him, squeezing his hand, and then moved past Sam and Payton in an overwhelming cloud of perfume. It reminded Payton of a teacher he'd had in school, the memory not an altogether pleasant one.

Walker turned then to greet them, his smile politically perfect, his gaze hard and assessing. "My people tell me you have some questions?"

Sam shot a look at flunky boy, and Walker dismissed him with the wave of his hand, then sat down on a tapestry-upholstered chair. "So, we're alone now. Why don't you tell me what this is all about?"

Sam sat on the sofa across from the senator, and Payton perched on the arm at her side. "I think you're already well aware that Ruckland, Dawson and Keith were working to make sure that certain agricultural subsidies were targeted to their home states. And that in doing so all three stood to gain considerably, both politically and financially."

"And if I tell you I have no idea what you're talking about?" the senator asked, his expression icy.

"Then we'll have to assume that there is evidence linking you to the conspiracy." Payton met the senator's stare full-on, remembering again why he disliked politicians.

"Which would mean a full-scale investigation," Sam said, following Payton's lead.

To the senator's credit, he didn't flinch, merely shrugged. "I assure you you're making more of my role than necessary."

"Maybe so. But at the moment, you're the only solid lead we have. And with your cooperation, maybe we can end this line of questioning once and for all. We have no interest in pursuing who was or wasn't involved with the pork, Senator. What we need to do is determine whether that bomb was meant for your colleagues."

"And you believe I could have had something to do with it, if it were?" he asked, hedging all the way.

"We know you were the reason the three of them were meeting. That you'd threatened to uncover their scheme if New Mexico wasn't included."

"You're half-right." Walker tipped his head, crossing his arms over his crisply starched shirt. "I was the reason they were meeting. But not to discuss some threat. We'd already reached an agreement."

"But Sloane said there was no way that Keith would work with you."

The senator laughed. "Sloane is a lackey. He knew only what Ruckland wanted him to know. And Keith knew which side of the bread his butter was on."

"So you're saying they'd already agreed to let you in."

"Ruckland had. And what Joe Ruckland wanted, he got. It's as simple as that. Whatever conspiracy existed, I was on the winning side, believe me. Which means I had absolutely no reason whatsoever to do anything to threaten that alliance. So unless I've missed something, we have no further business." He actually started to leave, his arrogance filling Payton with disgust.

"If what you're saying is the truth, Walker—" Payton stood up, his height and his scars playing to his advantage. Walker actually retreated a step, and Payton saw Sam conceal a smile. "—and I'm only saying *if*, then by my calculations, that would make you a target. If the bomber knew about Ruckland, Dawson and Keith's meeting, I'd bet my right arm that he knew about you."

Payton had the satisfaction of actually seeing the senator pale, but it was short-lived. "Bullshit. If he knew about me,

I'd have heard about it already. People like that are interested in one of two things. Money or power. And I have the ability to provide both. There's no need to kill me."

"Obviously you've never met a madman, Senator." Sam's voice was quiet, barely above a whisper, but it carried more force than if she'd yelled. The senator blanched again, his reserve obviously shaken.

"Then I assume the two of you will do whatever it is you do to make sure that I'm kept safe." He was back to arrogance. The idea that by sheer definition he deserved more protection than most.

"We've got everything covered tonight. After that, your people will be working with the Secret Service. Because you have seniority, and a sympathetic president, they'll watch over you."

"Fine." Walker stood up, his megawatt vote-for-me smile firmly back in place. "In case you haven't noticed I have people waiting for me. Which means we're finished here."

"Not quite, Senator." This time Sam's voice held a note of command, and Walker, despite himself, sat back down. "I need to know if this has any meaning for you." She held out a drawing of the Tai Chi. Walker took it from her, and held it out so that he could see it.

"I've seen it before, but I can't remember what it means."

"It's an Eastern symbol. Yin and yang," Payton allowed.

"Opposites or something, right?" Walker shot him a quizzical glance. "What has this got to do with the bombings?"

"The bomber left this symbol at both bomb sites." Sam wasn't revealing more than was necessary, as usual the consummate professional.

"Well, I haven't got any connection with it, if that's what you're looking for. I wasn't even sure what it was."

Sam studied him for a moment, then shot Payton a glance. He nodded, agreeing with her assessment that the senator was for once talking straight.

"If you can think of anyone in your organization that might have a connection with Eastern beliefs or philosophy, we need to know."

"Believe me, if there's a tie-in between my people and the man who killed Ruckland, you'll be the first to know. But I think you're on the wrong track. Despite the fact that we represent different parties, Ruckland and I were allies on more than just agricultural subsidies. Texas and New Mexico share similar problems. And even though the two states are perceived by some to be diametric opposites, the reality is that we're kissing cousins. No one in my employ would dare to harm that kind of symbiotic relationship.

"And now, I have to go." Without further comment, he stood up and strode from the room, leaving the two of them feeling like something momentous had happened.

Only of course, it hadn't. A particularly small little man had dismissed them. Nothing more.

"So you believe him?" Sam asked, looking up at him.

"Yeah. As much as I hate to say it, I think I do. If he was going to lie to us, he'd have come up with a hell of a lot better story."

"Do you think the bomber could really be after him?"

"I think it's possible. Hell, anything is possible. Especially where this guy is concerned. But we've done our homework, and the place is as secure as we can possibly make it. I guess the only thing left to do is to wait it out and see what happens."

"Pretty damn passive." Sam slammed her hand against the back of the chair.

"At the moment—" Payton shrugged "—it's all we've got."

"What if it's not enough?" She turned to face him, her expression grim. "Or worse, what if someone else has to die to prove the point?"

THE GUESTS WERE ALL SEATED, toying with their rubber chicken and pretending an enthusiasm nobody actually felt.

Sam and Payton had declined seats at a table in the corner. It made Sam think of *Animal House,* actually. The loser's table. She smothered a laugh, filled with nervous energy.

She hated playing defense, particularly when they were operating more or less in the dark. But as Payton had so succinctly put it, for the moment it was all they had.

The senator had started his speech, pontificating about country and apple pie, or something along those lines. She hadn't really been listening. Instead, she'd been watching the perimeter of the room, looking for something that seemed out of place or unusual.

She kept in contact with others in the room via her headset. Everyone was reporting all clear. The idea should have made her rest easy, but it didn't. She couldn't shake the feeling that they were waiting for the other shoe to drop.

Payton stood across the room from her, talking with a sergeant in the Albuquerque PD. Despite the conversation, he was aware of her scrutiny, because every few minutes he'd shoot a look in her direction. He obviously took the got-your-back thing very seriously, and surprisingly, the thought gave her a great deal of comfort.

She started to walk toward him, but turned at the sound of arguing. A rotund man was waving his arms at one of the security detail, his voice rising with each pass of the hand. Sam hurried in their direction, wishing suddenly that she'd brought a weapon.

An Albuquerque policeman had joined the security guard by the time Sam got there, the two of them physically restraining the man, whose face was red as a beet.

"Sir, if you can't calm down you'll have to leave the building," the security man said, his face brooking no argument.

But apparently the fat man wasn't buying. "Do you have any idea who I am?" The man was trying to wave his arm again, despite the two men holding him, his eyes disappearing into his face as he squinted up at the officer holding him.

"I own most of this fucking city." The man's words were slurred, but Sam got the gist of it, her heart rate immediately slowing.

They were dealing with a drunk.

"I wanna talk to the semator, righ' now." The man nodded toward the dais, his voice loud enough that people at the back tables were beginning to turn and look.

The security guy motioned to the policeman with a tilt of his head, and the two of them physically dragged the man out into the hallway. Sam followed, checking the perimeter again as she walked toward the door. Payton's gaze met hers across the room, and he nodded once. He'd obviously seen what was going on, and would take over coordination between teams until she came back into the room.

In the hallway, two uniformed policemen were in the process of cuffing the man. Still agitated, he weaved back and forth, yelling that heads were going to roll.

"You guys recognize him?" Sam asked the tuxedoed police officer, as he walked over to her.

"Winston Belker." The man grimaced. "Permanent pain in the ass. He's a local nut job. Shows up at political functions. Usually drunk and always pissed off about something. Most times he doesn't do more than mouth off a little too loudly. A night in the tank will cool him off."

"Most times?" Sam queried, not willing to take even the slightest chance that Belker could be involved.

The officer shrugged. "Sometimes he hits someone. More often than not some poor schmuck on the job. Fortunately, he never manages to get off more than a punch or so."

"So in your opinion, besides the pain-in-the-ass factor, this guy is harmless."

"Yup. Just a big mouth with a drinking problem, and enough money to cause problems."

"Fine," Sam said torn between relief and restlessness. She'd wanted things to come to a head, and part of her had hoped Belker would provide the key. "See that someone escorts him all the way to the station."

"No problem there." The policeman smiled. "I've had about enough of this bullshit anyway." He tipped his head toward the speaker in the hallway broadcasting Walker's speech. The man was still at it. "Seems like this has just been a huge waste of time."

Her sentiments exactly, but she wasn't about to admit it to a stranger, no matter whose side he was on. "Thanks for your help." She nodded to the two officers still holding the now-cowed Belker, and turned to head back into the ballroom. Maybe this would be the sum total of the excitement for the night.

Inside, the senator was saying something funny. Or at least the audience was laughing.

"Everything okay?" Payton's voice slid down her spine like warm butter. Even as tense as she was, she reacted to his nearness. Or maybe the tension was part and parcel of the attraction. No time to analyze it now.

"Yeah. Just a drunk. Locals were familiar with him. Nothing to do with our business."

Payton nodded. "Everyone's checked in and nothing's out of place."

"Maybe nothing's going to happen. Or maybe this is some kind of a ruse. Something to keep our attention diverted from the real target." The idea had been growing for about the last hour, but putting it into words made Sam feel sick. She hated having her chain jerked, and this guy was turning out to be really good at it.

"I don't know why he'd need a diversion," Payton said, his eyes narrowing as he considered the idea. "I mean, hell, we wouldn't have known where else to go anyway."

"Not a very flattering portrayal of our abilities."

Payton shrugged. "Unfortunately it's the truth. The only logic we've been able to find in all of this is the senators and their scheming. That makes Walker either a part of the solution or the problem and either way, our best lead."

"And since it doesn't seem to be panning out?"

"We say thanks that the man is still in one piece, and head back to the drawing board. Certainly it'd be worth a little more investigation into Senator Walker to make certain he's telling us the truth about being on board with Ruckland. But as I said before, my gut is telling me he's on the level."

"So we're back to square one."

Payton smiled down at her, his gaze rueful. "I'm not sure we were ever at square one."

"Great." Sam laughed, surprised at how much her tension eased with the action. "So now we're working from negative numbers."

"I guess we have to start somewhere."

Sam's radio crackled to life, and she turned her attention to the teams reporting in, watching as Senator Walker waved his hands at the two monitors over his head. She half listened to him talking about his new campaign commercials, and half listened as everyone systematically called in the all-clear.

The monitors flickered to life, and Sam frowned as the somewhat fuzzy picture of a suburban home filled the screens. The picture wavered for a moment, disappeared in static, and then reappeared, much clearer.

There was no soundtrack other than street noise around the house, some of it muffled by microphone feedback. Walker fumbled with the mike, and an aide hopped up to turn it off, the high-pitched humming stopping immediately. They turned to look at the screen, Walker angry, the aide clearly puzzled, and the audience began to whisper restlessly, all eyes still glued to the monitors.

It took a minute for Sam to realize what it was she was seeing, and her heart hit her stomach with a sickening thud, her knees buckling, even as her fingers tried desperately to remember how to make the buttons on her headset work.

"Sam?" Payton was beside her, his strong arm giving her renewed support.

She tried to wrench her eyes away from the screen, to tell him what was happening, but she couldn't. She just couldn't.

"Talk to me." It was his tone, more than his words, that finally reached her. She fought against the fear-induced paralysis holding her hostage.

"It's my mother, Payton." Sam said, pointing numbly at the screen. "That's her house."

As if waiting for her cue, smoke and flame filled the screens, the sound of the blast following a nanosecond later, the audience's screams ringing in her ears.

The other shoe had fallen.

CHAPTER TWENTY

IT LOOKED LIKE a war zone or the aftermath of a terror attack. Instead it was suburban Albuquerque, the Sandia mountains rising black against the night sky, an odd backdrop to the remaining smoke and fire.

The house had been destroyed. Unlike the bomb in Virginia, this one had been meant to annihilate, the visual as much a part of the package as the destruction. Payton stood next to Sam, who was issuing orders in an automated voice that said a hell of a lot about her state of mind. In truth, he was amazed that she was still functioning.

After the spectacle at the fund-raiser, the scene had been pandemonium. The social elite, running for the exits, security and police scrambling to try and find out where the feed had come from. It turned out to be simple. The small matter of some switched wires and a cable feed. Nothing that would have been noticed in a bomb search.

The camera on site had of course been sent to trace in the hopes that there would be a fingerprint or DNA evidence, but Payton wasn't holding his breath. This guy hadn't come so far by making elementary mistakes.

Hell, he'd been leading them around by the nose. Playing with the facts, setting the team up as easily as if they'd been cattle on the way to slaughter. And now he'd destroyed Sam. Taken her expertise and played it back against her. Killing her mother in a blatant attempt to show his superiority.

So far there had been no way to ascertain if there were bodies inside. But the two smoldering cars in what was left of the garage left little doubt. A partial plate identified one as Ruth Cramer's and Sam had ID'd the Saab as her mother's.

Coupled with Sam's earlier phone conversation, the evidence seemed to support the fact that the women had been inside. As soon as the residue cooled off a little, they'd know for certain. The bomb squad had already arrived on site, and were beginning to sift through the rubble, Sam directing the search with the precision of a general.

Despite the show of bravado, it was clear that she was hanging on by a thread. He could see it in the lines on her face, the creases around her eyes and the way her shoulders sagged when she thought no one was looking. It took everything he had not to pull her into his arms.

But he knew from experience that if he touched her, she could shatter. And he didn't want to do anything that would threaten her control. At least not here—not now. He clenched a fist, his anger needing physical release.

If he ever found the bastard, he was going to take great pleasure in making him pay for what he'd done. Not that it would undo the damage. Payton had played the revenge game before and knew that it didn't bring anyone back. But at least for a moment or two it provided release—and reset the balance.

Justice might be blind, but Payton's vision was just fine.

He'd called the team in San Antonio, and Gabe was on the way, Cullen figuring rightly that someone less involved would bring a clearer head. Harrison and Madison had wanted to come, too, but he'd convinced them that it was more important to have someone managing the operations there.

As soon as things cleared here, Sam would want the fragments sent to Austin. He knew her well enough to know that no amount of grief was going to stop her from finding the man behind this. She'd work night and day if she had to. All of which meant that their time in Albuquerque was limited. And frankly, the sooner he got her away from here, the better.

Standing there watching her mother's house burn to ashes wasn't something that she needed to see. Despite her professional involvement, it was too damn personal. Payton knew. He'd been there before, and he'd have given his life to somehow prevent the hell she was going through.

One of the bomb techs was walking toward her now, looking otherworldly in his Hazmat suit. He pushed back the visor, his face absurdly young. Payton read the expression in his eyes and hurried across to intercept him before he could reach Sam, but she'd seen him, too, and was making a beeline. They arrived at the same time.

She'd changed into a blue jumpsuit with the bomb squad's name stenciled on the back. The thing was about two sizes too big, and even with the sleeves and pant legs rolled up, it dwarfed her, making her seem fragile.

"What did you find?" There was an undercurrent of steel in her voice that dispelled any notion of weakness. She was one hell of a woman.

The tech shot a questioning look at Payton, who nodded slightly. Sam caught the interchange, anger flashing in her eyes. "I don't need mollycoddling. And I'll thank you both to remember that."

Payton shrugged, unapologetic. He'd be damned if he was just going to go about business as usual. He'd just have to get better at running interference.

Sam turned to the tech again, repeating her question, this time as an order. "Tell me what you found."

The kid stared down at his feet, then lifted his gaze to meet hers. "We found evidence of two bodies. Some tissue and bones. From the placement I'd say they'd been watching television."

Sam swallowed, the muscles in her throat convulsing, but except for the telltale motion, her face remained tightly shuttered. "Did you identify a seat?"

"Yeah." The tech motioned toward what had been the living room. "Looks like the blast emanated from the area around the television. We've got definite blast pattern, but we won't be able to establish the cause until we get the fragments back to the lab."

"My lab," Sam said, her eyes narrowed as she assessed the scene. "Is the M.E. on his way?"

"Her way," the tech corrected. "She gave an ETA of about fifteen minutes."

Sam nodded. "I want to know cause of death as soon as possible. And I need ID on the...bodies."

She stumbled over the last word, and Payton gave the kid a curt nod, motioning him to move on. He reached out to grab Sam's elbow, steadying her for a moment before releasing her. "You don't have to do this. There are other people here who can handle it."

"Not as well as I can," she snapped, stepping away from him. "If you'll excuse me, I need to get in there for a first-hand look."

"I don't think—" He reached out to stop her, but she batted his arm away, marching off in the direction the tech had gone. A part of his heart shuddered at the thought of what she was about to witness. No child should have to see a parent die. And thanks to some madman out there, that's exactly what Sam had had to endure, and now to add salt to the wound, she had to view the remains.

The world was sometimes too fucking cruel to believe.

He started to follow her, but stopped when he saw an altercation breaking out at the police barrier holding gawkers and the press at bay. Although he could only see the back of the policeman on guard, it was apparent that someone was trying to get past him. The officer held his ground, but from the sounds of the crowd, it was also evident that whoever was trying to get in wasn't about to give up.

He moved closer, partly from curiosity, partly to lend a hand should it be necessary. It wasn't unheard of for a bomber to turn up at the site of his handiwork. That kind of behavior was more likely from an arsonist, but there were certain personality similarities here.

Payton moved around a bomb squad tech who was busy photographing the scene, and headed for the barrier. It wasn't easy going, as the street in front of the house was littered with debris, some of it quite large. He stepped over a beam from the roof, shingles still attached, and headed for the altercation, still in progress.

The officer was getting agitated now, waving his hands, his tone threatening. Payton still couldn't see the person on the other side of the tape. But he could hear the voice.

Female.

Some premonition set his brain in gear, and he traveled the rest of the distance in seconds, coming to a stop beside the officer, his gaze locked on the woman standing on the other side of the tape. "What's going on here?"

"This lady refuses to stay behind the line. I've told her repeatedly that only authorized personnel can come past this point, but she keeps insisting."

Payton searched her face for some sign that he was right, a twist of the head, the color of her hair—something. She fit the age requirement. "Who are you?" he asked, ignoring the policeman and cutting to the chase.

"My name is Elizabeth Waters. And this is my house." Her eyes flashed in anger, the faded blue the exact color of her daughter's.

"Let her through," Payton ordered, his gaze still locked on Sam's mother.

The officer shot Payton an argumentative look, then evidently changed his mind, opening the barrier. The woman breathed the word *thank you* and was by him, running toward the house calling her daughter's name.

Payton sprinted after her, his heart stopping at the sight of Sam turning toward her mother, her expression first one of disbelief, and then, slowly, incredulity turning to joy. She ran to close the distance between herself and her mother, throwing herself into her arms with the abandon of a child. The two women embraced, mother and daughter locked together in reunion.

The killer was still out there. Two more notches on his belt. But Elizabeth Waters wasn't one of them. Whether it was an oversight, a twist of fate, or intentional, Payton had no way of knowing. And for the moment he didn't care. All that mattered was that the haunted look was gone from Sam's face.

At least, for now, things were right again in her world. Later she'd want retribution. For what had almost happened. For the two people who lay dead in the hollow shell of what had once been her mother's house.

But for right now, she simply wanted to feel her mother breathing. To know that the horror of the past few hours had been an awful mistake. That a miracle had occurred and her mother was alive.

Payton knew exactly what she was feeling. Or at least how he'd imagined it a million times. Nights when he'd wake suddenly from his nightmares, hoping against hope that it had all been nothing more than a bad dream. That Kevin was only a phone call away, and that Mariam would be sleeping next to him.

But for Payton there'd been no miracle.

Which, in some perverse way made Sam's that much sweeter.

"I STILL CAN'T BELIEVE IT." Sam was sitting across from her mother in a corporate suite Cullen had arranged. Typical of his usual attention to detail, the place was a palace, obviously the best Albuquerque had to offer. In addition to other amenities, it was situated on the top floor of a megasecurity high-rise.

With the added protection of the two guards outside, Sam felt certain that her mother was safe. Gabe and Payton hadn't been as positive, hounding them like shadows for the first hour or so since they'd arrived. But Sam had finally convinced them both that she and her mother needed a little privacy, and that had done the trick.

Although she'd heard Payton threatening the poor guy at the door with his life if he so much as let a fly past the door. Sam contained a smile. Despite the seriousness of the situation facing them, she couldn't seem to stop smiling.

When she'd seen the explosion on the monitor a part of her had died, her only thought all the things she wished she'd said to her mother. And now here they were sitting together and all Sam could do was babble about how happy she was.

"I'm not so sure I'm taking it all in either," her mother said, reaching for Sam's hand. "But I'm guessing the shock I had was nothing compared to yours."

Sam shook her head. "You lost everything."

"It's not the same as if I'd thought I'd lost you." Their gazes met and held, and Sam smiled through her tears.

"But I'm here and you're here, and…" Sam sobered, thinking of the two people who had lost their lives.

"Poor Ruth," her mother said, her own eyes misting over. "Such a tragedy. If only I'd insisted that they come with me."

Elizabeth's friend Kay had called to invite her to a movie. Ruth had been included in the invitation, but she'd declined, choosing instead to stay in with her boyfriend. Now they were both dead.

"There's no way you could have known what was going to happen. No one could have." Except maybe Last Chance, but Sam wasn't going to let herself go there right now. "At least you can take comfort in the fact that they went quickly."

Considering their proximity to the seat, and the condition of their remains, she was telling her mother the truth. The person who'd planted the bomb hadn't intended anyone to live through the blast. But then he hadn't counted on Sam's mother.

"I'm not blaming myself." Her mother shook her head.

"Not really. It just seems so sad. They had so much of their lives ahead of them."

Better them than you, Sam thought, then immediately was ashamed. It was a natural feeling, but one she wasn't proud of. No one had deserved to die here. And if she'd been more proficient at her job, maybe she'd have found a way to prevent it from happening at all.

"Now who's blaming themselves?" Her mother squeezed her hands and then released them. "I've been following this thing in the papers and from what I can tell you've done all that you could."

Sam was surprised to learn her mother was even aware she'd been on the case, but then again it would be hard to have missed the media frenzy surrounding the senators' deaths. "I know you're right. At least intellectually, I buy into the idea. But emotionally—oh God, Mom, I could have lost you."

"But you didn't. Honey, I'm right here, sitting in front of you, thinking about erecting a chapel in thanks to Kay Armstrong. It wasn't even a good movie." Her mother's smile was rueful, and despite the gravity of the situation, they both laughed. "Cullen Pulaski certainly knows how to put on the ritz." She turned to look around the lavish suite. "I doubt even Donald Trump lives this well."

"Cullen wanted you to be safe, and this is the best place until we can get you to Austin."

Her mother's expression turned mutinous. "I've already told you, I'm not coming to Austin. I'll just be in the way. I'll go to Maggie's. No one will think to look for me there."

Her mother's sister lived on a farm in the middle of rural Oklahoma. The nearest neighbor was about twenty miles away. When it came to secluded, Aunt Maggie and Uncle George had the corner on the market. But Sam didn't like the idea of her mother being out of sight.

"I'd feel better if you stayed with me."

"You're going to be busy trying to catch whoever did this,"

her mother said with a sigh. "There won't be time to babysit me. George and Maggie can watch out for me. Besides, that nice young man, Gabriel, said that he'd make sure I had someone to watch over me twenty-four/seven."

Sam doubted anyone had referred to Gabe as *a nice young man* in the past ten or fifteen years, but then again maybe it was all about perception. "I know he meant well…" she started and then trailed off at the stubborn look in her mother's eyes.

"Samantha, I'm perfectly capable of making my own decisions. This man, whoever he is, isn't going to start ruling my life. Besides, you said yourself he doesn't even know that I'm alive."

Payton had had the clarity of mind to make certain that as few people as possible knew who Elizabeth was, starting with the police officer who'd refused her entrance to the bomb site. The few who had seen her believed she was in fact Sam's Aunt Maggie. As far as the press and the public were concerned, Elizabeth Waters had died in the house along with Ruth and her boyfriend.

Cullen had pulled strings to make sure that forensics would concur. This way they could make certain that Elizabeth was safe until they apprehended the bomber. And in addition, the man would believe that he had accomplished his mission, which, hopefully, would buy Sam a little time to try and fit the newest piece of the puzzle into the facts they already had.

She suspected the bomber had believed that his latest act would clarify things, but except for his obvious intent to target her, she couldn't see a connection to the other two bombings. She'd had an attachment to Walter Atherton, certainly, but nothing like her relationship with her mother, and she'd never even met Ruckland, Dawson or Keith.

"I'm not going to change your mind, am I?" she asked, already knowing the answer.

"Not a chance." Her mother shook her head. "Like mother, like daughter."

There was truth in that, truth that Sam sometimes over-looked. But now that she'd been given a second chance with her mother she wasn't about to let it slip away.

"So tell me about your young man."

Again with the adjective. But this time her mother wasn't talking about Gabe. Sam swallowed nervously, feeling all of about sixteen, uncertain exactly what to say. Settling instead for denial. "He's not my young man."

"Well, he certainly thinks he is." Her mother settled back against the sofa cushions with a soft smile. "Reminds me of your father. He was always overprotective with me. Not that I really needed it, mind you. But it always made me feel so special to know that he cared that much."

Sam had always thought her mother allowed her father to push her around. That she'd been overshadowed by Bill's larger-than-life bluster. She'd never considered the idea that her mother's actions were conscious choices, decisions based solely on her love for Sam's father.

It put her mother in a whole new light, and Sam felt guilty for misjudging her.

"We all choose our path in life, darling. Mine was that I loved your father beyond all else. He made me happy. And so either I accepted him as he was, or I let him go. And the lat-ter was never an option. Your father was an adrenaline junkie. They didn't have a name for it then, but that was it just the same. He would never have been content to take a nine-to-five job and come home every night to his wife and daughter. Al-though if I'd asked it of him, I believe he'd have tried." Her mother smiled again, this time lost in memories. "But I never asked. Because I loved him. And because I wanted him to be happy. So I made a home, and I waited until he tired of his mil-itary adventures. He always came home to me, Sam. Always."

"But I couldn't live like that." She spoke the words before she had the chance to think about what she was saying, her thoughts centering not on her father, but on Payton.

"Of course not." Her mother shook her head. "You're your father's daughter. You like living on the edge as much as he did. But you've also got a deep sense of compassion, Sam. You have a great capacity to love. And it would be a shame if you let that slip away simply because you're afraid of commitment."

"I'm not afraid of commitment, Mom. I'm afraid that I won't be able to live up to what a man wants in a woman. That I'm too much of a free spirit. That I'm too ambitious and smart for my own good." It sounded sort of vain when she put it into words, and she stared down at her hands, wishing she'd kept her mouth shut.

"Honey, being smart and ambitious isn't a crime. It's just that some men can't handle a woman with beauty and brains. My guess is your Payton isn't one of them."

"He isn't my…" She started to deny it again, but saw from her mother's look that she wasn't buying. "I do care about him. But there's so much in his past. Things I'm not certain he'll ever be able to get over."

"There is a sadness in him. I could see it. But he also cares a great deal about you. I could see that, too. And I know that it's hard to believe, but it's possible to hold on to memories and still make a future. I'll love your father forever, Sam. But he died, not me. It took me a while to realize that. But now that I know, I'm not going to bury myself alongside him. It's not fair to him, it's not fair to you and it certainly isn't fair to me."

Elizabeth reached out to stroke Sam's hair, the sensation comforting in a timeless mother-daughter way. "Unfortunately you can't take away Payton's pain, or make him forget what's past. But you can show him that there's still something out there worth living for. Maybe it's as simple as that."

"Nothing with Payton is simple, Mother."

"Well, then, my darling," her mother said with an amused smile, "I'd say the two of you were made for each other."

CHAPTER TWENTY-ONE

"THIS THING IS GETTING REALLY UGLY. And I sure as hell don't like the direction things seem to be heading." Payton reached for his beer, his seat by the window of the bar giving him a direct view of the entrance to the building they were staying in. He could even see the armed guards standing just inside. Cullen, it seemed, had spared no expense. And for once Payton was in total agreement with the man.

"Targeting Sam, you mean." Gabe took a swallow from his beer, his eyes circled with exhaustion. The flight in had been grueling and then he'd spent another couple of hours dealing with the police and the press, sending out the story as they'd decided to spin it.

"Yeah. We know she was close to Atherton. And she had at least a tenuous relationship with Elliot. Add in the two bombs in her room, plus this latest attack on her mother and there's no avoiding the fact that this guy seems to be trying to get her attention. The sixty-four thousand dollar question, of course, is why…?" He trailed off with a shrug, the gesture reflecting a nonchalance he didn't feel.

"But she has no connection to Ruckland and his cronies."

"None that have been identified." Payton blew out a breath. "Hell, maybe the senators really were just in the wrong place at the wrong time."

"Maybe someone else was supposed to have been in the Prager that day. Someone with a connection to Sam."

"Like Atherton and the others."

"Exactly," Gabe agreed. "Or maybe there *is* a connection between Sam and the senators, something obscure enough that we missed it."

"Fucking son of a bitch." Payton slammed his hand down on the table, his control slipping. "I hate this. We're running around in circles trying to find answers, while this bastard sits back and pulls the strings. People Sam cares about are dying, Gabe, and I can't do a goddamned thing about it. Hell, for all we know, she could be next."

"We won't let that happen," Gabe said, his tone underscoring his resolve.

Payton met his friend's gaze, then looked away, pulling his emotions into control. What he needed was a change of topic, something that allowed him to sequester his fears and keep his mind clear.

"How'd the press conference go?"

"Could have been worse, I guess. Biggest problem really was Walker trying to play up the angle that somehow this was all targeted at him."

"A man with an ego the size of Walker's probably believes everything is about him. And since we can't do anything about it, I say we use it. Go ahead and establish the connection between Walker and Ruckland. It'll keep the media focused there, instead of on Sam and her mother."

"I've already done pretty much just that. I stopped short of announcing the Ruckland/Walker connection. I figure if we could connect the dots, the press will be able to do so, too. Which keeps Walker off of Cullen's back."

"I see you're becoming quite the diplomat." Payton wasn't sure he meant the remark as a compliment, and Gabe certainly didn't take it that way.

"I'm just trying to keep everyone happy." He took another long pull at his beer. "In the meantime, I'll spirit Elizabeth out of here tomorrow and see her safely to her sister's. Cullen's arranged for around-the-clock protection for the duration, but I want to make sure she gets there myself. It's the least I can do for Sam."

"I probably ought to be the one to go." He hated the idea of leaving Sam, but he wanted to make sure Elizabeth was truly safe.

"I'd rather you stick to Sam. Unless I miss my guess she's going to be hell-bent on taking this guy out, and I don't want her doing anything stupid."

Stupid wasn't a word Payton would ever associate with Sam, even when she was madder than hell. But he liked the idea of sticking close. All the better to make sure the bomber didn't get another chance at her. "All right then, we'll head back to Austin as soon as we know you're off safely. Sam's already sent debris from the bomb site to our lab. The rest is going to Georgia. I'm sure she's going to be anxious to get to work on it."

"How's she doing?" Gabe leaned back in his chair, his gaze somber.

"Hell of a lot better since finding out her mother is alive. I don't think she'd have forgiven herself if something had happened to her mom on her watch."

"There wasn't anything she could have done to predict what happened, Payton."

"Doesn't matter. She'd have held herself responsible anyway. As soon as she has a chance to get over the shock of today, I imagine she'll start blaming herself regardless, but at least the loss won't be as devastating as it could have been."

"Any connection between Ruth Cramer or her boyfriend and Sam?" Gabe asked with a frown.

"I don't think so. She says she'd never met either one of them," Payton said. "The boyfriend's name was Ronald Adkins. And according to Elizabeth, both he and Ruth were attending the University of New Mexico. They'd been dating about six months. Ruth was from Clayton, on the Texas border. Her parents own a feed store. Elizabeth thought the boy said something about being from Colorado, but she wasn't certain."

"The M.E. confirmed ID yet?"

"Yeah. Got dental from the girl from the university, and DNA on the boy." Payton sipped his beer. "It's a tentative match on the DNA pending more extensive testing but for all practical purposes we know who they were. Ruth's parents have been notified. And the Albuquerque PD is working on tracking someone down for Adkins."

"Talk about wrong place, wrong time..." Gabe's expression was grim.

"It probably sounds harsh, but I'm just grateful it wasn't Sam or her mother."

"It doesn't sound harsh at all," Gabe said, watching Payton through hooded eyes. "Bottom line, you care about Sam."

Payton considered pretending to misunderstand, but abandoned the idea. Gabe would only try another tack. The man was relentless when he wanted information. Better to face it head-on. "Yeah, I do. But it's nothing serious if that's where you're headed."

"I'm not heading anywhere." Gabe shrugged. "Just making an observation. And, for the record, I applaud your choice. Sam's a hell of a lady."

"She deserves better than anything I can give her," Payton said, surprised at how bitter he sounded.

"Give me a break. I know you, remember? You're one of the best friends I have. You and Nigel. And I'm not buying into the 'I'm no good for her' crap. Maybe the 'I'm scared shitless' crap—" He lifted his beer, his gaze slightly amused.

"Well, there is that." Payton smiled. Gabe knew him too damn well.

"So take what life is offering you. Give it a chance with Sam." Gabe held up his hands. "I've already said too much. You do what you have to do, okay? But in the meantime at least think about what I said."

"All right." Payton's answer was grudging, but he had to admit Gabe had a point. Maybe it was time to let it go and move on. Trouble was, he wasn't certain he knew how.

"So where do we go from here?" Gabe asked.

"We try to figure out why the bomber's targeting Sam," Payton said, pulling his thoughts back to the present. "It could be as simple as the fact that she's heading the investigation. Or maybe it's because she's the bomb expert. Harrison is still working on her list of enemies. Maybe we'll find something there. Or maybe there's a connection beyond all of that. Something personal. The use of the jack-in-the-box certainly seems to support that line of thinking."

"The truth is, this bastard hasn't left us with a whole lot to go on," Gabe said. "Basically what we've got is a bunch of spurious connections that may or may not mean something to this guy. And in order to figure out what his next move is, we're going to have to find a way to crawl inside his head."

"Easier said than done." Payton tightened his grip on the bottle, anger and frustration cresting inside him. "One thing is for certain though, when this guy tried to up the ante with Sam's mother, he changed the rules of the game."

"How so?" Gabe asked, his brows drawn together in question.

"He made it personal. For Sam. And more importantly, for me."

Because no matter how things turned out between them, Payton wasn't about to let anyone hurt Sam, not as long as there was a breath in his body. And truth be told, there wasn't a man alive who had made Payton an enemy and lived to tell about it.

SAM SAT IN A CHAIR she'd pulled up to the window, the mountains a dark shadow on the horizon, lights twinkling along the base where people were closing down for the night. She'd opened a window, the breeze cooling, the smell of piñon in the air. There was something about the high desert that made everything seem clearer.

Even sitting at the top of a high-rise in the heart of the city, she could feel it. Her mother was sleeping. The doctor had insisted they both take something for their nerves. Elizabeth had taken hers. Sam had not.

She wanted to keep her wits about her. But the trade-off was that sleep seemed impossible. She wondered if Payton and Gabe were settled into the suite next door. The guards were still standing at the door, and she simply didn't have the energy to deal with explanations should she decide to try and go over there. She'd face it all in the morning.

Tonight, she'd try and figure out what was on the bomber's mind. Why he'd decided to target her. And what, if anything, the tie-in to the senators was. The whole thing seemed so convoluted. And despite the fact that they were making progress, the man always seemed to be at least two jumps ahead of them.

Tomorrow she'd hit the lab, and hopefully she'd find the Tai Chi on one of the fragments from his latest handiwork. And there was still the car bomb to go through. Not to mention the two from her room. The ATF lab in Georgia was looking at debris as well, maybe they'd find something she'd missed.

She sighed and propped her feet up on the windowsill, staring out at the stars. Like everything else here, they seemed brighter. God, what she wouldn't give for some answers. She'd come so close to losing her mother. Too close. For a moment, she'd actually understood Payton's pain. Someone she loved had almost died, and no matter how badly she wanted to pretend otherwise, it would have been partially her fault. Either because of something she'd missed, or because the bomber had targeted her, and therefore her mother.

For the first time in her life, she found herself questioning her choice of career. Up until now the only chances she'd ever taken had been with her own life, and that was something she could live with. But now, conceivably, people she cared about had been targeted. Walter, her mother and, indirectly even Elliot.

And even if it wasn't personal, even if it was only about the fact that she was heading the investigation, it still had cost lives. She shook her head, trying to erase the notion, there were a million other reasons why Walter Atherton could have been targeted. He'd been investigating the bombings, too. His position with the FBI was certainly more prestigious than hers with the ATF.

It was only her experience with explosives, and Cullen Pulaski's clout that gave her seniority on the case. But when you added in the attempt to kill her mother, her friendship with Walter was suddenly suspect. She blew out a breath, closing her eyes and inhaling deeply, trying to clear her thoughts.

The problem with the whole scenario was that she didn't know the senators, and she had nothing whatsoever to do with their scheme to bring agricultural money to their states.

It was a conundrum of the highest order, but like every puzzle there was a solution, she just needed to find more pieces, and in the meantime, make certain her mother was safe. There was logic in her going to Oklahoma. Sam certainly wasn't going to be available to watch over her. But at the same time, she hated the idea of her mother being out of sight. As if by having her physically present, she could keep her safe.

The notion wasn't a practical one, and Sam was pragmatic enough to recognize the fact. Gabe would see her safely to Oklahoma, and she had no doubt that Cullen would take care of the rest. Besides, Uncle George wasn't the kind to sit on his ass and wait for something to happen. He'd make sure Elizabeth was safe.

She'd have better protection than a head of state.

Sam smiled and opened her eyes. Again caught by the beauty of the stars, and the crisp perfection of heavenly scent.

"Close the drapes."

Sam spun around, toppling her chair, crouched in position to spring, her heart hammering, only to find Payton standing at the door with a scowl that made his scar stand out more than usual.

"Jesus, Payton, you scared the crap out of me," she said, her own anger splintering through her with a force that surprised her.

Payton ignored her and crossed to close the window. "I would have thought you'd have more sense. Sitting there like a duck on a pond waiting for a hunter to blow you away." He jerked the drapes across, the drapery hooks protesting the rough treatment with a screech of metal on metal.

"He's a bomber, Payton. Not a sniper." She reached down to right the chair, and then turned to face him, arms crossed, ready to do battle. "And what are you doing sneaking in here in the middle of the night scaring me to death? Thanks to you I might just need that little pill the doctor gave me."

"I'm staying here tonight." He gestured to the sofa. "I'm not taking any chances."

"I see." His chivalry sort of took the wind out of her sails. Although she was still angry.

"Where's Elizabeth?" he asked, perching on the back of the sofa.

"Sleeping." Sam shrugged, feigning indifference. "At least she was. Your little surprise attack may have woken her."

Payton's eyebrows quirked in dispute, and then before she could stop him, he'd opened the door to her mother's bedroom and was peering inside. "She's still sleeping," he said, pulling the door shut again. "You should be, too. It's going to be a long day tomorrow. You need your rest."

"And you're not my mother." She sounded like a petulant child, but she was so tired, and so keyed-up, and sometimes he made her so damn mad.

"Fine. We'll stay up." He sat on the sofa this time, propping his feet on the coffee table.

"I don't need a babysitter." She sat back in her chair, purposely turning her back on him.

"The hell you don't." In one stride he was in front of her, and with one fluid motion he'd pulled her out of the chair. "In case you missed the fact, someone tried to kill your mother tonight."

"My mother. Not me." They were standing nose to nose now, her anger building to the bursting point.

"But it's pretty obvious this guy was targeting you. And now that he thinks your mother is dead, maybe you're next."

"If you're trying to scare me, it isn't working." Not exactly the truth, but she sure as hell wasn't going to admit it to him.

"Damn it, Sam, I'm trying to get you to realize that you have to be careful. You could have been killed sitting in the window like that."

She should have known better. And it galled her to think she'd been so careless. The realization should have made her less angry at him, but somehow, it only made her madder. "I can take care of myself. Like I said before, the guy isn't a sniper. He's not out there waiting for the right shot. I'm thirty floors up, for God's sake. I think it's okay to have the window open."

He closed his eyes, no doubt counting to three, then opened them, his expression grim. "I just want to make certain you're safe."

"Well I'm fine. Or at least as fine as I can be worrying about some jerk-off with a penchant for pyrotechnics who's decided to target me and the people I love. Hell, if anyone needs to be kept safe, Payton, it's you."

CHAPTER TWENTY-TWO

THE MINUTE THE WORDS were out, her heart threatened to stop. Right there on the spot, it wanted out of the whole equation. She'd just told him she loved him. In a roundabout way, certainly, but clearly she'd said it.

Silence reigned for a moment, and then to her utter horror, she began to cry. And not the slo-mo beautiful kind of tears from the movies. No, this was full-blown, water-in-the-nose, sniffing-to-beat-the-band, red-eyed crying.

Damn it all to hell.

He stared at her for a moment, as if she'd morphed into a stranger, and she angrily tried to push the tears away, but they weren't interested in retreating. And then he was holding her, his heart beating against hers, his arms feeling a whole lot like paradise.

And suddenly she recognized her anger for what it was. Tension and fear, and all the other emotions she'd suppressed since she'd witnessed the bomb blast. At first she'd managed by focusing on the scene, and then she'd held it together for her mother, and then, well, she'd simply held it together because that's what she always did.

She let herself cry a little longer, let the pressure inside her ease a bit, and then when she felt like she had control, she pushed away from him, drying her eyes with the sleeve of her shirt. "I'm sorry about that. I guess I'm more wound up than I thought." An understatement considering the fact that she'd blurted out her feelings for him. But maybe the significance of her words had somehow sailed over his head.

"You've been through a lot." He pushed the hair out of her face, his hands so gentle she almost wanted to cry again, but she resisted the urge.

"I've been through nothing," she said, squaring her shoulders. "It's my mother who lost everything, remember?"

"And it's you who thought you'd lost your mother. Things can be replaced, Sam."

That's basically what her mother had said. But the thought brought little comfort. "Nothing at all would have been lost if it hadn't been for me."

"You don't know that for certain." He was still cupping her face.

"Of course I do. I just don't know why. None of it makes sense at all, actually. But I can't avoid the fact that someone out there targeted my mother. I hardly think it was coincidence."

"I'm not saying that. I'm just saying you can't take blame for something some off-his-nut bomber is doing."

"We don't know that he's crazy. I mean, maybe I did something somewhere along the way that—"

"That what?" Payton interrupted. "Warranted killing your mother? That kind of thinking doesn't make sense. Sometimes things just happen. And no matter how much you wish you could control them, you can't."

"But I want to." She pulled away clenching her fists. "Damn it, I'm supposed to."

"No you're not. You do the best you can. And in your case, that means a hell of a lot. But you don't have superpowers, and you can't save the world."

"I don't want to save the world, Payton. I want to save my mother. And Walter. And… God, I don't know."

"You can't control everything." He sighed, letting his hands fall. "I know that better than anyone."

"So how do you stop blaming yourself?" she whispered, searching his face, hoping for something akin to absolution.

"You don't." He shrugged. "At least I haven't been able to. But that doesn't mean you give up either. Maybe it just takes time. Or maybe you learn to live with it."

"Or maybe you just forgive yourself?" They weren't talking about her anymore, and she reached out to touch his cheek, wondering if her mother was right, that it wasn't about forgetting so much as finding a way to move on.

"Maybe." He covered her hand with his, and leaned forward, his lips brushing hers.

She sighed at the contact, wanting him with a desperation that was born of desire, and need, and the remnants of her fear.

But he pushed away, his gaze holding regret. "You need to sleep."

She wasn't sure how to react. It was as if he'd slapped her, rejecting her in the most basic of ways. "Yeah," she said, dropping her hand. "I guess I do." She turned to go, heading for her room, tears forming again. This was turning into one hell of a night.

"Sam." He'd followed her, his words warm against her ear. She stopped, but didn't turn around, unwilling to let him see how upset she was. "I don't want to take advantage."

It wasn't anything at all close to what she'd wanted him to say, but it wasn't rejection. "It's a two-way street, Payton. If I'm offering, then you're not taking advantage."

It sounded sort of cold put into words like that, and it wasn't precisely true. Every moment she spent with him meant a tighter bond, which ultimately meant that it would hurt that much more when this was all over and he headed off for whatever adventure called next.

He put his hands on her shoulders, turning her around, his green eyes searching hers. "I don't want to make promises I can't keep, Sam."

"I'm not asking you to." She bit her lip, trying to find the right words, realizing that he *had* heard her declaration, and it had obviously scared him. "I just need you now, okay? Nothing more than that." It was a lie, and they both knew it, but she held out her hand anyway and he took it.

She led him into the bedroom, and closed the door. The men outside would look out for her mother, and the sleeping pill would no doubt last until morning. This was her time. And she intended to make the most of it.

They shed their clothes and climbed into bed, Payton holding her close, his body warm against hers. At first they just lay there, spooning as if they'd slept this way for years, and then he turned her so that they were face-to-face, his green eyes worried.

"I do care about you, Sam. More than I can put into words. It's just that—"

She covered his lips with a finger, shaking her head. "Don't. Let's just take the time we have. Okay?"

He nodded, but she could still see anxiety in his gaze. Payton Reynolds was an honorable man. And he didn't want to hurt her. There was comfort in the thought, even though it was probably too late.

She leaned over to kiss him, the touch starting out gentle, and then combusting into something neither of them could control. Whatever demons separated them, sexual chemistry was not the problem. She ran her hands down the broad planes of his back, reveling in his strength.

His scars felt raw and puckered beneath her fingers, and she marveled that a man could survive what he had. Suddenly she wanted to taste him. To memorize the feel and smell of him, as if by doing so, she could hold the memory forever in her heart.

She traced the line of his jaw with her tongue, his beard-roughened chin rasping beneath her touch. Then she tasted the hollow of his throat, and the line of his shoulder, stopping to caress the shrapnel-roughened skin.

Next she closed her mouth over his nipple, using her tongue to tease it to erection, delighting in his guttural reaction. She slid her mouth lower, then, circling the muscle-hardened skin of his abdomen, the edge of his belly button.

His penis jutted hard against her stomach, and she reached down to wrap her hand around it, stroking and kneading, delighting in the velvety feel of him. She wanted to explore every inch of him, leaving no territory uncharted, and she moved again, this time kissing the tender skin between his thighs, her breath teasing him as it passed.

With an audible groan he reached under her arms, pulling her along the length of his body, until they were again face-to-face. "I want you now." His voice was husky with need, and she felt the heat rising within her. He moved then so that he was poised above her, his gaze locking with hers. "Playtime's over."

For a moment he held his position, simply looking at her, his eyes greedy, his breath hot against her face. She clenched inside, her body threatening to climax on the spot. She opened to him, and everything disappeared except the passion between them. No bomber. No family. No nightmares.

Just the two of them. Body to body, soul to soul. A man and a woman as it was intended to be. Two halves of a whole.

He lifted and impaled her, the act at once conquering and surrendering. She drove upward in response, taking his penis deep inside her, striving for completion—this moment, this man, belonging to her.

Slowly they began to move, the friction building like the crest of a wave until she was riding high atop it, lost in the feel of his body moving within hers, his strength, her softness, the two becoming one. There was no quarter given and none taken. She gave as good as she got, knowing he was there with her, riding the same wave.

And still they moved, her body ratcheting tighter with each stroke, the pleasure building until it was almost unbearable. She reached up then, pulling him close, her lips meeting his, her tongue mirroring his body as it pounded into hers, thrust for thrust until the rhythm was the same and she forgot all logic, time disappearing into motion and sensation, every nerve in her body begging for release.

He reached between them then, his thumb finding the tender nub of her clitoris. He began to move and the world broke apart like crystal shattering against marble, the shards glittering as they spiraled into the night, raking through her body with an intensity that sucked her breath away.

Later, much later, she drifted down through the darkness, her contractions subsiding until they were only gentle undulations caressing his penis as it lay soft and contented within her. He clasped her face in his hands, his kiss gentle now, passion spent.

There might be no spoken covenant between them, but there were promises nonetheless. They were there in the tenderness of his kiss. In the way they lay together, spent but still connected. And in the deep, dark green of his eyes.

She wanted to hold him there forever. To stop time and keep this moment in a glass jar beside the bed. But even as she had the thought she knew it was ridiculous. Nothing lasted forever, and Payton wasn't a man to be caught and put on display.

So instead, she nestled her head against his chest, and fell asleep listening to the soft even sound of his breathing.

PAYTON LAY IN THE DARKNESS, watching shadows dance across the ceiling. The fierce independence that Sam maintained by daylight disappeared when she fell asleep. Her head rested on his shoulder, her arm flung across his chest, one slim thigh draped possessively across his leg.

He could feel her heart beating against his and the movement of her chest as she breathed slowly in and out, Morpheus holding her fast in his arms. The moon cast its rays across the bed, touching her hair and turning it to silver. It made him think of an old story from a book his mother had loved. *The Moon-Spinners.*

Supposedly you could run into them. Three girls holding three spindles, the threads rays of moonlight. They were spinning down the moon. Bringing darkness, and protecting the creatures of the night.

He couldn't remember any more of it, couldn't even remember if it was part of mythology, or just the fiction of a story his mother had read. Still, he loved the idea of it. Spinning the moon.

He hadn't thought of his mother in years. Not like that anyway. He kept her memory, of course, but he rarely allowed himself to call upon it. There wasn't much really. She'd been thin with dark hair. And she read a lot, and told him stories. She'd smelled of lavender, and Palmolive dish soap, and she'd had a way of stroking his hair back from his face that even now filled him with contentment.

He smiled in the dark, tightening his arm around Sam. Somehow, being with her filled him with the same sort of contentment. A deep peace that came with the knowledge that he was loved.

She hadn't meant to tell him, of course, the words coming out in anger. But the message had been there nevertheless, and he added the knowledge to the special things he kept in his heart. He could never give her what she needed. He wasn't the type of man who could deal with home and hearth, although at times he longed for both. Still, if he really was honest with himself, he'd have to admit that he cared for her.

Not that he could tell her. It would only raise false hopes. Living with him would make her a target. And he couldn't do that—not again.

Not ever.

He rolled away, careful not to wake her, already mourning the loss of her body wrapped around his, holding him secure against the night. She reached out in her sleep as if she too missed the connection, but settled down again when her fingers brushed against his thigh.

He started to roll back, to pull her against him, but memory tainted with guilt circled through his mind. There was so much to consider. Even if he accepted Kevin's death as something he couldn't have controlled, there was still Mariam.

If he hadn't met her, hadn't married her, she'd no doubt be somewhere today alive and well and working on acquiring her next Pulitzer. There was no way to avoid the fact that if it hadn't been for him, Mariam would never have been involved with Cullen's schemes, and, in so doing, murdered merely for that association.

And he couldn't do that to Sam.

As if she'd heard his thoughts, her eyes flickered open, concern washing across her face. "Did you have another nightmare?"

He shook his head, still staring at the ceiling. "I just couldn't sleep."

"There's a lot to think about."

He didn't pretend to misunderstand, just didn't say anything, and she snuggled close again, the warmth of her body comforting, her fingers splayed out across his chest.

"Are you thinking about Mariam?" she asked, her voice muffled against his neck.

"And Kevin—" he paused, sliding his arm around her "—and you."

"I don't know that I want to be in that group. Especially considering everything going on." There was a thread of laughter in her voice, combined with something deadly serious.

Payton fought for control over his rioting thoughts. "I wasn't thinking of you dead, if that's what you mean." He meant the words as a joke, but somehow the sentiment went flat.

"I certainly hope not." She rose up on an elbow, her

brows drawn together in consternation. "This thing with the bomber. It has you thinking about Iraq?"

"No." He shook his head, knowing that she could see right through him. "All right, I'll admit there are similarities, at least with regard to the fact that someone I care about is in danger, and I'm not sure what exactly I can do about it."

"I'll take that as a compliment." She smiled, obviously not realizing how difficult the words had been for him. "But maybe that's the point, Payton. Stuff happens and there isn't anything you can do about it. Isn't that what you said to me earlier? So maybe it's about faith."

"In what?"

"In chances. In relationships. Hell, in life. I don't know, I'm not the person to be asking these things. I'm the one who lines up when they call for a cynic."

"You couldn't tell it by me."

She shrugged. "I guess maybe you bring out the romantic in me."

Her laughter caressed him like a favorite blanket, and he marveled again at how comfortable she made him feel in his own skin. No need for apologies or excuses. She accepted him as is—period. And something about that fact made him feel whole again in a way he hadn't felt since before Iraq.

He rolled over, pinning her to the mattress, and the laughter in her eyes was replaced by something more primitive. Passion. Basic and earthy. Chemistry at its most elemental. They belonged together. At least in this moment.

Tomorrow would bring reality, and he knew that there was no such thing as an instant fix. Some wounds went too deep, the resulting scars twisting things until nothing was ever the same. And yet, as he moved inside her, a part of him honestly believed that anything was possible.

CHAPTER TWENTY-THREE

"YOU FOLLOW Gabe's instructions to the letter, all right?"
Sam stood in the living room of the corporate suite facing her
mother, her stomach in knots. Gabe and Payton stood closer
to the door, Gabe holding her mother's newly acquired suitcase. Sam wasn't sure how he'd managed to obtain clothes
and necessities for her mother so quickly, but she was relieved
that her mother wouldn't be arriving at her sister's with nothing but the clothes on her back.

Elizabeth nodded, her eyes twinkling, the gray wig making her look a lot older than sixty-two. "I'll hang on every
word." Despite the gravity of the situation and the fact that
she'd lost everything, her mother was treating the whole thing
like a grand lark. Agatha Christie meets Jessica Fletcher. "Really, this is so exciting."

"Mother," Sam said, exasperated. "This is serious stuff. We
don't want to tip anyone off to the fact that you're still alive."
Gabe contained a grin, and Sam shot him a heated look. "This
isn't a game."

"I know, darling." Her mother reached for her hand. "But
you can't blame me if I have a little fun with it. I mean how
often does a woman get to go incognito?" She reached up to
pat the Jackie O sunglasses perched on her nose. "I feel like
Mata Hari or someone."

Or someone was more like it, but even Sam had to smile
in the face of her mother's enthusiasm. Talk about rising to
the occasion. She had a moment's guilt at the thought of how

many times she'd categorized her mother as boring. Maybe she'd just never had her chance to shine. Or maybe Sam just hadn't been paying attention.

Either way, she was proud of her now. And worried.

"You'll call as soon as you get there?" Sam sounded more like the mother than the daughter. "Gabe's given you the satellite phone, right? I've got one, too, and we can talk as much as we like without there being any traceable record. No other phones, okay? And no other calls."

"Check." Her mother nodded, reaching into her carry-all to pull out the phone. "Secret agent phones. I love it." It turned out Gabe had been able to produce a lot more than just incidentals for her mother. Besides the phone, there was also a computer and a tracking device that would enable them to keep up with her mother's whereabouts. All this in addition to the detail of men assigned to guard her twenty-four/seven.

Actually, in thinking about it, it did have a sort of spy flavor. James Bond as a sexagenarian and recast as a woman. Her mother seemed to be fitting right into the mold.

Sam stifled a laugh, her gaze colliding with Payton's. His eyes crinkled in response and for a moment it was if they were the only two people in the room. She swallowed, and then purposely broke the contact. She had to stay focused on the business at hand, and Payton was one hell of a distraction.

"Okay, then, I think that's about it." She blew out a breath, wishing suddenly that she could keep her mother here, hidden away from prying eyes, but it didn't make sense. She had to go back to Austin. Had to start work on decoding the clues the bomber had left, and frankly her mother would just be in the way.

Oklahoma was the right place for her to be. Suddenly it just seemed really far away.

"I'll be fine, Sam. I've got you and your team looking after me." Her mother had always had an uncanny knack for reading her mind. "Not to mention your Uncle George. Heavens, I'll be knee-deep in men." She shot an admiring glance at Payton and Gabe. "Not that I'm complaining."

Again Sam realized she was seeing a side of her mother she hadn't even realized existed. This was a woman who was obviously capable of handling whatever was thrown at her with bravery and spunk, and unless she was missing the boat entirely, a bit of flirtation thrown into the mix as well.

"I'm sure you'll be fine. It's just that I worry. This guy is playing for keeps and I don't want you hurt." Sam squeezed her mother's hand. "I thought I'd lost you once. I couldn't bear it again."

"Well, I'm not too fond of the prospect myself," her mother whispered with a wink, then sobered. "The truth is, I'm not the one at risk, honey. You are. Which means you have to keep your wits about you and watch every step."

"I can handle it, Mom." Her tone was defensive, and she hated the fact.

"I'm not saying you can't. I'm just reminding you that no one is invincible. I don't want to lose you either."

"You won't. I promise."

"I'll hold you to it." Her mother smiled, pulling her close. "Just remember how proud I am of you. And how proud your father would be."

Sam nodded, letting her mother's words settle deep in her heart.

"I love you, honey. Don't ever forget that."

"Me too, you," Sam said, and then pulled back as Gabe nodded that it was time to go.

Her mother squeezed her hand again, and then turned to leave, stopping for a moment to whisper something in Payton's ear. Then with an audible click the door closed and it was just the two of them.

"I assume she told you to watch out for me," Sam snapped. Despite what she said, her mother obviously still didn't believe she could take care of herself.

"Nope," Payton said, his smile slow and a little bit provocative. "She told me to hang in there—that you were worth the effort."

J.T. PACED BACK AND FORTH across his living room with the determination of a caged cat. Everything had gone exactly as it was supposed to in New Mexico, but somehow the accomplishment wasn't giving him the same moment of exultation that the others had.

Maybe it was because it hadn't been part of the original plan, or maybe it was simply the fact that he honestly had no beef with Samantha's mother. But then, he hadn't had a problem with the senators either, and although originally that had been quite frustrating, now he was actually beginning to take pride in the fact that he alone had been responsible.

There was also the fact that other people had been killed in the blast. A college student and her boyfriend. He couldn't say that he had regrets about that. Relationships were something he'd never been able to understand. Physical ones in particular.

He'd seen the boy arrive, seen him kissing the girl, his hands pawing at her. The whole thing had been clumsy to the point of humor, except that it was so repugnant. J.T. shuddered delicately, and stopped to adjust the angle of the framed Nolan Ryan uniform on his wall.

He had very few possessions, everything chosen because it added meaning or value to his life. His small house was sparely decorated, each object placed with an eye to maintaining the proper balance and energy.

He particularly liked to make certain that things were kept immaculate. Everything was free of dust and in its place, the strict adherence to order giving him a sense of well-being. Even in his workshop there was order. Tools in their places, his workbench spotless. Only the far wall seemed chaotic. And even in chaos he'd created something beautiful.

A reflection of life. His and Samantha's.

He turned on the TV, flipping through the news channels, looking for something on the bombing, then clicked it off again. He'd only been back in Austin a short while, and he'd seen very little about the event. Just the fact that an explosion in Albuquerque had killed three people, and that the incident might be linked to the bombing that had taken the life of Senator Ruckland and his colleagues.

J.T. clenched a fist, then immediately released it, forcing his breathing into a slow, calming rhythm. There was nothing to be gained by allowing himself to be angry. Anger caused mistakes, and changed the field of energy.

He turned toward the statue of Kaun Yin, her compassionate face as always filling him with contentment. Sometimes he saw Samantha's face there, but not so much of late. It was almost as if she were pulling away from him, separating from what was ordained.

He frowned at the thought, his carefully won control slipping. Payton Reynolds was to blame. The man had glued himself to Samantha's side like the lovesick adolescent J.T. had killed in the bomb blast. The sight was revolting. He'd seen them on the news and in the paper, but seeing them together at her mother's house had been the worst. He'd wanted to stay and watch her work, watch her deal with the fact that his power was greater than hers. But the sight of Reynolds with his hands all over her had been more than J.T. could deal with.

So he'd left—taken the first plane home—and had been stewing about it ever since. The plan had always been for a final confrontation. Now that he had Samantha's attention, the time seemed perfect to lure her into the web before she figured out he was behind it all.

But he hated the idea of leaving anything undone. And Reynolds had upset the balance. J.T. sighed, letting the sound of the wind chimes on the porch soothe his roiling mind. There was only one thing to do, really.

No choice at all. Before he could achieve union, he must restore the balance. It would be a risk, certainly. The extra time a danger as she began to put together the pieces of the puzzle. But it was the only way.

SAM FOCUSED the microscope on the fragment from her mother's house. The metal had darkened with the blast, but beyond that there was nothing to see. No tool marks and no Chinese symbols—a paradox. On the one hand the work seemed to match that of the bomber, but on the other hand, this was the piece that should have the Tai symbol and it wasn't there.

She blew out a sigh, running her fingers through her hair, exhaustion playing havoc with her brain. Maybe she was just missing something. Or maybe they really were dealing with two separate situations.

She shook her head and removed the fragment, running her finger over it to try and feel for an indentation that might mark the etching. This was the same guy. She could feel it in her gut. She just needed to find the proof.

The symbols on the other fragments were tiny, barely visible to the naked eye. She'd never have seen either of them without the help of the microscope and computer enhancements. But now that she knew what to look for, she ought to be able to pick it up on her own.

At least with the help of the microscope.

But she wasn't finding a damn thing. Frustrated, she tipped back her head and closed her eyes, trying to think, her mind moving as slow as a fly in molasses. She grinned at the antiquated simile, thinking of her grandmother.

Tenacity and perseverance had been her favorite words. And Sam just needed a little of both. She opened her eyes and looked at the fragment again. The mark had to be there. She just wasn't seeing it.

She held it up to the light, the discoloration turning blue-black, almost iridescent in hue. She frowned, her brain finally clicking into gear. It was possible that the patina was masking the symbol. After putting the fragment carefully on the lab table, she walked over to a shelf and retrieved a small glass bottle. Returning to the table, she took a stopper full of the liquid inside, and carefully let a drop fall on the fragment.

She counted slowly to ten, and then took a piece of sterile flannel and carefully wiped the fragment clean, blowing on it in an attempt to get it to dry faster. Then with impatient fingers, she slid the fragment back under the microscope, centered the eyepiece and began to focus.

Nothing.

Determined now, she repeated the procedure, this time waiting a full thirty seconds before wiping the weak acid mixture away. She settled the fragment back under the microscope and peered through the lens, adjusting magnification, her heart accelerating as she saw the Tai come clear.

Sometimes it was all about a blinding glimpse of the obvious.

"You find something?" Harrison was standing at her elbow, his voice making her jump. Apparently he'd been taking lessons from Payton.

"The Tai." She backed off of the microscope, allowing him to have a look, waiting for his agreement.

"This one is different from the other two." He lifted his head, frowning.

"How so?" She asked, immediately taking another look at the magnified image.

"It's smaller for one thing. And the indentation is deeper. The symbol more defined."

Harrison was right. The detail was clearer. And the smaller size would account in part for why it had taken her so long to find it.

"You think he's evolving?" Harrison asked, his expression still puzzled.

"Maybe." Sam shrugged. "Or maybe he just wanted to come up with a better version. He's a perfectionist, remember?"

"Well, either way, I'd say it's a solid link from the Albuquerque bomb to the other two," Harrison said. "It must have been a relief to find out your mother wasn't in the house." There was a wistful quality to his voice, and Sam remembered the way his sister had died, the enormity of what had just happened to her hitting home.

"I was really lucky."

"Not sure I believe in luck." There was a trace of bitterness in Harrison's voice, something she hadn't heard from him before. Compared to Payton and Gabe he seemed so normal, as far from tortured as a man can be.

But then everyone dealt with life in different ways. Maybe Harrison hid behind his sunny facade.

"I've got something for you, too," he was saying, and she pulled her mind away from the complexities of human healing. What the hell did she know about stuff like that anyway?

"Something good, I hope?"

Harrison shrugged, with a grin, his countenance restored. "Depends on how you look at it."

"So tell me." She responded to his enthusiasm with a smile.

"While you were out battling the bomber, I was checking out the evidence from the remaining priors we isolated."

"And?" Sam felt the tingle in her bones that signaled discovery.

"And, Lubbock is a wash. Same as Brownsville, both ends welded, and no symbol. Add to that the fact that there was apparently real animosity between the night watchman and the night manager. Seems our watchman was hitting the sheets with the manager's wife."

"And they didn't suspect him at the time?"

"They did. Just couldn't prove it. Anyway, adding all the

factors together, I can say with almost all certainty that it wasn't our guy."

"I thought you said you had good news."

"No, you said that." But Harrison's grin gave evidence that she was right.

"Har-ri-son…." She narrowed her eyes, trying for stern.

His laughter indicated she hadn't achieved her aim. She punched him in the arm, then the two of them sobered as he pulled a photograph out of a file he was carrying. "I got this from the Bryan bombing."

"The barbeque place." She took the picture, holding it up to the light.

"Uh-huh," Harrison agreed. "Can you see that?" He pointed at the upper right quadrant of the fragment they were looking at. There was a clear blemish. What appeared to be something shadowed and round. "Here's an enlargement." He handed her another picture.

At this magnification, the blemish took shape, the circle of the Tai clear. It wasn't as sophisticated as his later work, but the symbol was clearly the same. "So he's got priors." It was stating the obvious, but she needed to say it out loud, let her mind center on the idea and its implications.

"At least one. I'm still waiting on the Abilene PD to send me what they've got. And there's still nothing from Refugio. They're supposedly still looking, but I'm guessing they're not going to come up with anything. Sixteen years is a hell of a long time."

"I still know a few people in Abilene, let me see if I can light a fire and get things moving."

"Sounds good. In the meantime, now that we've got another bomb, what does that tell us?"

"Nothing yet, except that the symbol probably isn't tied to the senators and their scheme. Six years ago Dawson wasn't even in office. Which means it's probably a signature of some kind."

"Or has meaning we haven't figured out."

Sam sighed. One step forward, two steps back. "Probably both. You get anything off of the frags from my room?"

"Nothing yet. I've been scouring the ones from the model car. But there are a lot of them, and when the information came in on Lubbock and Bryan, I figured that had priority."

"You figured right. But until we hear something from Abilene, let's go at it again. Maybe there's something there that explains why the bomber is targeting me."

"Well, considering the fact that he tried to off your mother, I'd say it's fairly apparent that he doesn't like you." Sam shivered at the thought of her mother, and Harrison immediately looked contrite. "I didn't mean to sound flip."

"It's understandable considering the circumstances. Besides you're right. This guy doesn't like me. The question is whether it's because I'm standing in the way of whatever goal his twisted little mind has cooked up, or whether it's something more personal, some link between the two of us that he can see and I can't."

"Considering that he's targeting people you care about, it seems to me that it's a hell of a lot more important to stop him than to worry about understanding him."

"That's just the problem, Harrison," Sam sighed, rubbing her temples. "Unless I can get a handle on why he's doing what he's doing, there may not be a way to stop him."

CHAPTER TWENTY-FOUR

PAYTON DROPPED his duffel on the floor of the bedroom in the new house Cullen had arranged for the team. "Mansion" was really a more applicable word—the sprawling house perched on the edge of a cliff overlooking a sea of trees.

There were three levels and something like eight bedrooms. He hadn't stopped to count, just picked the most isolated one. He'd told himself that he'd wanted his privacy, but knew that he was thinking of Sam. God, she could drive a man insane. In more ways than he could count. Most of them good.

He'd brought her suitcase here as well. Probably a bit presumptuous of him. But there was another room across the hall. So at least he'd left her an out. Or maybe he was leaving it for himself.

He wanted her. There was no question about it. His body ached at just the thought of her. And he cared for her, as well. There was no denying that fact. But there was still a gulf between them, one of his own making—and he wasn't sure it was something he could ever cross. Still, he wanted to be certain she was safe, and the best way to do that was to keep her close.

As a rationale went, it was solid. He grinned to himself, willing to admit in the privacy of his room that it was about a lot more than protection. That maybe Sam was the one protecting him. Keeping the devil at bay.

Unfortunately, he was afraid the devil in question might

actually be him. And that left a hell of a conundrum, one he wasn't about to tackle right now. There were too many other pressing issues, the first being to figure out who the hell was hounding Sam. And he wasn't going to get anything accomplished standing here being introspective.

Shaking his head at his own folly, he headed back up the stairs toward the living room, his thoughts turning toward the lab and Sam's work with the fragments. Hopefully the bomber had slipped up somehow, leaving trace evidence of some kind. Something that would lead them to his identity. The guy was good, but he wasn't perfect.

A noise coming from the room at the top of the stairs stopped Payton cold. He reached for the gun he had holstered in the small of his back, and stood listening. The house was supposed to be clean. No one in or out without proper authorization.

But Gabe was en route from Oklahoma. Madison had dropped their things off here and then gone to the airport to meet him. From there she was taking him straight to Cullen's offices. Harrison and Sam were at the lab working on the fragments. He'd dropped Sam there himself.

It was possible that he'd imagined the sound, but unlikely. Every nerve in his body was signaling that someone was up there. He analyzed the sound, running it through his mind, finally deciding that it had been a chair scraping against the wood floor.

Which could mean the intruder was sitting. More likely that he'd simply moved the chair for another purpose. Payton silently covered the next few risers on the staircase, and waited again.

Everything was silent.

Counting to three, he drew a breath and rounded the railing at the top of the stairs, his Beretta ready. "Don't move."

He swung into the room, centering the gun on the man sitting in the chair. He'd pulled it over by the window, the sunlight streaming through the glass washing out the intruder's features, leaving him in profile.

The man raised his hands, a deep-throated laugh filling the air. "I say, you always were good on your feet. I had no idea you were even down there."

Payton lowered the gun with a scowl, sliding it back into its holster. "What the hell are you doing here? This is supposed to be a secured location."

"Nothing is ever secured, mate." Nigel Ferris stood up with a shrug, the light shifting to reveal his craggy face and pencil-thin moustache, his casual stance deceptive. Nigel was MI6 to the core. He'd more than proved it the last time they'd all been together, his deception almost costing Madison her life.

"I repeat, how did you get in here?" The two of them stood facing off, the tension palpable. Despite what had happened in New York, Payton still considered Nigel his friend. Hell, Payton owed the man his life. But his loyalty to Gabe was greater.

"Cullen gave me clearance."

"Bullshit. Cullen can't stand you." The man had wanted to turn Nigel over to the authorities, and Payton couldn't say he'd disagreed. It was Gabe who'd wanted to turn the other cheek. Extreme loyalty had always been his best and worst trait.

"I didn't say the git loved me. I said he let me in. He understood that I needed to see you." The other man was looking uncomfortable now, and Payton allowed himself to relax. Despite the fact that they were sometimes on opposite sides of a mission, there was a hell of a lot of history there. And standing face-to-face with his friend, it was difficult to hang on to his anger.

"Me?" Payton sat down in an armchair, studying Nigel's face. "What the hell about?"

Nigel walked over to sit on the sofa across from him. "Iraq. I came across some information I thought you should know."

"It must be something pretty damn serious if it convinced Cullen to let you come here."

Nigel blew out a breath. "It's not something you're going to want to hear. In fact, at first Cullen tried to talk me out of telling you."

"But—"

"But I convinced him it was your right to know."

"All right then," Payton said, leaning forward, tension knotting through the muscles in his shoulders, "quit dragging it out. Just tell me."

Nigel pulled an official-looking file out of his briefcase, the red "eyes only" stamp covering the top third of the manila folder. The hair on the back of Payton's neck prickled and rose. "I've been working on something involving the same group of dissidents that kidnapped Cullen's exec in Iraq. They've been increasing in numbers, and Number 10 considers them as big a threat as al Qaeda."

Payton frowned, his frustration building.

Nigel recognized the signs and smiled. "Hang on," he said holding up a hand, "I'm getting there. As part of my operation, I've been digging into old MI6 files. The ones pertinent to this particular group. And I came across something about Mariam."

"That they killed her." The words were clipped and bitter.

"No. Actually, just the opposite." Nigel's gaze met his, a hint of compassion lurking in his eyes. "Mariam was on their payroll."

"What the hell are you talking about?" Payton exploded, standing up, his vision running red. "Mariam was betrayed like the rest of us. And when we succeeded, they killed her in revenge."

"Apparently that's what everyone wanted us to believe. Look, Payton, this isn't going to be easy to hear. I want you to sit down and try and avoid the urge to knock me senseless. I've got proof of everything or I wouldn't be here. All right?"

Payton nodded, unable to find words to answer, and sat back down, his fists clenched so tightly his nails were cutting into his palms.

"I don't know how much of this she told you, so for simplicity's sake I'll just start at the beginning." He opened the folder, consulting whatever was written there. "Mariam Akhtar Benold was born in Iran. Her father was a French trader and her mother was Persian."

"I knew that."

"Right." Nigel blew out a breath, and consulted the file again. "What you probably didn't know was that her father's work was really a cover. He was in fact working with the French underground against the existing Iranian regime. That's how he met Mariam's mother."

"So her family is known for supporting the old regime. That's not unusual."

"No, it isn't. Nor is it unusual for a daughter to share her family's beliefs. In the beginning she used her cover as a journalist for worthy endeavors. Things that she honestly believed would return things in Iran to the way they had been. But then I'm afraid she developed a taste for money, and started selling her services to the highest bidder."

"I don't believe any of this," Payton said. "I would have known."

"Love has the power to cuckold us all, my friend. Even the best of men." Nigel's steady gaze was damning. He wasn't the type of man to tell tales out of school, which meant that the file he held was not only accurate but corroborated.

Payton sighed and sat back, waiting for the rest, already guessing at where they were going.

"Right then," Nigel said, dropping his gaze back to the file. "She started selling information to the highest bidder. We got interested when she did some work for the Palestinians. Her efforts provided intel that brought down a busload of Israeli children. I'm not saying she knew that in advance. But she was involved. It's documented here. Anyway, there's a list of other incidents. And the allegiances are all over the board." He stopped reading and looked up at Payton, his expression grim. "All of this would have stayed buried, except for one incident."

"Iraq." Payton choked out the word, feeling as if he was drowning on a wave of conflicted emotion.

"Yes." Nigel nodded. "The intel she gave us was planted. She was working with the dissidents. Had been for quite some time."

"But they killed her."

"Actually not. It looks like that honor goes to the Israelis. Payback for the bus. Fortunately, for them, the Iraqis were a convenient scapegoat."

"But your government knew the truth."

"Yes, but revealing it would have put other sources in jeopardy. Especially if you'd gone hunting. It was better to let things stay the way they were." Nigel closed the file and sighed. "I had no idea about any of this. You've got to believe me. I wasn't even a blip on MI6's radar in those days. And I wouldn't have seen it now, except for the renewed interest in the Iraqi dissident group."

Payton sat perfectly still, trying to inventory his thoughts, his emotions, but it was too damn confusing. Mariam was responsible for Kevin's death. His wife had killed his brother. The idea was too repugnant to even accept.

"Everything is verified?" Nigel had already said as much, but Payton needed to hear it again, to force his mind to accept the reality of Nigel's words.

"Yes. And I rechecked it all just to be certain. There's no doubt."

"Why the hell didn't I know? I slept with the woman. I married her. Hell, I loved her." Payton closed his eyes, trying to find some sort of explanation for that kind of mistake.

"If it happened now, you would have figured it out. But not then. Payton, we were kids. We led with our guns and our cocks. Mariam was a beautiful woman, and there's no denying she wanted you."

"She loved me." He said the words, for the first time doubting them.

"If you want me to agree with that, I will." Nigel shifted uncomfortably on the sofa.

"But you don't."

"No. I don't. I think the two of you got carried away. Lust in the dust, so to speak. She was smart and she was charming as hell. And obviously really good at what she was doing. Look, everything is more intense in that kind of setting, and you know it. I'm just saying that it's easy to mistake need and desire for something more."

"But it was more than that." He wasn't certain who he was trying to convince, himself or Nigel.

"It became more than that when you were injured. Hell, it took on a life of its own. It was the reason you fought to stay alive. But the truth is, you invented a relationship that never existed. At least not on the level you created in your mind. If Mariam had lived, you'd have soon seen the truth of it. But she didn't. And there was no purpose served by our telling you. Not then."

"And after I knew she was dead?"

"There wasn't any talking to you then. You pulled away from all of us, remember? And besides, it wouldn't have changed anything. You'd still have blamed yourself. But this changes everything. That's why I'm telling you."

"So you think that telling me that my wife was the traitor responsible for killing Kevin and the others is somehow going to make me whole again?" Anger was mixed with frustration

"No. I just think it's best to face the truth head-on. And I know for a fact that you've spent the time since Iraq blaming yourself for something that never was your fault. But in light of this information I don't see how you could possibly blame yourself anymore."

"I married her. I brought her into our circle. Got her involved with Cullen's mission. Hell, Nigel, I gave her access."

"You didn't. She'd already infiltrated Delta Force. That's how she met you, remember? She was on base, covering the war. She was part of the press corps. If she hadn't found you, she'd have found someone else."

"Now there's something to hold on to."

"Damn it, man, you can't spend the rest of your life kicking yourself over something you couldn't possibly have controlled. I was there. I saw you pull your brother out of a firefight anyone else would have run screaming from. There is no blame here, Payton. Let it go. Let Mariam go. Let Kevin go. It's way past time. And one of them at least doesn't deserve the penance."

"Let me go." Kevin's voice echoed through his brain.

"Don't leave me," Mariam cried.

For the first time he really heard what she was saying—and the words were telling. In some twisted way she wanted to keep her hold. Or maybe he just wanted to hang on to the guilt.

"ALL RIGHT, so now that we're all together, let's see what we've got," Cullen said, sitting at the head of the conference table, leaning forward with his elbows on the table and his fingers steepled.

Madison sat next to Harrison, looking over his shoulder as he thumbed through some photographs. Gabe had just returned from his trip to Oklahoma and was sitting across from Madison with his feet propped up on the table.

Payton, as usual, was sitting apart from the rest of them, his hooded gaze resting on Cullen. He'd disappeared right after they'd returned to Cullen's headquarters, and since then he hadn't said much of anything to anyone.

A stranger sat next to Cullen, his beard and moustache neatly trimmed, his black turtleneck and pale skin out of place in the Texas heat. Sam had heard him saying something to Gabe earlier, and recognized the English accent. Unless she was mistaken, the man was Nigel Ferris. She couldn't think of anyone else who'd be allowed into the inner sanctum.

But according to both Payton and Gabe, he'd been exiled from the group for betraying them on a case, his actions indirectly threatening Madison. Maybe they'd all decided to let bygones be bygones. She shot a glance at Payton, surprised to see him frowning at Nigel.

Then again, maybe things weren't as forgive-and-forget as she'd thought. Not that she was surprised, really. Payton didn't strike her as a man who forgot anything.

Cullen recognized the direction of her thoughts, and waved a hand at Nigel. "Sam, I don't think you've had the chance to meet Nigel. He's flown in with some information for Payton, but in light of his experience with Special Forces and MI6, I thought it might be worthwhile to have him listen in." Cullen shot a glance at Nigel that could only be called speculative. Payton obviously wasn't the only one with a long memory.

"I don't know that I'll have much to offer," Nigel said. "But I'm happy to listen."

Gabe nodded, obviously much more accepting of his old friend. Madison, too, looked pleased. But then Sam doubted Madison held much of anything against anyone, her view of the world much more open-minded than the rest of them. Maybe because she knew better than anyone the atrocities man was capable of committing. Once you'd seen the work of a madman like the Sinatra Killer, you were more likely to cut someone like Nigel a little slack.

"All right, then. Sam, why don't you lead off with what we know." Cullen sat back, waiting, and Sam worked to order her thoughts, telling them first about the newest Tai and then moving on to the Bryan bombing.

"So we've got four bombings with the Tai, all of them with one end cap welded and no tool marks. They all seem to use electronics for detonation. But the actual device varies each time. Three of the incidents have occurred within days of each other, and the first one is six years old."

"Anything come back from trace?" Nigel asked.

"Nothing on the Virginia or the San Antonio bombs." Sam shook her head, impressed that he was already up to speed and moving in the right direction. "None of the parts are identifiable, and there are no fingerprints and no DNA. The ATF lab is looking at Albuquerque, but my guess is that they won't come up with anything. This guy is good. And getting better."

"What about the other possible priors?" Madison asked.

"We're still waiting for Abilene," Harrison answered. "Sam's put a call in to someone she knows there. And Refugio looks like a wash. They can't seem to locate the paperwork, and any evidence has long since been destroyed."

Madison frowned, her gaze shifting to Sam. "You know people in Abilene?"

"Yeah, I used to work crime scene investigation there way back when."

"And the Prager—have you ever been there?"

Payton's head popped up, his heated gaze settling on Sam.

She shivered, Madison's train of thought apparent. "I was there once. It's been years ago now. I attended an FBI seminar on bomb detection and removal. That's where I met Walter Atherton."

"Okay, I'll bite," Gabe said, leaning forward, his eyes narrowed in thought. "How about Bryan. It was a barbeque joint, right?"

"3D Barbeque, to be exact," Harrison offered.

Sam shook her head. "I don't know. I don't really like barbeque. But I did go to A&M. So it's possible, I guess."

"But not probable?" Cullen asked.

"I can't say for certain. I don't remember a place called 3D per se. The only place I remember was a beer joint where all the engineering students hung out. They had dollar pitchers, and pool. But that was in College Station."

Nigel's eyebrows rose in question.

"The two towns abut each other. College Station and Bryan. Anyway, the place I'm talking about was called the Blue Goose." She shrugged in apology.

"It was just an idea," Madison said.

"A good one." Payton was still staring at Sam. "If the bomber is targeting Sam, then it would make sense that the sites of the bombings have significance for her."

"But I haven't been to the 3D."

"Maybe the significance is all in the bomber's head," Madison said with a shrug.

"Well, whichever it is, I'm afraid there's more," Harrison said, producing the stack of photos he and Madison had been looking at earlier. "These are photos of one of the fragments of the model car that exploded in Sam's room." He waved them in the air. "I've taken the liberty of putting them on the computer."

He hit a button on his laptop, and an image appeared on the whiteboard behind his head. "When I first saw this etching, I thought it was the result of the blast. But on further examination, it appears to have form." He hit another button and the image changed, this time the anomaly looking more like a circle. "And when you enlarge it yet again." The picture switched, this time the crude etching coming clear.

"The Tai." Payton's voice held an edge of anger. "This bastard *is* targeting Sam."

Sam opened her mouth to refute the idea, but closed it again, her throat too dry to allow words.

"What about the fragments from the bomb in Elliot's car?" Gabe asked. "Anything there?"

"No." Sam shook her head, her mind still trying to make sense of this newest development. "There isn't much left. When the car exploded, the gasoline intensified the fire and most everything altered unrecognizably."

"How about information on Elliot Drummond?" Cullen asked.

Madison frowned. "I'm afraid I found something." Her gaze met Sam's, her expression apologetic. "Seems Elliot was in a bit of a fix. To the tune of fifty thousand dollars."

"Drugs?" Gabe asked, his eyes narrowed.

Sam wanted to defend Elliot, but obviously she hadn't known him as well as she thought she had.

"No." Madison shook her head. "Gambling. A little bit of everything. Horseracing, poker, even a stint in Atlantic City. Elliot had a definite problem, and unfortunately he picked the wrong people to do business with."

"So he had motive." The words came out on a whisper, Sam's mind scrambling to deal with the new information.

"And then some," Madison sighed. "I haven't been able to find anything to support the idea that he'd made a deal, but I didn't really expect that I would."

"But when you add up the facts, I don't think we can ignore the truth," Gabe said looking at Sam.

"Elliot sold information and it got him killed." Her heart twisted at the thought that he'd fallen so far. "I wish I'd known."

"There wasn't anything you could have done, Sam." Madison's voice was consoling.

"I know." She nodded. "Really, I do. It's just that he was my friend. And even if it was indirectly, I feel like I got him involved in all of this."

"But you didn't," Payton said, tension radiating from the line of his neck and jaw.

Sam nodded, knowing in her heart that he was right. But it still hurt.

"How about the confetti bomb?" Cullen asked, forcing their attention back to the bomber and his handiwork.

"I found a mark. But I can't make anything of it," Harrison said, switching to another photograph, everyone turning their attention to the screen. "This is from a piece of the box itself."

Sam stared at the image, her heart pounding in her throat, her vision swimming.

"Sam?" Payton was beside her in an instant, his hands on her shoulders. "What is it? What do you see?"

She shook her head, her brain screaming in denial, her gut churning with bile. "It's mine, Payton. My jack-in-the-box. That's an *S* and a *W*." She pointed up at the screen, the scratches clear only to her. But then she'd put them there herself, using her father's penknife. "Those are my initials."

CHAPTER TWENTY-FIVE

"WHEN DID YOU SAY the jack-in-the-box was stolen?" Cullen asked.

Payton was sitting beside Sam now, his leg pressed against hers in a subtle attempt at comfort. She'd regained her composure, but he could see the stress reflected in her eyes.

Gabe and Madison had wisely taken over the conversation, giving Sam a chance to pull herself together while they filled Nigel in. Cullen was pacing at the front of the room, Harrison as usual staring at his computer.

"About seven years ago. Right after I went to work for the FBI."

"Which means that it fits into the time line—if there is a time line." Cullen frowned, frustration apparent in his frenetic back and forth movement.

"Why don't we see if we can plot this out. It'll make thinking about it a lot easier," Madison said, getting up to walk to the whiteboard drawing a long horizontal line. "When were you in Bryan?"

"College Station," Sam corrected. "I was there four years, but it's been almost thirteen since I graduated."

Madison made a hash mark at the far left side of the continuum. "All right. And when did you go to Abilene?"

"Right after I graduated. I was there almost two years."

Madison made a second hash mark. "And that's when you went to the Prager?"

"No." Sam shook her head. "After Abilene I went to work

for the Houston bomb squad. They're the ones who sent me to the FBI seminar."

Madison nodded, and then made hash marks for Houston and the Prager respectively.

"And the seminar is where you met Walter Atherton?" Nigel asked, his eyes narrowed as he studied the whiteboard.

"Yes." Sam covered Payton's hand with her own, her nervousness reflected in the gesture. It was the only sign that she was reacting to their line of thinking, and Payton wasn't sure she was even aware of the fact. But it was telling—in more ways than one.

"And from there you went to work for the FBI, right?" Madison asked, already putting a hash mark in for Sam's job with ERT.

"And then four years ago I went to work for ATF."

"Right." Madison nodded, adding ATF toward the right end of the continuum. "Okay, Harrison, help me with the prior bombings, and for the time being let's assume that Abilene is in the mix."

"Well, the Bryan/College Station bombing—" he shot a grin in Sam's direction, but she missed it, her eyes still glued to the whiteboard "—was six years ago."

Madison inserted a hash mark for the barbeque bomb between Sam's ERT job and the ATF. "How about Abilene?"

"Three years ago," Harrison said. "But shouldn't you put Sam's Abilene bomb up there too?"

"Sam's bomb?" Gabe asked, his eyebrow lifting in question.

"The potential prior in Abilene was at the city complex. I worked a bomb there, too. But it was totally different. Not even a pipe bomb, and I successfully defused it."

"Did you find the bomber?" Payton asked, wondering if it could possibly be this simple.

"Yeah. A guy who'd been fired. Turned out he'd also lost his wife to cancer or something. Basically he had a total meltdown. He confessed and cut a deal, psychiatric help in exchange for time served. Look, I'll admit the guy wasn't a candidate for citizen of the year. But his bomb wasn't anything close to sophisticated. I'm not even completely certain it would have detonated."

"Meaning you don't think he had the potential to move up to the expertise of our bomber," Gabe said.

"No way." Sam shook her head. "I'd stake my life on it."

"Well since you are staking your life on it," Payton said, his tone dry, "why don't you let us check into the guy anyway?"

"Sure," Sam sighed. "His name was Henry Norton. If I remember right he was living in a neighboring town called Eula. But that was a long time ago."

"Should be easy enough to check out." Harrison jotted the information down, with a nod.

"And in the meantime I'll note it on the time line." Madison wrote it next to the hash mark for Sam's Abilene bomb, and added another mark for the Abilene prior. "Harrison, didn't you say there was another potential prior?"

"Refugio," Harrison answered. "It was sixteen years ago, but the records have been misplaced. So there's no way to check it for similarities."

"Have you ever been to Refugio, Sam?"

"With my mom and dad in the sixth grade. We did Goliad, San Jacinto and Refugio. Even the Alamo. My dad had a thing for Texas history. But I can't imagine that it's relevant." Her look said she was beginning to question the entire line of thinking, but Payton couldn't shake the feeling that they were on the right track, Refugio notwithstanding.

"I tend to agree," Madison said, "but I'll put it up there anyway." She extended the left hand end of the line and added Refugio to the list, once for the bomb and once for Sam's family vacation. Then she went to the other end of the board and added the San Antonio bomb, then the confetti bomb, followed by the bomb that killed Walter Atherton, then Elliot Drummond's bomb, the model car bomb and finally the one in Albuquerque.

"Is that everything?" Madison asked, her gaze encompassing them all.

"That's all I've got," Harrison said.

"All right then, people," Cullen said, resuming his pacing. "Let's connect the dots."

"Well…" Harrison squinted up at the whiteboard. "We've got the Tai on the three big bombs, and the one in Bryan, as well as the last one that went off in Sam's suite."

Madison made a circle at each appropriate hash mark.

"And we've identified the jack-in-the-box, and therefore Jack, as the one Sam had stolen in Virginia," Gabe said.

Madison marked those with Sam's initials.

"I guess we can mark a connection between Elliot's death and the model car used in the bomb in my room. They were the same make and model, and Jack seemed to be a surrogate for Elliot."

Madison nodded and linked the two events with a bracket. "All right, what else?"

"How about the robbery? Based on Sam's identification of the jack-in-the-box fragment, it looks like the bomber is also the one who broke into her apartment. How else would he have obtained the toy?" Payton asked.

"It's a bit out of character," Madison said. "Usually these guys keep a really low profile. But if he already knew of the box's existence, then maybe it wasn't such a stretch. I mean, he also broke into Sam's rooms at the hotel twice. So maybe he's just making damn sure no one is around before he makes his moves."

"He obviously got in and out of the control room at the Hyatt undetected," Harrison noted.

"Yes." Madison nodded. "He seems to be adept at blending in when he chooses to do so, which means he's more social than I'd originally profiled. At least more tolerant of people. I'd still say he's a loner though."

"All right, now that we've profiled the bastard, what else can we say about his work?" Cullen said, his pacing beginning to wear on Payton's nerves.

"This bugger's been really busy, with a marked escalation after the Prager," Nigel said, the crease between his eyebrows marking his concentration. "If we assume that the Abilene bomb fits the profile, then we're looking at a three-year gap between the first and second incidents, and again between the second and third. That's compared with a matter of days for the last two."

"So maybe the senators really were superfluous," Payton mused, trying to make sense of the facts spread out across the whiteboard. "Which means that we're right and our attention was focused in the wrong direction."

"So the guy takes out Walter Atherton in an attempt to get the focus back where it was supposed to be." Harrison's voice held a note of excitement they were all beginning to feel.

Everyone but Sam.

She sat staring at the board, still holding on to Payton's hand.

"It's going to be all right." The words were banal at best, but he couldn't stop his overriding need to comfort her.

"No." She shook her head, pulling her hand away. "It isn't. Not until we work this through and figure out who the hell is behind this." She crossed her arms over her chest, a defensive posture that spoke volumes to Payton, her gaze moving to Madison's. "Why Atherton?"

"I don't know. But looking at the continuum, I'd say it's related to the Prager. It's where you met the man, right?"

"Yes."

"Did you have a relationship with him?" Gabe asked, his gaze skimming the top of Sam's head, his face reflecting his distaste for the question.

"Of course not," Sam snapped. "He saw potential in me. We talked about bombs and the FBI, and as a result he offered me a position with ERT."

"While you were at the Prager?" Gabe queried, this time looking directly at her.

"No. A couple months later. But our meeting there is the reason why he even considered me."

"All right, so maybe killing Atherton was the best way to get you away from considering the senators and make you see the Prager in the proper context." Gabe shot a glance at his wife, who nodded in agreement.

"So what?" Sam asked, raising her hands in frustration. "None of this makes any sense."

"Well, we can add Bryan to the connection category." Harrison said, spinning his laptop around for everyone to see. "I just got verification that 3D Barbeque was actually in College Station. It occupies the same building as the now-defunct Blue Goose."

Sam shivered, her arms back around her middle. Payton damned the consequences and wrapped an arm around her, ready for her rebuff, surprised when she not only accepted the comfort but leaned into it. Across the room, Nigel lifted his eyebrows in surprise.

"All right," Madison said, turning to make the notation on the whiteboard. "That gives us three bombs, three years separating each of them, all at places that Sam has been to, quite possibly with some meaning to her. The job with the FBI, a favorite college hangout…"

"My first bomb scene." She moved away from Payton's embrace, her attention back on the board.

"Abilene."

"Yeah. I'd worked a couple as part of the crime scene investigation. But only after the fact. This was the first live bomb I ever worked with—officially."

"Okay so we have three significant events in your life," Madison summarized. "What if this guy knows that, and is playing off the fact by bombing those exact locations?"

"But I didn't even know about the first two until now. Hell, we haven't even ascertained for certain that the Abilene bomb is the work of the same man."

"But it fits the pattern," Madison insisted. "And my gut tells me we'll find the Tai when we get hold of the evidence."

"Hang on," Nigel said, holding up a hand. "Try this for size. What if the bomb in San Antonio was intended as a first and last act all at once?"

"You mean that the Prager was the last of the three bombs, but the first Sam was supposed to discover?" Gabe asked, already nodding in agreement.

"Right." Nigel stood up, and walked over to the board. "Let's assume for a moment that the senators weren't on-site at the Prager. That it had simply been a loss of property. You'd have found the Tai, Sam, and then the priors, and in that way you'd begin to work backward, until you uncovered the connection between the three bombs."

"And theoretically," Madison said, "the reason behind them."

"But the senators *were* in the Prager," Gabe said, building off of what they were all saying. "And so the message got lost. The masterpiece destroyed. Which meant our guy needed to get the focus back where he'd intended, quickly."

"So he picked Walter," Sam said, her voice quiet, her mind obviously grappling with the reality of this scenario. "But that didn't work either. Walter's work with the investigation into the senators' deaths colored my perception again."

"*Our* perception," Payton corrected. "We're all in this together, Sam."

"So he pumped Elliot for information," she continued, ignoring his comment, her focus still on the whiteboard, "then he killed him, and set things up in Albuquerque, knowing that I couldn't possibly miss the significance of my mother being targeted. Which leaves us with the inescapable conclusion that people are dead because some asshole out there has a problem with me."

"I'm guessing a fixation is more like it," Madison said, patting her pregnant belly thoughtfully. "If he had a problem with you, his attacks would have started out more violently. If you accept the train of our logic, the first three bombs weren't meant to have casualties. So he was merely trying to engage you. Not hurt you. If we're right about your connection to the sites, then it was more about pulling you into his fantasy. There's meaning for him, too, mind you. Some connection between the two of you. But at least in the beginning it wasn't intended to escalate to death."

"But the senators' presence upped the ante," Payton said.

"In more ways than one," Madison said. "He needed to refocus our investigation, but I also think he got a taste of blood and liked it. That's not unusual in the kind of personality we're discussing here. There's power in murder. As much or more as the destruction caused by a bomb. Combine the two, and in an obsessive compulsive, it can create a pretty powerful aphrodisiac."

"You're saying the guy is in love with Sam?" Cullen asked, his disgust evident.

"No." Madison shook her head. "He's in love with his work. And in his mind Sam is connected to that."

"Because she investigates bombings?" Nigel asked.

"I think that's part of it, but I also think there's something more personal going on."

"So how the hell do we figure out what it is?" Payton growled, everything in him screaming to grab Sam and get her the hell out of the way, but he resisted the urge, knowing damn well she would never allow it. Besides, he respected her too much to let his more primitive instincts take control.

"We start by getting a list of all the people attending that seminar at the Prager. And we compare that to the personnel roster of the Abilene PD when Sam was there. And then we cross that against the staff and students at Texas A&M." Gabe stood up, obviously ready to go to work.

"Do you have any idea how many people attended Texas A&M during that period?" Harrison asked.

"So we start with people in Sam's department. Engineering, right?"

She nodded.

"And maybe the staff in that department as well."

"I'd also look at the janitorial staff or security staff in the engineering building. I doubt this guy was a professor. Doesn't really fit the profile. But he could have liked hanging around the department. He definitely has the IQ for the work, just not the interpersonal skills necessary to maintain the ins and outs of college life."

"I'll get to work," Harrison said, with a wry smile. "Shouldn't take too long." There was irony in his voice, but it was tempered with enthusiasm. If anyone could pull it off in record time, it was Harrison.

"I can help," Madison offered.

"We all will," Gabe said, his gaze including Nigel who nodded in support. They all got up, and hurried out of the room, anxious to get to work, and realizing that Sam needed a little time.

Payton stood to go as well, but hesitated, not certain what he should do.

"Stay," she said, her gaze lifting to his. "I think I could use a little support."

For her to even suggest that she needed help was an indication of just how hard this had all hit her.

He adjusted his chair so that he was sitting across from her, reaching out to take her hands in his, leaning so close that their heads touched. "I'm not going anywhere."

"This all seems so surreal. I've had my share of death threats and angry perps, but nothing like this. Nothing at all. Payton, it's my fault all those people are dead."

"It isn't your fault. You heard Madison. This guy, whoever he is, has formed some sort of attachment to you. Something you weren't even aware of. There's no way in hell you can be held responsible for anything that's happened because of his insane fixation."

"Seems like I was just saying pretty much the same thing to you." She tried for a smile and missed. "About Iraq, I mean."

"So maybe you were right." His answer had been meant to comfort her, but he wondered if maybe there wasn't a little truth mixed in as well. A truth he'd avoided facing for one hell of a long time.

"And I've got some swampland for sale in Alaska." This time her smile was weak, but genuine. "Come on, we've got work to do." She lifted her head, squaring her shoulders, her battle face firmly back in place.

On anyone else he'd have figured it was a mask, but not Sam. She was the kind of woman who could rise to any occasion. Even one as frightening as this. His heart swelled, and if he'd been a schmaltzy kind of guy, he'd have said it was filling with love.

But he wasn't sentimental. Not at all.

Their gazes met and held, and for a moment, there was nobody in the world but the two of them. And despite himself, he leaned close, his breath brushing across her cheek.

"That's my girl," he whispered, knowing deep in his unsentimental heart that he meant every single word.

CHAPTER TWENTY-SIX

SAM SAT IN THE LAB with her eyes closed, trying to process the chain of events as Madison had described it. On the whiteboard it looked cold and logical, the puzzle pieces interconnecting to form a picture of sorts, but when she tried to apply it to her life, to put a face on the shadowy figure of the bomber, it all fell apart.

How could someone she knew—someone she'd obviously trusted with the details of her life—how could this person have twisted it into some horrible nightmarish fantasy? It just didn't make sense. Or maybe she just didn't want to accept the fact.

Despite what Payton had said, she did blame herself. If this guy had fixated on her, then maybe she'd given him a reason. Her brain cautioned that this was a predictable reaction, and that nothing she'd done could possibly have warranted this kind of behavior, but her heart wasn't convinced.

Which made it hurt—hurt for Walter, for Elliot, for her mother's friends and for three senators she didn't even know. She blew out a breath, rubbing the bridge of her nose, the throbbing pain in her head showing no sign of subsiding despite the handful of pain relievers she'd swallowed earlier. No rest for the weary—or was it the wicked? With a sigh she opened her eyes and looked down at the evidence report she'd just received from the ATF lab on the Albuquerque bomb.

As expected, there was nothing from trace. The fragments they'd identified and the camera were all clean. Like the others, the Albuquerque bomb had no identifiable tool marks or parts. That much she'd already been certain of.

The report also speculated about detonation. It had definitely been an electronic ignition, this one more complex than the others because it appeared to have been triggered by a relay from the audio equipment at Senator Walker's fundraiser. When the commercials had been cued, the camera at the site had started broadcasting, and using infrared and cable wire a signal had been sent to the house, detonating the bomb.

It would probably be weeks before they could reconstruct the exact way the wiring had worked. But as a working hypothesis, it was supported by evidence at both the bomb site and the hotel. Based on the combined experience of the folks working the site, Sam suspected they were correct.

"Is this a bad time?" Nigel Ferris stopped in the doorway, his brows raised in question.

"No, it's fine." Sam forced a smile she didn't feel, swiveling around in her chair so that she could better see him.

"I really don't want to interrupt anything." He moved closer, his gaze falling to the report in her lap.

"You're not interrupting. At least not anything important. I'm supposed to be studying this report, but to be honest with you, what I've mainly been doing is trotting out all the people I've ever known and considering them as suspects. Including Billy Fletcher, the first grade bully at Sunset elementary."

"And how's it look for Billy?" Nigel asked, his moustache twitching with amusement.

"Not good. He was really a fiend. Although I suspect he'll wash out when we check into his IQ. If I'm remembering correctly, no one could accuse him of being overly intelligent."

"Oh, well, back to the drawing board then." There was something commiserative in his tone. As if he understood only too well what it was to be hunted by someone you didn't know. But then in his line of work, he probably encountered that sort of thing all the time. Still, she found herself comforted anyway. "Actually, I thought maybe you and I should get to know each other a little better. After all, I know everyone else on the team."

"Or maybe you're here to talk about Payton." It was just a guess, but when she'd left Payton he'd been his usual caustic self, and when he'd returned in Nigel's company, he'd been subdued to say the least.

"Gabe was right, you're very perceptive. Not unlike Madison."

"We both spend a lot of time trying to crawl into the minds of dangerous men."

"Well, I've great respect for Madison. And from what I've been hearing, I suspect there are similarities. However, you're much more brash than Madison."

"I blame it on being an army brat."

Nigel's lips quirked up at the corners. "I believe I know the species."

"So tell me why you wanted to talk to me." She met his gaze head on, seeing nothing but concern reflected there.

"Right." He nodded. "Cut to the chase and all that. I should tell you that I'm here at Madison and Gabe's urging, which leaves me a bit uncomfortable, to tell you the truth. I'm not in the habit of sharing confidences."

"Then why do so now?" She tilted her head, reading nothing but honesty in his face. At least at first blush, Nigel Ferris was the kind of man she'd want in the trenches with her. Right alongside Gabe and Payton.

"Because second chances don't come around that often, and I'd hate to see something I've done affect Payton's."

At just the mention of his name her heart started to hammer, her mind jumping to all kinds of things Nigel could be talking about, not the least of them warning her off of his friend. "I'm not sure exactly what you're getting at."

"Nothing to do with you," he reassured, like his friends, quick to read her thoughts. "It's something to do with Payton."

"Is he all right?" she asked, frowning now, her brain on high alert.

"Not to worry. He's fine. At least physically. Emotionally, I'm afraid I may have upset the applecart." Nigel paused, studying her face. "God, this is more awkward than I thought. I can see in your face you care about him, but in telling you I'm afraid I'm overstepping my bounds." It seemed to be a trend with Payton's friends. First Gabe, now Nigel.

"Well you've started now, you can't just leave me hanging." In light of the worry in Nigel's eyes, she wished she hadn't been so flip, but the whole thing was rather unnerving, and in truth she wished he'd just spit out whatever he had to say and be done with it.

"I suppose not." He sighed, and shook his head, looking very much as if he'd just signed his death warrant, which depending on what he was about to reveal, Sam supposed could have some merit based on Payton's overwhelming need for privacy.

"Look, if it helps, I already know about what happened in Iraq." She wasn't sure why she was trying to help him, except that he looked positively miserable, and he seemed like a good guy all in all. ﹘

"I know. Gabe told me. That's why I thought it might be helpful if I told you the rest of it."

"The rest of it?" She frowned at the thought, wondering how the situation could possibly get any worse.

"I don't know if anyone told you, but I'm with MI6. And as such have a rather high security clearance."

Sam nodded, having no idea at all where they were headed, but her curiosity was piqued.

"I had the opportunity to research some old classified documents, and as part of that exploration I came across evidence, purely by chance you understand, that Mariam Reynolds was in fact the person who betrayed us in Iraq." He went on to share the details, all of them damning.

Sam wasn't sure which she wanted to do more, dig up the dead woman and give her a piece of her mind, or kill her all over again. She'd seen the pain that Payton carried with him. Seen the toll it took on everything he did. And at least some of it was based on a lie.

A lie Mariam Benold Reynolds had perpetrated on all of them. Gabe, Nigel, Kevin, even Cullen. But most of all Payton. Sam drew in a breath, her anger pulsing inside her. "How did he take it?"

"He asked a few questions, uttered a few choice oaths, but overall I'd characterize his reaction as stoic. But then Payton is an expert at hiding his feelings. So that doesn't mean a goddamned thing."

"Surely you or Gabe would be better suited—" she began, only to have Nigel wave her quiet.

"I'm not asking you to deal with the fallout. Unless Payton is prepared to let you in. I just thought that you'd want to know. Gabe says the two of you have grown close. And I saw him in there with you just now…" He trailed off with a shrug. "I came here to help. Payton means a great deal to me. And if he cares about you, then you need to know. It's that simple."

She was humbled by his faith, and terrified that somehow she'd let him down. Or worse still, that she'd let Payton down. Everything had gotten so complicated. Or maybe it had always been that way. She always had been one to gloss over the parts in life she simply didn't want to see. Which went a long way toward explaining why she was still alone.

That, and the fact that she defused bombs for a living.

"I appreciate your faith in me," she said, licking her lips, feeling really uncomfortable with the whole conversation.

"But…" Nigel prompted, the corners of his moustache twitching again.

"*But* I'm not exactly certain where Payton and I stand. And frankly, the fact that Mariam was a traitor might be exactly what he needs to send him running for deep cover."

"Look, use the information or don't," Nigel said, holding up his hands in submission. "I just want what's best for Payton. And if that's you, then I didn't want to blindside you."

"Thanks. I think." Despite the gravity of the situation, Sam smiled. "I do care about him. It's just that I don't know where we're going."

"Who the hell ever knows that?" Nigel's smile was gentle. "Look, I've said my piece, and you've got work to do. Why don't I just get the hell out of here?" He turned to go, and Sam found herself wondering if she'd ever had friends like Nigel and Gabe.

"Nigel," she called, before her better sense could stop her. "I meant what I said—thank you."

His smile was crooked, somewhere between wistful and sexy. "If things don't work out, remember there are always other options."

This was the kind of banter from a guy she could handle. "It's a lovely offer, but I'll stick with what I've got." *A big fat nothing,* the little voice in her head cautioned, but she blatantly ignored it.

"For what it's worth, Sam," Nigel said, a twinkle in his eye, "Payton's one hell of a lucky man."

Now if only someone would share the fact with Payton.

"DID YOU KNOW about Mariam, Cullen? When I was in the hospital, did you know then?" Payton placed his hands on Cullen's desk, leaning down so that his gaze locked with the older man's. He'd accepted the information Nigel had on Mariam as the truth, if only because Nigel would never have brought it to him unless he was certain. But he was also wise enough to realize that what the British had, the United States had as well.

Which meant that Cullen had to have known.

"What do you want me to say, Payton?" Cullen asked, spreading his hands, his expression apologetic.

"The truth would be nice."

"I knew about it."

"And Gabe?" Payton felt as though someone had sucker-punched him, the blow interfering with his breathing.

"He knew what you knew. Nothing more."

Payton nodded, relieved at least to know that Gabe hadn't lied to him. But Cullen had. "So why the lie?"

Cullen shrugged, his eyes still dark with remorse, the two expressions at odds with each other. "Partly because the information was need-to-know. And partly because I wanted to protect you."

"Protect me?" Payton's voice raised to an octave he hadn't known he possessed. "How the hell did my thinking I killed Mariam protect me?"

"In the beginning, you weren't thinking like that. In fact, she was the reason you survived."

"Until I found out she was dead." Even after all this time it still hurt to remember. He could see Gabe and Nigel standing by his hospital bed uncomfortable in their own skins in a way he'd never seen before.

"And seeking revenge for her was the only thing that kept you going for a hell of a long time. If I'd told you, you'd have had nothing."

Payton stared at Cullen, his nemesis for so long. He'd hated the man, blamed him for Mariam and Kevin's death as much as he'd blamed himself. And now it turned out it had all been a lie. Mariam had double-crossed them all. Lied to them, betrayed them and made a mockery of Payton's young heart.

"Payton, I've never met anyone like you in all of my life," Cullen said. "And believe me, I've met a hell of a lot of people. Your loyalty is unwavering, your life attached bodily to the people you love. I couldn't take that from you. You have to understand. It was my fault that I sent you and Kevin and the others into such a volatile situation. Hell, it was my fault my employee wound up there in the first place. I couldn't take away the only thing you had left."

"My hatred?"

"Yes. Because in the end, it's just a crazy circle. Hate, love, all of it. You needed a reason to live. I let you have it. It's that simple. If you can't understand that, then so be it. If I had to do it all over again, I'd do it just the same."

"But she was a traitor."

"And she paid for it in spades. People do things for all kinds of reasons, Payton. We'll never know hers. But remember that one person's traitor is another's hero. Just look at Nigel."

Payton nodded, his thoughts still on the woman who had been his wife, his chest tightening at the implications of his involvement with Mariam. "I didn't know."

"Of course not. No one ever thought you did. There was a cursory investigation, of course, but it was dropped almost immediately. Your patriotism was never questioned, Payton. Until it suited you to put it in doubt."

The last was a reference to the fact that most of what he did was government-ordered, not government-sanctioned. If something ever went wrong, Payton would be hung out to dry. And frankly, until recently, the notion had suited him just fine.

"So what happens now?" He knew the answer, but he needed to hear Cullen say it.

"Nothing. It was all over a long time ago. No one cares anymore about our little expedition. We'll remember forever, of course, but no one else gives a damn. The fact that Nigel told you has no bearing on how the rest of the world will perceive what happened."

"So that's the end of it."

"Is it?" Cullen asked, sitting back in his chair, his eyes narrowed as he studied Payton's face. "Are you ready to let it go?"

"I don't know. I only just found out the truth." He frowned, trying to decipher the true meaning of Cullen's words.

Cullen sighed. "I think the importance of the revelation, now, is that you've got nothing else to hang on to. You almost lost your life trying to save your brother."

"But I failed."

"Yes, you did, but not for lack of trying. And no matter how much you beat yourself up about it, you can't bring him back. And I can't believe for a moment that he'd want you to throw your life away."

"I haven't been throwing it away." Payton hated the defensive note in his voice, but Cullen was hitting too close to home.

"I saw you in the jungle, remember? You were just a hairsbreadth away from blowing yourself to oblivion."

"Along with about fifteen of the baddest hombres south of the equator."

"You know what I mean." Cullen sat back, his face full of compassion. "Let the news of Mariam's betrayal put an end to this. Take your life back. Even if you did have a debt to pay, you've more than paid it."

"So I'm just supposed to pick up and go on?"

"People do it every day. And most of them don't have someone like Sam waiting in the wings for them."

The mention of her name sent a strange sense of calm flooding through him. As if just the thought of her was enough to ease his tormented spirit. Payton looked up to meet Cullen's somber gaze, and for the first time, he saw a man, not a mogul. A man who, for better or worse, had made decisions based on an attempt to protect Payton from himself.

"Thanks for your honesty." It had never been easy for him to thank anyone, and the idea that he was thanking Cullen Pulaski didn't sit all that well. But it was the right thing to do, and, in a way that nothing else could have, it brought a form of closure. The past for once was just that—the past.

And if he wanted a future, it was time to reach out for it with both hands.

CHAPTER TWENTY-SEVEN

SAM DROPPED DOWN onto the bed, exhaustion warring with concern over Payton. She'd noticed that both their bags were in the same bedroom, and while some part of her insisted that for propriety's sake she should move across the hall, she simply couldn't find the energy to do so. And considering everything that had happened today, she didn't really want to.

She'd left Harrison and Madison upstairs playing cards. The two of them had tried to entice her into joining them, but she was simply too exhausted to try and keep up with the intricacies of playing poker.

There were guards at the gated entrance to the house, and armed men at the doors. Cullen was leaving nothing to chance. The house itself was situated at the end of a cul-de-sac on an out-of-the-way road that no one would be able to find unless they knew it was there.

Which meant that, for the moment at least, she was safe. Although she had to admit she'd feel better when Payton got home. Not that she was expecting him anytime soon. He and Gabe had gone out with Nigel. For all she knew, they'd stay out a good long while. It was pretty obvious they'd had things to talk about.

There was something compelling about the kind of friendship the three men had. Sam had never experienced anything like it except maybe with her father, and as close as they were, it was still different from the bond that Payton, Nigel and Gabe shared.

She'd simply never had the opportunity to form that kind of relationship with anyone. Since she'd been a kid, she'd always been on the move. Different bases, different towns, hell, different countries. Somewhere along the way, she'd learned to insulate herself. To make sure that she didn't connect with others in a way that would ultimately mean the pain of separation. What had started as self-defense had wound up a personality trait. She simply didn't know any other way to operate.

And until recently, she hadn't really cared. But now for the first time in her life she had someone worth keeping around, and she wasn't really sure how to proceed. Of course, the ball wasn't exactly in her court. She needed Payton to engage. And although she was certain he had feelings for her, she wasn't as certain that he would ever acknowledge them.

At least with any permanence.

Not that permanent was in the cards if the bomber had any say about it. She'd been over it all a thousand times, and there wasn't really anything new she could add to the mix. Someone out there was playing a game—it was as simple as that. And Sam always played to win. It's just that at the moment, she wasn't even certain what game they were playing.

She blew out a breath and sat up. Despite her exhaustion, she wasn't going to be able to sleep. What she needed was a distraction. She toyed with the idea of going back upstairs to Harrison and Madison, but rejected the idea. Casual banter wasn't what she needed. Instead, she reached into her bag for the cell that Gabe had given her. Maybe talking to her mother would help calm her nerves.

And if not, at least Sam would be certain her mother was all right.

Elizabeth answered on one ring. "I was just going to call you."

Sam let her mother's voice wash over her. Even with the distance, she felt immediately better. "I wanted to be sure you were okay. Gabe said the trip was uneventful."

"Actually, it was sort of exciting. But then I guess you're used to that sort of thing." She could hear the smile in her mother's voice. "He's a nice man, Gabriel. He told me all about his wife, and how they met. Sounded a little like you and Payton."

Sam considered the notion and then rejected it. Madison and Gabe were polar opposites. What he lacked, she provided, and vice versa. It was nice to see them together. "They complement each other, Mother. Payton and I are more like mirror images."

"It takes all kinds. And you've never been the type to choose an easy relationship."

There was definitely truth in that, but Sam didn't want to discuss it. "How are Aunt Maggie and Uncle George?"

"Enjoying the notoriety, even if no one else can know about it. We've got men stationed at the house, and several more patrolling the property. Aunt Maggie spent the afternoon cooking for them all."

"I'll bet that was a hit."

"It was." Her mother laughed. "Only George is worried that they'll all lapse into food coma, leaving him to defend the womenfolk."

Sam sighed. "In an insane kind of way, it sounds wonderfully normal."

"You don't sound so good." Her mother as usual could sense what she was feeling. "Something more to do with the bomber?"

"Just general concern, I guess." She had no intention of worrying her mother with their latest theories about the bomber's motives. At least not unless it was absolutely necessary. "I just keep feeling like I'm missing something. Like the answer is staring me in the face, but I'm not interpreting it right. Does that make sense?"

"Perfect sense. I think the hard part about what you do is working backward. You've got an answer but no question, which has got to be frustrating as all get-out."

Sam swallowed her surprise. It seemed her mother not only followed her career, she actually understood it. "Yeah, and this one is worse than most."

"Honey, don't let the fact that he's targeting people you care about distract you. That's how you make mistakes. Just concentrate on the facts and let them tell the story."

"I'm trying, Mom, but it's hard. I just keep seeing your house on that monitor. I couldn't even breathe."

"But I wasn't hurt. I'm sitting right here talking to you, on our supersecret spy phone, I might add. It's going to be all right, Sam. You just have to keep your focus and everything else will fall into place. The bomber may be good at what he's doing, but you're better. Don't forget that. It doesn't take all that much to destroy things. It's the people like you, who fight to stop them, they're the ones who really matter. And in the end, I honestly believe you'll win the day."

"I wish I had your confidence." Sam lay back against the pillows, moonlight streaming across the bed. "I just feel like this guy has me by the balls."

"Well, there's your first problem. He can't have that kind of hold on you, Sam. You don't have balls."

Sam smothered a ripple of laughter. She'd never heard her mother use crass language before. "Well then he's got me by the hair. Is that better?"

"He hasn't got you at all. That's what's driving him crazy. And I'm betting that's why this thing keeps escalating. He's trying to get your attention. And when you figure out why, you'll figure out who he is."

There was truth in the idea, but she was just so far away from understanding his reasons. "Well, I'm just sorry you got caught up in all of this."

"Better that than the alternative." Again her mother's voice was purposefully light.

Sam shivered, thinking of Ruth and her boyfriend. "I feel sick about your friends."

"Me, too. But like I said before, the only person responsible here is the man who planted the bomb. And when you find him, I've no doubt in the world that he'll get his due." Her mother's voice had turned serious, tight with emotion. "The important thing now, honey, is to take care of yourself. Let Payton and the others watch your back. This is not the time for mavericking."

It wasn't like she hadn't considered the idea. Sam had always preferred to work on her own, but somewhere along the way, she'd come to depend on the people she was working with. Maybe Last Chance was about more than solving crimes. Maybe it also offered hope to terminal loners.

"Sam? Are you listening? I want your promise, that you'll play it safe."

"I hear you, Mom. And I promise I'll be careful." It was as far as she could go. There was nothing safe in anything she did.

"Even if you're afraid of whatever it is between you and Payton, you can't lose sight of the fact that you need his help."

"I swear, Mom, I'll keep him close no matter the cost." The idea was actually somewhat appealing. Not that she was going to admit it to her mother. "Are you happy?"

"I'll only be happy when this is over, Sam. When I know you're safe."

She nodded into the phone, then realized her mother couldn't see. "I love you, Mom." And she realized that for the first time in a long time, she really meant it. Whatever gulf had opened between them with her father's death was gone now, closed by the necessity of pulling together, and by the fact that Sam was seeing her mother in a whole new light.

"I love you, too." The smile was back in her mother's voice. "And remember, honey, I'm right here anytime you need me. I mean, how many mothers and daughters have their own special hotline."

Sam clicked off, her heart feeling a little lighter. She might not know who was behind the bombings, but she was getting closer. And for once, she wasn't alone. She had her mother, and her new friends—and Payton. She snuggled down into the sheets, letting her eyes drift shut.

Her sleep was fitful, filled with images of a faceless man holding a detonator, his laughter sending bolts of icy fear chasing through her. Then suddenly, Payton was there, his body warm against hers as he slid into the bed, and she relaxed, her nightmares fleeing in the wake of his strength. She nestled close, settling into the curve of his arms, and sighed, knowing they should talk, that she should ask about Mariam.

He kissed her hair, and told her to sleep, and she did, dreamlessly, waking much later to the feel of his hands on her body, his lips on her face, his penis hard against her thigh, and she opened herself, letting him make love to her.

The ferocity of their earlier couplings was gone, in its place a tender intensity that filled her with wonder and incredible joy. This was a union of both spirit and body. Sam recognized the walls that were tumbling down, and she let him take her, heedless of anything beyond the two of them.

This was a safe place, where nothing could touch them. Not the past, not the future, not the bleak darkness of their nightmares. There was only love. The two of them, moving together, faster and faster, until they found release, pleasure whispering through her like a summer breeze.

Afterward, they lay together, limbs entangled, bodies intertwined, and Sam relished the rise and fall of his chest beneath her cheek. "I know about Mariam." The words came out of their own volition, somehow in the afterglow of their lovemaking not quite as fearsome as she'd thought they'd be.

"I know." He kissed the top of her head. "Nigel told me."

"I'm here if you want to talk about it."

He was very still, and she bit her lip, her heart pounding

for fear he'd shut her out again. Then he tightened his arms around her. "I haven't really processed it yet. It's like finding out that your whole life has been based on a lie. Every decision I've made since I got out of the hospital was predicated on the fact that I'd been responsible for Mariam's death. Mariam's and Kevin's."

"And now?" she prompted.

"And now it seems that honor belongs to Mariam, and I don't know what that means for me."

She waited for him to say more, stroking the scars on his arm, her fingers tracing the jagged patterns in his skin. "And me? Where do I fit into all this?"

"You don't."

She froze, her heart constricting with agony, unable to say anything. She started to jerk away, to break all contact, but he pulled her around to face him instead, his gaze locking on hers.

"You're not part of my past, Sam. You're part of my future. And nothing that happened before can affect how I feel about you. I want you in my life. And nothing, not Mariam's betrayal, not Kevin's death, not a twisted lunatic with a bomb is going to get in the way of that. Nothing."

She started to breathe again, tears filling her eyes.

"So will you stay?"

It wasn't a declaration of love, but it was a beginning. "As long as you want me." They were the same words he'd used with her earlier, and somehow they seemed right. A promise of things to come.

He cupped her face, his gaze tender, and then they kissed, their passion rising anew, and he smiled, his expression turning a little wicked. Sam laughed, pulling him close, feeling him harden inside her, and as he started to move, she concentrated on the sensation, allowing it to carry her away, her last clear thought that, at least for the moment, everything seemed to be right with the world.

J.T. LOWERED HIS BINOCULARS and sat back in the darkness, anger filling him beyond all measure. He'd managed to elude the guards at the perimeter, at least enough to get a quick look at the house. He doubted he could gain access, but that hadn't been his objective.

All he'd wanted was a look at Samantha, his need overriding all caution. And he'd gotten an eyeful all right. He clenched his fist, forcing himself to retreat, to pick his way back down the outcropping of rock, before the guards made another circle.

His mind played and replayed the image of Payton Reynolds with his hands and mouth all over her. He'd only seen a glimpse, but his mind supplied the rest, and the images gagged him, the idea of their coupling so base that it was almost beyond comprehension.

He wasn't certain who it was he wanted to hurt the most. Samantha for her betrayal, or Reynolds for daring to touch what belonged to him. Not that it mattered, because they'd both have to pay.

A frond of cedar slapped him in the face, but J.T. pushed onward, telling himself it was the branch that had caused his tears, that no one, not even Samantha, had the power to make him cry.

He pulled in a breath, arriving at the bottom of the hill and his well-hidden car, his mind already working out a solution to his problem, a way to find retribution and still keep to his plan. It wasn't that he wanted Samantha. Not in that way. But she was his soul mate, and J.T. couldn't stand the thought of Reynolds rutting on top of her like a bull in heat. He shuddered at the memory, his heart skipping a beat.

He fumbled with his keys, almost dropping them, the lights of an oncoming car sweeping across the road. There was no way anyone could see him, but J.T. stepped back anyway, the action helping to center him.

He never should have come. He'd known better than to give

in to his need. It was a hungry thing, never satisfied, and if he allowed it to gain control he had no doubt that he'd be destroyed.

As soon as the headlights faded away, J.T. slid into his car and started the ignition, repeating his mantra over and over, the refrain working to still the demons within him, to soothe the sleeping dragon.

He had been tested, certainly. Samantha, too.

But where she had failed, he had triumphed.

Every action had consequences. It was part of life's circle. And unfortunately for Samantha, sometimes the consequences were lethal.

CHAPTER TWENTY-EIGHT

SAM SCANNED THE PHOTOS the Abilene PD had sent, finally finding the one she wanted. An old pal had already called to say that they'd found the Tai, but she needed to see it with her own eyes.

The mark was similar to the one at the Prager, the fine edges much more refined than those on the Bryan bomb. She'd been reading about yin and yang, trying to find some way to fit the idea into the scheme of things. Originally she'd been thinking about the senators, but now she was working to put the information she'd gleaned into the context of her own life.

The obvious answer was something to do with good and evil, the two opposites as part of a continuum. Elliot had hit on the idea, and she hadn't ever really let it go. Refining the thought a bit, it was possible to see the link between someone who made bombs and someone who defused them.

There was certainly a circle of sorts there. But it didn't feel right. There had to be something more, something that specifically tied her to the killer. But despite the fact that she'd been working on the problem all morning, she hadn't come up with a damn thing.

Cullen had asked Payton and Gabe to accompany him to a briefing for key government officials, obviously feeling the need for reinforcements. Nigel had gone along for the ride. The plan was to keep things focused on the senators and their pork-barreling scheme. Walter's death could be explained by his involvement in the investigation, along with Elliot's. Her mother's supposed death was attributed to an attempt to warn Sam to stay away from the investigation.

There were holes in the theory, certainly, but with the added information about Senator Walker's involvement, attention would hopefully turn to Washington. At least for the moment. Anyway, she was delighted she hadn't been drafted to attend.

Payton's stoicism would no doubt be quite useful in that kind of situation. She smiled at the thought, the memory of his far-from-stoic performance last night still resonating inside her. There was undeniably a physical connection between them. But there was more than just that, and last night Payton had proved it with his actions, if not his words. It might not have been an out-and-out declaration of love, but there'd been a breakthrough. Enough to give her hope.

And hope was a powerful thing.

"You verify the Tai Chi?" Harrison asked, slipping up behind her, his gaze curious.

"Yeah." She held out the photograph for him to see.

Madison looked up from the printout she was studying. "So it's definite?"

"Looks like it." Harrison stared down at the photo in his hand and then looked up at Sam. "Makes all the hypothesizing yesterday seem pretty damn accurate."

"I don't know if I'm relieved that we found it or disappointed," Sam admitted with a sigh, rubbing the small of her back.

"Probably both," Madison said. "You'd be some sort of automaton if you weren't just a little bit worried about this guy."

"More than a little actually." Sam took the photos from Harrison, and laid them on the lab table. "I mean he's got all the advantages. He knows the rules and I don't. It's not exactly a fair competition."

"You'll rise to the occasion," Harrison said. "I've seen you in action."

"I wish it were that easy." Sam shook her head. "But without knowing who this guy is, or understanding what the hell is driving him, there's no way on earth to predict his next move."

"We're closer than we were a couple of days ago," Madison said, waving the printout. "With this we've at least got a chance of finding him."

"Any luck?" Sam asked, her skepticism evident in the tone of her voice. Madison and Harrison had been running names, trying to find someone who'd been present in Bryan, Abilene and San Antonio when she'd been there.

"Not as much as I'd like." Madison shrugged. "But I have managed to rule out Henry Norton. According to the folks in Abilene, he died two years ago of a heart attack."

"Was he still in Eula?"

"Yeah. Same house, even. Anyway, we can cross him off the list. Unfortunately that's all I've got so far. I had two matches between Abilene and the FBI seminar, but no tie-in to the university." She pushed a notepad in Sam's direction. "I wrote them down anyway. Harrison's checking details just in case. Either of the names jump out at you?"

Sam glanced at the sheet of paper, recognizing both names. "I just got off the phone with Joe Franklin. He's senior officer on Abilene's bomb squad. I've worked with him off and on over the years. No way it's him."

"We can't discount anyone, Sam." Madison's expression turned serious.

"I know. But it isn't Joe. I've seen him work. The guy is all about taking bombs apart, not constructing them. Besides, he's happily married. Three kids last I heard. It just doesn't fit your profile."

"What about the other one? Randy Howson?"

Sam frowned down at the name. "He worked arson for the fire department. I didn't really know him all that well. We served on a task force together once. The arson angle would explain why he was at the seminar in San Antonio, though. There's a lot of crossover between fires and explosions."

"You've got a good memory," Madison nodded.

"And we've got nothing," Harrison said, pulling a fax off the computer. "I checked on both of them. And you're right about Joe Franklin, he seems to be held in high respect, especially by his family. Howson is more of a loner, but he left Abilene about three years ago to take a job in Fargo, North Dakota."

"Kind of a long way to come for a vendetta."

"Yeah. According to his boss, he hasn't had time off in a couple of months."

"So that's it then." Sam ran a frustrated hand through her hair.

"Maybe not. I've been thinking about what Madison said about the bomber wanting to hang around engineering students," Harrison said, his brow furrowed in thought. "And it occurred to me that maybe we were being too narrow in our search."

"There's certainly truth in that," Sam said, anger mixing with frustration. "When you get right down to it, it could be almost anyone. Someone I worked with, someone I put away, hell, the guy who bags my groceries."

"It's not quite that broad," Harrison said with a smile, and Sam was immediately embarrassed by her outburst.

"Sorry. Guess I'm a little more tightly strung than I'd like to admit." She shot Harrison and Madison a crooked smile.

"No problem. Comes with the territory." Harrison as usual took everything in stride, and Sam found herself wondering if he ever got ruffled. "Anyway, I was thinking that it might help if we got a list of the employees at the Blue Goose around the time that Sam was there. Maybe one of them had a particular interest in engineering. Specifically, wiring things to go boom," Harrison said, his eyebrows rising to emphasize the last word.

"So let me see the list." Madison reached out to take the

sheet from Harrison, scanning it almost before she had possession. "Hang on." She picked up the printout, flipping a couple pages in. "There's a match here. At least to Abilene." She scrunched her nose, as she flipped to the end of the report, her mouth screwing up with disappointment as she kept reading. "The name doesn't match with anyone at the seminar."

"So maybe we're being too narrow there, too?" Sam asked, her gaze meeting Harrison's.

"Maybe," he said. "What's the name?"

Madison consulted the list. "James Riker."

Harrison walked over to the phone, and dialed, turning his back on them when someone answered, one hand over his ear.

"The name ring any bells, Sam?" Madison asked. "According to this, he was a bartender at the Blue Goose for about six months during what would have been your senior year."

Sam shook her head. "Never heard of him. But then I wasn't exactly making time with the staff at the bar. What did he do in Abilene?"

"He's just listed as part of the department." She thumbed through the printout. "No wait a minute, he's listed as working in the evidence room."

"No memory of him. Sorry." She chewed the side of her lip, running the name through her brain to no avail.

"Well, it's still something we should pursue," Harrison said, hanging up the phone with a smile.

"So what'd you find?" Sam asked with a smile. Harrison was like a dog with a bone when it came to ferreting out information.

"Well, I figured not registering for the seminar didn't rule out his being at the Prager at the same time."

"So you called for the records."

"Yup, and considering their recent loss of property, they were only too willing to help." He reached over to the fax machine and took a sheet before it could drop into the tray. "I give you one James Riker." He held the piece of paper out to

Sam, bending at the waist with the aplomb of an overexuberant butler.

She took the sheet, scanning the registry card. "This lists an address in Houston." She looked up, her troubled gaze meeting Madison's.

"Surprise surprise. The same town you were living in. I'd say we've moved a ways away from simple coincidence."

"Except that I've got absolutely no memory of this guy. None at all. Is there a picture?"

"No," Harrison and Madison answered together.

"But I'll get to work on it." Harrison was already heading toward the operations room and his computer. "Along with a current address."

"Whose address are we looking for?" Payton dodged Harrison as he passed, his dark brows raised in question, Gabe following right behind him.

"We think we've found someone who fits the profile. At least with regard to location." Madison stood up to give Gabe a hug, and Sam felt a wash of envy at the ease with which the two of them expressed their feelings.

"Someone you know?" Payton had moved to stand beside her, his eyes, if not his actions, reflecting the fact that he cared.

"No." She shook her head. "At least not by name. He evidently was a bartender at the Blue Goose."

"And an evidence clerk in Abilene," Madison added. "We've also got him staying at the Prager at the same time that Sam was there." She handed the faxed copy of the registration to Gabe. "What we don't know is why he was there, or how any of this connects to Sam."

"That's where Harrison was going in such a hurry," Gabe said with a smile.

"Got it in one." Sam nodded. "How was the press conference?"

"Cullen was magnificent, as usual. And totally full of shit," Payton said, but instead of his usual cynicism toward the man, there was actually a note of genuine amusement. "And more importantly, I think the media bought it."

"For now," Gabe said.

"Where's Nigel?" Madison asked, her hand linked with her husband's. "He didn't leave without saying goodbye?"

"Actually he's staying." Payton sounded pleased with the fact, which meant that at least some of the problems between them were on the mend. "He seems to think he can help us."

"I say the more the merrier." Gabe, too, seemed pleased that Nigel wasn't heading back to London. "Anyway, he's still with Cullen. The two of them have a meeting with a bunch of politicos. I think Cullen thought Nigel's international connections would impress them." His wry expression saying exactly what he thought of the notion.

"How you doing?" Payton's words were for her ears only, the question about more than just the case.

"Except for the fact that some lunatic is tormenting me, I'm doing pretty good." She smiled up at him. Whatever happened, she wasn't going to regret spending time with Payton. Life was about taking chances, and while she did it every day in her professional life, she'd opted for the safe route in her personal life, but Payton had made her realize she wanted something more, and the intimacy of his gaze made her believe that it might just be possible.

But first she needed to find this James Riker and put an end to his games once and for all.

"Did you find a picture?" Madison's voice pulled Sam out of her daydreams and she turned around to find that Harrison was back.

"Nope. No dirt either. Although I'll keep digging. But I've got something that just might be a way to skip that whole process and get our information straight from the horse's mouth, so to speak. I traced our Mr. Riker through a series of forwarding addresses, some concealed better than others. A couple in Houston, three in Virginia, and this latest one—just outside Austin. Place called Liberty Hill." He held a slip of paper out to Sam.

"Seems like maybe it's time to pay Mr. Riker a visit." Payton said, his muscles tensing in anticipation, the hunter readying himself for the hunt.

THE HOUSE WASN'T actually in Liberty Hill. It was off a county highway, at the end of an unpaved, rutted road that wound its way through the cedar and scrub of the Texas hill country. In springtime, the countryside would be covered with bluebonnets and Indian paintbrushes, but the rains were gone now, and the land was dusty and dry, the heat rising in waves off the hard-packed clay road.

They'd left their cars a half mile back or so, not wanting to spook Riker—if he was there. Personally, Payton had his doubts. This was going down entirely too easy. Madison's take was that the man wanted Sam to find him, that that had been the plan from the beginning.

In some sick way, Payton supposed, it made sense, but he still didn't like the feel of it. The guy had been toying with them from the beginning. First by leading them all over the country to clean up his handiwork, and then leaving puzzle pieces for them to try and put together.

If this was a game, then Payton didn't believe for an instant it was going to end with an arrest at some farmhouse in the middle of fucking nowhere. But that didn't mean they weren't treating the possibility seriously. He tightened his grip on his assault rifle, signaling Gabe and Nigel to advance.

They'd split up to cover the house more effectively, Sam backing him up as they edged forward. It was odd working with her this way, part of him wanting her to stay at the operation room with Madison and Harrison, and the other part delighting in the fact that she was as competent out here as she was at a bomb site. They worked together as if they'd been doing it for years rather than days. He motioned toward

a stand of brush up ahead, and she nodded in acknowl-
edgement.

The house was a low-slung affair, probably built in the
twenties or thirties. It had definitely seen better days, needing a new roof and a coat of paint. But for all that, it was clean,
the yard cleared of brush and graveled in, partially surrounded
by an adobe wall. Despite the obvious Mexican influence, the
place had a Zen feel about it, the gravel garden in particular.
There were fresh rake marks, and everything was arranged
strategically around a central statue.

From here Payton couldn't determine for certain but he
thought it might be a Buddha, which supported the fact that
they'd come to the right place. The Tai Chi was only part of
a greater philosophy and Riker at least from first glance
seemed to have more than a passing acquaintance with the *I
Ching*.

Gabe indicated that he and Nigel were heading around the
back. Payton nodded, following Sam to the right side of the
adobe wall. There was an arched gate, and a pathway leading to the front door. With a tilt of the head, Payton signaled
that they should move.

Leading the way, his rifle held ready, Payton stepped up
onto the front porch with Sam right behind him. They flanked
the door, backs to the wall, and Payton reached over to knock,
the sound hollow as it echoed through the house.

Nothing moved, even the air was still, the only sound the
mockingbirds in the juniper. Payton reached for the door handle and turned it, then used his foot to push the door wide,
swinging into the opening, ready for attack.

"Clear." He spoke both to Sam and the microphone that
connected him to Gabe and Nigel. He stepped into the room,
rifle still at the ready, Sam following him, pivoting to check
the corners, her gun hand steady.

Moving quickly, they searched the other rooms in the same
fashion, meeting Nigel and Gabe in what obviously served

as a living room. There were five rooms in all. The living room and a parlor, kitchen and two small bedrooms. All of them were empty.

"There's no one here," Payton said to no one in particular, his gaze searching the room, taking in the careful arrangement of furnishings and art. There was a framed baseball uniform on one wall, an ornate carved screen in the opposite corner and a Chinese statue on a table in the corner. Other than that there was little ornamentation. The furniture was equally simple. A room designed for function and form, uncluttered, so that the energy flow was unobstructed.

He'd seen it over and over in China, the need for spiritual wholeness overriding the normal human desire for possessions. An admirable trait. Even in a bomber.

"I'm guessing we're at the right place," Sam said, picking up the statue. "Except for the baseball uniform, this room feels like it was transplanted straight from the Orient. Do you recognize her?" She held out the little deity, and Payton smiled.

"Kaun Yin. The name literally means 'she who hears the weeping world.' Pretty ironic to find her here, actually. She's the goddess of peace and compassion."

"Obviously not a role model." Nigel's tone was dry.

"Westerners rarely understand the workings of Eastern philosophy. They tend to pick the parts they like and abandon the rest." Payton shrugged. "Beyond his penchant for feng shui, I don't see a hell of a lot here that could be tied to the bombings."

"There's a shed out back. I didn't see any tools, but then we only had time to give it a cursory look," Gabe said, pulling a book off the shelf.

Tao Te Ching—the Book of the Way. Payton had first read it after Kevin's death. In the original Chinese. In many ways, the words there had saved his life, made him see a way to exist outside of the pain. He didn't buy into the concept of organized religion—East or West—but he believed there was a higher order. The idea was at once perplexing and comforting, and it had seen him through his darkest days.

Payton sighed, pushing away his thoughts, forcing his attention to the situation at hand. "We'll check it out." He headed to the back door without waiting to see if Sam was following, restless energy demanding action of some kind.

It was always like this when he was hunting, his mind honing in on the prey, his body preparing for the kill, and this one would give him particular pleasure. The man had threatened Sam, and Payton intended to make certain he paid for his obsession.

But first he had to find the bastard. And it sure as hell wasn't going to be here.

"We've got to look, Payton. Something here might tell us where he is." Her hand on his arm was gentle, hesitant, and he worried for a moment that he had frightened her. His stillness did that to people. Usually to good advantage. But it was important to him that she not feel like that.

His gaze met hers, his breath releasing on a whisper of relief. Her eyes were clear and steady, her expression conveying only her own frustration. He covered her hand with his for a moment, and the connection was as complete as if he were making love to her. Then he pulled away, breaking the spell.

Emotions were a liability. Especially in a situation like this.

"Let's go." He motioned toward the back door, and strode through the kitchen. Like the living room, the kitchen was simply furnished. Basic cabinets and appliances. A small table. No ornamentation at all.

He pushed open the back screen, the heat of the day rushing up to meet him with the intensity of tarmac in Mosul. The shed sat almost immediately behind the house, attached by a covered walkway.

"Not much to look at," Sam said, following him down the

path. "But I agree with Gabe, it's as good a place as any for a workshop."

Payton pushed open the door and they stepped inside. There wasn't much there—a rake, a broken spade, a hose and a couple of bags of gravel. There was also a scattering of paintings, crudely done, the artwork painted directly on the woodwork. Chinese deities. Gods and goddesses smiling benignly down at them from the shed walls.

Seems Riker was an artist, among other things. Not that it did them a bit of good.

"Nothing." Sam echoed his thoughts, clearly as disappointed as he was. "Maybe we've got the wrong guy."

"Or maybe he was expecting us." Payton bent down to have a look at the end of the rake. There were still bits of earth clinging to it, and a couple of grains of gravel caught in the tines. The dirt was dry, but that really didn't mean anything in this heat.

"Something isn't right here," Sam said, frowning. She walked over to the back wall and stared at the adjacent window. "This isn't aligned right. No one puts a window flush to the corner like this. There isn't even a frame on the left side." She reached up to trace the line of the glass with her fingers. "There's air penetration, too."

"It's a false wall. Look at the other side, the painting of the dragon isn't aligned right either. See, half of his tail is missing." Payton started running his fingers along the surface of the wall, feeling for a point of entry or a catch of some kind.

At first all he felt was the natural indention of the planks used in the wall. But about two-thirds of the way across he felt the faint difference in texture that signaled a door. "It's here." He tried to manually pry it open with no luck, then took the rake Sam offered and tried to wedge it in the crack.

"It's no use." He dropped the rake, blowing out a breath in frustration. "It's either locked from the inside, or works on some kind of mechanism."

Sam turned to consider the shed. "This guy is a whiz at electronics, remember? My bet's on a mechanism." She reached down to shift first the hose and then the spade. Nothing happened. Then she went around the room, pressing on the various paintings, all to no avail.

Payton turned to the sacks of gravel in the corner.

"It's got to be something more obscure than that," Sam said, coming up behind him as he leaned down to move the first sack.

It was unopened and surprisingly heavy, but there was nothing behind it. The second sack was almost empty, so much lighter, and once he'd shoved it aside, it revealed another painting in the corner. This one of Hotei—the laughing Buddha.

"This could be it." Sam reached around him to press the little Buddha's fat stomach. Behind them, something clicked and whirred, and when they turned back around, the door was open. Payton started forward, anxious to see what the man had so carefully hidden away, but Sam stopped him with her hand.

"Wait. It could be booby-trapped." She walked forward slowly, inspecting the door frame first with her eyes, and then carefully with her hands. "There's nothing here, but that doesn't mean we're home free. Move carefully."

Payton nodded, and started forward, stepping into the room, his eyes drawn immediately to the mural on the opposite wall. At first he thought it was another of Riker's paintings—a large rendition of the Tai Chi—but then his brain registered what it was he was looking at.

An elaborate collage. The lighter half of the circle was made up of articles about the bombs. Bryan, Abilene, San Antonio, Virginia. They were all there. A tribute. Blood, or something that looked a hell of a lot like it, was smeared across a picture of Senator Ruckland.

But it was the other half of the circle that frightened him the most—the shaded half. It was almost completely covered with photographs of Sam. Some were from the newspaper, but others were clearly shots that Riker had taken without her knowing. There were articles, too. Chronicles of Sam's career.

Yin and yang. It finally made sense. And it shook Payton to the core. He moved immediately, trying to stop her from seeing it. But the gesture was telling, and she pushed past him, coming to a full stop about four steps into the room.

"Oh my God." Her hand came to her throat.

"I know." He nodded, his voice clipped as he tried to control the rage that threatened to consume him.

She shook her head, her face going ashen. "It's not the Tai. It's the floor."

His eyes dropped to her feet, and he saw immediately the depression where her left foot touched the floor. It looked as if a tile had been set off level.

"It's a pressure plate." She said, her voice totally devoid of emotion. "I should have been more careful."

"It didn't blow. That could mean it's a dud."

"No way in hell." She shook her head slightly, careful not to move more than necessary. "I'm guessing it's either set to detonate when I lift my foot—or it's on a timer and I've started the clock. Either way, we're in deep shit."

CHAPTER TWENTY-NINE

"I'LL RADIO Gabe and Nigel and tell them to get back."

"No." Sam shook her head. "Radio waves can set off a bomb. You'll have to go to them, and then I want all three of you to get the hell out of here. All the way to the cars. No telling what he's got rigged, but I guarantee you it's meant to blow the hell out of this house and workshop."

"I'm not leaving you." His face was tight with worry, but it was also mutinous.

"You have to. Gabe's got a baby coming, remember?" She'd picked something she knew he wouldn't be able to ignore, and watched with satisfaction as he accepted the truth of what he had to do.

"I'll be back." He disappeared from the doorway before she had time to tell him otherwise. Stubborn man.

Sam fought against her emotions, working to maintain control. It wasn't over until the last man was out, and even though her stupidity had gotten her into this mess, she'd escaped from worse and lived to tell the tale. Still, it was the mistake of a novice and it pissed her off.

Releasing a slow breath, she surveyed the room, trying to figure out something she could use to replace the pressure of her foot. But there was nothing within reach. Her internal clock ticked loudly, her mind counting down minutes and seconds with annoying precision. If there was a timer, then she figured she had maybe ten minutes.

If it was a pressure plate, then it was all about endurance.

As long as she stood firm—literally—she had time. But there was no way of knowing which way the plate worked without testing it, and just at the moment, she wasn't fond of the odds.

There was a table off to her right, bits of wiring and welded metal littering the surface. There was, however, no sign of any tools. No welding torch, nothing. Which meant that Riker either stored things somewhere besides the secret room, or Payton was right, and he'd been expecting them.

Just at the moment, it was the least of her concerns. Time enough to puzzle that out later. If there was a later.

"All right," Payton said, his voice coming from behind her. "They're not too happy about it, but they're away. What do we do now?"

"Get blown up together?" A bubble of hysteria started its way up her throat but she quashed it. "Sorry. Nerves." She forced a smile, turning her head so that she could see him. "I thought I told you to beat it, too?"

Payton shrugged. "You should know by now how much I hate missing the action."

That was an understatement, but despite her fear for him, she was glad he was here.

"I think our best shot is to try to find something to displace my weight Indiana-Jones style." Whatever mechanism was involved, it was located underneath the pressure plate, and there was no way to access it to disarm. Their only option was to buy enough time to get out of there.

Payton stood silently, his eyes searching the room for something that might work.

"There's nothing here that weighs enough." Sam shook her head to emphasize the point. "I weigh around a hundred and eight pounds, so we're going to need something pretty hefty."

"Like me." He moved forward, and she held up her hand with a shake of her head.

"Too much weight. These things can be really sensitive."

He walked out of the room again, returning a minute later with the unopened bag of gravel. "This says it weighs ninety pounds, I'd say it's as close as we're going to get."

She nodded, watching as he set the bag next to the plate. "How much time do you think we have if it's a timer?"

She figured about five or six minutes had elapsed since she'd first stepped on the plate. "I'm thinking four or five minutes."

He nodded, adjusting the gravel so that it was about an inch from the ground. "On three?"

She nodded, her heart racing. "My count." Their gazes met and held, and she shook her head at the emotion reflected in his eyes. No way in hell was she going to act like this could be the end. "One, two, *three*."

She stepped off the plate, just as he dropped the bag on it. Nothing happened.

They shared another look. "There could still be a timer," she breathed, pulling them back to reality.

"All right, then," he said, grabbing her hand. "Let's get the hell out of here."

They ran outside, dashing across the overgrown backyard. They stopped short at a barbed wire fence, hesitating a moment before Payton literally tossed her across, following her in one swift motion.

They'd made it about another hundred feet when the ground shook and the deafening roar of the explosion knocked them to the ground, Payton's big body covering hers. Sam could feel the heat, and bits of debris rained down on their heads, but experience told her that they were far enough away to escape the brunt of Riker's handiwork.

Payton shifted and Sam rolled over, the sky above her thick with smoke, nothing left of Riker's house and workshop but charred pieces of wood and masonry. She'd been right. He'd intended for the whole thing to be destroyed.

No evidence.

And no Riker.

"You were right about the timer," Payton said, his breath hot against her neck. "We could have skipped the gravel."

"Not necessarily." She pushed up to her feet, shading her eyes with her hand, her eyes on the fiery debris. "Could have been a double trigger. I wouldn't put it past him. Anyway, there's no way to know now. And frankly, I think all that matters is that we're standing here discussing it."

Payton had risen as well, his arm sliding around her shoulders. "There's a hell of a lot more that matters here," he said, his face grim. "But before we discuss it, I want to string this bastard up by his balls."

"Nice sentiment." She looked up into his face, her breath quickening at the ferocity reflected in his eyes. Payton Reynolds wasn't a man to mess with. And the fact that she was the reason he was so angry sent her heart fluttering. "But to do that we've got to find him. And something tells me James Riker doesn't want to be found."

"So WHAT have you guys got on Riker?" Sam strode into the operations room, adrenaline pumping at a rate that had every neuron in her body firing at once. Anger mixed with frustration and relief made her almost dizzy.

Madison looked up from the computer with a frown. "What happened to you?"

"Riker left us a little present," Nigel said, following Madison into the room. "He blew up his house with Sam and Payton in it."

"Is Gabe okay?" Madison half rose from the table, her eyes going wide with fear.

"He's fine. Honestly." Sam held out a reassuring hand. "He and Nigel were well away from the blast."

She sat back down again, her hand on her belly. "Thank God. And you're all right, as well?" Her eyes searched Sam's for any indication that she was holding back.

"Just bruised a bit here and there." Sam gingerly rubbed the back of her neck for emphasis. "And Payton is the same."

Her heart swelled at just the sound of his name. She hadn't really had the chance to talk with him alone since the bomb had exploded. She'd spent most of her energy on organizing the investigative team, making sure the techs were briefed on what kinds of things to look for.

Payton had been huddled with Gabe, no doubt discussing ways to find and destroy James Riker. Payton was a man of action, and at the moment there wasn't a lot to do, at least not on a level that would help him discharge some of his rage. Then they'd split up, Gabe and Payton heading for Cullen, she and Nigel finishing up at the site and taking the other car back here.

"He and Gabe have gone to meet Cullen downtown," she said, pulling her thoughts to the present.

"Another press conference?" Madison's fear had receded, her mind returning to the job at hand, and Sam admired her ability to stay focused.

"Right," Nigel said, perching on the edge of a desk. "A pre-emptive strike. Since word of the explosion is bound to hit the ten o'clock news, Cullen wanted experts there to deal with questions."

Madison frowned. "Wouldn't that be you, Sam?"

"I don't do the press. At least not if I can help it. I get tongue-tied or angry or both, and either way I tend to say things I wasn't supposed to." She shrugged. It was mostly the truth. If she were totally honest, she'd have to admit that she tended to exaggerate the trait. Fact was, she hated anything to do with the media and avoided contact like the plague. She and Payton had flipped to see who had to bite the bullet and go with Gabe. He'd lost.

"So why don't you all fill me in on the details?" Madison asked, her forehead creased by a frown.

While Nigel gave her the basics, Sam checked the lab and

the conference room for Harrison. His computers were all running, but there was no sign of the man.

"Where's Harrison?" she asked stepping back into the operations room, her frustration barely leashed.

"He's gone over to DMV to get Riker's photograph." Madison's look was apologetic. "Massive red tape. They wouldn't fax it over. I know he's got more biographical information, but to be honest we weren't expecting you to need it in a rush."

"We wouldn't have—" Sam let out an explosive sigh "—if I hadn't fallen into Riker's trap. Thanks to the explosion any evidence we might have had has been blown to bits."

"Surely they'll be able to salvage something?"

"Nothing that's going to give us any kind of lead on where he's going or what he has planned next," Sam said.

"Seems to me like he wanted us to find his house, even see his workshop." Nigel had moved over to a chair, tipping it back against the wall.

"And then he wanted to erase the memory," Sam said, taking a seat next to Nigel, anger mixing with trepidation at the thought of what could have happened.

"No," Madison said, swiveling around to face them. "I don't think he wanted to kill you. Or at least he wasn't trying to do it overtly. I mean, if he'd wanted to kill you, the guy is perfectly capable of rigging up something that would have exploded on contact. But he didn't."

"You mean you think he wanted to give us an out?" Sam asked.

"I think he wanted to give *you* one." Madison scrunched up her nose, obviously trying to sort through her thoughts. "Look, if we accept the theory that this guy is obsessed with you—and after what you told me about the Tai Chi in his workshop, I'd say that seems like a pretty safe bet—then it follows that he wanted you to figure out who he is. Maybe even find him. That seems to have been the goal of the original bombs. Starting with the Prager and working backward, you should have been able to find out who he was. Only the senators got in the way and it took a little more effort to get your attention."

"But once he had it, you got there pretty damn quick," Nigel interjected with a smile.

"Not as fast as I should have." Sam shook her head, wincing with the motion. "But there's not a lot I can do about that now."

"Hindsight and all that," Madison said, her smile rueful. "I know you blame yourself for all of this, but you know that it's not true."

"Unfortunately my heart isn't listening. And even if I could absolve myself of the other deaths, today was clearly my fault. I know better than to go charging into a room like that. When I was at Redstone, I sailed through room 402."

"402?" Nigel asked.

"It's a booby-trapped room the FBI uses for hazardous device training. Actually it's a complex of rooms, and they're loaded with every conceivable kind of trap. Trip wires, exploding doors, pressure plates..." She trailed off, wishing she could call back time and do it all again.

"You were distracted by the photographs," Nigel said, his tone matter-of-fact. "Manipulated, actually. Riker would have to have known you'd react that way, and so he used the fact to his advantage."

There was truth in that, but it still rankled. "Well, no matter how or why I did it, I single-handedly managed to destroy any chance we had at figuring out what his agenda is. Not to mention evidence that could have convicted him, if we ever find him."

"So we'll find something else." Madison as usual was pragmatic. "The point I was trying to make, though, is that I think finding out about his obsession is part of the plan. He wants you to know how he feels. He's been planting clues from the beginning."

"So you think he's playing me?" Sam asked, frustration welling.

"To some extent, yes, I do." Madison shrugged. "He knew you'd find the workshop. And he knew that you'd be upset enough by it to be careless. Remember, Sam, this guy has been studying you for years. He knows your work, your temperament, probably even your idiosyncrasies."

"But he couldn't have known for certain that I'd have stepped on the pressure plate. Or even that I'd find the workshop."

"No. But he made a calculated guess. And adding your friends to the mix—" she shrugged, her expression telling "—Riker was probably anticipating that they also would respond to the photographs in anger."

"So if I didn't trigger it, Payton would have."

"Or Nigel or Gabe," Madison said, a shadow crossing her features. "For all we know there were more devices hidden, more booby-traps. If you hadn't triggered that one, you'd have hit another. The point is that he wanted to show you who he is, but at the same time he couldn't allow any evidence to survive, so he set the equation to accomplish both objectives at once."

"And potentially kill us in the process." Sam blew out a breath, pushing out of the chair to resume her pacing.

"He's killed before, so he certainly wouldn't see that as a barrier. But I think his gamble was that you'd be smart enough to get yourself out of the trap if he gave you a little time."

"The timer." Sam worked to keep her voice calm, her anger simmering just beneath the surface.

"Right. As I said before, we know he's got the ability to blow you all up if he chooses to do so. But he didn't—"

"You're making this guy sound like an uber-villain," Nigel said, his brows drawn together in a frown.

"He doesn't have superpowers, if that's what you're getting at." Madison smiled, then sobered. "But he is smart. Way beyond average. Which means he's calculating every move.

Even when things go wrong, he's managed to get back on track, to get you back where he wants you."

"So how do I beat him?" Sam asked, frustration cresting

"I don't know for sure. But I do think he's got a finale planned." Madison sat back in her chair, her hands resting on her belly. "I've been reading about the Tai, and although my survey has really only been superficial, I was taken with the idea of opposite forces working against each other in an integrated way. You know, the old idea that without evil there can be no good. So maybe Riker's seeing you as part of himself. One half of a whole. He builds the very thing that you try to destroy. But neither of you can exist without the other."

"So he's creating these bombs so that I'll have something to do?" Sam snapped, tension coiling tight inside her.

"I think that's oversimplifying it," Madison said. "It's more about his viewing your lives as a circle. He honestly believes that you can't exist without him, and that he can't exist without you. What I don't know is whether his goal is to bring the circle to completion or closure."

"You're saying you don't know whether he wants me to live or die."

"Not just you. Him, too. Remember, in his mind, you're intrinsically linked."

"But this is all just speculation," Nigel said. "We don't know for certain that any of it is true."

"No, we don't," Madison sighed, her tone indicating that she'd fought tougher skeptics than Nigel. "But it's not like I'm shooting in the dark. The man has practically drawn me a picture, and combining that with years of experience, I'd say the profile is fairly accurate."

"I wasn't trying to question your abilities." Nigel shook his head, running a hand through his hair. "I just don't like the picture you're painting."

"Believe me, neither do I." Madison's gaze was almost apologetic.

"Well, if you're right and all this is leading up to some kind of finale," Sam said, "then we've got to go on the offensive."

"But we can't do that without more information on Riker. It's a Catch-22." Nigel dropped the chair legs onto the floor and pushed away from the table. "We're stuck here chasing our tails while the bastard moves around like a bloody ghost."

"So maybe I can help give him a little substance," Harrison said, striding into the room. "He's not the easiest man to run to ground. I'll admit that. But I've managed a thing or two. Anyone want to see what I've got?"

THE CAMERA CLOSED for a tight shot of Cullen Pulaski at the podium, his face reflecting the bland neutrality that characterized most politicos. But J.T. didn't care about Pulaski. He'd learned a long time ago that men like him made promises that would never be kept. Offered banal words of encouragement that meant absolutely nothing.

Walter Atherton had been such a man. J.T. suppressed a smile, and focused his energy on the picture, muting it so that the endless stream of rhetoric wouldn't distract.

He searched the faces of the people flanking the podium, looking for Samantha. He was already fairly certain she wasn't there. He'd seen her at his house. Watched from the safe distance of the overgrowth as she'd walked through his sanctuary—following the trail he'd left her—and then stepped neatly into the trap he'd laid.

But just as he'd expected, she'd risen to the occasion, her experience and instincts coming together to save her from destruction. He'd stayed to watch as she shook off the effects of her ordeal, her strength of character filling him with pride. She'd passed his test with flying colors. Not that he'd ever doubted her.

He'd hated destroying his home. Especially Nolan Ryan's uniform. It had been a prized possession for many years. His first conquest. But the Tao taught that a man must keep his needs simple. And that meant sacrificing everything in his search for completion.

His thoughts turned again to Samantha.

He'd wanted to stay, to see her begin to unravel his latest puzzle, but the longer he remained the more he risked exposure, and like Samantha, he was shrewd enough to know when it was time to retreat.

He'd bought the trailer three months ago, paying cash, and parked it on an isolated parcel of land that hadn't seen human habitation for fifty years or more. It would provide a safe haven for operations, his beloved tools all safely housed here until he could complete his mission. The fact that it was less than half a mile from Samantha's safe house was an added bonus, a quirk of fate that only underscored what had been destined from the beginning—a cosmic connection that he could neither deny nor sever.

They were one and the same, he and Samantha. And though the plan had been altered, the goal had never changed. All he had to do was remove one last obstacle. To save Samantha from her own misguided libido. He'd been angry at first, but then he'd realized that it wasn't entirely her fault—temptation could be a very seductive thing. She just needed him to help her find her way, and that's exactly what he intended to do.

J.T. turned his attention back to the television. Pulaski was still talking. Answering questions as if he honestly had answers. J.T. swallowed a laugh.

Payton Reynolds stood with Gabriel Roarke just to Pulaski's right. Muscled minions—nothing more. They were like powerful puppets, jumping whenever men like Pulaski crooked their fingers. J.T. had encountered the type often. In grade school they were bullies; in high school, jocks who took pleasure in tormenting others; in college they had been frat boys; and in the army, platoon leaders. Whatever their title, the role was always the same. Follow orders, fit the mold. Deviation meant rejection.

Oh yes, J.T. knew the type well. And despised it.

He shook his head, forcing himself to focus. Retribution was almost at hand, his plan carefully set into place. But as with everything in life, timing was crucial. Like jumping rope, you had to feel the rhythm—waiting, waiting—until the moment was right, and then you moved.

He knew that Samantha was at Cullen's headquarters. The receptionist there had verified the fact without even asking for his name. *Stupid bitch.*

He'd thought the real trick would be finding Payton. The man was an expert at disappearing, after all, but he needn't have worried, since Payton had just presented himself front and center on the television, a lackey's lackey, waiting for his master's orders. It was almost as if fate had ordered him there just for J.T.

The bobble-headed Nolan Ryan nodded in agreement, and J.T. sighed. Some things he simply could not part with. He glanced back at the TV, excitement swelling inside him. All the pieces were in place, the players exactly where he wanted them to be.

It was time for action.

He reached for the photograph of Samantha he kept by his bed, letting his gaze linger on the smooth curves of her face. She smiled up at him, her eyes full of promise, and he closed his eyes, imagining that she was waiting for him.

Soon, Samantha. Soon…

CHAPTER THIRTY

"THERE'S NOT AS MUCH about him as I'd have liked, but there's enough to establish that the guy's a perpetual loser." Harrison opened the file he'd brought, spreading papers across the table. "James Riker is officially James Thomas Riker. Known as J.T. to his friends. Which, if I had to call, I'd say numbered in the single digits."

"Fits my profile of him," Madison said, her tone matter-of-fact.

"J.T.?" Sam asked, the skin on her arms crawling.

"Yeah, seems like it started out as a nickname. I've got references to it from Abilene and even the Blue Goose, but employment records refer to him as James Riker, and then apparently when he moved back to Texas from Virginia, he changed everything, including his driver's license, to J.T. Took a while to verify the connection between the names. But I've got it now. J.T. Riker and James Riker are definitely one and the same."

"You recognize the name?" Madison asked, her gaze appraising.

"I think so." Sam nodded. "There was a guy in Abilene. His name was J.T. I never knew his last name. So I didn't think to make the connection to James Riker. Did you get the driver's license?"

"Yeah." Harrison opened a file folder. "But I can do you one better. Abilene sent his personnel photo." He pulled out a fax and a photocopy and handed it to Sam.

She stared down into the face of her nemesis. Even though the picture had been taken years ago, Sam remembered the man. Not so much for anything he'd done. It was rather the fact that he hadn't done anything at all. Simply been there. A shadow in her life. A presence she should have noticed, but somehow had dismissed as unimportant.

The second photo was a balding version of the first. Riker hadn't aged well. Whatever promise the man had shown in Abilene, it was gone now.

"I recognize him," Sam said, looking again at the first photo. "He was always underfoot. I put it down to misguided enthusiasm. He wanted to work crime scenes, but hadn't been able to make the team."

"Were the two of you friends?" Madison asked.

"No. I wouldn't even call us acquaintances really. He just hung around the lab, and so I talked to him from time to time."

"How about from the Blue Goose? You remember him there?" Nigel asked.

Sam shook her head. "No. I think if I'd known that, then I'd have attached more significance in Abilene. Or maybe not." She sighed. "It's amazing how people can manage to slip under the radar."

"Sometimes it's not that hard," Madison said. "Unfortunately, it's a by-product of our society that people who are neither beautiful nor charismatic, or even hideously deformed, get lost in the shuffle. Average can be the key to invisibility."

"Obviously a benefit if you're planning to become a bomber." Harrison sat down at the table.

"Or the reason you do it in the first place," Madison responded. "What do we know about Riker's past?"

Harrison consulted his notes. "He was born in Detroit, the son of an assembly line worker and a beautician. He had five siblings. And despite the double income, money was apparently tight. They headed south when the American auto industry hit the skids, and landed in Houston. Riker was five. I've got school records here, and they match a lot of what you said, Madison. The guy was bright—his grades in elementary and the beginning of middle school topped the charts, but then they start to drop, and according to this—" he pulled out a report "—he started isolating himself from the other students. Never a problem in any kind of Columbine way, but I'm betting he had the same kind of thoughts. There are eight incident reports in his ninth grade year alone. Mainly bathroom shenanigans."

"He was bothering other kids?" Sam asked.

"No." Madison shook her head. "He was the target, right?"

"Yup." Harrison nodded. "This guy evidently took the idea of dweeb to new levels."

"And the seeds for his need to fit into the macho world were sewn. Any evidence of military service?"

Again Harrison nodded. "Enlisted right out of high school. Army. But he washed out in less than a month."

"How about college?" Madison's eyes narrowed in thought.

"He got in to A&M. Long before you were there, Sam. And declared himself an engineering major. But he didn't last there either. Three semesters." Harrison consulted his notes. "He had good grades, but evidently couldn't cut it."

"Same pattern." Madison nodded. "This guy wants to fit in. Maybe to be like his father, I don't know. But he's definitely got a macho complex going. It's there in the choices he makes. The army, wanting to do police work. Even his preoccupation with bombs. It's a pretty testosterone-driven field." She shot an apologetic glance at Sam. "And it takes a certain amount of brains as well."

"So why didn't he succeed?" Sam asked. "I did."

"Any number of reasons, really. But I'm betting it had to do with his inability to be part of a team. The guy's social skills are probably stunted at best. He's lived on the outside looking in for such a long time that fitting in has become an impossibility. At least at the level it takes for something like ordnance work."

"So he turned to bombing?" Harrison asked.

"Probably the other way around. I suspect he made bombs first, and then in his effort to belong, he thought he could fit in by using his expertise for good. But when that was thwarted, he sank back into his hole."

"And fixated on Sam," Nigel offered.

"Actually, I think the fixation is on her success. She is what he wanted to be, and so in creating his fantasy, he's cast himself as her opposite. Which based on his fascination with Eastern philosophy would make him a part of that success."

"Especially in a situation where she shines due to something he's done?" Nigel asked, his brows drawn together in thought.

"No." Madison shook her head. "I think that's oversimplifying. These bombs are about more than giving Sam something to do, even about more than showing her his power. I think they're stair steps to something more. Something bigger. He wanted to prove his power certainly, but he also wanted her to know who he is. To find him, actually."

"So we're back to the idea of a finale, but we still don't have anything to help us figure out what the hell it's going to be." Sam slammed her hand on the table in frustration. "There are APBs out everywhere, but no one's found a thing. The guy's just disappeared into the woodwork again."

"He's had years to perfect that," Madison said. "But he also knows that time is running out, and, unless I miss my guess, he still wants an ending. Which means that whatever he's planning, he'll have to act soon. And maybe that means he'll be rushed into making a mistake."

Sam wasn't as optimistic, but it seemed like their only hope at this point. Riker seemed to hold all the cards. She looked down again at his driver's license photo.

It had been taken two years ago, and despite the fact that DMV photos always sucked, there was a hint of something in his eyes. Something cold and focused. Clarity. The man was far from insane, and that meant that, despite his fantasy, he was still playing with a full deck. A dangerous adversary.

A phone rang, and Sam jumped. Nigel crossed the room to answer it, listened for a moment, then hung up, his expression grim. "There's another bomb. This one unexploded."

"And they think it's tied to Riker?" Harrison asked.

"They're certain." Nigel nodded. "There's a Tai on it. This one large enough to see without the microscope."

Madison frowned. "Seems a bit obvious."

"Maybe it's his way of saying 'check,'" Harrison said. "He's been playing a game from the beginning. So maybe this is the final move."

"Maybe." Madison didn't look convinced, but as far as Sam was concerned the answer wasn't relevant, stopping the bomber was.

"Where is it?" Sam asked already halfway out the door.

"A day care on West Lynn. The bomb is in one of the classrooms. A worker found it."

Sam's heart skidded to a stop. "Are there children present?"

"Yes. Three- and four-year-olds. Apparently the bomb is rigged so that when the door shut it was armed. Open it and—" Nigel shrugged.

It was her worst nightmare—again. First the dead children in Oklahoma City. Then recently, the bomb in Waleska. He obviously knew all about Georgia, the similarity in setup far from coincidence, and she'd bet her life that he'd upped the ante, learning from Frank Ingram's failure. There wouldn't be any open windows this time.

No, this was a showdown. His abilities against hers. And this time he was giving her the opportunity to make a move. The only question being whether or not she could pull it off.

The stakes were high. Lives in jeopardy. And not just any lives. *Children's.*

Riker knew her well. Knew that she'd be willing to do almost anything to save the day. Which meant that there was a twist somehow. Something he had waiting for her. Something she had to decipher before it was too late.

Riker, after all, intended to win the game.

But then again, so did she.

THE QUESTIONS SEEMED to be going on forever, but Cullen was handling things with the polished precision of a professional. Although he had deferred to Gabe several times during the first few questions, he seemed to be holding his own at the moment, and Payton wondered why in the world he'd agreed to come along.

He'd much rather be with Sam and the others trying to draw a bead on Riker, but Cullen had requested his presence with his usual take-no-prisoners attitude, and so Payton had complied. He'd left Sam at work on the remains of the house, trying to pull a phoenix from the ashes, something that would lead them to Riker.

He reached for his cell phone, thinking to call her, then abandoned the idea. He'd see her soon enough, and she'd be safe surrounded by bomb techs. He'd already placed several calls, using stateside contacts to try and run Riker to ground, but he hadn't managed to turn anything up. It seemed James Riker wasn't on anyone's radar.

If he'd been a career criminal, or involved in subversive activities, there'd be a record, but the man hadn't so much as raised an eyebrow, which meant Payton's contacts were all but useless, his training and abilities even more so. This was not a jungle in Peru, or the mountains of China, and even though he could hunt a man in urban environments, he couldn't find a ghost. And the idea of Riker maintaining the upper hand galled him.

Payton had run into men like Riker before—men who didn't have the balls for face-to-face combat—and he despised them. Always one step removed from the damage they inflicted. Determined at all costs to keep the blood off their hands. Sometimes they used other men to do their dirty work, sometimes other means—like bombs. But no matter their method of operation, the primary objective was to keep distance from the havoc they wreaked.

Chickenshit sons of bitches.

Payton clenched a hand convulsively, thinking of Kevin. Of Mariam. She'd been one of the game players. Trading other people's lives to line her own pockets. And despite what had been between them, he knew she'd gotten what she deserved. If he'd known the truth, he'd have done it himself.

His heart twisted at the thought, and he forced himself to center his thoughts on Riker. The man was playing a game with Sam, hurting the people she loved along the way. The idea that he had to sit by idly waiting for the man's next move didn't sit well at all.

As if in answer to his frustrated musings, his cell phone vibrated in his pocket. Certain it was Sam, he nodded to Gabe, and then stepped back into the shadows, out of reach of the furiously flashing cameras.

"Reynolds."

"Mr. Reynolds," a male voice said. "This is Rob Mathis. I work for Mr. Pulaski. Mr. Ferris asked me to call and let you know that there's been another bomb threat."

"Tell me about the bomb."

"I really don't have much information. Only that an undetonated bomb has been detected and that it's tied into the other bombings somehow. Ms. Waters has already gone to the site. I think she's hoping to disarm the thing. Mr. Ferris said you'd want to be there."

"Where's Nigel?" He relaxed slightly, knowing that if the situation were really bad, Nigel would have called himself.

Still, despite the fact that he knew she could probably handle it, he didn't like the idea of her out there working with an unexploded bomb.

"He's gone with Ms. Waters. I have an address if you want it."

The man sounded as if he'd much rather hang up the phone, his timidity crossing the telephone lines loud and clear. Payton sighed, forcing a more pleasant tone. No sense in shooting the messenger. "Go ahead."

Rob gave him the address, and Payton wrote it down on a scrap of paper, then disconnected the call. On a whim, he hit Caller ID and got the private number display. Typical Cullen.

Turning to Gabe, he motioned for his friend, his mind already on the bomb site, his thoughts centering on Sam. "There's been another bomb attempt. Sam and Nigel are there now. I'm on my way. I'll be more useful there than here." His tone left no room for argument.

Gabe nodded in agreement, and Payton gave him the slip of paper. "Here's where we'll be. Come as soon as you've finished here."

Payton headed out the back way, the sound of voices vying for the right to ask a question signaling that they most likely wouldn't be finished anytime soon. Not that Payton cared. All that mattered right now was getting to Sam. He needed to be with her, to watch her back. James Riker meant business and whatever trap he'd set for Sam, it wouldn't be something she could easily outwit.

The stakes were high, particularly when he considered the fact that he could lose her. Most people didn't get second chances in life, and Payton sure as hell wasn't going to let his slip away without a fight.

CHAPTER THIRTY-ONE

SAM STOOD in the alley looking into the toddler room through a set of barred windows. The locks were rusted shut, and at least for the moment no one seemed to be able to locate the keys. A crew had been called to come and cut the metal, but before they could do so, Sam wanted to be sure that there were no trip wires.

Inside the room a teacher sat on the floor playing with several kids. The look she shot Sam was just this side of hysteria, but she forced a smile, and circled finger and thumb to signal okay. Three other children were playing with blocks in a corner, a second teacher keeping their activities closely monitored and low-key.

From this vantage point, Sam could see the box that held the bomb. The carving was clearly Oriental, and even from this distance she recognized the Tai. Two wires ran out from the bottom of the box, one curving upward to attach to a black box on the door, a static red light indicating it was armed, the other snaking out along the perpendicular wall to disappear behind a bookshelf.

Based on simple observation, she had to believe it continued on to the windows and possibly another trigger attached to the frame, meaning any vibration of the glass could potentially set the thing off.

The teacher by the blocks looked up, their gazes meeting. Sam tilted her head, calling for the woman to come over to the window. Moving with careful steps, the woman stopped about two feet away.

Sam nodded her approval, and mouthed instructions, having to repeat herself several times before she was understood. Finally, though, the teacher nodded, and set off to follow the wire's path, tracing it past the bookcase and picking it up on the other side. She returned to the window, her face whiter than before, and mimed the shape of a second trigger, pointing first to the one in Sam's line of sight, and then to an area just to her right of the window.

Even without seeing it, Sam felt her heart sink. She had a sealed room with two triggers, two adults, eight children and a live bomb. Not exactly the best of scenarios. Her gaze shot upward toward the ceiling and the acoustical tiles that covered it.

"Is there access from the ceiling?" She turned to the janitor, an elderly man who seemed genuinely horrified by the unfolding events. He was nearing the tottering stage, long past retirement age, and Sam guessed that had he been working for anything other than a day care, he'd already have been put out to pasture.

At the moment, it was clear from the little steps he kept taking backward that he was more than ready to take retirement on the spot if it got him the hell out of here. Not that she blamed him. Only a crazy person walked into a situation like this willingly.

A crazy person—or Sam.

She swallowed a smile, and refocused her attention on the old man.

"I think so," he said, his bushy eyebrows scrunching together as he thought about it. "There's a crawl space between the second floor and this one. All the ductwork runs through there, so they had to allow for workmen."

"All right," Sam said, her mind already formulating a plan. "I'll need you to tell me how to get into the crawl space."

The old man nodded, and started off toward the front of the building. Sam headed after him, motioning for Nigel, who was diligently trying to calm the understandably frightened administrator, to follow.

"What's up?" Nigel asked, falling in step beside her.

"Looks like there's no cutting the window bars. There's another trigger. Any vibration of the glass could set the thing off. But, there's a crawlspace in the ceiling. If I can access it, then maybe I can drop down in the room with a disrupter, and take the thing out."

"Seems kind of risky," Nigel said, shooting a look at the building. "You don't know how sensitive the triggers are."

"I don't see that we've got any other choice. Anything I do in the ceiling is going to be a lot less dangerous than trying to get through the windows or door. It's worth a shot. If I can get in and ascertain that everything is stable enough, maybe I can even boost the kids out before using the disrupter. That possibility alone makes it worth trying."

"Then let me do it," Nigel said, his dark eyes somber.

She shook her head. "Thanks for the offer. But I weigh about half of what you do. Less chance that I'll set something off with my movements. Besides, Nigel, this is what I do, remember?"

"Payton will never forgive me if something happens to you," Nigel said, but dipped his head in acceptance anyway.

"Payton and I can argue about it tomorrow, okay?" She sounded more confident than she felt. But that was par for the course in a situation like this, and she'd learned long ago to shut out all emotion. There simply wasn't room for anything even resembling fear.

"That's it," the old man said, coming to a full stop at the bottom of a weathered ladder that resembled a fire escape. "That's the door."

The ladder extended just above the level of the first-floor ceiling, the metal door at the top looking nearly as rusted as the grill covering the window. "Is it locked?" Sam asked skeptically, her heart sinking.

"Nope." The janitor shook his head. "The latch sticks, but it ain't locked."

"How about access once I'm inside?"

"There's four openings. Yours should be the third." He didn't sound as positive as she would have liked, but there wasn't time to try and jar his memory further. She'd just have to send up a prayer that the man was remembering correctly.

Sam nodded, then signaled for a tech, explaining what she needed. The man returned in record time, handing her a portable PAN disrupter. Weighing in at twenty pounds, it wasn't easy to lug around, but still considerably better than its bigger brothers and sisters. In addition to the disrupter, he'd also brought a portable X-ray machine that would help her see inside the box with the bomb.

She slung the X-ray machine and disrupter over her shoulder, and reached up for the ladder.

"Wait a minute," Nigel and the tech both called at once, and she swung back around irritated at the interruption.

"Aren't you forgetting something?" Nigel held out her bomb suit, his eyebrows raised in rebuke.

Sam shook her head. "Don't want to deal with the extra weight. Besides, if that thing goes off while I'm in there, there's not a bomb suit on the planet that can save me. Might as well be naked." What she didn't say was that she didn't want to live through it if she was responsible for killing those kids. No point in even going there. Better to concentrate on the job at hand, and hopefully they'd all come out of it in one piece.

Giving Nigel a thumbs-up and no more chance to argue, she started up the ladder, stopping at the top to work the latch free. The old man hadn't been exaggerating. The latch might as well have been a lock. But with much determination and a little help from an old screwdriver on the landing, she got it open.

Once inside, she was relieved to see that it was passable by merely leaning over. A taller person wouldn't have been able to fit, but she traversed the space with only one or two places where she had to drop to her knees and crawl. The children should be able to make it through with no problems—assuming that was an option.

She almost missed the first opening, the cracks that marked the trap door covered with grit and dust. Kneeling beside it, she opened it to reveal an eight-inch space between the door and the acoustical tile below. It was tempting to practice here, but time was of the essence, and she didn't want to take the chance.

The passageway veered off sharply to the left just past the first access point, and she had a moment's worry about the old man's memory. She was now well away from the room she needed. Probably across the hall.

The second opening was more clearly visible, and she didn't bother to open it, instead moving forward, grateful when the crawl space veered back to the right again. The ceiling was lower here, and she dropped to her knees, holding her equipment securely under her left arm, slowing her approach so that there were no sudden shifts causing vibrations below.

The third trap door resembled the first, obscured by debris and dust. She carefully placed both the X-ray machine and disrupter on the floor near the opening, and then taking a deep breath for luck, she pulled the handle upward.

The wood groaned in protest, but opened relatively easily, and she leaned into the open space and grabbed the tile, lifting it upward and laying it carefully on the floor of the crawl space.

A curious face appeared below her, the toddler tipping his head from side to side trying to figure out what to make of her. Sam smiled, hoping she looked more reassuring than she felt. The child's face was replaced with a teacher's, and Sam quickly handed down her equipment. Then holding onto the sides of the opening, she lowered herself into the room, the teacher helping her descend.

After instructing the teachers to move the kids to the far side of the room, she walked over to the bomb, visually inspecting it. There wasn't much to see, the box obscuring a true look at the mechanism inside.

The steady red light on the trigger was definitely connected to the door. Any attempt to open it would clearly detonate the bomb. Her movements however, did not seem to affect the trigger. A good sign as far as evacuation was concerned.

She crossed over to the pair of windows and again watched for any change in the trigger light there. It continued to shine steadily, only blinking slightly when she accidentally brushed against the frame.

So far, so good.

She smiled at the group of kids, giving them a thumbs-up, and walked back over to the bomb, debating the wisdom of using the X-ray before trying to evacuate the kids, but decided it would be better to get them out first.

She signaled to the teacher who'd helped her down, and the woman slowly crossed the room toward her, her face a mixture of determination and sheer terror. Sam was impressed at how well both teachers had held it together, and grateful. Hysterical victims could cause a situation to sour faster than any other variable.

"We're going to evacuate the children," Sam whispered, nodding toward the hole in the ceiling. "I want one of you to go up first and the other to stay here and help me. We'll boost the kids up and then they can crawl out."

The teacher nodded, her eyes glued to the box with the bomb. "What about you?"

"As soon as everyone is out of here, then I'm going to disarm the thing."

"Wouldn't it be easier to just do that now?" The woman asked, eyeing the crawl space with trepidation.

"Don't want to take any unnecessary chances," Sam said,

already focusing on the task at hand. "Look, I'd take them out myself, but I don't want to risk trying to come back in here. I'm not certain how sensitive these things are." She shot a look at first one trigger and then the other. "So you'll go. All right?"

The woman nodded, her emotions back in control. "How do you want me to get up there?"

Sam eyeballed the woman, she was taller and a little heavier than Sam, but not by too much. "I think I can boost you up, if you can pull yourself into the crawl space."

"Fine." The woman nodded, removed her sweater, and then pulled the back of her skirt through her legs to tuck into her waistband, creating an improvised set of culottes.

Sam crouched, braced her hands on the woman's thighs, whispered a count of three, and lifted. The first attempt failed, and the light near the door flickered ominously, but nothing happened, and Sam sucked in a breath and repeated the lift. This time the woman managed to pull herself up and into the crawl space, the trigger light remaining steady.

After that is was short work to boost the eight children up and into the space. They weighed next to nothing and Sam's heart lightened as the last one went through the opening. The second teacher had been standing near the center of the room, eyes glued to the two triggers. Now Sam motioned her over to the opening.

Unlike the first teacher, this woman was much bigger. Sam guessed she outweighed her by at least a hundred pounds, and she had a good six inches on her. The woman looked up at the hole and her colleague's worried face, then back at Sam, her expression resolute.

"I'm not going to be able to do this. At least not without making enough vibrations to bring the building down. Angela," she called to the woman in the crawl space, "take the children and get out of here. I'll stay with her."

Angela opened her mouth to protest, then evidently thought better of the idea, instead nodding at her friend. Sam hated the idea of having a civilian in the room, but had to agree that there was real danger in trying to get the woman out via the crawl space.

There was a faint scraping noise as the children filed away, and Sam turned toward the window and Nigel's anxious face. She signaled that the children were on their way, and he nodded, showing her the face of his watch and then holding up five fingers.

Five minutes.

She nodded in return, and he disappeared.

"They'll be all right?" The older teacher was standing by her elbow, her face shadowed with concern.

"Absolutely. If something was going to happen it already would have." She gave the woman a smile. "We've just got to wait here until I get the signal that they're clear."

The woman nodded, wrapping her arms around her ample middle.

"What's your name?"

"Melanie Johnson. But everyone calls me Mel." The woman offered a weak smile.

"I'm Sam Waters." Sam held out a hand, and they solemnly shook. "What I'm going to be doing in a minute is X-ray the bomb to see what's inside, and then, using this disrupter, I'll disarm it."

"Disrupter?" Melanie looked at the machine in confusion.

"It's like a really powerful water pistol. Only it shoots at something like five hundred feet per second. I'm going to use it to take out the bomb's power source."

"Sounds very sci-fi." Melanie's curiosity was obviously piqued, the distraction working.

Nigel's face reappeared in the window, a thumbs-up indicating that everything had gone smoothly. Score one for the home team.

"All right, Melanie—Mel," Sam said. "I want you to go over there in the corner, and cover yourself with those pillows."

The woman's fear returned.

"Everything is going to be fine," Sam soothed. "I do this all the time. But better safe than sorry. Okay?"

Melanie nodded, and dutifully headed for the corner, gathering pillows on the way. Sam blocked the woman from her mind and turned her concentration to the bomb. Gingerly, she placed the X-ray film behind the bomb encasement, and then moved back to the base unit to take the picture. Then she grabbed the film, slid it into the appropriate slot and a few minutes later a grainy black-and-white image appeared on the monitor.

The key now was to interpret the thing correctly. She could see the explosive and blasting cap in the upper right hand corner, and the power source in the upper left. The wires were there, too, clearly attached to the battery and explosives as well as the triggers.

Something at the lower left was too fuzzy to make out, but she'd seen all the pertinent parts. It should be an easy target.

Too easy.

She studied the X-ray again, trying to see something that she'd missed, something that would bring this bomb up to the level of expertise she'd seen in Riker's other bombs. This was an amateur effort at best. Effective if triggered, but easy to disarm if someone with even minimal expertise was called in.

Riker didn't seem the type to take the easy way out, and he certainly always seemed to have method in his madness.

Which meant there was something here.

She looked at the image, her intellect assuring her that her assessment was correct. Maybe there was a secondary device. She stood up and carefully followed the wires extending out of the box. The first led straight to the black box attached to the door. The second wire followed the course of the south wall, making the corner to hook into the second box attached to the window frame.

Sam searched the rest of the room, Melanie's eyes, just visible above the pile of pillows, following her every move. There was nothing visible. No trip wires, no hidden apparatus, nothing that she could see that could be a threat.

She considered the possibility of a copy cat, and then dismissed the idea as too coincidental. So why would Riker set this up? He'd gone to great lengths trying to get her attention, hurting the people she loved—

Sam stopped, her heart dropping to her stomach.

Payton. This was about Payton. Riker's bomb here had been meant as a distraction. Something to keep her busy while he...

She grabbed the disrupter, and using the laser site centered on the upper left corner of the bomb. The power source. Praying that she was right and not simply reacting on emotion, she shot, the water knocking the box over, the lid flipping off.

Nothing happening.

On an exhale of breath, she counted to three and then looked at the triggers. They were black. The red lights gone. Her heart was pounding now, beating off seconds and minutes. Time wasted. Time lost.

Payton.

She walked over to the door and forcing focus, turned the handle and slowly opened it.

Again nothing.

"Melanie, go," she ordered, her voice hoarse with emotion.

The woman shot out of the pillows like a cannon, running through the door and down the hallway. Sam followed, sprinting out the door, skidding to a momentary halt beside Nigel. "Everything is fine. I disarmed it. But it was a ploy. I think Payton's in danger. Stay here and finish up. I've got to find him." She didn't wait for Nigel's agreement, just ran for her car and her cell phone.

Her fingers were shaking so hard it took two times to dial headquarters, but Madison answered on the first ring.

"Madison, it's Sam. Is Payton there?"

"No. He's supposed to be with you." Sam could hear the frown in her voice. "I just got off the phone with Gabe, and he's on his way, as well."

"They're not here." Her heart was threatening to break free of her chest.

"Gabe wouldn't be, he was just leaving the press conference and it's clear across town, but Payton should have been there a while ago."

"Well he's not here." Sam swallowed a wave of panic. It wouldn't do to lose it now.

"Hold on. Harrison didn't give me your location, so I asked Gabe for it. Maybe they got it wrong somehow." Sam could hear paper rattling and then Madison was back on the phone. "End of Orchard Street, just off Fifth, right?"

"No." Sam's breathing was coming in gasps. "I'm at Enfield and West Lynn."

"What's happening, Sam?"

"I think Riker pulled a fast one. He suckered me into believing this was the finale, but it's not. There's still one more distraction. One more person I love."

"Payton." Madison's voice echoed Sam's horror. "I'm pulling up a map now."

"Never mind. I know where it is," Sam said, already turning onto Fifteenth. "Call Gabe and tell him I'm on my way."

"I've got it on the computer now. You're much closer than he is. So you'll be there first. Do you want me to call for backup?"

"Not yet. Just call Gabe. He's already on the way, and for all I know this is just another of Riker's tricks. I'll try Payton's phone, and see what's what. If I can't reach him, or if Gabe isn't there when I get there, I'll call and you can send in the troops."

"Okay, sounds like a plan. But call me the minute you know anything. And be careful."

"Will do." Sam disconnected the phone, and stepped on the accelerator, her panic dissipating with the action.

The game wasn't over until it was over. And she'd be damned if she was going to lose Payton now.

CHAPTER THIRTY-TWO

ORCHARD WAS a short little road that dead-ended into the railroad. Payton was supposed to have been able to access it from Fifth, but had somehow managed to miss the turnoff twice, finally reaching it via Walsh and Fourth.

He pulled the car to a stop, his heart pounding at the sight of the charred remains of a warehouse sitting adjacent to the tracks at the end of the street. Images of Sam trapped in a blast slammed through his brain with 3D intensity, threatening to rob him of breath.

He was out of the car in less than three seconds, running across an empty lot and into the warehouse, and then reality slammed into place. There was no sulfur in the air and no debris. Nothing to indicate a recent explosion. In addition, he'd passed no cars. No people. The warehouse was, in fact, eerily silent.

If Sam had been here, she was long gone.

Payton walked farther into the gloom of the building, searching for something to give him a clue. The floor groaned under his weight, parts of it misshapen and missing. He bent down and picked up a burnt cinder. It was cold. Damp, actually. Rotting like the floor.

Whatever had happened here, it had obviously happened a long time ago.

Something in the back of the warehouse rattled, and then was still. Payton froze, starting forward, then stopping again, his mind trying to sort through various options. Two stood out as primary candidates for the truth. Either the tip had been a bad one and there hadn't been any bomb. Or the person who'd called him—Rob Mathis—in reality had nothing whatsoever to do with Cullen Pulaski.

He remembered the private number notation on his caller ID. He'd thought at the time that it suited Cullen to have an unlisted number. But what if it had been someone else calling. What if it had been Riker?

Something moved again against the far wall, and Payton took another step forward, straining to see through the gloom. Off to his left, something shifted, rattled, and beady eyes peered at him from under a pile of burned boards.

A rat.

Apropos. If Riker had lured him here, it was obviously a diversion. Something to keep him away from Sam. Unless of course Payton was the target.

It wasn't likely. But not impossible. If Riker knew about his relationship with Sam, then he might see Payton as a rival. There was validity in that line of thinking, but Payton's gut said this was about diversion, and he'd fallen neatly into the trap. But there was no way to know for certain without talking to someone.

He flipped open his cell phone, started to turn it on, but closed it again instead, remembering Sam's warning about radio waves in Riker's workshop. No sense in taking chances.

He strode across the floor and out of the warehouse, squinting in the bright light of the sun. If there were a bomb and they were setting a perimeter, he figured he needed to be at least five hundred feet from the bomb before using his phone. The quickest way to achieve the distance and still keep the warehouse in sight was across the railroad tracks.

So he sprinted across the warehouse yard, through an open gate and across the tracks to the field on the other side. The wind had picked up, the sky turning a murky gray, the heat-laden air heavy with moisture. Thunder rolled in the distance, and if Payton had been a man of faith, he'd have taken it all as a sign.

But he was pragmatic, and his only concern at the moment was for Sam.

He pulled out the phone, and flipped it open, waiting as the device searched for service and fed into the network. Finally, the signal was established, but before he could place his call, the hollow moan of a train whistle split the silence. He looked up with a frown, the first cars of a freight train already rolling past. He'd obviously missed it coming in his haste to get far enough away from the bomb site to call.

It was moving slowly, and seemed to stretch on forever. The noise was deafening, and he immediately headed toward the far side of the field where he hoped he'd be able to hear. It was only when he had moved another twenty yards or so that he realized his access to the warehouse had also been cut off.

If he was right about either of his theories then his being cut off wouldn't matter. Sam, along with other experts, was working on a bomb somewhere else, and he was out of harm's way. But the hairs on the back of his neck refused to take comfort in the thought. He couldn't shake the feeling that something was in play. The question was, what?

Flipping open his phone again, he dialed.

J.T. SAT IN the little room in back of the warehouse watching the train go rattling by. His finger was still on the detonator. A flick of the switch and he'd have been able to take Payton out. Instead, they were separated by the rusted metal cars of a fucking freight train.

He'd watched Payton come into the building, his triumph almost complete. He waited as the man moved forward, inch by agonizing inch. Just a few feet more and it would have all gone according to plan, but then the rats had startled the prick, and his head had obviously cleared. J.T. had been counting on Reynolds's possessive nature, and his oversexed need for Samantha, to color his judgment, the hero riding to rescue the damsel in distress and all that bullshit.

Only Payton Reynolds was no hero, and Samantha was not in distress. In fact, if he had to call it, he'd say she was just now figuring out that she could use the crawl space to access the room and evacuate the children.

He'd planned it all to a T. His diversion complex enough to take time, but obvious enough for her to eventually put it all together. Too late.

Or at least that had been the plan.

He released the trigger, and slammed his hand down on the table, the violence of the action surprising him. He was not usually given to fits of anger, but he hated it when his plans went awry, and this one was turning into a comedy of errors.

And now the bastard was across the way, no doubt using his cell phone to verify the call. There was no way it could be traced, of course, he'd seen to that. And Rob Mathis really did exist. But the administrative assistant was off for the afternoon. A doctor's appointment. These people were really too damn free with information. Especially considering their boss was someone like Cullen Pulaski.

J.T. smiled. It would take at least an hour just to track the kid down and get his story, but that didn't mean that Payton would be back. He'd find out that Sam wasn't here, and if he acted true to form, he'd be off to make sure she was all right.

As if she needed his help. Anger washed through J.T. again, and he repeated his mantra under his breath, trying to find his center. Nothing was ever accomplished in the heat of anger.

Nothing.

While J.T.'d obviously predicted Reynolds's Neanderthal reaction to hearing that Sam needed him, he had also apparently underestimated the man's intelligence. The idea sat bitterly in his throat. But there was no way to avoid the truth of it. It had only taken moments for Reynolds to figure out that something was off, and he hadn't made it far enough into the warehouse for J.T. to be certain that detonation would have taken him out.

He tipped back his head, trying to figure out what to do next, calling on the gods to help him find the true path. His union with Samantha was so close he could smell it, but Reynolds seemed to present an insurmountable barrier.

He fingered the bomb's control again. He'd rigged it to a timer. Once Reynolds had been in place, J.T. had planned to detonate, the timed delay giving him the precious minutes he needed to escape.

But he'd failed. Again.

All his careful planning had come to nothing. Sam would disarm the bomb at the day care, and Payton would be there to hold her in his arms. The train rattled by, the cars still stretching back as far as J.T. could see.

His vision ran red, his mind filled with images of Payton and Sam—naked, writhing. It wasn't fair. She belonged to him. The gods had deemed it so. Fate had foretold it. And he was following the path that would bring it all to fruition. He had done his part, and still he had failed, thus making a mockery of all that he believed.

A sound in the warehouse caught his attention. A voice he recognized. Chills raced down his spine, and he sent a prayer winging off to the east.

Samantha was here.

Fate had spoken.

His pride had gotten in his way, his need to destroy Payton interfering with the divinity of their joining, the simple beauty of his plan. This, then, was the truth. The real path. The fates after all had been kind. They had delivered her to him.

And even better, Payton Reynolds would be forced to watch.

With a smile, J.T. reached out, setting eternity in motion with the flick of a finger.

SAM STOOD in the middle of the warehouse, calling Payton's name. His car was outside, so she knew he had to be somewhere in the vicinity of the building. He had to be. The alternative was something she couldn't contemplate.

The warehouse shook with the sound of the train rumbling past, and she turned slowly, her eyes darting around the burned-out building, searching every shadow for some sign of Payton. She'd tried his cell phone on the way over, but she'd been switched immediately to voice mail, which meant his phone wasn't on.

When she'd arrived, she'd called Madison as promised and requested backup. Gabe should be arriving any minute, and Nigel and the others were no doubt on the way. If she'd been playing it by the book, she would still be waiting in her car, but she wasn't used to sitting on the sidelines. So she'd waited all of about two minutes and then headed in here, certain that Payton was in trouble, that Riker had done something to him. But there was nothing here.

The warehouse was empty. There was no sign of Payton or Riker. Her heart stuttered at the thought that perhaps Riker had taken him somewhere, but then she rejected the idea. Payton wasn't the type of man to go without a struggle and there was no sign of it here. Besides, Madison had said Riker liked to attack from a distance.

She turned to go, thinking that she'd try and call again. She'd left her cell phone in the car. So maybe it was providential. She'd wait for the team to arrive, and in the meantime hopefully get through to Payton.

"It's too late now to leave."

She pivoted at the sound of the voice, her gaze locking with a lanky man standing a foot or so away, the light from the window bouncing off the gun in his hand.

"Riker." He was taller than he looked in his pictures, but the rest of the features were the same. The sunken eyes, the sallow skin and the receding hairline.

"You don't remember me." His tone was flat, with maybe a hint of disappointment.

"No. At least not beyond what I've learned about you in the past few days. I did know you. In Abilene, right?" she asked, playing for time. She didn't think he'd shoot her, but she didn't want to take the chance. "My memory is hazy."

The train whistle blew again, the sound farther away. Sam could still hear cars passing outside, but the noise had changed, lighter somehow, the end of train approaching.

"I remember *you*," Riker said, his mouth softening, as his gaze devoured her. "I've followed every moment of your career. Every triumph. Every failure."

She thought of the photographs in his workshop and shuddered. "You've been stalking me."

"How can you possibly think something like that?" he snapped, his anger apparent. "I've a right to your life, just as you have a right to mine. We are part of the same whole, Samantha. Surely you can see that. After everything that has happened between us."

"Nothing has happened, Riker. It's all in your head."

"No. It's here." He pounded his heart. "It's real. You just can't see it. Your lust for Reynolds is clouding your vision."

"What have you done with Payton?" She bit out the words, her own anger matching his.

"Nothing. Not for lack of trying I might add." His smile broadened. "But in the end he provided us with the perfect ending."

"What the hell are you talking about?" She backed up a

step, holding her hands up, trying to figure out the best way to make a break for it.

Riker shot, the bullet hitting her in the thigh, pain shooting like wildfire through her leg. Sam hit the ground, fighting for breath.

"I told you it was too late to leave." He moved closer, kneeling beside her, a flash of regret crossing his face. "I didn't want to hurt you. But you don't have to worry. It'll all be over soon."

He reached out to stroke her hair, and she batted his hand away. "What do mean by that?" Even before she finished the words, she suspected the truth. Riker wouldn't use the gun to kill her. He didn't have to.

He smiled, rocking back onto his haunches, the gun still in his hand, but his finger slack on the trigger. "By my count we have about sixty seconds, and then we will be joined for all time."

"So that's what this has all been about. Some sick kind of sexual fantasy?"

"Of course not." Riker's eyes widened in horror. "The connection between us is far greater than anything physical pleasure can provide. It's spiritual. I am you and you are me. One infinite circle. You are yin to my yang. Can't you see, Samantha? We have no need of anything more than each other."

"If you're part of me, my other half, then how can you even contemplate killing me?" She spoke before she had time to think, her mind busy with a mental countdown, but she forced herself to focus as Riker's face changed from one of certainty to one of doubt.

"It won't hurt." It was poor comfort and he knew it, his eyes searching her face, his frown indicating her words were something he'd never considered.

"It doesn't matter though, does it? You'll still have killed me."

The gun dropped, and Sam scooted away using her good

foot to propel her along. She'd made it about four feet when he caught up to her. "The bomb will only set us free. Allow us to unite in fire as one."

"The bomb will destroy us." She continued to move toward the open doorway, the distance to safety still seeming miles away.

He moved along beside her, making no move to stop her, his brow crumpled in contemplation. "But in destroying we will be released."

"I don't know where you're getting all of this, Riker. But if the bomb goes off we'll be dead. Finished. Kaput. Nothing more. I repeat—you will have killed me."

His expression had changed to one of confusion. "You're wrong. You just don't believe."

"There's nothing to believe in, Riker. You've based your fantasy on delusion." Now there was an understatement. "Stop the bomb." She continued to crawl, knowing that she'd never make it in time.

"I can't," he whispered, his eyes reflecting the truth of his words.

She tried to force her muscles to respond, to convince her leg to move and support her, but to no avail, she couldn't even feel it, let alone use it. "Then we're going to die."

Everything after that happened in a blur. She heard Riker yelling "No!" and felt the weight of his body as it hit hers, the sound of the blast reaching her before the floor shimmied with the resulting force.

Something splintered and it felt as if the floor had broken away, and she was falling—floating free—Riker's body ripping away. She could see his face. See the horror in his eyes.

And then there was nothing but pain and fire and smoke, and as the blackness came rushing up to meet her—her thoughts reached out to Payton one last time, praying that he knew how much she loved him.

CHAPTER THIRTY-THREE

THE LAST TRAIN CAR passed the warehouse, just as the building blew sky-high. Payton could feel the heat of the blast from where he stood, his eyes locked not on the building, but on Sam's SUV. He was in motion before his brain even had time to click into gear, his heart hammering not from exertion but from absolute fear.

Riker had played his last card, and it seemed that Payton had managed to fail Sam in the same way he'd failed Keith, allowing her to fall into a trap that had no doubt been intended for him. He'd talked to Madison, who'd explained about the setup, telling him that Sam was en route.

Obviously, she'd already arrived.

He reached the entrance to the warehouse, timber blazing all around him, bits of debris still hurtling from the sky. There was no way anyone could have survived the blast, but he had to know for certain. He started in, but was stopped when an arm wrapped around him, the steely grip preventing forward motion.

"You can't go in there." Gabe's voice sounded as tormented as Payton felt, and he whirled to face his friend.

"Was she in there?"

Gabe shook his head. "I don't know. I got here just after it blew. I didn't see her. But there's nobody here, so I'm guessing…" He trailed off, his eyes dark with anguish.

"No." Payton spit the word out, breaking Gabe's hold, dashing into the burning building before his friend could stop him. The air inside was thick with acrid smoke, and he pulled his shirt over his face to help him breathe.

It was hard to see. Even with the roof gone the smoke obscured the light, and Payton bent low in an attempt to escape the worst of it. A splintered beam from the ceiling broke free and fell, raining hot embers as it tumbled through the air. Payton twisted to the left, managing to miss the wood as it crashed to the floor.

"Sam?" His voice seemed unusually loud after the roar of the explosion. The sound of falling debris was muffled by a thick layer of dust, and he waited, forcing himself to breathe slowly and listen.

"If she was in here, she's dead, Payton." Gabe had materialized at his side again.

As if in testament to his words Payton stumbled over something, his eyes riveted to the charred remains of what was clearly a body. His stomach clenched, bile burning his throat, and automatically he steeled himself for the worst.

Gabe stepped around him, blocking his view. "Let me do it."

Payton managed to nod, his throat so tight it was impossible to breathe. He wasn't a devout man by any standard, but he sent up a prayer anyway.

Please, please, please don't let it be Sam.

Gabe rolled the body over, shaking his head. "I can't ID it. The face is gone. But it's definitely a male."

Air rushed into Payton's lungs and he breathed again. "Sam," he screamed. She had to be here. Had to be alive. There was no way this could happen again. Not again.

He rushed forward, searching through the smoke and burning debris. Looking for something, anything to indicate where she might be. "Sam? Can you hear me?"

The smoke was beginning to clear a little, and Payton could see Gabe on the opposite side of the blast, searching among the rubble. Their gazes met across the room, and Gabe shook his head.

Nothing.

"Sam? It's Payton. Sweetheart, I need to know where you are." He waited, listening.

Please, God, he prayed again, his cynical heart breaking. *Please.*

And then he heard it. A tiny whimper. So soft he thought, at first, that he might have imagined it. But it came again. Behind him, near where the other body lay.

"Sam?" he yelled, motioning for Gabe to be quiet. "Where are you?"

The whimper came again, this time a little louder, accompanied by a banging noise.

"Did you hear that?" Payton asked Gabe, not quite daring to hope.

His friend nodded, and the two of them followed the direction of the noise, stopping when they reached a gaping hole in the floor.

"Sam?" Payton dropped to his knees, searching the darkness for some sign of life. "Are you down there?"

"Here, Payton." The words were weak, barely more than a whisper. "I'm here." A shadow moved in the darkness. "Stuck."

"I'll get help," Gabe said. "There should be rope and a flashlight in Sam's SUV." He sprinted away, smoke and dust still swirling.

"Sam?" Payton called, almost afraid to hope. "Gabe's gone for help. We'll have you out of there in no time. You've just got to hang on. All right, sweetheart? Just hang on."

He waited for an answer, but everything had gone quiet, the only sound now the frantic beating of his heart. He fought the urge to plunge into the darkness after her, breaking a leg wasn't going to help either of them. "I'm still here, Sam. I'm still here," he crooned, not sure if he was trying to soothe her or himself. Not really caring.

Gabe was back in record time, Nigel and Harrison behind

him. Payton didn't even bother to ask how they knew to come. He was just grateful to have his friends there to help him. He grabbed the flashlight from Gabe, and let the light play over the collapsed floor and the basement below. There was debris everywhere, and at first he couldn't find her, but then the light caught the gleam of her hair.

Sam.

Grabbing the end of the rope Gabe and Nigel had secured, he lowered himself into the hole, the flashlight hooked to his belt. He hit the ground with a thud, and made his way across the debris pile with adrenaline-injected speed, throwing the splintered and burning beams and boards out of his way.

Finally he reached her, his heart twisting at the blood on her cheeks and chest. A large chunk of rebar-encrusted cement lay across her legs, a blackened beam beside her acting as a buffer to keep the broken piece of support column from crushing her.

"Sam, sweetheart, can you hear me?" He knelt beside her, brushing debris from her face with gentle fingers.

Her eyes fluttered open, and he could see the spark of joy. "Payton," she whispered.

"Can you move?" He already thought he knew the answer, but he was having trouble finding words, his only thought to get her the hell out of harm's way.

She shook her head. "Took a bullet in my leg. Lost a lot of blood." She spoke slowly, each word an obvious effort, and his concern deepened. "Something's on top of me."

"You're caught between the girder above you, tumbled stones from the wall, and a beam."

She nodded her understanding. "What about Riker?"

"He's dead, Sam. His body is upstairs." There was of course no proof of the fact, but Payton was pretty damn sure, and she needed to believe the bastard was dead.

"Good." The word was little more than a breath of air, but he heard her.

"I'm going to need help to get you out. Can you hang on until I get back?"

"Hurry," she said with a brief nod, her determination evident even in the shadows.

"Sam." He leaned close, his gaze locking with hers. "I love you. And I'm not going to lose you now. Okay?"

She nodded again, her smile weak but genuine. "Love you, too." Her eyes fluttered shut, but her chest was still moving.

Payton moved back to the opening above, calling up to Gabe, then waited for his friends to haul him up.

"She's stuck between chunks of debris, the biggest pieces a stone girder and a fractured beam. It's like a Chinese puzzle, each piece supporting the other. We move one, and the others are going to fall." He didn't finish the thought, but it was clear his friends got the picture.

"We could wait for the paramedics. They're on the way," Nigel offered, not looking as if he really endorsed the idea.

"No time. The bastard shot her in the leg. She said she's losing blood, and I think she's already going into shock."

"All right then, we go down," Harrison said, leaving no room for discussion. Gabe and Nigel nodded their agreement.

Ten minutes later, they were all in the hole, a variety of makeshift tools accompanying them.

"She's out cold," Payton said, his fingers reassuring him that Sam's heart was still pumping.

"Probably for the best," Nigel said, squatting down to examine the debris trapping her. "The more of this she can forget, the better."

Nigel was right, of course, but her deathly stillness, coupled with the garish crimson of her blood frightened Payton more than he wanted to admit, and all he was seeing was the result of a gash on her head. It was hard to even contemplate what might be happening beneath the broken girder.

"I think if we can lever the beam up at this end," Harrison was saying, his eyes narrowed in concentration, "then we should be able to slide her out without shifting the girder. But it's going to be really heavy, so we'll have to move fast."

Gabe held up a crowbar. "I found this in the car. Think it will be strong enough?"

Harrison nodded. "If we combine it with this piece of rebar." He held up a long length of metal.

"You really think it will work?" Nigel asked, shooting a doubtful glance at the chunk of girder.

"It has to," Payton spat, not even considering the alternative.

"It's all about the fulcrum," Harrison said, ignoring Payton's outburst. "I think we can do it."

The building groaned as the debris settled, and a huge chunk of flooring broke free and fell to the basement floor, the pieces splintering like shrapnel. Harrison ducked, just missing the sharp edge of one flying missile.

"If we're going to do it, I say we hurry," Gabe said. "This place is ready to come down any minute."

"All right," Payton said, taking charge, focusing his mind on the task at hand, for the moment shutting out his fears. "Gabe, you and Harrison work the levers and then Nigel and I will pull her out."

Harrison and Gabe moved quickly into place, Gabe shifting slightly on Harrison's instructions. Nigel and Payton bent down to each slide their hands under Sam's arms.

"On my count," Harrison said. "Wait for the lift, Payton. One, two, *three.*"

The beam groaned as it was forced upward, its massive weight moving the cement above it fractionally. It was enough. They pulled Sam free, sliding her along the floor until she was clear of the beam and girder.

The minute she was out of the way, Gabe and Harrison released the crow bar and rebar, the beam dropping heavily back to the ground. There was a moment of silence and then the weight of the girder finally took over, splitting the beam in two, the cement hitting the floor in a cloud of dust.

Payton covered her as best he could, waiting for the dust to clear, then sat back to visually assess her wounds. The gash to her head had clotted, the worst of the damage above her hairline. It was already turning a mottled shade of purple, as were several places on her arms and chest. Nothing seemed to be broken, though. Her pants were torn and soaked with blood about eight inches above her knee.

"That's the gunshot wound," Payton said to no one in particular.

Gabe was shinnying up the rope to check on the emergency personnel while Harrison and Nigel huddled close to help in any way they could.

Payton carefully pulled back the torn pieces of her jeans, baring the wound, his breath escaping on a hiss at the sight of her torn flesh, and the pulsing blood bubbling up from the bullet hole.

Reacting on instinct, he pressed two fingers against the wound, trying to manually stanch the flow of blood, his heart pounding in time to the pulsing of her artery. "We've got to tie this thing off quickly or she's going to bleed to death."

"One step ahead of you," Nigel said. He had pulled off his shirt and ripped it into ragged strips. Balling three of them together, he handed the field dressing to Payton, who pressed the material against Sam's wound. Harrison then bent and wound two strips of Nigel's shirt around the balled material and Sam's thigh, creating a makeshift pressure bandage. Nigel then tied a third strip of cotton above the wound, forming a tourniquet.

"That should hold her for a little while. But her pulse is really sketchy," Nigel said, his face creased with worry. "I think you're right, she's going into shock."

"Where the hell are the paramedics?" Payton yelled, anxiety mixing with frustration and impotency.

"They're here," Gabe called from the opening in the floor.

"They've rigged a pulley system and are sending the stretcher down now."

Harrison made his way over to the hole and helped guide the stretcher to the floor, an EMT sliding down the rope at the same time. When they'd both hit bottom, the EMT and Harrison carried the stretcher over to Sam.

Payton held her hand, whispering nonsensical words of love, willing her to be strong—to live. "Hang in there, sweetheart. We've come too far to let Riker beat us now."

Her eyelids fluttered in response, and he thought that maybe she'd tightened her fingers around his, but then it was time for her to go, and the stretcher was up and away.

Payton stood at the bottom of the rope, looking upward, knowing that his entire life was on that stretcher. That she was all he'd ever wanted. That nothing, not the horror of his past, the uncertainty of the present or his fear of the future could be allowed to stand in their way.

She had to live.

Otherwise it had all been for nothing. And he couldn't believe God could possibly be that callous.

THE HOSPITAL WAS COLD and smelled of antiseptic and illness, the scents blending together into a bittersweet stench that left Payton feeling empty inside. He'd given up pacing an hour ago, sitting now in the waiting room chair, his head buried in his hands.

Sam had been in surgery for almost two hours, the surgeons trying to repair the damage to her artery. She had come close to bleeding to death, but thanks to Nigel's field dressing, and the quick work of the paramedics they'd been able to stabilize her for the ride to the hospital. But she was weak and in shock, and still bleeding. The doctor hadn't minced words, the odds weren't good.

"She's a fighter, Payton." Madison patted his shoulder, as usual reading his mind.

"I know." He nodded. "It's just been so long."

"It's complicated surgery," Harrison said, his shirt still streaked with Sam's blood. "But the prognosis is good. Think of all that they're doing with vascular surgery these days."

Payton nodded, as if he understood, which of course he didn't. Or maybe it was just that he wasn't capable of taking anything in at the moment. He'd replayed the scene at the warehouse over and over in his mind, trying to find a way he could have prevented it all from happening.

But there was simply no way he could have predicted what happened.

"There's no point in blaming yourself," Nigel said. It seemed everyone was a mind reader. "What happened, happened. What's important now is the future."

"If there is a future," Payton said, immediately regretting the words, as if his doubt had the power to hurt Sam.

"Mr. Reynolds?"

Payton jerked his head up, rising from the chair to face the blood-spattered surgeon. "Is she... I mean..." Madison's hand slipped into his, and he held on for dear life.

"She came through the surgery with flying colors." The man smiled, his eyes tired. "The bullet shredded the artery, but we managed to repair it. She's lost a lot of blood and been through quite an ordeal, but with proper care, I don't anticipate any problems."

"Is she awake?" Payton asked, his heart pounding in his ears, his relief making him lightheaded.

"Yes. She's groggy, but she's asking for you."

He shook the surgeon's hand, and then hugged everyone within reach. Tears blinded him as he followed the nurse down the hall to Sam's room, his mind chanting *thank you* over and over again.

He pushed open the door, then stood hesitating in the entrance. She looked so tiny against the stark white of the hospital sheets. Blood dripped from a bag down a tube connected to her wrist, and another with clear fluids attached somewhere along the way.

Her head was wrapped in gauze, and her leg was elevated in a sling, the bandage around her thigh thick and uncomfortable-looking. He took a step back, suddenly not certain what he wanted to say. Afraid that she'd blame him for letting her down.

"Payton." She turned her head, her blue eyes open, her lips curving upward into a smile. She held out her hand and he crossed the room, kneeling beside her, closing his fingers around hers.

"I was so scared." The words came of their own volition. "I thought I'd lost you." He laid his forehead against the edge of the bed, fighting to control his emotions.

"Not a chance," she said, her hand stroking his hair. "You told me to hang on, and so I did. Besides, unless I was hallucinating, you told me you loved me. I wasn't about to check out after that."

He lifted his head, his gaze meeting hers, the love reflected there humbling. "I do love you."

Her smile broadened, a hint of mischief shining through, her fingers tightening around his. "Well then, what do you say we spend the next sixty years or so finding out just how much?"

EPILOGUE

"WE'VE ALL GOT TO STOP meeting like this." Nigel stood in the hospital room doorway holding a huge stuffed panda, the bear almost bigger than Nigel. Harrison shifted over to allow room for the latest arrival, which wasn't easy when one considered the number of plants and balloons and flowers that filled the room.

Sam sat on Payton's lap, the cane lying against the wall the only remaining physical reminder of the ordeal James Riker had put them through. In another couple of months she wouldn't even need that.

"Glad you could make it," Gabe said from his permanent perch at the head of the bed. Madison was propped up against the pillows, looking impossibly put together for a woman who'd just gone through eighteen hours of labor.

"Wouldn't have missed it for the world." Nigel put the bear on the floor next to a giraffe of equal stature, Harrison's gift. Next to the giraffe was a lion—Payton's contribution. Andrea Roarke was going to have a menagerie before they were done. Her father's friends all seemed to have a penchant for stuffed animals of gargantuan proportion.

Baby Andrea cooed contentedly against her mother's breast, and Gabe reached over to pick up his daughter, his big hands dwarfing her. "Want to hold her?"

Nigel frowned at the baby, as if unsure exactly what to do, but then held out his hands palms up, as if he were forming a shelf for her to lie on.

"She's not going to break, Nigel," Madison said with a sleepy smile. "Just pick her up."

Nigel shot Payton a bail-me-out-of-this look, but Payton just smiled and shrugged. "You might as well get used to it. Madison's already told me we're all on deck for babysitting."

"Or maybe the two of you could work on a playmate?" Madison raised her eyebrows in speculation, and of course everyone in the room turned to look at them. Except Nigel, who was totally captivated by the baby in his arms.

"I only just got back on my feet again," Sam protested, feeling her face go hot. "We haven't even had a honeymoon yet."

"Well it's something to think about." Her new husband's arms tightened around her, and the kiss he dropped on her neck was far from platonic. "And you know what they say?" His breath caressed the soft skin of her neck, and her cheeks grew even hotter.

"Practice makes perfect?" Nigel was back with the program, little Andrea still cradled in his arms.

Laughter filled the room, and Sam sat back, letting the sound fill her with happiness. Life was good. She'd hit the jackpot, actually. Riker hadn't meant for it to turn out the way it had, but he'd been right about one thing.

There was joy in unity. Hers and Payton's.

And in some perverse way, she'd always owe a part of that joy to James Riker and his insanity.

She settled back against her husband, relishing the feel of his chest rising and falling against her back. Life was for cherishing. And now that she and Payton had gotten a second chance, she wasn't about to waste a minute of it.

"I'm thinking maybe we should all try for a vacation in the tropics. Somewhere with white beaches and mai tais," Nigel was saying. "We deserve a celebration."

"Well, I'd hold that thought if I were you." Cullen stood in the doorway holding a stuffed gorilla a head and a half taller than the giraffe.

"Oh, great," Harrison groaned. "Don't tell me, there's a plot against the president and he just can't make it through the day without our help."

"Actually, it's NORAD. They seem to have misplaced some missiles, and well—" Cullen shrugged, his expression faintly apologetic "—someone's got to find them."

*Turn the page for a look at Dee Davis's next
heart-stopping romantic thriller
EXPOSURE*

coming from HQN Books in September 2005

"I NEED MORE EXPRESSION. Something that makes it look as though you're enjoying your work." Melissa Pope adjusted her camera lens, the shot going wide over the woman's shoulder, focusing on the charts on the far wall.

The UN logistics officer beamed for the camera, her smile luminous. The photograph would have been wonderful, except that Melissa had gotten the shot she needed a half hour ago, and was now concentrating on the more inanimate parts of the office.

The last of the autumn sun beamed through windows of the United Nations Secretariat, the glistening East River rolling placidly by. Each office here was very much like the next, cubicles and tiny offices fronted with metal dividers and standard-issue 1950s furniture. The only thing that seemed to have changed from Cary Grant's *North by Northwest* days was the addition of computer equipment—in this case, a state of the art think pad with a 17-inch flat screen monitor. Obviously the IT department was intent on dragging the UN into the new millennium despite the dismal decor.

What Melissa needed was five minutes alone with the computer. But that wasn't going to be easy with this woman. Despite her glowing smile, she was, in fact, quite territorial. Every time Melissa moved too close to the desk or the information tacked on the walls behind it, Idina Meloski shot her "the look."

Of course the camera lens was impervious to that sort of

thing, but it also wasn't able to turn on a computer and search through the files. What Melissa needed was a diversion. She scanned the office looking for coffee or water and found no beverages of any kind. Not even a cup. It wasn't exactly Sydney Bristow, but she had a hunch it would work.

Sucking in a breath, she began to cough, pulling all the way from her diaphragm for effect. Bending over for theatrical impact, she shot a look at the woman through her hair. Idina had risen to her feet, her eyebrows raised in alarm.

"Miss Pope, are you all right?"

Melissa nodded, but continued to cough, straightening enough to hold out a hand gesturing that she needed water.

Idina swallowed the whole act, rushing from the office with the assurance that she'd be right back. Hopefully, it would take a little while to find a cup and water. Hopefully.

Melissa moved quickly around the desk to the computer, tapping instructions to bring up the woman's data directory. She'd already learned that most UN staff logged on to their computers first thing in the morning and stayed connected for the rest of the day, which meant that daytime was her best chance for access, averting the need to secure passwords or try to end-run past them.

Unfortunately, Idina's files looked pretty pedestrian. Not that she expected the woman to have labeled something *Subversive Efforts to Undermine the UN*. Still, there could be a clue, it was just a matter of finding it. With a couple of keystrokes she changed directories, again with nothing interesting to report. Standard requisition forms, labeled sequentially, and a bunch of letters applying for various other UN positions. Apparently Idina wasn't all that satisfied with her job.

Popping a CD into the appropriate drive, Melissa ordered the computer to copy a series of files relating to Idina's most recent operations, just in case there was a pattern here she was missing. If nothing else she could compare it to similar files of other UN employees with the means to be a part of the smuggling operation.

While the files were copying, she entered a code her handler had given her, the miniprogram designed to find and open any encrypted files, but the resulting search came up empty. If Idina was working with terrorists, she certainly hadn't left a paper trail. Not that Melissa had really expected to find anything.

Although Idina's job as a junior logistics officer for UN Peacekeeping Operations gave her the necessary access to information that could be useful in the illegal transport of arms and munitions, she really didn't fit the profile of a woman on the take. And more importantly, she didn't have the necessary skills to pull off a scam of this magnitude.

But Melissa had learned the hard way that acting on assumption alone was never enough in this business. It was the kind of mistake that could get a girl killed actually, so she ran the program again, just to be certain. No hidden files. No secrets stashed handily on the office computer. Which meant either Idina was smarter than she looked, or she wasn't the one.

Melissa was betting on the latter.

Grabbing the CD, she slipped it into her pocket and was just rounding the desk summoning up a renewed chorus of coughing when Idina returned, water glass in hand, Alexi Kirov, her boss, following right on her heels.

If Idina was territorial, Alexi was expansive. He'd practically given her the key to the proverbial front door. Partly, she suspected, because he didn't seem to care a whole lot about his job. Despite the fact that he was senior staff, his motivation for excellence had been left behind in his native Russia. Still, he was on the list, and sooner or later she intended to have a look at his files as well.

Right now, however, she needed to do her best Camille. Coughing to beat the band, she took the water, and gulped it, gasping for breath in a way she hoped signaled the choking was at an end. "Thank you," she panted. "I'm not sure what happened. Something going down the wrong way, I guess."

Idina fluttered around her, patting her back and mumbling what sounded a hell of a lot like Czech endearments. Melissa choked down some more water, and lifted her gaze to meet Alexi's. As always, it was difficult to read his expression. Amusement surely, but just for a moment she thought she saw something else in his eyes.

Melissa shook her head, and smiled, patting the still flustered Idina. "I'm fine now. Honestly. Sorry to have frightened you."

"Maybe you'd better call it a day." Alexi was still watching under hooded eyes.

"I can't." Melissa shook her head, patting her camera. "Deadlines. There are proof sheets to go over, film to develop and I'd still like to get a few more shots before this light is gone." She waved absently at the window, wondering what in hell had made her think this assignment would be less stressful than her usual fare. Give her a war zone any day. At least there, you were dodging bullets not people.

"Surely you're allowed to take a break now and then?" Alexi sounded just a bit too interested for Melissa's taste, but she'd learned a long time ago never to say never when opportunity presented itself.

"Now and then," she grudgingly admitted. "In fact, tonight I'm actually attending a party as a guest and not a photographer."

"What kind of party?" Idina asked, her mask of composure firmly back in place.

"It's in honor of the Swiss delegation. I'm going as a guest of my brother-in-law."

"Your brother-in-law?" Alexi asked, one eyebrow raising with curiosity.

"Yes, he's with the diplomatic corps. Assigned to Brazil at the moment, but he and my sister are here on leave."

"Not much of a vacation," Alexi snorted. "The Swiss minister is a noted bore."

"So tell me what you really think." The words were out before she realized what she'd said. Europeans, especially eastern ones, were often slow to get American humor, and she usually tried to refrain from making flippant comments in case she was misunderstood.

She need not have worried with Alexi, though. His laughter erupted in full force. "I'm sorry, I spoke out of turn, but then that is, how do you say, par for the course for me."

"Well done." Obviously Alexi had a solid grasp on American slang. Part and parcel of a permanent assignment to New York no doubt. "Anyway, regardless of the host's personality flaws, it'll be nice to leave the camera at home for once."

"And I'm sure you'll clean up beautifully." Again with the innuendo, and this time there was no mistaking the appreciative glint in Alexi's eyes.

Idina made a noise somewhere between a snort and a harrumph, making a play of moving the stacks of paper on her desk, her expression even more forbidding than usual. Melissa toyed with the idea that the woman was jealous, and then dismissed it. Idina wasn't the jealous type. And especially over Alexi Kirov. There was certainly still no love lost between the Czech Republic and the remnants of the Soviet Union. So despite the fact that he was good looking in a blond and blue-eyed kind of way, Melissa doubted Idina was pining away for him.

Anyway he had a weak chin and his handshake was a lot like a limp noodle. Not that a handshake was the be-all and end-all of a man, but it was a good indication of where he was coming from. And besides, Idina probably had the handshake of a national league linebacker.

Shaking her head at her own folly, Melissa drank the last of her water, and handed the glass back to Idina. "Let me just get a last shot of you at your desk, and then I really ought to be going." After all, there was a CD burning a hole in her pocket, and the longer she stood there chatting, the more likely it was she'd be discovered.

She'd been doing this kind of thing for a long time, but sometimes she wondered how the hell anyone in the Company ever managed to take themselves seriously. Clandestine work was fodder for situation comedy, *Get Smart* being a lot closer to the truth than some of the more frightening flicks people thought of as tributes to the kind of work she did.

"Will you be back tomorrow?" Idina asked with about as much enthusiasm as if Melissa were a dentist holding a drill. Melissa clicked the shutter and lowered her camera.

"No." She shook her head for emphasis, and the other woman immediately relaxed. "I think I've got everything I need from you. I might be back in a week or so for reshoots. But in the meanwhile, Alexi, I do still need to get some shots of you."

The Russian smiled, the gesture transforming his expression into something that bordered on charm, but then he frowned, and looked down at his watch. "I'm swamped with detail work at the moment, everything due at once. So I'll have to check my calendar and then get back to you." She waited for him to click his heels and bow, but instead he tipped his head, his expression quizzical. "Why don't I phone you and we'll set a time?"

"Of course," she said. "I certainly don't want to do anything to interrupt your schedule. I can always shoot background rolls in the meantime."

"Wonderful." He seemed distracted now, as if his mind had preceded him from the room. "We'll talk tomorrow."

"Absolutely." She nodded, shivering as his chilly gaze swept over her one last time. Maybe she'd been too flip earlier in dismissing the dangers of her job. Fingering the CD in her pocket, she nodded goodbye to Idina, and turned to go, suddenly wanting nothing more than to get the hell out of Dodge.

"LOOK WHAT THE CAT dragged in." Madison Roarke warmly embraced first Ryan and then Payton. Madison was a new mother, a profiler with the FBI and the wife of Nigel's friend Gabe. All three were difficult roles, but together they probably qualified Madison for sainthood.

"How's the baby?" The last time Nigel had seen Andrea Roarke she was about three months old, chubby, cheerful and very fond of tugging on his mustache.

"Not so much a baby anymore. She's pulling up, and crawling everywhere in sight. And Gabriel swears she said *daddy*. Although I'm pretty sure it was only a burp." Madison's smile was beautifully maternal, and Nigel felt an absurd sense of longing. Fortunately, it never lasted long.

"How was the flight in?" she asked.

"Bumpy." Nigel hated flying and Cullen's private jet only made it slightly more palatable. "But as usual Cullen's accommodations were top-notch."

At the mention of his name, Cullen Pulaski looked up from the document he was examining and smiled at the assembled company. "Nice to all be together again."

Cullen was a king-maker of sorts, the kind of man who stayed behind the scenes but still managed to control almost everything he touched. Last Chance was no exception. His idea from conception, he left the dirty work to the team, but was always there for moral support and to provide an endless bankroll, which helped immeasurably when it came to cutting corners and actually getting things done.

"Almost all," Harrison Blake corrected, getting up from his laptop. Harrison was a genius when it came to bits and bytes, his ability to manipulate a computer taking on more legendary proportions with each operation. He'd never met a puzzle he couldn't solve, and his tenacity had bailed them out on more than one occasion. "Gabe's flying in later today, and Sam's tied up with a case and won't be in for a day or so."

Payton groaned at this last bit of news. For all practical purposes he was still a newlywed, but between his wife's job as an ATF explosives officer, and his work for the CIA, the two of them were often separated for long stretches at a time, making Last Chance operations that much more attractive for both of them.

"Well, since we've got a majority, why don't I go ahead and fill you in on what we know? Payton, you and Madison can brief your spouses when they arrive."

Payton nodded, his expression as guarded as usual, his scar shining white in the fluorescent light.

"Works for me," Madison agreed.

Cullen laid down the sheaf of papers he was holding and crossed his arms. "We don't know nearly enough. Four days ago three canisters of R-VX were stolen from the storage facility in Shchuch'ye, Russia."

"R-VX?" Madison queried.

"Nerve agent." Payton's tone was grim. "One of the most deadly. VX can kill within minutes if inhaled or deposited on the skin."

"It was accidentally released in Utah in 1968, killing thousands of sheep, some of them as far as forty miles from where the gas escaped," Cullen said. "Imagine what that would mean in a crowded city."

"And worse still, it contaminates everything it touches, and remains dangerous for several days," Nigel added. "It was created by British scientists in the '50s. The only verified sources for its existence today are in the U.S. and Russia."

"The R in R-VX is for the Russian variety, I take it." Harrison was already typing the name into his computer.

"Exactly. The chemical makeup is apparently somewhat different—" Cullen leaned forward, his palms pressed to the table "—but the effect is every bit as deadly."

"So why is it still in existence?" Madison asked. "I thought there were agreements to get rid of the stuff."

"There are," Cullen said. "But unfortunately chemical

weapons aren't easy to destroy safely. And it can be quite costly. The deadline for destroying stockpiles is 2007, but there's little likelihood that either side will be able to meet that date."

"Which means that places like Shchuch'ye serve as one-stop shopping for terrorists." Payton's voice was filled with contempt. "The place is practically falling down, and the binary weapons are just lying on shelves waiting for someone to come along and pick them up."

"You've been there?" Cullen queried, his eyes sparkling with interest.

"Once." As usual, Payton chose not to elaborate. Not that Nigel doubted him. He'd never been to Shchuch'ye but he'd seen similar storage facilities.

"But surely there's security?" Harrison frowned.

"Not much," Nigel answered. "The truth of the matter is that the new Russia simply doesn't have the money or personnel to deal with Soviet stockpiles, whether we're talking about conventional weaponry or chemical and biological ones."

"So someone just walked into the facility at Shchuch'ye and helped themselves?" Harrison had stopped typing, his brows drawn together in frustration.

"More or less," Cullen agreed. "They had help. A man named Yuri Dynkin. He'd worked as a guard at the facility months earlier, and was fired for insubordination of some kind. Apparently, the man held a grudge."

"Or was looking to make a quick buck," Payton said, ever the pessimist.

"I'm afraid we'll never know for certain. Dynkin was killed on-site. A bullet in the back."

"From which side?" Nigel quipped. "Not that it matters."

"No way to know." Cullen shrugged. "And unfortunately the rest of the party got away, along with three canisters of R-VX."

"Just the nerve agent?" Payton asked, his eyes narrowing in thought.

"No." Cullen shook his head. "The canisters are actually binary warheads."

"I'm not sure I'm following." Madison leaned forward, elbows propped on the table.

"Basically the warhead acts as a chemical reactor," Nigel explained. "Two substances are stored inside separate containers. When the thing is detonated the wall between the two canisters collapses and substances mix and the nerve agent is formed."

"So all someone has to do is shoot the thing?" Harrison asked.

"Or blow it up. There are really any number of ways it can be used." Nigel sighed, the reality of the situation beginning to sink in. "Do we have any idea who took it?"

"No," Cullen said, tipping back his head and rolling his shoulders. "No particular group has claimed credit. But they had help from the Kurds, so we're guessing Islamic extremists. And the chatter internationally seems to support the idea."

"So why were we called in?" Madison asked. "Surely there are international groups more equipped to handle something like this?"

"There are." Cullen nodded to emphasize the point. "But despite the fact that no one is claiming responsibility, we've got very credible intel that the stolen R-VX is headed for the U.S. Most probably here in New York. We believe the canisters are being routed through the Black Sea. I've got sources trying to confirm the fact now. But if we're right about the U.S. being the target, then we've got to move fast."

"It'll be like finding a bloody needle in a haystack." Nigel's frustration was echoed on the other team members' faces.

"Maybe not quite that bad." Cullen actually smiled. "The CIA has an ongoing covert investigation into the possibility that someone at the UN, specifically someone working for the UN Peacekeeping Operations, has been using peacekeeping transports to smuggle weapons and other illegal goods."

"Do they have proof?"

"Nothing verifiable, of course, or they'd have taken action. But I'm told they're getting close. They have someone working on the inside now. And I've arranged a meet. Her position is, as you can imagine, very vulnerable. So there's no way to just call her in. But her handler has arranged for one of you to connect at a diplomatic party."

"So who's going?" Harrison asked, looking like he'd rather eat nails than attend. Not that Nigel felt all that differently. Socials dos weren't really his cup of tea, although in his line of work they were often unavoidable.

Cullen's gaze settled on Nigel.

"Not me," he groaned.

Madison laughed, although she at least had the good sense to hide it behind her hands.

"Unfortunately, you're the perfect choice," Cullen said. "It's unlikely that anyone will connect you with us, and you're certainly not American, which is a plus." He actually said it as if in normal circumstances being a non-American was a detriment. To date, Nigel had found the opposite far more likely to be true, unless one happened to reside in Nebraska. "Gabriel and Madison will accompany you. Madison's father will be there, so that gives them legitimacy."

"You knew about this?" Nigel's gaze locked with Madison's.

"About the party?" she asked with a debutante smile. "Yes."

"I didn't bring a tux." He sounded sulky and he knew it. But bloody hell, he hated getting trussed up like an overstuffed pheasant.

"Not a problem," Payton said with a rare smile. "We're about the same size. You can wear mine."

"Wonderful." Nigel sighed, accepting the inevitable. "You said my contact is a woman?"

"Yes, but I don't know much other than that. As I said, they're trying to keep her exposure to a minimum. Anyway, she'll have a description of you. And there'll be a signal of some sort."

"The red salmon are running in Peru?" Payton's smile turned to a grin. "Hell, why don't you just have her carry a neon sign or something?"

"Look, there wasn't much time to get this all arranged. And the thought was that the easiest way to deal with this was for her to find you, give you the signal—and then you can talk." Cullen waved his hand through the air in dismissal. "I'll leave the details up to you."

"So what is the signal?" Nigel asked.

Cullen actually had the decency to look embarrassed. "She'll ask you how you like the weather in New York, and you'll respond that it's much colder in Spain."

"You'll be a regular Eliza Doolittle," Payton said with a laugh and Nigel shot him a look, wondering what the hell he'd been thinking agreeing to help out. This operation had disaster written all over it. He hated tuxedos, he hated society parties and he hated playing James-fucking-Bond.

HQN™

We *are* romance™

From the *New York Times* bestselling author of
Secondhand Bride comes the latest title in the
McKettrick family saga!

LINDA LAEL MILLER

Independent and strong-willed Lorelai Fellows has had it with
men, but setting fire to her wedding dress probably wasn't
the best way to make her point. Yet when Holt McKettrick
comes to town looking to save his best friend from the
gallows, the sparks between him and Lorelai are flying...
and two people determined never to believe in love can't
believe they've gone this long without it.

The wayward McKettrick brother is back in town,
and things will never be the same....

McKettrick's Choice

Available in hardcover in bookstores this June.